THE TIN HORSE

The

TIN HORSE

A NOVEL

JANICE STEINBERG

RANDOM HOUSE

NEW YORK

Copyright © 2013 by Janice Steinberg

All rights reserved.

Published in the United States by Random House,
an imprint of The Random House Publishing Group,
a division of Random House, Inc., New York.

RANDOM HOUSE and colophon are
registered trademarks of Random House, Inc.

LIBRARY OF CONGRESS CATALOGING-IN-PUBLICATION DATA
Steinberg, Janice
The tin horse: a novel/by Janice Steinberg.
p.   cm.
ISBN 978-0-679-64374-6
eBook ISBN 978-0-345-54028-7
1. Twins—Fiction. 2. Reminiscing in old age—Fiction.
3. Missing persons—Fiction. 4. Jewish fiction. 5. Boyle Heights
(Los Angeles, Calif.)—Fiction. 6. Domestic fiction. I. Title
PS3619.T476195T56 2013
813'.6—dc23   2012020156

Printed in the United States of America on acid-free paper

www.atrandom.com

2 4 6 8 9 7 5 3 1

FIRST EDITION

Book design by Barbara M. Bachman

FOR JACK,
MY BASHERT

I shoved on back into the store, passed through a partition and found a small dark woman reading a law book at a desk. . . . She had the fine-drawn face of an intelligent Jewess.

RAYMOND CHANDLER, *The Big Sleep*

We tell ourselves stories in order to live.

JOAN DIDION, *The White Album*

THE TIN HORSE

CHAPTER 1

ELAINE

"ELAINE, WHAT'S THIS? POETRY?" HE SHOOTS A GLANCE AT ME, HIS face so young, so eager. Then his eyes return to the folder he's opened on the dining room table.

"Let me see it," I say, but he begins reading aloud.

" 'Each fig hides its flower deep within its heart—' "

"Josh!" I reach out my hand and give him what my kids call the Acid Regard . . . even as I feel, against my back, the trunk of the fig tree in our yard in Boyle Heights; feel for a moment, stirring in my bones, the impossibly tender eighteen-year-old self who wrote those words.

"Sure, okay, if you want to look at them first." He hands over the folder but adds, "These belong in the archive." He's well named, Joshua; didn't he make the walls come tumbling down?

I thought it was a godsend when the library at the University of Southern California asked me to donate my papers to their special collections. I'd been considering moving to a senior apartment at Rancho Mañana, or, as I can't help calling it, the Ranch of No Tomorrow, and I dreaded having to sort through all the papers and books accumulated during more than half a century of living in my house in Santa Monica. USC volunteered the assistance of a Ph.D. student in library and information science, an archivist, and I jumped at the offer.

I did have a twinge of misgiving. It's one thing to expose my professional life to strangers, but USC doesn't just want material from my legal career; they're interested in my personal papers, things from my childhood and family. Well, I figured the library science student would be a docile young woman who wouldn't put up a fight if I chose to keep something private, someone with whom the process of excavating my past would be a sort of surgical procedure: clean and impersonal. I of all people—after a lifetime devoted to fighting prejudice—fell into such hasty stereotyping. And I'm paying for it. My not-at-all-docile archivist, Josh, sees every scrap of paper as a potential gold mine, and if his abrasive curiosity pokes an old pain or anger, he's delighted; my annoyance doesn't intimidate him, it just makes him push harder.

Not that I can hold Josh responsible for the nostalgia that ambushed me as I opened a box of my kids' childhood drawings, or the stab of grief when I came upon letters I'd exchanged with Paul—dead four years as of last month—when he was in the army in World War II. And now my teenage poetry. I suppose it's just as well that Josh isn't a sensitive, bookish type who'd try to comfort me every time some piece of my past touches a nerve. I prefer sparring to sympathy.

"Is that everything from my office?" I ask briskly. That's who I am, Elaine Greenstein Resnick, a brisk, no-bullshit woman, not a girlish poet whom every memento leaves undone.

"Let me check." He jumps up. He's quick and efficient—thank goodness, since I did decide on the senior apartment. I put my house on the market, and I'm moving to Rancho Mañana in mid-December, just six weeks away.

As soon as he's left the room and I'm alone, I peek at the first poem. "Each fig hides its flower deep within its heart. I have no such art of concealment. The flower of my love . . ." Could I ever have been so young and vulnerable? Where did that girl go? I can look back at the Elaine who wrote her first idealistic letter to a newspaper at eleven and draw a line to the crusading attorney I became. The seeds were there, even if it does astonish me that the quiet, reflective girl I was learned to be such a fighter—what did the *Los Angeles Times* call me, "the city's go-to progressive attorney for decades, from the McCarthy witch hunts to the civil rights, anti–Viet Nam War, and women's movements"?

But the gentle poet who once lived in me, what became of her? I can name the date I stopped writing poetry: September 12, 1939. I was eighteen. Whether or not I kept writing, however, what happened to that gentleness? Did I just outgrow it? Did I wall it off? I have a sense of something calling to me from those forgotten poems. But what nonsense! I chide myself. An old woman's sentimentality. I close the folder and put it in the wicker basket of things I want to look over before releasing them to Josh for the archive. Not that I have any intention of giving him the poems. I plan to "misplace" them.

After the surprise of finding the poetry, I'm wary when Josh returns to the dining room carrying two department store boxes—though the boxes themselves set off no warning bell, no frisson of alarm.

"Where did those come from?" I ask.

"Closet shelf, way in the back. There's a stack of 'em."

"Maybe they're things of Ronnie's." My office used to be my son's room. I expect moth-eaten camp clothes or a comic-book collection.

"No, they're full of papers."

Josh puts the top box—it's from Buffum's—between us and lifts the lid, and now the memory stirs: of my younger sisters and me cleaning out our mother's apartment after she died. That was more than thirty years ago, and what an ordeal it was. In the clean-lined apartment in West Los Angeles to which we moved Mama after Papa died, she had re-created the overstuffed claustrophobia of our house in Boyle Heights. Mama's death, ten years after Papa's (he'd had a stroke), was a shock. Still vigorous at seventy-six, she was out taking her daily walk, and a drunk driver ran her down. Going through her apartment in a blur of grief, Audrey, Harriet, and I came across two—four? a dozen?—boxes from now-defunct department stores in which Mama kept papers, and who knew what else. None of us could bear to go through them at the time.

I have no memory of doing it, but we must have thrown the boxes into my car, and somehow they ended up in my son's closet.

"Hey, is this Hebrew?" Josh holds out a letter he's unfolded and tries to hand me a pair of white gloves. It doesn't matter how often I tell him I have the right to touch my own things; he brings a second pair of gloves every time.

I scan the Hebrew letters. "Yiddish. It must be from my mother's family in Romania."

"You can read Yiddish?"

I discover I still can.

"What's it about?"

"Family news—somebody got married, somebody else had a child." Typical of what we heard from our Romanian relatives in the 1920s. During the thirties, their letters became anguished pleas for us to get at least the young ones out. We succeeded with my cousin Ivan; my family sponsored him to come to Los Angeles. And after the war, two cousins made it to Palestine, and three others went to our relatives in Chicago. But the rest were gone.

"Well, these are definitely keepers." An acquisitive gleam in his eyes, Josh holds a stack of letters, all neatly saved in their original envelopes. He reaches for one of the plastic bags he uses for items to place in the archive.

"Wait, I want to read them!" I doubt I'll have time to do more than glance through the letters. But this is my family, my history. Mine and Harriet's. Of the four of us, the Greenstein girls, she and I are the only ones left. I don't know if Harriet ever learned any Yiddish, but I need to share the letters with her, to let her at least touch these things Mama cherished, before they become source material for someone's dissertation.

"Sure, of course." Josh slips the letters into the bag, labels it, and hands it to me. "Just keep them in here when you're not reading them."

Along with the letters, the box contains stray notes, receipts, and newspaper and magazine clippings that have no obvious reason for being saved. "Someone was a pack rat," Josh says happily, but even he consigns much of the contents of the box to the recycling container at his side.

We move on to the second box, this one from May Company. It's a treasure trove. Mama dedicated this box to us, her daughters. I discover report cards, school papers, crayon drawings. Here's my letter of acceptance from USC, with the promise of a full scholarship. And here, neatly saved in a manila envelope, my articles from the school newspaper and the letters to editors I wrote with Danny, pleas for America to respond to the plight of Jews in Europe. Yes, of course, I tell Josh, I'll give him the articles and letters after I'm done with them; and after I've shared the box with Harriet.

I keep digging and come upon a packet the size of a half sheet of paper, held together with a rubber band. When I pick up the packet, the rubber band crumbles, and out spill . . . oh, it's the programs from Barbara's dance recitals. There are a dozen or more, with artfully hand-lettered titles, printed on thick, good-quality paper.

I open one of the programs, and I'm sitting in the dark, watching my sister dance. Not just admiring her but *feeling* her movements in my body—though I could never have danced with her abandon and fire. I craved private moments, whereas Barbara came alive in the spotlight.

"Elaine," Josh says, and I realize I've been miles—years—away. "Did you dance?"

"No. My sister Barbara." My throat goes rough with the threat of unexpected tears.

"Ballet?"

"Modern," I choke out.

"Did she ever do anything with it? Have a career?"

"She did what most of the women of my generation did. Got married, raised a family." Lying, the words come more easily. Still, I have a sudden image of standing on the bank of the Los Angeles River during a storm, the water churning and my nerves alert for signs of a flash flood. Nonsense! I tell myself again.

He asks if he can take the programs for some kind of dance archive at USC, and I say fine—what would I do with them?

Then the box yields a fresh challenge to my equilibrium: Philip's business card.

Josh whistles. "Wow! What did your mother have to do with a private detective?"

I mumble something about my having worked for Philip when I was in college. That spins Josh into fresh questions, and he mentions a name, someone I've never heard of, written on the back of the card. I blurt that I've come down with a splitting headache and rush him out the door. Then I stop fighting and let the flood come.

I'm expecting some kind of violence, that I'll break into wild weeping or hurl a vase across the room. Instead, there's a sense of surrender as I let myself be carried by the river of sorrow and rage and regret and love, the river of Barbara.

CHAPTER 2

ZAYDE
THE PILOT

AT 11:52 P.M. ON MARCH 28, 1921, BARBARA WRIGGLED OUT OF
Mama into the brightness of White Memorial Hospital on Boyle Avenue in
Los Angeles. Seventeen minutes—but the next day—later, I swam after
her. Did she shove me aside? Did I, suddenly shy of the world, hold back?
But Barbara always arrived ahead of me. She balanced on a bicycle half
an hour before I did, and everyone was so busy congratulating her, they
didn't notice when I climbed onto the bike we shared and wobbled to
the corner. People always called us Barbara and Elaine, never Elaine and
Barbara. And though I met Danny first, Barbara was his first love.

We were fraternal twins, not identical. Still, no one would have doubted
that we were sisters. We both had thick, curly dark hair (hers slightly curl-
ier and mine with redder highlights, of which I was vain), gold-flecked
hazel eyes, and largish but thankfully straight noses. When we got into
our teens, I shot up to five foot three, which was tall for our family;
Barbara was an inch shorter. Our most obvious physical difference lay in

the architecture of our faces. She had soft apple cheeks like Mama's, while my face was narrow, with Papa's deep-set eyes; long before I had to start wearing glasses at eleven, people rightly pegged me as the serious one. Did we grow into our faces, or did they express our natures from the beginning? Both of us spoke at a medium pitch and "so clear, like bells! You girls should go on the radio!" Papa, shamed by his parents' and Mama's accents, polished our articulation by having us declaim poems. While I kneaded my thoughts into sentences deliberately, Barbara never hesitated. And she could sing, with what matured into a throaty, torch-song voice, while I could barely croak out a tune.

We have the same smile in photographs, the same gap between our front teeth, inherited from Papa. A film, though, would have shown that she was quicker to smile. If one quality most described my sister, it was quickness, in every sense of the word. Barbara was spontaneous, eager, vital, warm, someone who constantly came up with games and mischief, making her a natural leader of the band of kids in our neighborhood. She was also impatient, impulsive, reckless, and hasty to judge. Mercurial, even cruel, a quick-change artist of affection who adored you one day and, worse than anger or hatred, forgot you existed the next.

And she could leave havoc in her wake, a talent I witnessed for the first time when she caused the stock market crash of 1929. Of course, I was old enough at that time—eight and a half—to understand that cataclysms in my family didn't affect the entire world. Yet I always associated Black Tuesday with the storm that hit our house the same day because of what Barbara did to Zayde.

Zayde Dov, Papa's father, lived with us. In fact, our house was the same one Zayde had moved into when Papa was seventeen. But Zayde wasn't from Los Angeles. He had crossed the ocean to come to America. And before that, he'd had to cross a river. A trifling distance, to be sure, compared to the Atlantic that churned beneath him for two weeks, an ordeal that made him refuse to set foot in a boat ever again, not even the little rowboats in Hollenbeck Park. But crossing the river was harder. The first wrenching away from everything he knew and that knew him, a seventeen-year-old boy with his mama's kugel still warm in his belly and the fresh damp of her tears wetting the scarf she'd knotted around his neck.

And Zayde's river was no country trickle, but the mighty Dniester, which swept from the Carpathian Mountains past his village in the Ukraine to the Black Sea. Then there was the fact that he had to swim across the river on a March night—the water icy, the current at a gallop from melting Carpathian snow—so the dogs wouldn't pick up his scent. The dogs and the men with them, men who carried cudgels and guns.

Zayde always paused at this point. And Barbara and I always demanded, breathless as if the dogs were after *us*, "Why were they chasing you?"

"Ah," he'd say, taking a sip from his cup of tea, laced with whiskey. "A great crime I committed, girls."

No matter how many times I heard the story, I could never erase the picture that jumped into my mind, of Zayde Dov in his house slippers vaulting onto a horse with the loot from a bank robbery, like the Wild West bandits I saw in the movies.

Until he continued, "I fell in love."

The girl's name was Agneta. She was the daughter of one of the farmers who came into town on market day, an event that over time, between Zayde's storytelling and my imagination, became so real I almost felt as if I'd been there, as if I'd witnessed the scene that sealed Zayde's fate. Market day in Zayde's village was busy and noisy, what with the jostle of peasants selling what their farms produced and the Jewish villagers offering goods such as tea, salt, and lamp oil. The villagers also provided the services of craftsmen such as Berel the tinsmith, who was Zayde Dov's father.

Berel, an enterprising man, had recently bought a grinding machine and branched into sharpening. And scissors, appropriately, proved the instrument of Dov's *estrangement*—such a rich word, signifying both that you become a stranger to others and that everything around you, everything you see and hear, even what you smell, is alien. No more do your nostrils suck in the precise odors that emanate from *this* soil and vegetation, *this* method of cooking and of handling trash, the perfume, however foul, of home. If only Dov could have foreseen what he was about to lose, would he have acted differently the day Agneta came into the tinsmith's shop wanting her scissors sharpened fine enough to cut the challis she'd just bought for a best dress?

It was nearly dusk, and Dov was tending the shop alone. He pumped the foot pedal to start the grinding wheel and held the blades of Agneta's scissors against the stone. He was more aware at first of the work than of the pretty peasant customer.

"I liked using the grinder," he told us. "It's the one thing I was good at. My father said he'd never seen such a schlemiel at working tin."

He tested the scissor blades with his finger, then ground them a bit more and buffed them with a clean rag until they gleamed in the thin light of a late January afternoon. "Perfect, see?" he said, and demonstrated by snipping a piece of paper and displaying the crisp edges. Agneta, who was shortsighted, leaned close to look, close enough that he smelled her: a scent of rough soap, the dried rosemary she'd carried in bunches to the market, and sixteen-year-old girl.

"Show me on this." Plucking a parcel from the basket she carried over her arm, she unwrapped the brown paper and freed a corner of the fabric, a bright blue that matched her eyes; it was soft to his touch when he held it and aimed the scissors at it. "No, silly, not that much!" she cried, and snatched the wool from him, her fingers grazing his, her blue eyes teasing.

Emboldened, he handed her the scissors, their touch lasting perhaps two seconds this time. "You do it."

Agneta folded the fabric back into the brown paper and reached behind her for the braid that fell halfway to her waist. Flourishing her rosemary-scented blond hair between them, she sliced a dozen strands from the end of her braid and held them out to Dov.

"You understand, girls? Agneta was a goy, a Christian. She thought she could say anything she wanted, because I was nobody, a Jew."

Dov Grinshtayn didn't believe in such distinctions, however. He intended to abolish them; everyone did at the socialist meetings he snuck off to. And he was a strong, good-looking boy, fonder of walking in the forest and (luckily, as it turned out) swimming in the river than spending all day shut up in the rabbi's study hall. In a photograph taken in New York a few years later, his jaw is firm, his shoulders solid, and his eyes, under thick, wavy black hair . . . Even though the photo is slightly out of focus, you can see the challenge in his eyes. The kind of look I pictured him giving Agneta.

"Here," she said when he just stood there instead of reaching for the lock of hair. "Take it."

"Why would I want it?"

"To think of me." She tossed her head, even as the disdained hair grew damp with sweat from her fingers.

"Why would I want to think of you?"

Her jest turned against her, Agneta's smile lost its courage and became the sucked-in lips of a child fighting tears. And Dov experienced in one telescoped moment everything that was fine and everything that was mean in himself. "Ai, I felt sorry for upsetting her. But living in America, girls, you have no idea. Christian boys used to beat us up; they did it in plain sight of adults and got away with it. Sometimes mobs of Christians attacked all the Jews. It was called a pogrom. Every minute of your life, you were afraid."

Given the perpetual anxiety of being at the mercy of the Christian peasants, Dov couldn't help but savor his taste of power over one Christian girl . . . until tears brimmed in her eyes. Then his heart melted. Gravely he held out his hand. Agneta pressed the lock of hair into his palm. He twisted the hair into a triangle of paper and slipped it in his pocket.

They spoke now only of their transaction.

"Are they sharp enough?"

"Yes, they're fine."

"Shall I wrap them?"

But every word carried poetry in its arms.

"Agneta, what's taking you so long, girl?" A man's voice at the door, thick as if he'd just come from the tavern, and that was when Dov learned her name.

"Coming, Father," she called.

"Wait. Take . . . ," Dov said, before he had any idea what to give her. "Here!" A pencil from his pocket, almost new and hardly chewed at all.

"Oh." She looked at the pencil as if she didn't know how to use one. Was she even literate, this girl who was going to hurl him into exile? She thrust the pencil into her basket and scurried out the door.

She came back two weeks later with a pot to mend, but the shop was busy, and he had to focus on the work under finicky Berel's eye. Nervous, he burned his fingers with solder, but that hardly aroused his father's suspicion, as it happened all the time.

He was luckier on the next market day. When he passed the stalls in the town square, on his way to deliver tin pails to the dairy, he spotted her and caught her eye. She slipped off and followed him. In a stand of beech trees, he and Agneta were alone at last.

"Did you kiss?" we asked. We went to the movies. We knew what happened when people were in love; not that we saw this kind of behavior between Mama and Papa!

"The ideas you girls have. Once, I kissed her." But they didn't dare linger and risk being seen. And she had important things to tell him: how to recognize her farm, at what time she came out to feed the chickens, and that she had a secret place in the woods at the edge of the farm, where no one else ever went.

Since their first meeting, Dov had saved bits of tin and wire, scraps left from trimming pots or punching holes in colanders. He'd snuck the leavings into his pocket, where he also kept the lock of Agneta's hair. Once he had enough scraps, he devoted himself to tinsmithing as never before. His father was right, he had little talent. But despite his lack of skill, not long after he'd first kissed Agneta, he was ready. The next Shabbos, when he had the afternoon free, he walked by her farm three times. Each time, he continued a hundred yards past the house, then turned and—heart pounding, terrified that every one of her four brothers had seen him—passed again. At long last, Agneta came out carrying her bucket of chicken feed. She raced into the chicken house and a moment later, never glancing his way, hurried toward the woods. She stayed within the fence; Dov paralleled her on the road. Once they were out of sight of the house, he climbed over the fence to her . . . and gave her his gift, a tin menagerie.

"Oh!" Agneta clapped her hands. "Oh!" She marveled over the rooster with a flared comb, the curly-tailed lamb, and the horse. But she most adored the ungainly creature, a lion, that he'd done his best to copy from a drawing in a magazine. He had given it a mane by soldering thirty bits of wire to the massive head as if each wire were an individual hair. He kissed

Agneta a few more times that day, and two weeks later when they met in the woods again.

Some dozen kisses were all they had (at least all Zayde admitted to) before the lion betrayed them. Agneta found the spiky-maned beast so strange and wonderful, she couldn't resist showing it to her closest friends. Soon her brothers found out, and where could she have gotten tin animals but from the Jew tinsmith? Gnarled old Berel? Ridiculous. But didn't Berel have an apprentice, a son? They grilled Agneta; I imagined her tears and blood from her fingers drenching the tin lion she wouldn't let them rip from her grasp. Then they came after Dov.

Zayde's family got warning barely in time for him to pack a small bag and for his mother to make a secret pocket in the lining of his coat and sew in three gold coins. The money seemed a fortune until he had to use one entire coin to bribe his way across the Austro-Hungarian border. Then came the train ticket to Rotterdam. With little money left, he shoveled coal to pay off his steamship passage. Two weeks of sweating and vomiting in the pits of hell, and he stumbled rubber-legged onto Castle Garden, the island at the tip of Manhattan where immigrants were processed then, sure of two things: he would never have anything more to do with boats, and he would never work tin again.

The first vow he had to break almost immediately, but just once, and briefly, to take the barge from Castle Garden to the mainland. The second one he kept for forty-five years, until Monday, October 28, 1929. And breaking it led to one of the times when the story of my family collided with history—the story of the whole world.

"I'm not a tinsmith, I'm an idea man," Zayde would insist when Barbara and I begged for our own tin animals.

Our father had another way of describing him. "He's a *luftmensch*," he used to say to Mama in Yiddish, the language of secrets. We knew *luft* meant "air" and *mensch* was "man," and at first we thought the word, and the fact that Papa half whispered it, meant Zayde was an airplane pilot; maybe he had flown missions that still couldn't be talked about, even years after the Great War. Zayde had done so many things in America—sewing suspenders and then pants, having a garlic route, rolling cigars, even having his own cigar factory. And after the family moved to Los Angeles because our grandmother, who died before we were born, had consumption, Zayde built the West: he had an egg ranch that supplied eggs to half of Los Angeles, and he played his part in the housing boom by buying and selling furniture. "There's always money to be made," he said. Now he sold books, except that when we asked to visit his bookstore, the way we sometimes went to Uncle Leo's bookstore on Hollywood Boulevard, everyone shook their heads and acted mysterious. With Zayde having had so many different jobs, some of them hushed and secret, why couldn't he have been a pilot, too?

It was Auntie Pearl, Papa's youngest sister, who told us the truth. And Barbara who turned it into catastrophe.

Both of us adored Auntie Pearl, a flapper with bobbed brown hair, daring skirts that barely covered her plump knees, and merry eyes. Pearl sewed most of our clothes, and on that Monday in October 1929, Barbara and I had gone to her apartment after school so she could finish our navy winter skirts. I was standing on a box so Pearl could pin the hem of my skirt, when something about Charles Lindbergh came on the radio.

"Does Zayde know Mr. Lindbergh?" I said.

"Charles Lindbergh, the pilot?"

I nodded.

"What has your *zayde* been telling you?" Pearl laughed, but not in a happy way. She and Zayde hadn't spoken for the past two years, not since a scandal so huge that even though the adults whispered, they couldn't keep Barbara and me from hearing. Pearl's husband, our uncle Gabriel Davidoff, had left her for another woman, a goy! A worse scandal followed. For a girl as young as Pearl, even a girl who'd been married, it wasn't respectable to live on her own. But Pearl hadn't moved back in with her family. Instead, she'd stayed in the apartment where she'd lived with Gabe and started a custom tailoring business. Zayde now refused to see her.

"Nothing," I said, sorry I'd brought it up. We weren't supposed to say anything about Zayde to Pearl, just as we had to pretend around him that a new skirt or jacket had been bought at the store.

But Barbara, who'd already had her navy skirt pinned, piped up, "Isn't Zayde a *luftmensch*?"

This time Pearl's laughter was genuine, booming so hard she dropped the pins and rocked back onto the floor. "A *luftmensch*! A *luftmensch*!"

"That's what Papa says," I said when she'd quieted down to a few chuckles.

"I'll bet he does." Pearl, who moved quickly and sharply even though she was a bit *zaftig*, gathered her legs under her and hopped up. "Barbara, honey, pick up those pins for me. And Elaine, hold still. Just a few more and we're done."

Pearl waited until she finished pinning my hem and I changed back into my old skirt (also navy, which Mama considered an appropriate color for young girls—and it had the advantage of not showing dirt). Then she told us to sit in her tiny living room, she and Barbara on the frayed gray love seat and I on the room's one chair.

Pearl lit a cigarette, another of her scandalous habits. "Darlings, do you know what a *luftmensch* is?" she said.

"Isn't it a pilot?" I said.

"Of an airplane? Whatever made you think . . . oh, of course, 'air man,' how clever of you. But a *luftmensch* doesn't fly in the air. It's a person who you can't imagine how they make a living. It's like they live on nothing but air. Someone who's always got this big scheme or that big scheme, but the schemes never work out. A *luftmensch* . . ." She stared at the ash growing on the end of her cigarette, and her voice turned bitter; the harshness from my usually cheerful aunt upset me almost as much as what she said. "He borrows money from all the relatives to start a cigar factory that's going to make them rich, but surprise, the man who promised to sell him tobacco at a huge discount takes the money and disappears. He brags about how he's going to send his children to university, even his daughters, or that he'll be the egg king of Los Angeles. The egg king! More like egg on his face . . . Oh, girls! I didn't mean . . ."

I don't know about Barbara, but I was crying, and Pearl must have suddenly realized she wasn't recounting the litany of broken promises to her friends, adults who understood why Zayde might live on the air of dreams.

"It's just that people like your *zayde*," Pearl said, "they come to America and try different things. But it's not easy. No matter what they heard about America in the old country, look outside—do you see any streets paved with gold?"

"Papa showed us the egg ranch!" Barbara said, focusing with an eight-year-old's moral absolutism not on the nuances of immigrant hopes but on the black and white of whether we'd been lied to. "Uncle Leo took us on a drive into the San Fernando Valley, and Papa showed us where the ranch was."

"Honey, of course we had the egg ranch. It's not that Zayde—"

"Why don't we have it anymore?" I demanded, suddenly seeing the holes that always gaped in Zayde's stories. If his businesses were so successful, why did he keep abandoning them? If there was always money to be made, why weren't we rich? Why, if we needed to go someplace by car, did we have to ask Uncle Leo—the bookstore-owning husband of Papa's other sister, Sonya—to drive us? Why, as Mama never stopped complaining, did Papa break his back working for Mr. Fine at Fine & Son Fine Footwear, instead of having a business of his own like Leo did?

"Having a ranch with dozens of chickens," Pearl said, "it's not like people who have a little chicken coop behind their house. We didn't know enough, or we were just unlucky. The chickens got sick and died."

"What about the bookstore?" Barbara asked.

"The bookstore?"

"Where Zayde works now."

"*Gevult*, what nonsense have they been filling your heads with?"

Pearl told us the truth gently, but she overestimated our maturity, our ability to balance the wrong done to us with understanding of the fragile pride that had motivated it. Barbara in particular heard what Zayde really did with the passion and violence of betrayal with which children experience any departure from their certainties about important adults in their lives.

"I'm going there," Barbara said as soon as we left Pearl's.

"We can't, we aren't supposed to," I protested, even as I followed her to Brooklyn Avenue.

She charged down the street, which was busy with women shopping and newsboys screaming about problems with the stock market.

"Don't you want to get buttermilk?" I grabbed her hand. Pearl had given us pennies, and we could treat ourselves to delicious paper cones of buttermilk at the dairy store.

Barbara stopped for a moment, turned, and thrust her face into mine. "I'm going. You can do what you want!"

It may sound as if I'm trying to avoid my share of guilt for what happened. Actually, I'm exposing my particular guilt at being a child who was cautious by nature. Everyone is fond of plucky children, kids who launch into adventures, even (within reason) kids who sass back. What about the girl who sits for a long time and watches other children going down the slide, whose legs quiver just from imagining how it will feel to stand at the top of that silver swoop into the unknown? I made up for it in time, I learned bravado—but back then I was my brash sister's follower.

Barbara pushed through a nondescript door just past a dress shop—we kids all knew where these places of adult misdoing were located, just as we were aware of the bootleg schnapps Mr. Zakarin concocted in his tub—and ran up a dark, narrow flight of stairs. Then she paused at the threshold of a room. Standing a few steps behind her, I couldn't see inside, I could only smell a fug of cigar smoke and hear what sounded like a radio.

"What can I do for you, sweetheart?" The man who spoke came over, and even though his words were friendly, he posed his thick, squat body in the door in a way that made Barbara take a step backward.

"Is Dov Greenstein here?" she said.

The man looked relieved. "You looking for Dov? You've come to the wrong place. Say, I'll get word to him that you want him, okay? You girls go on home now."

"Where is he, then?" Barbara said.

"I told you, be good girls and go home."

This man was clearly used to children who were more docile than Barbara. While she declared that we would try every place like this on Brooklyn Avenue, so he might as well tell her which one Zayde worked in, I escaped into the radio broadcast, a baritone voice crooning, "In the fifth, it's Excelsior, Excelsior takes first at six to one. That's a six-to-one win for Excelsior. The favorite, Patrician, has to settle for second this time around, and Irish Eyes, beautiful Irish Eyes, comes in third."

Barbara got the man to tell her where Zayde worked, and we stormed down Brooklyn and up another tight stairway with what sounded like the same radio broadcast playing at the top. We didn't hesitate in the doorway this time but burst into a low-ceilinged room that smelled like a combination of cigars and my school classroom. The classroom smell came from a big chalkboard, where a man with a mustache stood writing in a hand that would have gotten an A from my teacher. *Excelsior*, I read in his perfect script, and *Irish Eyes*, as I took everything in with a time-slowed-down clarity: the radio perched on a filing cabinet, a tree hung with coats and hats, a droopy-eyed man sitting at a table strewn with dozens of what I recognized as the racing forms sold by the newsboy outside the ice cream parlor. Another messy table abutted the first at a weird angle, as if someone had just shoved both tables into the room and wherever they landed, they stayed.

There was a third table, but it was lined up squarely with a corner of the room, and its dozens of papers were stacked as neatly as Zayde kept his room at home.

He didn't notice us. Chewing on a pencil, he stared at a piece of paper on the table with the kind of intense concentration he brought to our games of gin rummy. I expected Barbara to say something, but she must have exhausted her first wind simply getting us here.

I broke the silence. "Zayde!"

He jumped up so fast his chair fell over. "Girls! Is everything all right at home? Is someone sick?"

Barbara found her voice. "Why did you tell us you worked in a bookstore?"

"Is someone sick?" he repeated, although he was quickly realizing we hadn't been sent here because of a family emergency. That *this* was the emergency. "Who told you to come here? This isn't a place for children."

"You said you worked in a bookstore, not a bookie joint!" Barbara accused.

"Oy, you thought . . ." Laughing—shifting his strategy with the quickness any immigrant learns if he wants to survive—Zayde walked around the table toward us. "You don't think I *work* here? That's a good one, isn't it, Mr. Melansky?"

"A good one." The droopy-eyed man guffawed. "That's rich, that's a good one."

"I just come by when I have a little extra time and give my friend Mr. Melansky a hand."

"That's the ticket, ha ha," Mr. Melansky chimed in.

"But . . . ," Barbara sputtered. Zayde's initial defensiveness hadn't rattled her; it was the same way we reacted when accused of anything. But now he'd outflanked her.

"Barbara, Elaine, say hello to Mr. Melansky," he said. "And Mr. Freitag," he added, nodding toward the man who'd kept writing on the chalkboard through all of this—he couldn't stop, since race results were still coming in over the radio.

"How do you do?" we said, temporarily cowed by the rules hammered into us by our parents and teachers: *Be polite to grown-ups. Never make a scene.*

"Girls, why don't you get yourself a treat?" Zayde reached into his pocket, took out a fat roll of bills, and peeled one off for us. The bills were all ones; I'd seen him roll them at the kitchen table when he was finishing his breakfast and preparing to go out and build the West. Still, to us, a dollar was a fortune.

I looked at the characteristically tidy table where he'd been sitting, lit by a small lamp I remembered from our living room, and my legs shook the way they had the time I finally climbed to the top of the slide and stared down that shimmering Niagara, so bright with reflected sun it made me dizzy. There was also a calm, however, an elegant beauty, in holding the solid physical evidence against his mere words of denial. Later I thought of that vertiginous moment as the first time I reasoned like an attorney.

"Zayde, it's not true," I murmured, more sad than angry.

"What?" He crouched, hands on his thighs, to look me in the eye (he was sixty-two then, but vigorous and surprisingly limber). His eyes, hazel like mine, warned—begged?—me not to go further. Or was he asking me to free him from this deception?

Whatever he wanted, I couldn't turn back. I was standing at the top of the slide, the kid behind me on the ladder pressing into my calves. The only thing I could do was force my wobbly legs onto that terrifying cataract and let go.

"You don't work in a bookstore," I said. "You work here."

"A little respect your *zayde* deserves!" Mr. Melansky huffed, but Zayde held up his hand.

"Why don't I walk you girls home?" he said. Without a word to the other men, he put his gray felt homburg on his head and guided us to the door. His hand on my shoulder trembled, but in the street he had a chuckle in his voice.

"Since when do eight-year-old girls know about Melansky's?" he said.

"All the kids know," I said. "Don't they, Barbara?" My sister was too quiet.

"You kids, you're so smart. Your mama and papa and me, we thought, a bookie shop, a bookshop, see? Almost the same English. We thought, not until you're a little older. So smart! You want ice creams from Currie's?"

"Yes, please." I accepted the peace offering, even better than a cone of buttermilk.

"Better you shouldn't have been there, though," he said. "How about you don't mention it to your mama and papa?"

"What about your egg ranch?" Barbara said, too sweetly.

"In the valley?"

"I want chocolate," I said, tugging on his sleeve. "Barbara always gets strawberry."

She said at the same time, "You supplied eggs to half of Los Angeles, isn't that what you told us?"

"Who have you been talking to? One of your aunts?"

"The chickens died!"

"Sweetheart, keep your voice down." Zayde glanced uneasily at the women milling around the fish barrels outside Rosen's.

"And what about the cigar factory?"

He yanked us into a doorway between Rosen's and the next store. "Barbara! What did I just tell you?"

"Lies!" she spat back. "You told us lies."

Sweat beaded on Zayde's brow and he leaned against the wall.

"Barbara, stop it," I pleaded.

"No, it's fine," Zayde sighed, and wiped his face with his handkerchief. "It's America, people can speak freely. And any accused person has the right to answer charges made against him. The egg ranch, you want to see where it was? You want I should ask your uncle Leo to take us there?"

"But you didn't supply eggs to half of Los Angeles," she persisted.

"When Harry was there we did a good business."

A hush always fell at the mention of Zayde's firstborn son, who died in the Great War. But not this time.

"Agneta's hair," she said. "Where is it?"

"What?" Zayde said.

"The hair she gave you. I want to see it."

"You think I kept a few hairs from a kid I knew when I was seventeen?"

"Then how do I know any of it is true?"

"Are you calling your *zayde* a liar?"

Even Barbara hadn't said that; she had only said he told lies. It was a crucial distinction for us, and the irreversibility of that word, *liar,* stopped her in her tracks. For a moment.

"What were the tin animals you made for her?" she asked.

"What, you don't remember?" He wiped his face with his handkerchief again.

Rooster, lamb, horse, lion. Did I say it or only think it?

"Make them for us," Barbara said.

"Didn't I tell you, when I stepped off the boat onto America, I promised myself I would never work tin again?"

"The only thing I've ever seen you do with tin is open a can of vegetables."

Zayde's face went white. "Go home," he said.

Barbara, her face as stunned as Zayde's, turned and ran.

"Zayde!" I cried.

"Go home!"

I pretended to leave, but I hid among the fish and pickle barrels outside Rosen's. When Zayde started down the street, taking big, fast strides, I trotted a little behind him. I felt as if the harm Barbara had done was mine to repair, or at least—since I had no idea how to fix this damage—not to abandon. He went into Elster's Hardware; I lurked a few doors away. Ten minutes later, he emerged carrying a brown paper sack and went straight home.

I lagged a few minutes behind. When I entered the house, I could hear Zayde talking to Mama in the kitchen, too low for me to know what they were saying. Then the voices stopped. A minute later I peeked in. Mama asked about my day at school. Zayde wasn't there. He must have gone into his bedroom off the kitchen. I sat at the table and read my latest library book, *Treasure Island*, so I could keep watch. His door remained closed.

He didn't come out for dinner. He hadn't been able to resist having a corned beef sandwich at Canter's on his way home; that's what he'd told Mama. She might have started in on Barbara and me, picking at our dinners in guilty silence, but she and Papa were preoccupied with the stock market. Their investments, although modest, represented almost all of their savings.

Barbara and I barely spoke as we got ready for bed. I don't know what was going through her mind, but I was shocked by what had happened—and heartsick at having hurt the one person in our house who adored me. Mama might cuddle me one moment and slap me the next, and Papa tended to be stern. But everything I did had delighted Zayde.

Sometime during the night, I woke up feeling scared. I crept into the inky unfamiliarity of the house in the middle of night, from our bedroom into the hallway, where I felt my way by touching the wall, then through the living room and into the kitchen. A light came from under Zayde's door, and I heard rustles of some kind of activity going on. I lingered outside his door for a few minutes, but I was afraid to disturb him.

In the morning, Papa found Zayde asleep in his chair, slumped over the small table in his room. On the table were metalworking tools, scraps of solder, remnants of the tin cans he had cut for materials, and three crude but recognizable tin animals: a rooster, a lamb, and a horse.

Zayde woke up when Papa came into his room. He rose and started stuffing his belongings into a potato sack; he was moving to Aunt Sonya and Uncle Leo's, he announced. Sonya was always after him to live in her house, so much nicer and bigger than ours, but he'd said Sonya kvetched so much, she would make his ears fall off. Papa kept asking him what was wrong. All he said was, "A man deserves respect."

He was already gone when Barbara and I came into the kitchen for breakfast. Papa brought out the tin animals and asked what was going on. "Nothing," we both replied.

Barbara waited until Papa left the room. Then she asked Mama, "Could I have the horse?"

Mama eyed her suspiciously but said, "Yes, all right. Elaine, what about you?"

"I want the rooster." I would have liked the lion, but that was the one animal Zayde hadn't made. Maybe he fell asleep before he got to it, but I suspected that treasure was for Agneta alone.

Terrified of discovery, I waited until Barbara and I were a full block away from home, on our way to school, before I pounced on her.

"Look what you did!" I said, distressed by everything that had happened and frantic to push the blame onto her.

She tossed her head. "What *I* did?"

"You accused him of lying about Agneta."

"Well, you didn't say you believed him. You didn't say anything."

These distinctions of culpability meant nothing to Papa, of course, when he found out everything from Pearl. He rarely hit us, but that night he spanked Barbara and me so hard that we wept. Then he stood over us while we wrote letters of apology to Zayde. I meant every word I wrote. And in spite of my misery over hurting him and getting punished, I was deeply relieved that his story about Agneta, at least, was true. I think Barbara felt that way, too, because she cherished the tin horse. She kept it on her side of the dresser we shared and got furious if she thought anyone had moved it an inch.

Our letters, along with Aunt Sonya's carping and her mediocre cooking, persuaded Zayde to move back to our house two weeks later. But everything had changed by then.

The day after Barbara goaded Zayde into breaking his vow never to

work tin again had swelled into a national uproar: Black Tuesday, the col-
lapse of the stock market. Men on Wall Street jumped out of windows, and
people all over the country—including us—lost their savings. Somehow,
in my imagination, my sister had precipitated that disaster. Mingled with
my horror was awe at Barbara's power.

CHAPTER 3

BOYLE
HEIGHTS

Boyle heights sits on the east side of the los angeles river. That means nothing anymore, since the river's course was fixed in concrete by the Army Corps of Engineers, a project that began when I was in high school and was completed around 1960. My granddaughter once asked about the concrete ditch we were driving over, and her older brother informed her, "That's where they film car chases."

The river once meant a great deal, however. In fact, as Papa used to tell us, the river ruled Los Angeles.

"Where do you live, girls? What's the name of your city?" he would begin one of our history lessons.

"El Pueblo de la Reina de los Angeles," we learned to answer.

"What language is that? What does it mean?"

"Spanish. It means 'the Town of the Queen of the Angels.'"

"And what was the queen of the Town of the Queen of the Angels?

Why did they put the center of Los Angeles twenty miles inland, instead of on the ocean?"

"Because of the river?"

"That's right."

Papa's lessons took place erratically. Fine & Son Fine Footwear stayed open most nights until nine, and Papa often had to work in the evening. "Mr. Julius Fine gets to go home and eat with *his* family!" Mama fumed as she put our dinner on the table at six and shoved a plate for Papa into the oven. (The son in the store's name didn't yet work there. He was barely older than Barbara and me.) On nights when Papa wasn't working, though, he spent half an hour after dinner instructing us in history, poetry recitation, or mathematics, depending on his mood.

Zayde told his stories to remember who he was and where he'd come from. Papa taught us who he expected us to be: American girls. Yet in Papa's lessons, too, I glimpsed his younger self: winner of the first prize in elocution in his tenth-grade class, his last year of school before his older brother, Harry, joined the army, and he had to take Harry's place at the egg ranch. Papa almost sang his story about the river, which came from the speech he had written for the elocution competition. Though there were many words I didn't understand, I didn't dare interrupt him.

"The river was the true *reina*, the queen, of El Pueblo de la Reina de los Angeles," Papa said. "She brought water to the settlers' vineyards and orchards through irrigation ditches called *zanjas* that fanned out from the great Zanja Madre, the Mother Ditch. The river created woodlands with sycamore, live oak, cottonwood, and wild roses. And there were turtle-doves and quail. Can you imagine, girls? That was right here in Boyle Heights.

"The river can also be an angry queen," Papa said. "During the dry months, she can't even maintain a permanent channel, but in the rainy season, she covers a huge floodplain. You know never to go near the river when it's been raining, even if it's not raining that day? You know about Micky Altschul?"

We were only babies when it happened, but every child in Boyle Heights had heard of Micky Altschul, who went to play with a paper boat in the river the day after a big storm. It was a clear day in the city, but it was still raining hard in the mountains, where the river started. Water flooded down from the mountains and swept Micky away. His body was found halfway to San Pedro.

In the olden days, Papa said, the river divided Los Angeles into two very different cities. A prosperous white Los Angeles flourished on the west side of the river; to the east, everyone was Mexican or Indian, and all of them were poor. The division was so extreme that not even one white person lived east of the river until the 1850s, when an Irish immigrant bought a vineyard on the river's east bank. The Irishman also bought the hilly land beyond the vineyard, and he built his house there and lived among the Mexicans and Indians.

"What was the Irishman's name, girls?" Papa asked.

"Andrew Boyle."

We learned that Andrew Boyle was only fourteen when he and his seven brothers and sisters sailed to America in 1832. Motherless children, they had come in search of their father; he had left Ireland after his wife's death and vanished into the New World.

"How could he vanish?" I asked. "Did something happen to him?"

"It doesn't matter. The point of the story is Andrew Boyle coming to America. So Andrew and his family—"

"Why didn't he send them a letter?"

"Maybe he went someplace on the frontier, like Alaska, that didn't have mail service." Papa frowned, and I knew I should stop, but hearing about the vanished father touched a primal fear of abandonment. A fear and a premonition?

"Did he get killed by Indians?" I said. "Or eaten by a bear?"

"Enough, Elaine! And Barbara, pay attention!"

The Boyle children spent two years on the East Coast looking for their father, then moved to Texas, Papa said. (I bit my lip to keep from asking if they'd left some way for their father to find them, like children dropping bread crumbs in a fairy tale.) Andrew joined the U.S. Army to fight in the Texas Revolution, and his life almost ended then. His company was losing in battle and surrendered in exchange for the Mexican general's promise to spare the men. But the general lied. Once the Americans surrendered, the general had them all shot. All except one: Andrew Boyle. The general had at one time stayed in the town where Boyle's family lived; they'd treated him kindly, and he'd told them he would help Andrew if he ever had the chance. That promise he kept. He let Andrew go.

"You see, girls," Papa said, "Andrew Boyle survived because his family was kind to Mexicans. And later he chose to live with Mexicans and Indians as his neighbors. Remember, I showed you his house on Boyle Avenue? That's why, in Boyle Heights, we have so many different kinds of people and we all get along."

The real story, I learned when I got older, was far less pretty than what I'd heard from Papa. Andrew Boyle may indeed have been a paragon of tolerance, as Papa said. But after Boyle died, his son-in-law literally gave away plots of land to attract "desirable" neighbors. At first the plan succeeded, and the son-in-law's friends built the grand Victorian mansions around Hollenbeck Park (named for one of the friends). But Boyle Heights was still on the wrong side of the river. Eventually it filled up with cheap little wood and stucco houses and with undesirable people like us— and our Mexican, Japanese, Russian, Armenian, and black neighbors. Papa wouldn't have told children such an ambiguous tale, of course. And whether it reflected Andrew Boyle's populist spirit or was simply a happy accident, Papa was right that our involuntary League of Nations formed a surprisingly harmonious community. When I was growing up, Boyle Heights was home to people from fifty different ethnic groups. And we didn't dissolve into some kind of treacly melting pot; each of the largest groups—the Mexicans, the Japanese, and especially the Jews, who were over half of Boyle Heights' residents then—had its own neighborhood.

The Jewish area was centered at the intersection of Brooklyn Avenue and Soto Street. Brooklyn is now called Cesar Chavez Avenue, and Boyle Heights is entirely Hispanic, but back in the 1920s and '30s, you could walk in either direction from the corner of Brooklyn and Soto and pass kosher bakeries and delicatessens with barrels of sharp-smelling pickles and *matyas* herring sitting out front. Canter's was the deli where all of the junk men had breakfast and a shot of whiskey every morning at six, and every year before Passover it was the site of the crying man—a man who sat on the sidewalk in front of Canter's grinding horseradish, tears running down his face. There was also the notorious chicken store, where

Jews from all over Los Angeles came on Thursdays to buy kosher chickens
for their Friday dinners. You pointed to a live, clucking chicken, the unfor-
tunate bird was then taken into the back room and hung upside down,
and a religious butcher called a *shochet* slit its throat. At some point, every
child became aware of what went on in the store's back room and refused
to eat chicken for several weeks; some stayed vegetarians for years.

Stores had signs in both English and Yiddish, and there were Yiddish
workers' societies, community centers, and socialists debating outside the
vegetarian cafe. Boyle Heights had many synagogues, too; we lived on
Breed Street, a block from the majestic Breed Street Shul, and sometimes
went there on the High Holidays. That was the only time we went to syna-
gogue, though, and a number of our neighbors didn't go at all. We were
modern Americans; what did we want with Old Country superstitions?
We didn't need to pray to God to relieve the misery of our lives. What misery? In America, Jews could even own land and build their own houses—as
Aunt Sonya and Uncle Leo did on Wabash Avenue in Boyle Heights.

Sonya and Leo built their house in 1926, when Wabash was just being
developed. Approaching their brand-new house, you smelled the delicious
sweet scent of fresh wood and heard a symphony of clanging hammers,
rasping saws, and the shouts of men swarming over the construction
sites—carpenters, plumbers, stuccoers. And what a feast for the eye, the
bright facades of the just-completed houses. So modern, so proud.

Sonya and Leo moved into their house in March, just before Barbara
and I turned five. Mama, with us in tow—and our new brother or sister
huge in her belly—went there almost every day that spring. Sometimes
Sonya had summoned her to witness the house's latest adornment. More
often Mama was simply drawn there, as if under some compulsion to go
the six blocks from our house (not new or owned, but rented and in need
of repair) and torment herself with her sister-in-law's affluence.

"I need to walk! Hurry, girls!" Mama would cry. We'd grab our sweaters, and sometimes persuade her to take us to Hollenbeck Park, where
we'd happily spend hours hurtling into space on the swings. Or we might
go visit Auntie Pearl, who delighted in playing with us. Mama and Pearl
laughed together, whereas Sonya got on Mama's nerves.

Most of the time, though, when we took a walk, Mama's feet turned toward Sonya's. Sonya was twenty-four then, but no one would have believed she was only a year older than Pearl. Sonya was settled, with her fine house, her two-year-old son, Stan, and her husband, Leo, a stolid, gray-haired man who constantly complained about his dyspepsia. In some ways, Sonya was the better-looking of Papa's sisters; a "handsome" woman, she wore her brown hair elegantly pinned up, and even at twenty-four her plumpness made her seem important and matronly. (Sonya eventually served as the president of more than one women's organization.) In contrast, Pearl often looked like she'd just emerged from a hot kitchen, her hair in unruly tendrils and her face shiny.

The first thing Sonya always said to Barbara and me when she greeted us at the door of her house was not to get anything dirty. And then she'd turn her attention to Mama.

"Charlotte, did you notice the chandelier? It got delivered yesterday," Sonya would crow. "Well, how could you not notice? Thirty-two pendants of Czechoslovakian crystal! Two men it took to bring it into the house and hang it!"

"Beautiful. So elegant," Mama said of every new item. Then, unable to help herself, she always added, "Can I ask, what did it cost?"

"We got a bargain, someone Leo knows in business," Sonya said of every item, before proceeding to reveal the price. Along with bragging about her acquisitions, she'd point out the room she was fixing for Zayde, because of course he'd prefer living in her spacious new home rather than the room off our kitchen.

Mama was called Charlotte, but her real name was Zipporah, which is Hebrew for "bird," and she sounded like a bird twittering whenever we walked home from Sonya's. "Dreck," she'd mutter. "All that money, and not a shred of taste . . . If she thinks Zayde is going to trade my cooking for hers . . ." Mama had started talking to herself a few months earlier, around the time when Papa announced, "Your mama is growing a little brother or sister for you in her tummy!"

Papa was usually calm and dignified, but often during that winter and spring, instead of giving lessons after dinner, he took us for walks. He said we were going out "to give your mama a little peace." But I felt he had to move because he had so much excitement inside him. It felt almost dangerous to walk after dark with this man I did but didn't recognize, a jolly Papa—a Papa who whistled! If we ran into a person he knew, he called "hello" in a big outdoor voice. "My girls," he introduced us, always adding, "And there's a new one on the way." And on Saturday afternoons, he gave Mama peace by taking us to the movies at the Joy or the National Theater. Barbara liked the Joy because it showed cowboy movies. I favored the National because before we went in, Papa bought each of us a little bag of sunflower seeds at the candy store next door; I ate the seeds during the movie, cracking the shells with my teeth and spitting them onto the floor—an act that felt thrillingly mischievous, but no one punished me for it! That's because everyone did this at the National; by the end of the movie, there were shells all over the floor, hence the theater's nickname, the Polly Seed Opera House.

In the spring, Papa and Zayde, who seemed equally delighted with Mama's pregnancy—he kept smiling at Papa and patting him on the back—planted a vegetable garden by the fig tree in the yard. We helped them water the new shoots coming up and pull out weeds. And I hadn't known Papa could draw, but sometimes he sat at the kitchen table and practiced fancy lettering. He made a beautiful alphabet for Barbara and me and did each of our names with curlicues and flowers coming out of the letters. One day I saw a drawing he'd done of a storefront with fancy lettering on the window. I hadn't yet learned how to read, but I recognized our name, *Greenstein*, and I knew *& Son* from seeing it on the sign at Fine & Son Fine Footwear.

Did I feel a sting of rejection, confronting this evidence that Papa wanted a son? Was there already a bud inside me of the attorney who would champion feminist causes? What I remember is that I, too, wanted a boy. I already had a sister. And, in my ignorance of human reproduction, I simply assumed that since it was what we wanted, the baby inside Mama was a little brother.

At the same time Papa became so cheerful, Mama seemed to be sucked inside her own thoughts. She burned things on the stove or got the buttons wrong when she dressed us or forgot to make us lunch. Worse than her distraction, however, were the times she did notice us. She'd always had a temper, but now if we took too long in the bath or we talked too loud, she'd pinch or slap us.

I say "we" and "us"—Barbara and I both referred to ourselves that way—but of course we weren't the same person. Nor did Mama treat us the same. Her punishments for me could be arbitrary, as if she simply needed to relieve some anger and her eyes happened to light on me. I walked past her in the kitchen one day that spring, and out of nowhere she grabbed my shoulders and shook me for what felt like forever. Then, as if a storm had passed through her, she softly touched my terrified face and said, "You just looked like you needed a good shaking."

But between Mama and Barbara, a clash could turn into war. Like what happened on the day Sonya showed off her telephone, the first phone I'd ever seen in a person's house.

"Here, Char, call someone." Sonya plucked the receiver from its cradle on the wall.

"No, thank you," Mama said, but Sonya pressed the instrument into her hand.

"You hold it up to your ear," Sonya said.

"I know how to use a telephone! But who do you want I should call? The mayor? The . . ." The idea of telephoning anyone was so foreign, Mama couldn't even think of whom else she might call.

"Call Canter's. Look, I have their number right here. I call and order a pound of corned beef, they send a boy to deliver it. So much easier when I'm busy with Stan."

"You'd buy a pound of corned beef without looking to make sure they give you fresh and trim off the fat?" Mama sniffed and handed her back the receiver.

"You think they'd give anything but their best to a customer who telephones an order? In fact, I think I'll order some now." Sonya made a show of placing the call and telling the man at Canter's to send her their leanest, most tender corned beef.

On the way home, Mama grumbled to herself more than ever. "The airs she puts on, you'd think she was the Queen of Sheba. . . . Who cares that Leo is forty-two and he's got fat, pudgy fingers, and he laughs like a wheezing donkey? At least he has a head for business. . . . And I thought I was too good for Slotkin."

Barbara and I had both gotten good at pretending not to listen to her muttering. We chattered to each other or chased one of the goats that grazed on the unpaved streets near Sonya's new house. We scampered around Mama as she walked, spinning in circles until we staggered from dizziness. But sometimes, if she said something like, "Nine kids like my mother, I'd kill myself first," my eyes leaped in search of Barbara's; she was looking for me, too, and we exchanged frightened glances.

We *knew* not to respond when Mama talked to herself. So I was shocked when Barbara said this time, "Mama, who's Slotkin? . . . Mama?"

For a moment Mama looked dazed, as if she were swimming out of a dream. Then she stared daggers at Barbara. "Was anyone talking to you?"

It wasn't too late; Barbara could have backed down. Instead she repeated, "Who's Slotkin?"

"What are you talking about?"

"You said Slotkin. And you said Uncle Leo laughs like a donkey. Hee haw, hee haw!" She skipped a few steps ahead.

Mama was seven months pregnant, and she'd been complaining that she could barely move, but she swooped forward with astonishing speed and grabbed Barbara's elbow, then marched her the two remaining blocks to our house. All the while, Barbara kept defiantly braying, "Hee haw!"

I trotted behind them, trying to *will* Barbara to be quiet . . . at the same time as I was transfixed by the drama. I'd never seen Barbara so naughty. Or Mama so furious.

Mama kept her grip on Barbara as she pushed through our front door and into the hall.

"Hee haw!"

Mama slapped her. Then she flung open the door to the hall closet and shoved Barbara inside. Coats and jackets were jammed into the closet, hanging on a rod. Barbara fell into them, and for a moment it looked as if the coats would push her back out. But Mama slammed the door, grabbed the key hanging on a nail, and locked her in.

"No!" Barbara pounded her fists against the door.

"I can't stand to have you in my sight!" Mama yelled.

"Let me out!"

"Elaine!" Mama commanded, and I jumped. I hadn't done anything, but that wouldn't save me if her wrath turned toward me. All she said was, "We're going outside."

Trembling with the effort of not crying, I followed Mama into the kitchen. She got us glasses of water, then went into the backyard and lowered herself heavily into one of the beat-up wooden chairs Papa had found in the street and placed under the fig tree, next to our garden.

Fruit trees—figs, apricots, peaches, loquats, pomegranates—grew in the yards of many houses in Boyle Heights. Our tree was a Black Mission fig, with purplish skin and fruit that was amber with a touch of pink. I thought of the tree as Zayde's. The tree was the reason he'd chosen our house to rent when he moved the family to Boyle Heights, he said, and he sometimes sighed in contentment and said something (which I learned came from the Bible) about dwelling under his vine and his fig tree. Zayde tended the tree carefully, checking it on summer afternoons for the wilting leaves that meant it needed water and harvesting the figs just when they were ripe, not letting them spoil on the tree.

I usually loved to sit beneath the fig tree, lounging on one of the chairs or, even better, sitting on the ground, where I'd find a perch in a crook of the twisty roots. When I began to read, it became one of my favorite places to retreat with a book.

But today I wanted to be anywhere but here. I could still hear Barbara screaming. And Mama said, "Sit down. Sit! And don't you move, or I'll put you in there."

I sat.

Now that it was May, Mama, Papa, and Zayde often lounged beside the garden after dinner. The early evenings were pleasant, just cool enough for a light jacket or sweater, the air scented with night-blooming jasmine from the bushes along the back of the house. In the middle of the day, though, I was soon hot and uncomfortable. Mama had to be hot, too. She kept fanning her face. But she didn't say a word; she just sat and stared at nothing.

There were things in the closet behind the coats, dark old things whose musty reek mingled with the sickly sweet odor of mothballs. And there were spiders. Once Mama was getting her coat out, and she screamed at a giant spider on the sleeve. Thinking about it, I felt like it was me trapped in the dark, with horrid things I couldn't see crawling on me.

And worse than that fear was the way I felt toward Mama. Like any child, I accepted the behavior of adults in my world even when it baffled me. But imprisoning Barbara in the closet on a sweltering afternoon . . . Yes, I knew that Mama's upbringing had been harsh, and in the 1920s there was no such thing as "parenting"—parents simply reared their children, they didn't have bookstore shelves filled with expert advice. Still, in what Mama had done, even my five-year-old self recognized a streak of irrationality that terrified me. A wave of dizziness sent me pitching out of the chair.

I crouched on the ground, drenched in sweat, and cast a frightened glance at Mama. Would she put *me* in the closet for leaving my chair?

But Mama's eyes were closed. She was asleep.

Carefully, not making a sound, I stood up, planning to return to the chair.

She didn't stir.

I took two steps away. Mama continued to sleep. Another step. Then, moving as silently as I could, I sneaked back inside the house.

Into the hallway. Something odd had happened. There were bits of white stuff on the floor. I got closer and saw that the bits were plaster. They had come from a hole in the wall about the size of a potato next to the closet door.

There was no sound from inside the closet, and for a moment I imagined Barbara had squeezed herself out through the potato-sized hole.

"Barbara?" I whispered. "Barbara?"

Two fingers poked out from the hole. I reached for them, and our fingers locked. Hers were clammy, as if she had a fever. And she hadn't said a word.

I looked at the key, on its nail above my head. If Mama had thrown Barbara in the closet for sassing her, what would she do to me if I . . . ?

I kissed Barbara's fingers. She whimpered.

"I'm going to get you out. I promise." I had to pull to loosen her grip.

I went into the kitchen to get a chair. Peeked into the yard. Mama didn't stir. I pulled the chair into the hall, climbed up on it, and got the key. Climbed down and opened the door.

Barbara flew out as if something were chasing her. I slammed the door to keep whatever it was inside. She was sour with sweat, her bangs plastered to her forehead. She still didn't say anything.

"I'll get you some water." I took her hand and led her into the kitchen.

Oh, no! Mama was coming in! She was already through the door, and it was too late to hide.

But Mama wasn't mad. Instead, she cried out, *"Oy, mein kind!"* and ran to put her arms around Barbara as if she hadn't been the one who locked Barbara in the closet. Barbara flinched for a moment, but then started to sob and let Mama kiss her and smooth her sweaty hair.

That's how it was between Mama and Barbara. Barbara challenged Mama more than I did, and Mama punished her more harshly. But she was also more affectionate toward Barbara. And it seems bizarre to call Mama *indulgent*, but how else could you describe the way she sometimes went along with Barbara's fancies? Like when we went to the party Aunt Sonya and Uncle Leo gave in June to show off their new house.

Mama planned for us to wear our good Kate Greenaway dresses. She took the dresses out of the closet but left us to step into them and do each other's buttons—she was now in her final month of pregnancy and had already packed a bag with the things she'd need for the hospital. I donned my dress happily; I loved the soft green color and the fancy smocked bodice. Barbara, however, left her blue Kate Greenaway lying on the bed. Instead she put on her white middy blouse with the navy sailor collar and matching navy skirt.

"What are you wearing?" Mama said the minute Barbara emerged from our bedroom.

"I want to wear my middy blouse."

"This is a party. You don't wear just a blouse and skirt."

"It's my *middy* blouse."

"I'm not bringing my daughter to a party at Sonya's fancy new house in a blouse and skirt. Go put on your good dress."

"It's my middy blouse!" Barbara stood with her legs planted.

Mama lurched heavily across the room, a storm gathering on her face, and I tensed, sure that she was going to slap Barbara for sassing. Suddenly, though, her eyes went soft, as if her gaze were filled with honey, so warm and sweet I yearned for a taste of it. She shook her head and smiled at Barbara. "My headstrong girl." She didn't say another word about the middy blouse.

THE HOUSEWARMING PARTY took place on a hot day, and all of the children—there were a dozen of us in those fecund times—were sent outside to the back. Anna, the daughter of Leo's brother and the oldest of us at eleven, was told to keep us in the yard.

Anna was a bit strange. She rarely looked straight at anyone, and if any attention came her way, her face scrunched like she was going to cry.

"Let's play hide-and-seek," Barbara said.

"Where?" One of the boys scanned the yard, which was no larger than ours.

"We're supposed to stay—" Anna tried. Even at twice our age, she was no match for Barbara.

"You're it." Barbara pointed to a girl.

"I don't want to be it. You be it."

"I'll be it next time." Barbara flashed the girl a dazzling smile. "What's your name?"

"Judy. Promise you'll be it next time?"

"Promise."

Judy put her hands over her eyes and started counting.

I glanced at Anna. She'd retreated to the side of the yard.

"Five, six . . . ," Judy said.

The other kids were scattering, a couple of the littlest crouching by the back steps but the rest running around the side of the house toward the street. I ran, too. Glimpsing a bigger girl, I followed her down the block toward the new construction. We'd been forbidden to play around the construction because we might step on stray nails, but I had to find a hiding place! Besides, the rule about nails made no sense. As the daughter of a salesman at the best shoe store on Brooklyn Avenue, I was never allowed to go barefoot, not even on a hot day like this.

The bigger girl turned toward a house that was almost done, the stucco walls already constructed and framing set up for the porch. I made for a site two doors down that was still skeletal, just a slab and some wooden joists, with big stacks of two-by-fours over to the side. I squeezed between two piles of wood into a perfect hiding place, just the right size for a five-year-old. Judy would never find me here.

The wood, warmed by the afternoon sun, smelled intoxicating. Zayde always talked about the forest outside his village, how beautiful it was, how cool on a hot day. I had never been to a forest, but, hunkered in the shade of the fragrant lumber, I imagined I was in Zayde's woods. My feet felt hot and itchy, and I took off my Mary Janes and my socks; I couldn't step on any nails if I was just sitting.

The women had all baked for Sonya and Leo's party, and I had three different kinds of cake in my stomach, all of them sweet and delicious and heavy. And it was such a warm, sleepy afternoon . . .

"HEY! GIRL!"

Startled awake, I started to jump up, but someone grabbed my shoulders to stop me.

"Don't, you make fall." The boy's accent was like Zayde's, but his English wasn't as good.

I sat up, careful not to disturb the wood, and stared at the boy crouching next to me. About my age, he had cat eyes, their irises weirdly light compared to his olive skin and black hair.

"What you do here?" he said.

"I'm hiding."

Fear leaped into his eyes. "Why? Pogrom?"

"No, silly. Hide-and-seek." I'd heard the word *pogrom* from Zayde and Mama, and I knew it was a very bad thing. But it only happened in the old country. What a strange boy, to think of that. Was he one of Anna's many cousins? Except he wasn't wearing dress-up clothes, like all the other kids at the party. This boy's thin shirt looked the way our clothes did when Mama said they'd gotten too old to mend and we should give them to the poor.

I noticed a sack behind him. "What's that?"

"Nothing." Suddenly furtive, he shifted his body so I couldn't see the sack anymore. "You Elaine?"

"How do you know my name?"

"They call. You don't want they find you?"

"Don't you know how to play hide-and-seek? What's your name?"

"Danny."

"Do you live on this street?"

He looked secretive again but then declared, "Going to. This house, here. My father builds. Big house." Prouder and prouder, as if with each word, the house became more solid, his future life in it brighter. "You live over there?"

"My aunt and uncle. They're having a party."

"Ela-aine!" I heard from my hiding place. It was Barbara. Why was *she* looking for me, when Judy was it? And why the note of urgency? "Elaine, are you there?"

"Over here," I called in a whisper-shout. "Here! Here!" I crept to the edge of the stack of wood and waved. I couldn't go out until I put on my shoes.

"Everybody's looking for you. Are you okay?" She came and stood at the end of my hiding place. And spotted Danny. "Who's that?"

I looked at him. He was staring openmouthed at Barbara, who sparkled in the bright sunlight in her middy blouse with its jaunty sailor collar.

"Just a boy," I said. Not wanting to share him. Thinking of him, already, as "my boy."

Someone yelled, "Barbara! Did you find her?" An adult voice.

"She's here," Barbara called back. And said to me, "Hurry."

I scrambled out from my burrow. A woman screamed, "Thank God, she's all right!" Then a pack of people rushed at me, and Papa hugged me so tight I couldn't breathe. He carried me back to Sonya and Leo's, he and everyone else yelling at me.

"Where were you?"

"Didn't you hear everyone looking for you?"

"Look at your dress, filthy."

"Where are your shoes?"

"Did you want to kill your poor mother?" a woman scolded, and when they brought me into the house, I was terrified I had done just that.

Mama was lying back in a chair, her legs splayed and her arms limp over her huge belly. Aunt Sonya was fanning her with a magazine, but Mama didn't move. Her face looked yellow-white like old candle wax.

"Mama!" I howled, and ran to her. And then stopped, horrified by the puddle of water on the floor by the chair. Had Mama peed herself . . . like I was doing now, wet shame squirting down my legs even faster than the tears gushed from my eyes?

"Lainie." Mama opened her eyes and took my hand. I steeled myself for her fury, but something must have been terribly wrong. She smiled at me.

Then she was gone, driven by Leo to the hospital.

I hadn't hurt Mama, Pearl assured me. Her water had broken, and it meant she was going to have her baby.

But I didn't stop crying until Barbara came and blew on my face to cool me down. When the adults weren't looking, she took my hand and we snuck back to the house under construction to get my shoes. She acted like I'd done something bold and exciting, and I stopped feeling guilty and came to see that day as an adventure. For the first time, I saw a little something bold in myself.

AFTER OUR BABY SISTER Audrey was born, we didn't go as often to Aunt Sonya's. Still, every Monday afternoon, when Sonya had "the girls" over to play cards, Mama carried Audrey, and we walked there. All of the women brought their children. They put the babies down in Sonya and Leo's bedroom, and the rest of us played in the yard. By August, the house where I'd hidden was completed, and a family moved in. I walked by and watched for my boy, Danny, but I never saw him. He had appeared so fleetingly, with his cat eyes and his air of mystery, that I thought I might have dreamed him, except that when Barbara had taken me back to get my shoes, I saw that he'd left his sack; it held a few pieces of scrap wood and some nails, and I took one of the nails. I hid it in my treasure box, a gift from Aunt Pearl.

I might have dreamed jolly Papa, too. Now, on the nights he came home for dinner, he gave us lessons again or sat in his chair, absorbed in the newspaper. Occasionally, if Barbara or I asked very, very nicely, without pestering, he took us for a walk, but he no longer called out to people or whistled. And he paid little attention to baby Audrey.

He lost interest in the garden. Barbara and I kept on taking care of it, with Zayde's help. We had green thumbs, Zayde said. He said we grew the best tomatoes and cucumbers in Los Angeles.

CHAPTER 4

DAMAGE?

I SIT FLOATING ON MEMORY AS THE AFTERNOON GIVES WAY TO DUSK. And then the pull of the past is done with me . . . or maybe it's just my eighty-five-year-old bladder that insists on yanking me back to the present. After using the bathroom, I gather up Mama's daughter memorabilia to share with Harriet.

Everything except Philip's card, one more piece of detritus that Mama saved simply because she couldn't throw anything away. I pick up the card to drop it in with the recycling, but didn't Josh say that something was written on the back?

Kay Devereaux
Broadmoor Hotel, Colorado Springs

The handwriting looks like Philip's, but I've never heard of Kay Devereaux. I wonder why Philip gave the card to Mama. Maybe this Kay was a lead who didn't pan out, a chorus-girl friend of Barbara's; the name sounds like a stage name.

And then a memory slams me: I see Barbara and me painting on our scarlet Coty lipstick—the precious tube we shared, hidden in the toe of a shoe—and making up movie star names for ourselves. *Diane Hollister. Priscilla Camberwell. Nola Trent* was my favorite, a no-nonsense type who'd had a brilliant New York theatrical career and only did films with clever repartee. *Kay Devereaux* is just the kind of name Barbara would have chosen. Could Philip have found her?

I run for the phone, call information, and ask for Kay Devereaux in Colorado Springs. Even as I recognize—and loathe—the prickly feeling surging through me. It's the charge I felt the first year or two after she left, every time I raced for a ringing telephone or snatched up the mail, or we got a tip that someone in Hollywood or San Francisco or Tijuana had spotted her.

We searched for her like crazy back then, no matter that in her note she'd said not to worry and that she was fine. As Aunt Sonya never tired of saying, an eighteen-year-old girl on her own—or worse, *not* on her own— how could she be fine? Look at the job she'd had, singing and dancing in the chorus at a Hollywood nightclub, her legs and everything on display and her silly head filled with dreams of breaking into the pictures. "A girl like that doesn't have the best judgment, does she?" Sonya said again and again, until one day Mama screamed in her face.

We talked to every one of her friends and ran personal ads in the newspapers in the biggest cities in California. Papa went to the police, too, but they didn't do anything, not when they heard about the note and her job at the nightclub. We tried one more time when Philip offered to help, though by then she'd been gone for two years. (I didn't lie to Josh. I *did* work for Philip, but it was a trade, a way for my family to pay him for looking for my sister.)

Along with the prickle of hope, I got used to the crash that followed, when the mail contained no word from her, or the "Barbara" spotted working as a waitress in Newport Beach turned out to be a middle-aged Mexican woman, and the man who'd given us the tip had vanished with his twenty-dollar reward.

Within a few months, even a hint of hope and I was already plummeting. The pattern became so fixed in my nervous system that it kicks in now, more than sixty-five years later, when I ask the recorded voice for Kay Devereaux. And of course, there's no listing. She would have married and changed her name. Moved. Died.

I could check the Internet. I jump up to go to my office.

"Stop it!" I say it out loud and will myself to sit down.

What the hell does it matter what happened to a woman named Kay Devereaux? That woman can't be Barbara, because if she were, Mama and Papa would have told me.

I pour myself a Scotch. It's almost time for *Jeopardy!*. I should get myself some dinner and get settled in front of the television. But for just another moment, I'm drawn back to the May Company box; there are things I haven't looked at yet, below Barbara's dance programs and Philip's card. I get to the bottom without finding anything else about the mysterious Kay—not that I was hunting for anything, of course not. But to think that the box sat for decades on the closet shelf and I never opened it.

And Josh brought in just two department store boxes, but he said there were more. What other riches did my mother squirrel away? I go into my office. Josh left a chair just inside the closet. I hop up on it . . . and wobble. Oh, no! Gripping the back of the chair, I plant both feet on the ground. I can't afford another broken leg like last year, or, kiss of death, a broken hip. That's the main reason I'm moving to Rancho Mañana, so I won't have to worry about stairs, and so in case anything does happen, my kids won't have to put their lives on hold to take care of me. Carol did that when I broke my leg; she came down from Oregon for a month.

I should put some food on top of the Scotch. The refrigerator yields half a turkey sandwich, left over from going out to lunch yesterday. I take the sandwich into the den, turn on the TV, and match wits against the contestants on *Jeopardy!*.

Once I've eaten (and aced Final Jeopardy!), I brave the chair again. I find another three department store boxes, one so heavy it almost sends me tumbling. No wonder, the box is filled with books. "Papa!" I murmur. I can almost smell him as I lift out the poetry anthologies he had us recite from, and his beloved histories of Los Angeles, everything friable with decay. I open one of the poetry books, glimpse a title, and discover I can recite the poem by heart. I wonder if Harriet will be able to do that, too.

She has to see this! I call and invite her to come over for lunch after our water aerobics class tomorrow.

I LEARNED TO SWIM at Venice Beach—Papa taught me when I was little—and there's still nothing I love more than to walk into the ocean, out to where the waves lap just above my waist, and then dive in. The exhilaration of that first cold immersion! The bubbly tickle of salt water on my skin and the blurry (without my glasses) vastness ahead of me. A whiff of the beach, and my nose still comes up like an eager dog's. The first time I swam in a pool, when I was a student at USC, I felt claustrophobic and my skin itched for hours. Since then, I've come to appreciate the unique pleasures of pool swimming—in particular, that the pool at the Westside Y, where Harriet and I take water aerobics twice a week, is blissfully warm.

I don't see Harriet in the locker room. My baby sister, twelve years my junior, has probably come early to swim laps. Sure enough, when I go out to the pool, I spot her cutting through the water, a zaftig seal in her fluorescent green suit and matching cap. I put on booties, ease into the water, and greet the half dozen other regulars who are already there. A few minutes later, Harriet swims to the shallow end and joins us, stripping off her swim cap and shaking out her long gray hair.

Anytime I've attempted to go gray, the word *schoolmarm* immediately comes to mind. That's why I get to the salon every six weeks for a feathery cut and to keep up my color, which has gotten lighter and lighter; it's now a sort of cocker spaniel blond. On Harriet, though, wild gray locks suggest a free spirit who still puts marijuana in her brownies and has a diverting sex life. The look is perfect for her workshops, "Wise Woman: The Deep Knowing of Age." Sounds like psychobabble, but Harriet really is a wise woman, and not only because she's a respected psychotherapist; she sees beneath the surface of people and relationships and comes up with insights that amaze me. Not that she often exercises her skill on the family. Refraining from analyzing us is part of her wisdom.

We prance—well, Harriet prances; I shuffle—in the pool for an hour to music that runs from big-band tunes to the kind of songs my grandkids listen to; then we take showers, dress, and meet back at my house.

"Wow. You're really doing this!" Harriet surveys the living room, which already feels bare, though all I've done so far is empty bookshelves. Every piece of furniture, however—except for the few things that will fit in the apartment at Rancho Mañana—has been assessed by a sweet but ruthless woman named Melissa who bluntly told me what's worth placing in her consignment store and what's so pathetically outdated I should just give it away.

"Sure you don't want to move in with me?" Harriet says.

"I'm sure. But thanks!" I think of Harriet's household—her forty-two-year-old son who moved back home after getting laid off and the not-much-older man with whom she does, in fact, have a diverting sex life—and experience a moment of profound gratitude that I can afford my own apartment at Rancho Mañana.

Over lunch, I tell her about the boxes. Then I make tea and show her the gems I've found. I start with the daughter box, though I'm surprised, going through it with Harriet, to realize Mama saved far less ephemera of her life than of Barbara's, Audrey's, or mine. There are report cards and class pictures, but nothing more personal.

But what really stuns me is when we turn to Papa's books.

"Remember Papa's poetry lessons?" I say.

"What poetry lessons?"

"Didn't he have you recite poems?" She looks blank, and I continue, "It wasn't just because he wanted us to speak well. He loved to recite. Remember, he won a prize for elocution when he was in high school?"

"Did he?"

"Harriet! The story of Papa's prize is a Greenstein legend."

She laughs. "They say—and I guess this proves it—that every sibling grows up in a different family. That if someone asked you or Audrey or me what it was like growing up, we'd have wildly different stories. It has to do with birth order, temperament." She picks up the tag on the end of her teabag, starts shredding it. "And of course, most of my childhood was after Barbara left."

I think of Philip's card and the wild idea I had that I'd stumbled on Barbara's new identity. "What if we could find her now, if she's still alive?"

"Why, so we could confront her with the damage she did?" Harriet snaps.

Her ferocity stuns me. As does what she says next.

"I used to make movies in my mind, of Audrey being so anxious it was torture for her to get out the door to go to school, or Papa when he came back from the morgue—remember, he nagged the police so much that for a year or two they called him every time they found some poor, nameless girl dead in an alley? He'd walk in the door, and his face was gray, like *he* was dead. I'd fantasize about forcing her to watch them. . . . Shit! I thought I'd worked through this in therapy a few decades ago."

"I had no idea it hit you that hard."

"Elaine! She left when I was five, and after that everyone in the family . . . well, it created a few abandonment issues after everyone shut down in one way or another."

"I didn't mean . . . I just wish I'd known. I could have done something. I knew Audrey was having a lot of problems, but I thought of you as Little Mary Sunshine—you were cheerful no matter what."

"I *was* cheerful. I'm cheerful by nature. Just like poor Audrey was always a bundle of nerves."

Poor Audrey, indeed. Audrey struggled all her life with severe anxiety and eventually with a dependence on the Valium that used to be handed out like candy to jittery housewives. Still, even I know enough psychology to understand that while my family recognized Audrey's fears and tried to soothe them—and acknowledged the particular distress I felt as Barbara's twin—we shortchanged Harriet.

"I'm sorry," I tell her. "For what it's worth all these years later, I really am."

She squeezes my hand. "Apology accepted. And I did work through a lot in therapy . . . But why did you ask about Barbara? Did you find something?"

"It's just . . . going through all this stuff stirs up memories." By this time, I've Googled "Kay Devereaux" and gotten nothing. And I looked up the Broadmoor Hotel; it's still there, a five-star resort whose website displays stately Italianate buildings with "purple mountain majesties" soaring behind them. The site offers the fascinating tidbit that the woman who composed "America the Beautiful" wrote it after visiting the area.

"Now, this book I remember." She picks up one of Papa's histories of Los Angeles, written by a grandson of Andrew Boyle. "We studied it in school."

The Boyle book came out in the mid-1930s, when I was working at Uncle Leo's bookstore, and I bought it at a discount for Papa's birthday. I don't recall actually reading the book, but I had already heard the exciting part of the story, about the founder of Boyle Heights, from Papa.

"It used to upset me," I say, "hearing about Andrew Boyle's father, who left his kids in Ireland and vanished."

"Yeah, but Boyle found him eventually."

"The father? No, he didn't."

"Lainie, I'm sure of it. I feel like I know exactly where to find it." She starts paging through the book.

"I'll bet you a ticket to the symphony that I'm right." Just thinking about the forsaken brothers and sisters sparks a whisper of the uneasiness the story caused me as a child.

"You're on." She slows her flipping. "Ha! I win." She reads aloud, " 'He'—Andrew Boyle—'finally arrived in New Orleans and there found his father, the cause of the family migration to America.' "

I reach for the book and read the sentence for myself. Just that one sentence? And not a word more? I skim the next several pages; the long-lost father no sooner enters the narrative than he disappears again.

"Where's the rest of the story? Finding his father, it's like something out of a myth. What was the father doing all that time? And how did it happen? Did they just run into each other on the street in New Orleans?"

"That's, as they say, all he wrote," Harriet replies. "That's why it stuck with me. Kids in my class asked the same questions as you, and the teacher gave us some lame answer, like the author didn't go into detail because it was a private family matter. Then she gave me one of *those* looks. Everyone knew about Barbara—certainly all the teachers did. Another subject that took hours of therapy."

I had escaped that burden, being branded as a girl whose sister had run away and never come back. In our neighborhood or among childhood friends, yes, people saw me and thought of Barbara being gone—just as, all the time I was growing up, they knew me as her twin, seeing her next to me even when I was alone. But I was already going to USC when she left, already spending most of my waking hours beyond the fishbowl of Boyle Heights.

"Even as a kid," Harriet says, "I knew the real reason the grandson didn't say anything about a joyous reunion. Because it wasn't joyous. How could it be? No matter how happy they were the first minute they laid eyes on each other, how long would it take before Andrew looked his father in the eye and asked, 'Why?' And from the father's perspective— think about it—having Andrew back in his life threatened his exercise of Americans' most precious right."

"The pursuit of happiness?"

"The right to reinvent ourselves . . . Which brings us back to your question. How would I feel if we could find Barbara now? Profoundly ambivalent, I think. Finding her might lead to a wonderful relationship for the time we have left. But that isn't the only possible outcome."

As I said, Harriet is a wise woman.

She's not, however, infallible. After she leaves, I go back to her comment that after Barbara took off, everyone in the family shut down. It's not true. We were all upset, of course, scared something terrible had happened to Barbara, and that was why we hadn't heard a word. At the same time, we were hurt and angry to think *nothing* had happened, and in that case how could she lack the decency to let us know she was all right?

But *shutting down*, that's a term from Harriet's world of psychotherapy. And I never saw any point in spending time on a therapist's couch dissecting my reaction to Barbara's leaving. Any time, energy, or money I put into the mystery of my twin's disappearance went toward hiring detectives to look for her—really hiring them, paying a generous fee, not like the trade I did with Philip, who squeezed in the favor of looking for Barbara during spare moments between bread-and-butter jobs. I did it the first time about fifteen years after she left, when Paul and I had gotten on our feet financially; and again in the early 1980s, when my law firm started working with a detective who was a wizard at locating things in public records. Nothing ever panned out.

Did Barbara's leaving "damage" me? Did something shut down in me . . . and never come back to life? I think of my youthful poetry—odes to the glories of nature, impassioned empathy for the suffering of the world, and of course love poems. Thank God the sweet girl who wrote those poems turned into a strong woman!

"It's called growing up," I say out loud as I straighten up the stuff Harriet and I looked through.

If I became not just strong but tough, was that because of Barbara? Or was it *my* nature, along with the fact that I went to law school and made it as an attorney at a time when not just the law but all of professional life was a men's club? A pundit for a conservative rag once described me as "a brainy ballbuster who gets energized by outrage as if chronic anger were a steak dinner. Bring on the bromo." Paul and I laughed so much over that one that I had it framed.

But it's true that a tough cookie, a scrapper who didn't run away from a fight—even, perhaps, an angry woman—was what I had to be in my working life. And if I didn't just leave it at the office, if I was a scrapper at home, too, well, Paul dove into our spats with as much gusto as I did. We honed our ideas, our characters, by butting heads. Couples did that in our day, they gave each other edges. Maybe because it was harder to divorce, we didn't tiptoe around each other, cordial and careful and dull.

I miss Paul! Life is so quiet without him. If, early in our marriage, I ever wondered if I'd made the right choice, there was one crystalline moment when every doubt disappeared. Ronnie was six or seven, and he was having an asthma attack, heaving as he coughed phlegm into a pail. Paul and I knelt on either side of him, each of us with a hand on his back. Our eyes met over our son's gasping body. In Paul's gaze, I saw love, concern, a steadiness that told me this man would never, in any of the big things, let me down. But it was more than that. At the risk of sounding mystical, I felt like I was getting a message from God: that I was one of those rare, favored people who had truly found her soul mate.

I did all right with Ronnie. But Carol . . . My sensitive firstborn was the daughter of the poet I once was. And I wish I had summoned some of that young poet's softness for her. Maybe if I'd worked part-time when she was little . . . But I mentor young women attorneys; even now, the mommy track is no real option for any of them who wants to be taken seriously. And I loved working; I would have gone crazy at home. Like a lot of working moms today, I managed thanks to Mexican nannies. I was lucky— I found girls who were both affectionate and reliable. And the kids learned to speak fluent Spanish; Ronnie is now an attorney specializing in contracts between U.S. and Latin American companies. Yet there were times when I saw how naturally the nannies cuddled my children, how the kids flopped like puppies in their arms, and I wished . . .

But I'm hardly going to blame Barbara for my disappointments or roads not taken, any more than I'd give her credit for my triumphs. All of it is *life*. Eggs break in life, and if you're smart, you make an omelette. Life gives you lemons; you make lemonade. Clichés, yes, because they're deeply true. And it's the way we lived our lives, not just Paul and I but our generation.

Look at Harriet, whose husband in the late 1960s started wearing love beads over his dental smock and then left her, with three young kids, for his twentysomething hygienist. She was devastated at first, naturally. Then she picked herself up, went back to college, and became a psychotherapist.

And Paul—he *did* have someone to blame, Joe McCarthy and his vicious Red-baiting cronies, for destroying his dream of being a history professor. He was studying for his Ph.D. at UCLA when the State of California demanded that all university faculty, even teaching assistants like Paul, sign an anti-Communist loyalty oath. Though he'd quit the Party by then, he refused to sign because the oath was an outrage. That put an end to UCLA. At first he found a job teaching history at a private high school, but his politics got him in trouble there, too. He ended up going into his father's scrap metal business. Scrap metal was honest, he said; it required no ideological purity test. I was furious on his behalf; it was one reason I jumped to take McCarthy cases. Paul, though, didn't look back. He genuinely enjoyed the business, the salt-of-the-earth people he dealt with every day. He fulfilled his love for teaching, too, by starting a workers' university, where he taught two evenings a week for the rest of his life. He'd come home electrified, continuing class debates with me as we drank a nightcap; ah, some of our best lovemaking took place on those nights.

I've divided the things from Mama's boxes into several piles: mementos of Audrey to give to her kids, Boyle Heights items for the Jewish Historical Society, Papa's poetry books for Carol.

I hesitate over the book by Andrew Boyle's grandson. I'll give it to the Jewish Historical Society, but do I want to read it first? Funny how I insisted to Harriet that the father never turned up. The story I heard when I was so young, the children's plight so poignant that it had the truth of lived experience. I wonder what else I've been dead wrong about.

I drop the book into the pile for the Historical Society. It won't tell me the one thing I really want to know: what *did* happen when Andrew asked, "Why?"

Not why she left in the first place, nor why she didn't contact us for a year or two—those things I can understand, the desperation of a teenage runaway terrified someone would force her to return home. What I can't fathom are the years and the decades after, when she lacked the compassion to let us know she was all right; lacked even the curiosity to find out what had happened to us.

Better, perhaps, if Andrew Boyle had never found his father, because no answer could satisfy that question. No love could survive its being asked. Better to think his father was devoured by a bear in the Alaskan wilderness. Better if he had been!

CHAPTER 5

OUR FIRST DAY OF SCHOOL

AFTER AUDREY WAS BORN, ON JUNE 12, 1926, PAPA CHANGED BACK to the way he used to be before Mama got pregnant. Mama changed, too. But she became someone brand-new. Forceful, purposeful, an arrow whizzing toward one gleaming target—our first day of school, which she had circled in black ink on the calendar page for September, the day after Labor Day.

"Charlotte, it's only kindergarten," Aunt Sonya said. "They don't learn anything. They just play."

"And where does this just-playing take place?" Mama retorted.

"The elementary school."

"See! The Breed Street Elementary School," Mama said, as if that settled it.

"Yes, but kindergarten . . . Believe me, Charlotte, if you'd ever gone to school, you'd understand." Sonya patted Mama's hand.

Mama stood up abruptly. "Girls, we have to get home." She didn't even bother to wipe our fingers, sticky from the orange slices we'd been snacking on. And when we started walking, her legs pumped so fast, even as she carried Audrey, that we had to trot to keep up.

What had Sonya meant by that—*if you'd ever gone to school?* I wondered. Everyone went to school. We often walked by the middle and high schools that Aunt Sonya and Aunt Pearl had attended after Papa's family moved to Boyle Heights; and Uncle Leo once drove us by the high school in the San Fernando Valley where Papa won the elocution prize. Mama had grown up in another country, Romania, but didn't Romania have schools? Her apparent rage made me afraid to ask.

Mama's anger didn't stop Barbara, however. "Mama, didn't you go to school?" she asked.

"Can your mama read?" Mama demanded as she charged down the street.

"Yes," I said quickly. Barbara, to my relief, didn't mention that if Mama picked up the *Los Angeles Times*, which Papa brought home at night, she often threw it down in disgust. I never saw her open any of Papa's books, and she spent a long time perusing letters written in English from our cousin Mollie in Chicago. She had no problems, though, with letters in Yiddish from other relatives or with the signs, in both Yiddish and English, in shops. And Mama read to us from picture books. Still, only Papa read aloud from books with words all over the pages, like *Alice in Wonderland* or *Peter Pan.*

"Can I do sums?" Mama said.

"Yes," I said. Sums, she could do in her head. She corrected shopkeepers if they tried to overcharge her, and they always ended up shaking their heads and saying, "You're right, Mrs. Greenstein, to the penny."

"So." She stopped so suddenly that I kept walking for several steps and had to come back.

"You girls know I grew up in Romania?" Mama said. "And it was very bad for the Jews there?"

We had heard Mama's stories of how the Romanians hated the Jews, though Papa tried to stop her from telling them. "Don't fill their heads with the idea that we're less than anyone else. We're Americans," he'd say. "We're not Jews?" Mama replied. Still, she usually told the stories when Papa wasn't around.

I knew that Mama's father, my other *zayde* whom I'd never met, used to own a tavern, but then the Romanian government made a law saying Jews couldn't sell alcohol. They even sent soldiers to make Mama's family, who lived at the tavern, leave. Mama did the strangest thing whenever she told that story. When she said "soldiers," she spat. Not wet spit so it landed on anyone; but she made a sound—*ptui!*—so rude and shocking that if she'd said she had killed the soldiers by spitting at them, I would have believed her.

Mama started walking again, but this time at a normal pace. "In Romania when I was a girl," she said, "they made a law that only a few Jewish children could go to their schools. We tried to start our own schools, but they wouldn't let us do that, either."

"How did you learn?" I asked, bolder now that she was calm.

"Ah! You think, like your silly aunt Sonya, a person's brain only works inside a building that says *school* on the front of it? Is that what you think?"

"No." Although I had thought just that.

"I learned to read Yiddish and Romanian at home, and to do sums," Mama said. "And English reading, I learned from your cousin Mollie, when I lived with Uncle Meyr in Chicago. You remember, I've told you about my brother Meyr? The happiest day of my life was when he sent for me to come live with him in America."

"Meyr the *fusgeyer*!" Barbara and I sang out together. The silly-sounding Yiddish word means "foot-wanderer," and we had learned it from Mama's favorite story, about her beloved brother Meyr.

WHEN MAMA WAS EVEN younger than Barbara and me, it got so terrible for Jews in Romania that many of them wanted to leave for America. If they could reach the port cities of Hamburg or Rotterdam, wealthy Jews would pay for their passage on ships. But it was a long way to the ports, and most Romanian Jews were too poor to afford even the cheapest train tickets. Then some clever young people came up with a way to turn their poverty into adventure. They decided to band together and go on foot. Calling themselves *fusgeyers*, they built their strength with daylong marches through the countryside. "Imagine!" Mama said. "The Romanians thought all Jews were weak. They couldn't believe it when they saw these Jewish boys and girls marching past their farms. Or when they heard that the Jews planned to walk all the way across Europe!" The *fusgeyers* didn't actually have to go that far; once they crossed the border into Austro-Hungary, Jewish organizations gave them train tickets to the ports. But they would have walked every step, Mama said. Some groups made themselves uniforms with jaunty caps, like Scouts. And when they took to the road in Romania, they raised money by staging theatricals in Jewish towns. Bands of foot-wanderers formed in town after town. There was even a "Song of the *Fusgeyers*" that Mama sang when she was especially happy.

One of the first of these bold pioneers was Meyr Avramescu, a strapping nineteen-year-old with a big, sweet laugh. Meyr was loved more than any young man has ever been loved by his baby sister, Zipporah—"That was my name, girls. It's Hebrew for 'bird.' " From the moment his finger wiggled over her cradle in the final year of the nineteenth century, Mama was captivated by her big brother. And he doted on her. He, the golden firstborn son, could have chosen any of his eight siblings to favor, but it was little Zipporah, the seventh child for whom no one else had time, who captured his heart. "From the moment I could crawl, I followed him everywhere. And he used to pick me up and throw me in the air. 'My little bird's flying!' he'd say." Mama laughed, and her eyes shone. I laughed, too, as if I were the one being tossed in the air. I loved hearing the *fusgeyer* story not only because it was exciting, but for the thrill of seeing Mama transform into a lighthearted girl whose soul brimmed with love.

Zipporah was three when Meyr joined a group of *fusgeyers* in their village, Tecuci. She didn't understand what it meant, but she loved the excitement when he got ready for an outing and the songs he sang when he came home. He played the accordion, and when he practiced for the group's theatricals, she clapped her hands and danced.

One Saturday night in the late spring, the whole village had a big party, and the *fusgeyers* entertained. Meyr played a special song, "for my little bird," and beckoned her to join him on the stage of nailed-together boards. She danced, and everyone cheered.

The next morning, Meyr hugged her so tight she could barely breathe. "I'll write to you, little bird," he said. "Every week. And I'll send for you, I promise." Why was he crying? He picked up his satchel and strode off, like he always did when the *fusgeyers* took their hikes. But everyone was weeping and acting strange. And Meyr didn't come home that night.

"Where's Meyr?" she demanded.

"Off to America," she was told.

That meant no more than hearing her brother had gone to the next village. But after two days passed and still he hadn't returned, she stopped eating for a week.

True to his word, Meyr wrote to her weekly; there was always a special note for her in the envelope with a letter to the rest of the family. At first one of her older siblings read his letters aloud to her and penned her reply. Soon she was able to correspond with him herself. Now she understood what he had meant about sending for her, and her heart fastened on America just as she had grabbed Meyr's finger above her cradle and not wanted to let go.

"He promised to send for me when I was twelve," she told us. "And he said I should learn to sew, that skilled seamstresses did well in America."

An older sister, Dora, was apprenticed to a dressmaker and sewed beautifully. Zipporah begged for lessons, but no matter how many times Dora explained or placed her hands on Zipporah's to guide them, her stitches sprawled crooked and ugly. "Oy, Zippi, a girl with no skills ends up a housemaid," Dora declared in exasperation—though she took it back immediately, stunned by her own meanness; the shame of being sent out to domestic service marked both a girl and her family as failures.

Zipporah tossed her head. What was the story the rabbi in their village told? About Rabbi Zusya saying that when he got to heaven, they weren't going to ask, "Why weren't you Moses?" No, they'd ask, "Why weren't you Zusya?" Zipporah Avramescu clearly wasn't meant to be a seamstress. God intended her to be . . . why not an actress? Because didn't the whole village applaud when she danced with Meyr? And what better talent for a *fusgeyer*, since new groups kept setting out for America? Dora and two of their brothers emigrated when she was eight. They tried to persuade the rest of the family to come, since some groups, less jolly than Meyr's, now included whole families. How could they leave, her parents protested, when they'd just gotten back on their feet with a cafe after the government had taken their tavern, and Zipporah's grandmother and her brother Shlomo were ill, and . . . the arguments went on for hours. Zipporah cajoled and wept and raged to be allowed to go with Dora and her brothers on her own, but she was too young, her parents said.

As it turned out, Mama's skill, the one that paved her way to America, lay in neither needlework nor theater. Instead, it was the art she had first exercised in her cradle, when Meyr adored her, and it flowered in her family's cafe. It was her ability to charm older men. This gift, like her infant winsomeness, she possessed in all innocence. How could a scrawny child, wielding a birch-twig broom taller than she, inveigle the pennies that were invariably slipped into her pocket? She wasn't a cheeky child, either, a bold girl who got herself noticed by talking back or joking. Why, when she couldn't even be seen—her arms plunged into dishwater in the kitchen—would Avner Papo the housepainter ask to have the little girl come stand behind his chair when he played cards? And she must be the one to fetch him a bowl of her mother's stew or a glass of the home-brewed schnapps they sold, illegally—"the Romanians even made a law against Jews doing that!"

Other than an occasional wink, Avner Papo barely acknowledged Zipporah's presence. But he claimed she brought him luck. And he *was* lucky; he often won. He always gave her some of his winnings, too. Of course, she had to turn the money over to her parents; why else would they let her waste her time standing behind Avner's chair when there were carrots and turnips to peel and dishes to wash? Once Avner realized what was happening, though, he always gave her an extra penny just for herself. She put all the pennies in a little purse Dora had sewn for her; they were her savings for America, to add to the money Meyr would send her when he was ready.

Meyr lived in a city called Chicago. He married a Jewish girl whose family came from Poland, and they had one, then two, and soon four children—he sent a photograph when each new baby was born. Now that Meyr was a busy husband and father, his letters came only once a month or even two months apart. Still, he had sent money to help his parents start their cafe, and even though Dora and their brothers paid their own way, Meyr helped them get settled once they got to Chicago.

Zipporah lived for her twelfth birthday. And she died a little when, even after her beloved Meyr sent the money for her steamship ticket, her parents insisted she was too young to travel on her own. And they needed her in the cafe. "I cried and cried. But I kept taking long walks in the hills because when I had my chance to be a *fusgeyer*, I was going to be ready!"

One day a few months later, Avner the housepainter came into the tavern and announced, "This will be my last card game here."

"What? You're sick? You're dying?" someone asked—"I remember it was Reuven, the barrel maker. He always drank too much and his friends had to carry him home."

Avner just grinned.

"Has the rabbi turned you into a pious man? No more cards? Not even any schnapps?" Zipporah's father winked as he filled a glass for Avner.

"I'm going to America!" Avner said.

The broom crashed from Zipporah's hands. Her legs dissolved to jelly and could barely hold her.

"What's wrong with you?" her father demanded.

She snatched up the broom. Then she swept again and again by the table where Avner talked about his American cousins who were going to help him get started and the opportunities in pharmacy, which was Avner's real profession. He had become a painter after the Romanian government passed a law saying Jews couldn't own or manage pharmacies; he'd decided that painting houses was a better day's work than making money for the Christian who had taken over his business.

Fusgeyers from another village were going to pass through Tecuci in two days, Avner said. A friend of his was in the group, and he planned to join them.

In all of the hours Zipporah had stood silently behind Avner, bringing him luck at cards, she'd come to know every wart and freckle on the housepainter's thick, strong neck. She had scrutinized his dandruff-dusted shoulders and his shirt collars, soiled because he had no wife to scrub them—Avner's wife had died giving birth to their only child, a girl who was already dead when the midwife pried her from her mother. That had happened ten years ago, and no one had washed Avner's shirts properly since.

Another thing Zipporah had learned about Avner Papo was that he was kind, and not in the show-offy way of some people, who made a fuss so everyone would notice their good deed. Avner was kind in his heart. If Pinchas, who was simple, was doing some small job in the cafe and someone made fun of him, Avner interrupted by telling a joke, so as not to shame either Pinchas or the man who had mocked him. Once Zipporah was crying behind the cafe after a beating from her mother. She looked up, and Avner was there. "He didn't say a word about me crying. He just reached toward my ear, and there was a penny in his hand!"

Avner asked Zipporah's father if she could stand by his chair for his "last card game in Tecuci," a phrase that brought groans from his friends . . . and set Zipporah's nerves on fire. She stood patiently while the men played cards, containing herself until Avner heaved himself up from his chair and lumbered to the outhouse. Then she slipped outside and danced from one foot to the other beside the outhouse, waiting for him to emerge. Everyone had been buying him drinks, and he staggered and didn't hear at first when she said, "Reb Avner! Reb Avner!"

She pulled at his sleeve. "Reb Avner!"

"Wha—?" He wiped a hand over his eyes, as if brushing a cobweb away. Then he recognized her and smiled. He leaned forward, hands on his thighs, to bring his face close to hers. "What can I do for you, my luck-giving friend?"

"Take me to America!"

Zipporah had scarcely ever spoken to Avner, only to tell him in a near whisper what kind of soup her mother had made that day or thank him for a penny. Now all of her longing, all the fierce wanting forbidden to girls in the shtetl—*why want when you can never have?*—slammed into those four words.

Avner reared back as if she'd shoved him.

"Take me!" she repeated.

"But how can . . . Your parents . . ."

As Avner groped for words, she rushed on, "My brother's there, you remember, my brother Meyr? He sent for me to live with him. All you have to do is take me with the *fusgeyers* and on the ship."

"I'm sorry. I can't. But here, to remember me . . ." He reached into his pocket for a penny.

"Reb Avner!" She grabbed his arm to make him look at her again, and fixed all the force of her soul into her gaze. "I'll bring you luck."

" 'I'll bring you luck'—that's what I said to him," Mama told us, all those years later. "He scratched his head, the way he did in a card game when he was figuring out how to play a difficult hand. Every clock in the village stopped ticking, I was sure of it. And I felt so light-headed, my feet must have left the ground. And then he said . . ." She paused.

"He said, 'Do you have money?' " Barbara and I chorused.

"And for a moment, I was so excited, I didn't even understand what he was saying. As if he was already speaking English!"

AVNER PAPO DIDN'T JUST bring Mama to America. He bestowed on her a talent that lay hidden . . . until the summer before our first day of school.

With both Papa and Zayde working, Mama didn't need to have a job. A lucky thing, she said, since there was nothing she could really do. Before marrying Papa, she'd worked in a dress factory, but, true to her early attempts, she was never a good seamstress. And "it takes a different kind of man than your papa to start his own business where I could keep the books, for instance, or help with the customers." Whenever she said that, Papa winced. He wanted to open a business someday, and he and Mama and Zayde often talked about it, but he never felt he had enough money— though Zayde said it wasn't money Papa lacked but chutzpah, a word I heard so often that I was surprised to find out it wasn't English but Yiddish. It meant "courage, nerve."

Thanks to the hours spent behind Avner's chair, however, Mama did have one surprising way to earn money, a skill that she unveiled in the service of our debut at Breed Street Elementary School.

She was a genius at playing cards. No matter what the game—bridge, hearts, poker, gin rummy—she seemed to have a magic power to see straight through the backs of the cards and know what was in everyone's hand. And she strategized her own play as if she could picture the final trick in a game before she even laid down the first card. She'd always played cards socially, either with Papa and other couples in the evening or with a group of ladies in the afternoon. But she'd hidden her brilliance, like a hustler who fumbles through a few games, then swoops in for the kill. Except that Mama had groomed her marks over *years* of adequate but unexceptional playing. It made her devastating.

I got the first hint of Mama's virtuosity one afternoon at Sonya's in late June. She, Sonya, and two other ladies were having their Monday afternoon hearts game, while the children (all of us except the napping infants) played in the yard. Suddenly, louder than our shouting in a game of Red Rover, came shrieks from our mothers. We tore into the house like the small animals we were, quivering with worry at the sign of adult distress. But the women were laughing. And Sonya, Mrs. Litmann, and Mrs. Zinser were all looking at Mama.

"How did you do that?" Mrs. Litmann said.

"Do what?" Mama replied, with a smile that didn't show her teeth.

"Charlotte, you look like the cat that ate the cream," said Mrs. Zinser.

Did Sonya have a cat? Why hadn't she let us play with it? My eyes darted around the room looking for a hiding kitty.

"Shooting the moon once, all right," said Mrs. Litmann. "But four times?"

Ah, I knew they weren't talking about the moon in the sky, but the game of hearts. Likewise, there was no cat at Sonya's.

"You're going to think my sister-in-law is some kind of cardsharp." Sonya glanced uneasily at Mrs. Litmann, one of her new neighbors whose husband owned a men's clothing store.

"Don't be silly," Mama said. "It's just my lucky day."

"I'll say," Mrs. Zinser grumbled. She took her wallet out of her handbag. "How much do I owe you?"

Mama made almost two dollars that day, and she gave a nickel to both Barbara and me.

But Mama owed her success to more than luck. That Saturday night

she and Papa played bridge with several other couples, and the next morning Papa couldn't stop talking about how brilliantly they'd played. "That
five-clubs bid, I never thought we'd make that. And when Arnie had all
those high spades, but you kept trumping him. The look on his face! Guess
how much we won, girls?"

"Two dollars?" I said.

"Two dollars and seventy-five cents." He started to hand us quarters,
but Mama stopped him.

"A nickel each is plenty. That's the school fund," she said.

After a few more afternoons and evenings like that, Mama started carrying a special purse, the very one made by her sister Dora, inside her
handbag just for her winnings. She even got Zayde to invite her to games
with his poker cronies, which Papa thought not quite nice. In fact, once
Mama's "luck" became a streak, Papa didn't think any of it was nice. "These
are supposed to be social games. You keep taking everyone's money, no
one's going to invite us to play," he said.

Mama laughed. "They want to see if they can beat me."

"You need money for nice school outfits for the girls?" Papa persisted.
"A few dresses for five-year-olds, how much can it cost?"

"More than Julius Fine pays you!"

Papa raised his newspaper and pretended to read it, rather than repeat
that familiar argument.

Mama's skill did enhance her social standing. Mrs. Litmann played
hearts with Sonya on Monday afternoons and bridge with a different
group on Thursdays. One of the Thursday ladies moved, and Mrs. Litmann invited Mama to that group, which even included a doctor's wife
who drove to Boyle Heights from Hollywood in her own shiny yellow car.
The minute Sonya heard that Mama was invited to the Thursday group,
she was so upset she put Stan in his stroller and walked to our house in the
midday July heat.

"You've got to get a telephone, Charlotte!" Sonya fanned her red face
and gulped the cold lemonade Mama had poured for her.

"What is it, Sonya?"

"You ought to be able to afford one, all the money you're taking from
my friends at cards."

"What do I need a telephone for? To call Canter's and have them send me corned beef without the fat trimmed off?"

"Charlotte, I just moved to a new house. I'm just getting to know my neighbors. I'm asking you. Stop with the cards."

"I will," Mama said. "As soon as I get what we need for school."

"Your darling girls, I love them like they were my own. Why don't you let me treat them to some school outfits?"

Mama stood. "Sorry to rush you out, Sonya. I have so much cleaning to do this afternoon."

"A few blouses and skirts," Sonya said, and echoed Papa. "How much can that cost?"

Actually, Barbara's and my school clothes weren't expensive, nor were the fancy extras Mama bought us—hair ribbons and ruffled ankle socks, as well as sweaters and jackets for cooler weather. How much did it take to look well turned out when our new Mary Janes, bought at a discount at Fine & Son Fine Footwear, already elevated us above some of our class-mates, who would come to school barefoot?

Mama's project, however, was to outfit "us" for the first day of school. Not just Barbara and me, but Mama herself.

In early August, when Mama's take added up to twenty-seven dollars, with still more card parties to come, she bought some plum-colored silk shantung and took it to Mrs. Kalman, the dressmaker that Sonya's neigh-bors swore by. (A year later and she would have gone to Aunt Pearl, but Pearl was still married at that time and was a housewife; she hadn't yet started her dressmaking business.) Mama huddled over pictures in fash-ion magazines with Mrs. Kalman, a thin woman whose mouth was per-manently pursed from holding pins between her lips; she would have seemed withered except for the delicious flowery perfume she wore. Bar-bara and I could still sniff Mrs. Kalman's fragrance in each other's hair for hours after we'd gone there; and it scented Mama's suit when she brought it home. Appropriately for a school outfit, Mama had gotten a "smart suit." Mrs. Kalman called it that, and Mama echoed her proudly during the weeks of measuring, fitting, making a white silk charmeuse blouse, and purchasing accessories—calfskin pumps with the fashionable new spike heel from Fine's, a calfskin pocketbook, silk hose, and tan silk gloves. Naturally, the ensemble would include a new hat as well. Aunt Pearl was going to help Mama choose one, and whenever they talked about it, they whispered and giggled like Barbara and me.

Mama picked up the suit from Mrs. Kalman a week before the big day. That evening she modeled it for us. Mama was nice-looking, but most of her clothes were made of cheap fabrics that made her slightly plump figure look a bit dumpy. The new suit had a swagger jacket tailored to hug her hips—"just like the latest fashions in New York and Paris," as Mrs. Kalman frequently remarked. A daring skirt, that came to just below her knees, showed off her shapely calves, made long and elegant by her spike heels. Uncle Gabe, invited with Pearl for the occasion, gave a wolf whistle when Mama came into the living room in her new outfit.

Papa grumbled, "Does this mean you'll finally stop cleaning up on our friends at cards?" Still, he couldn't stop staring at Mama.

And she hadn't finished astonishing us. The next day, Pearl came over after lunch to stay with Barbara, Audrey, and me. She and Mama whispered together, and Mama said, "Pearl, are you sure?"

"Positive," Pearl replied. Finally Pearl said, "Charlotte, go already!" and almost pushed Mama out the door.

I was on the porch when she returned, walking fast and dabbing her handkerchief at her eyes. "Mama!" I cried, but she ran up the steps into the house and let out a sob. I ran in after her, but I was too frightened to ask what was wrong.

Pearl rushed to Mama, too, and hugged her. "Don't worry, Charlotte. It's how I felt right after, too. Everyone does. Oh, I can tell already it's gorgeous."

Pearl eased off the wide-brimmed summer straw hat that Mama had pulled down so it covered her whole head.

She had cut her beautiful hair. The heavy, dark, wavy blanket that she let me brush sometimes had been shorn into a flapper's bob. Pearl's hair was bobbed, but Pearl was different—she and Gabe danced the Charleston, and she smoked cigarettes. And her bob clung sleekly to her head, only poufing out a little when she set it in pin curls. Mama's hair, cut short, was thick and springy, as if the energy that used to wiggle to the end of each hair no longer knew where to go, and now the strands shot out from her head.

I couldn't help it. I gasped in horror.

Pearl gave me a dirty look and fluffed Mama's bob with her fingers. "It's perfect! I knew you had the right kind of hair, Char. So much better than mine—you've got that beautiful natural wave. Doesn't your mama look beautiful, Elaine?"

Barbara—where *was* she?—might have zipped past the crack that opened in the world, through which I glimpsed the broken places in my mother and knew I had to fix them. But what about the rip threatening to open inside me, the sense of betraying some essential Elaine-ness, if I said what they wanted to hear?

"Yes, beautiful!" I tried to sound enthusiastic, and even though I'd hesitated, Pearl smiled, and Mama said, "I'm a modern lady now, aren't I?"

"Like a movie star," I said.

"See?" Pearl said. "Let's see how it looks with this." From a big shopping bag she'd brought with her, Pearl took out a hatbox.

"Oh, Pearl!" Mama clapped her hands. Pearl had bought Mama a dark brown bob hat, its bell shape fitted close to her head to show just the edges of her hair at her cheeks.

Barbara came in then; she must have been in the garden. "Let me feel," she said, and ran her hands through Mama's bob. It hadn't occurred to me that the wiry helmet would feel anything like hair.

Mama seemed happy until Pearl had to go home to make dinner. "Can't you stay just a little longer?" she asked.

"Don't worry, Bill will love it," Pearl said. But Pearl knew, just as I did, the story of how Mama and Papa had met—that she took the English class he used to teach at night, and he noticed the dramatic fervor with which she recited poems . . . and her abundant, almost-black hair.

I heard later that Pearl went straight from our house to Fine's and warned Papa that he'd better compliment Mama, or Pearl would make him sorry for the rest of his life.

We didn't need to worry about Papa. No matter how attractive he had found Mama's long hair, his passion was for modernity. "No more old country," he said.

It was Zayde who murmured, "Your pretty, pretty hair." Still, Zayde—who was, after all, an older man, for whom Mama had her greatest appeal—liked everything she did. In fact, he wanted her to keep coming to his card games, but she'd promised Papa she would stop when she got the money for school outfits, and she declared herself finished with all that.

The minefield of the bob crossed, Mama threw us into a euphoria of anticipation. She lectured us constantly on how to behave in school: Always respect our teachers. Never hit or push other children. Never, never fight with each other the way we did at home. She patted her hair and tried her new lipstick, and at least once a day she went to the closet and ran her hands over the plum silk of her smart suit.

On the Saturday of Labor Day weekend, three days before our new lives as students were to begin, a vicious Santa Ana wind from the desert invaded Los Angeles. The sun scorched everything it touched, and there was no escaping it on streets whose only trees were skinny palms. Five minutes outside, and my head felt like a warm melon ready to burst. Our wooden house groaned in the dryness, the white paint baked to flakes. Papa limped home from work that day after fitting shoes on an endless stream of kids whose parents were making last-minute school purchases, and he lay on the floor as he always did when his back ached—but he wore only his underwear! Audrey wailed so much that even patient Zayde flinched and said, "Can't you give her a drop of whiskey, Charlotte, to calm her down?" Mama did it, too, because she had a terrible headache; every so often, she whimpered in pain.

Night, which had been invisible—you closed your eyes in the dark, and then you opened them and it was morning—became a torment of minutes and seconds, a misery of sweat-damp sheets, harsh air from the fires that were burning in the forest to the east of the city, and nasty stickiness whenever Barbara or I shifted positions and any part of our bodies touched in bed.

During the day, our crankiness flared into war. Everything either of us did annoyed the other and provoked yelps of outrage, even though Mama begged us to be quiet because of her headache. If one of us was asked to help with anything, we whined that it was the other's turn. On Labor Day, our family took refuge in Hollenbeck Park with its shade trees and pond. But Barbara and I started a tickling match that soon exploded in screaming and hitting, and Papa marched us back to the stifling house. Exhausted, Mama didn't murmur a word about how to behave in school when she bathed us that night. She only spoke to tell us to lift an arm or turn so she could reach another part of our feverish bodies.

None of it, however, not even another uneasy sleep, mattered in the morning. Finally, the giant circle on the calendar marked *the* day, when we woke before six, the momentousness of the first day of school pounding through our veins so hard, our small bodies could barely contain it. Mama poked her head into our room and said, "You're awake already, too, aren't you?" She helped us put on our nicest school clothes, drop-waisted gingham dresses, Barbara's in red and mine blue. Brushing our hair, she hummed the *fusgeyer* song. Then she went to get ready herself, while Papa made us breakfast and Zayde took charge of Audrey.

We were set to go—Barbara and I fed and clothed, Mama beautiful in her suit and new hat with her curls peek-a-booing on either side—almost an hour before we needed to leave. "Well!" Mama said. "Your teacher will notice the children who arrive early, ready to learn." She picked up her gloves.

"Not this early, Charlotte." Papa's tense undertone said that he was afraid she was going to make us look ridiculous. "You'll just be standing on the playground in the heat. Why don't I read to the girls for a little while?"

"Yes, all right." Carefully smoothing her suit, Mama sat on the sofa and automatically reached for the sewing basket next to it. But she didn't take any work out of the basket; she just sat and stroked the fabric of her jacket.

Even Papa got infected by our delirium. Reading from *The Secret Garden*, he sometimes read the same line twice or skipped a word. Every so often he glanced at Mama and said, "Don't you want to take off your jacket for now? Or your hat?"

"I'm fine," Mama said, although her face looked red and sweaty.

At long, long last, we were on our way to Breed Street Elementary School two blocks from our house. Mama had Barbara and me walk on either side of her, holding her hands. Her hand in mine trembled a little. I felt the same trembling inside me. I was alert and happy and scared at the same time. And I noticed a heavy, flowery smell—Mrs. Kalman's perfume, infusing Mama's suit and heightened by the warmth of her body under the sun, which was already brutal at eight-thirty.

Even after delaying our departure, we were among the first to arrive at the school. An older boy, maybe ten years old and looking very important, stood at the entrance to the playground and asked Mama what class we were in. "Both of 'em in kindergarten?" he said. "You sure?"

"They're twins," Mama said.

He scrutinized us. "No, they're not."

"Fraternal twins, not identical," Mama said, her voice asking permission in our first encounter with the school's authority, albeit in the person of a ten-year-old child.

"Huh, never heard of that," the boy said, but he pointed us toward the kindergarten table, one of half a dozen tables set up outside.

Mama looked around at the other mothers on the playground. A few had dressed nicely, but no one looked as nice as Mama, and many of the women wore the same dresses in which they'd probably clean their houses when they returned home. "Old country," Mama sniffed, regaining her courage.

A pretty blond lady who looked barely older than a teenager stood behind the kindergarten table. Our teacher? I hoped so!

"What a beautiful ensemble," the lady said when she saw Mama.

Mama beamed, then introduced us. "Barbara Inez Greenstein and Elaine Rose Greenstein."

The blond lady leaned forward a little and talked directly to Barbara in a voice like bells. "Barbara, your teacher is Miss Madenwald, in room eleven. I'm Miss Powell, I'm a student teacher, and I work with Miss Madenwald. We're going to have such a lot of fun." Then she spoke to me. "Elaine, you're in Miss Carr's class. That's in room twelve."

Miss Powell's smile traveled to whoever stood behind us, but Mama didn't move.

"They're both in the kindergarten," she said.

"Yes, I know," Miss Powell said. "Some of the older children are inside, Mrs. Greenstein. They'll help you find the rooms."

"They're twins, the same age, five," Mama said. "They're both in the kindergarten class."

"Oh, yes." Miss Powell smiled, understanding now. She explained slowly, as if Mama were the kindergartner, "We have two kindergarten classes. One teacher is Miss Madenwald, and the other is Miss Carr."

"Why put sisters in different classes?" Mama set her jaw the way she did when she challenged a sum at the market. But her accent got stronger, and sweat beaded her face.

"We always put twins in different classes. It helps them make friends with other children." I noticed now that Miss Powell was sweating, too. I followed her nervous gaze down the line of children and parents that had formed behind us—and spotted Danny, *my* boy from Aunt Sonya's party! But I just glanced at him, because the argument between Mama and Miss Powell required all of my attention.

"I know my daughters. They should be together," Mama said.

"Mama, I'll be fine," Barbara chirped, smiling at—allying herself with—Miss Powell. Why not? She had the teacher with the musical name, Miss Madenwald, as well as pretty Miss Powell. Who knew what my teacher, named like an automobile, would be like?

More than that, all of my life so far had been lived as "we" and "us" and "you girls." In every mental picture I had created of school and classroom, Barbara and I were there together. It wasn't that I was afraid of walking into a classroom without Barbara at my side; I simply couldn't conceive it. My personal geography needed to change to allow kindergarten to mean Barbara and me both being at Breed Street Elementary School but in different rooms, with different teachers and classmates. As if I needed to reconstruct the world as I knew it in the few minutes between being on the playground and entering my class.

"Can you remember, Barbara, you're in room eleven?" Miss Powell addressed Barbara, ignoring the stubborn immigrant who was ruining her first hour of being a student teacher. "And your sister is in room twelve?"

"Yes, Miss Powell. Eleven and twelve. Come on, Mama."

Mama let Barbara lead her inside, but not because she had conceded to the wisdom of American pedagogy concerning twins.

"Why not tell you to put your legs in one class and your arms in another?" she fumed. "And how am I supposed to meet my children's teacher if it's two different people?"

"Here's my room, Mama," Barbara said, pointing out a sign that had a big 11 in red crayon, with designs of flowers and animals, in front of the doorway. Papa had drilled us on our numbers up to twenty.

"No, it's not," said Mama, and pulled us across the hall to a similarly decorated sign with a green 12. "Here, you're going to be in this class."

"Can't we both be in Miss Madenwald's class?" I said.

"With that Miss Powell who doesn't know anything?" Mama led us inside room twelve.

"Hello, children." Miss Carr had a pleasant round face. But I was already in love with Miss Powell and Miss Madenwald.

"Elaine Rose Greenstein, ma'am," I mumbled when she asked my name.

"I'm very pleased to meet you, Elaine," Miss Carr said, then turned to Barbara.

"Barbara Inez Greenstein, ma'am."

"You came to bring your sister to her class, how nice," she said to Barbara.

"Miss Carr, I'm Mrs. Greenstein." Mama extended her hand in its beautiful if sweat-damp silk glove. As Miss Carr shook her hand, Mama announced, "I want both of my girls to be in your class."

Miss Carr, clearly more experienced than Miss Powell in dealing with parents, didn't argue with Mama. She simply directed us to the school office to talk to the principal, Mr. Berryhill.

Mr. Berryhill wouldn't be available for a few minutes, said the lady who spoke to Mama from behind a chest-high counter in the large, busy office. She told us to wait in wooden chairs lined up with military precision along one wall. None of us—not Mama or Barbara or me—had ever heard of being "sent to the principal's office," but a few minutes in those chairs, catching pitying or condescending looks from people who came in for one thing or another, and we were squirming.

"Mama, I don't mind not being with Elaine," Barbara said. "I just want to go to my class."

"Me too," I lied.

"We're going to talk to this Mr. Berryhill." Mama fanned herself with her pocketbook. Her face no longer looked red but pale. Conceding a little to the heat, she took off her hat, but then she took out her smart new compact and peeked at herself in the mirror. "My hair," she murmured. Her sweat-drenched bob clung to her head. She jammed her hat back on.

A bell rang. All three of us tensed and then drooped, ashamed. Our first day of school had started, and we were late for class.

A few minutes later, a gangly man with salt-and-pepper hair strode out from behind the counter. "Mrs. Greenstein?" He extended his right hand. "Delighted to meet you. Delighted!"

Mr. Berryhill had a husky smoker's voice and the brightest, bluest eyes I'd ever seen. He ushered us into his office—and transformed our seemingly relentless march toward greater humiliations into a treasured experience that Mama would recount for years.

"He was like the rebbe in my town," Mama told Aunt Pearl later. "You could tell he understood things that you never even thought about. And the books in his office! Like the rebbe's study, books everywhere."

The principal didn't even say the word *twins* at first. He spoke to Mama about the importance of parents being involved in their children's education and nodded at her in her smart suit as if to say he knew that a person who had taken so much care on her daughters' first day of school must be an exemplary parent. By the time he explained that it was school policy to separate twins, Mama was already saying what a fine idea that was, and she'd considered the possibility all along but worried that we'd be afraid.

"You'll be surprised," he said. "Am I correct that one of your daughters is quieter than the other, and stays more in the background?"

"Yes, my Elaine."

I stared at the floor, ashamed for not being louder, but I could feel Mr. Berryhill looking at me, and when I glanced up, his blue eyes twinkled.

"You wait and see," he said. "Elaine is going to blossom."

I felt myself blossoming right at that moment, and even more when

Mama took me to my classroom with a note Mr. Berryhill had written to excuse my being late. "You met Mr. Berryhill!" my teacher said.

I blossomed all morning, quietly, like the first shoots coming up in our garden. My happiness brimmed over when school let out at noon and I saw Danny—barefoot, his tousled black hair uncombed, just as when we'd met in my nest among the stacks of wood. "Danny!" I exclaimed, full of my new boldness, and ran toward him.

He started to look toward me. Then someone else called him, and he hurried in the other direction. I followed him—to Barbara.

"This is Danny Berlov. He's in my class," my sister said possessively.

But Barbara didn't need to lay claim to him. Danny had already chosen. He was hers.

CHAPTER 6

DANNY
THE PRINCE

DANNY BERLOV WAS POOR AND HAD NO MOTHER. EVERYONE KNEW that. Danny's father taught Yiddish classes at the Yiddische Folkschule on Soto Street and tutored religious boys in Hebrew, and what kind of living was that? He and Danny lived in two rented rooms that had a sink but no tub; on Friday afternoons, they went to the Monte Carlo Baths.

Danny's family hadn't always been poor, though. His grandfather was the richest man in . . .

Whatever he said, his accent, which had nearly vanished now that we were in the first grade, suddenly thickened.

"Where?" I said.

"Vilna. It's in Lithuania."

"Oh." I had never heard of Lithuania, but I understood it was one of those places that people's parents or grandparents had come from, like Romania. I also sensed that if I challenged Danny, he might clam up.

And I was thrilled to have Danny to myself. He often came over to play with Barbara and me, but on this particular rainy February afternoon, Barbara was confined to bed with a cold. Even better, with the drizzle keeping Danny and me inside, Mama gave me permission to use the Zenith radio. Bought a month earlier with Papa's 1928 New Year's bonus and some money from Zayde, the Zenith in its handsome walnut console was a magical addition to our house. I made a show of turning the radio on and finding a station playing beautiful piano music.

That was when Danny mentioned his rich grandfather.

"Josef Berlov, his name was."

"What did he do?"

"He was a fur trader. He had the biggest house in Vilna. With a Zenith radio in every room."

THAT WAS ALL DANNY said the first time. Gradually, though, the story gained detail and luster, and it became not just the tale of the Berlov family's former riches but the tragic explanation for Danny's absent mother.

Being a fur trader, I learned, meant that Josef Berlov traveled around the countryside buying the skins of minks, sables, and rabbits from people who trapped them, and he sold the skins to furriers in the city, who made them into coats. Even though the trappers were Christians, they liked and respected Josef because he could beat any man at arm wrestling, and he was always fair in business with them. They loved his horse, too, a fast brown stallion named Star. Danny's father, Gershon, sometimes went with his father if he didn't have to be in school. He had his own horse, a pinto named Frisky because he was hard to ride, except Gershon could always calm him down.

The trappers liked Josef so much they saved their best skins for him. That was what made him rich. He supplied finer skins than any other trader, and the furriers paid him whatever he asked. In fact, they made just a few coats every year using only skins that he brought them, instead of mixing them with inferior skins. These 100 percent Berlov coats were very special and expensive. If someone died and hadn't put in writing who was supposed to get his Berlov coat, the family argued over it for years.

One day a messenger arrived at Josef's house from the king of Vilna. The king wanted to have a Berlov sable coat made, and he insisted on picking each individual skin himself. Josef and Gershon, who was now a young man, carried four big bundles of sable skins to the palace. The palace was very grand, with door handles made of gold, and the room where they were taken to meet the king was bigger than most people's entire houses.

Josef, who had the gift of being at ease everywhere, from the simple huts of the trappers to palaces, smiled and said hello to the king. Gershon wasn't nervous, either. But then a girl ran into the huge room, laughing— the most beautiful girl he had ever seen. Stunned by her beauty, Gershon dropped his bundles. Sable skins spilled over the floor. He had to get on his knees to gather them up, his face burning as the girl laughed more. But it wasn't a mean laugh; she was just a merry girl. She was also wise and kind. Quickly she knelt on the floor beside him and helped him pick up the furs. "Beautiful," she said, holding a piece of lustrous sable up to her cheek. Then she met Gershon's eyes.

The girl was the king's daughter, Princess Verena; the sable coat was being made for her. A king's daughter and a Jewish boy? Even if he was the son of the richest man in Vilna, it was impossible. Ah, but impossible or not, they fell in love. When Gershon came to deliver Verena's coat, she jumped onto Frisky with him, and they fled into the woods. The trappers, who loved Gershon and knew of the princess's kindness, protected their secret. They lived in a tiny cottage, and for a year they were very happy. That was when Danny was born. But that winter Verena fell ill. The cold was terrible, and Gershon wrapped her sable coat around her. Still, she couldn't stop shivering. He added his own coat and his body, but Verena turned to ice in his arms.

Gershon moved to America because it was a country that didn't have kings or queens and therefore held no danger that he would meet a princess who might remind him of his lost love. He decided to live in Los Angeles so that he would never lose his and Verena's son to the cold. And he could no longer bear the touch of fur or of any heavy, rich fabric. That was why he wore only simple cotton shirts and threadbare pants now, instead of the fine clothes he could afford.

———

BY THE TIME I was nine or ten, I had heard Danny's story multiple times. And I'd noticed it wasn't always the same. Sometimes Princess Verena ran away from the palace on her own horse. Sometimes the king threw Gershon's father in prison and the family lost all its money. In some tellings, one of the trappers, an evil man whom nobody liked, betrayed them, and they had to run away from the king's soldiers, and that was when Danny's mother died of the cold.

It hadn't escaped me that the plot sounded just like a fairy tale or that the Lithuanian horses had names straight out of cowboy movies. And I heard Mama whisper to Pearl in Yiddish, "You know, the wife just took off one day."

I had also gotten to know the story's hero, Gershon Berlov. Mama took to inviting him and Danny to our Friday night dinners and beach outings, at first out of sympathy for Barbara's and my motherless playmate and soon out of fondness for the Yiddish teacher, with whom she and Zayde could relax into the *mamaloschen*, the mother tongue. "Poor Mr. Berlov," Mama referred to him with a sigh, and not only because he was raising Danny on his own. Among Boyle Heights' up-and-coming merchants and manufacturers, Mr. Berlov was a shtetl Jew, shuffling down the street, his shoulders hunched and his suit shiny with wear. If only I could say he made up for his lack of worldliness by being a born teacher, one of those people who blazed to life like a searchlight heralding a movie premiere the moment he entered a classroom. But his classes at the Yiddische Folkschule—which I insisted on attending, despite Papa's objections to studying the language of superstition and poverty when we were privileged to speak the tongue of Shakespeare—ricocheted between boredom and the chaos that erupted when one kid's naughtiness infected a few others, and with unstoppable momentum we all spun out of control.

Danny, however, did shine like a beacon, like the king's son hidden in a rude woodcutter's hut, clothed in rags, who grows up unable to disguise his inherent nobility. Even as I saw holes in his story, I didn't challenge him because I recognized the truth of Danny Berlov as deposed royalty.

And I lived in a world of tales about the old country, a mythic place that gave rise to stories whose details might flicker and shift, but always there was a core of truth. Look at Zayde and Agneta! Zayde really had made those tin animals. I saw beneath the surface fantasy in Danny's stories to their emotional authenticity—as Barbara, with her quickness to judge, couldn't have done. That was another reason I didn't question Danny: because he told his story to me alone. It was our secret, a continuation of the bond we'd formed the first day we met, between the stacks of wood down the street from Sonya's. The rough pine had long since become the Eppermans' house, but now Danny and I talked in a corner of the school playground or in my house if no one was in earshot. Or we went for long walks at Ocean Park, which on summer weekends became "Boyle Heights on the sea."

Our walks drove Barbara wild. "Where were you? I looked all over," she accused us when we reappeared after one walk at the family encampment of chairs and beach umbrellas.

Danny grinned. "We were wearing invisibility capes."

"You were gone for an hour. You need to tell someone if you're going to be gone for an hour at the beach." She glanced toward the umbrellas, hoping for adult support.

We had a different adult contingent every time, depending on whether Papa had the day off from work, and if Aunt Pearl or Zayde—though never, after Pearl's divorce, both of them together—joined us. The two constants were Mama and Mr. Berlov, who turned out to be a surprisingly enthusiastic beach-goer. Taking off his shoes and socks and rolling his trouser legs, he would sit in a sagging yellow canvas chair and chat with Mama or Zayde in Yiddish, or just lean back blissfully and stretch his thin, hairy toes into the sun, as if he could never get warm enough—perhaps remembering that winter when Princess Verena died.

"Yeah, I can tell how worried they were," Danny teased, glancing at the only adult present, Mr. Berlov, who lounged with his eyes closed and drew contentedly on a cigarette. Mama was off splashing with Audrey at the water's edge, and Papa was swimming his mile.

"Well, what about Elaine?" Barbara jerked her chin toward me. "She's my sister. What if she drowned?"

"Does Elaine look drowned? Do you think she's a ghost?"

"I don't know. Elaine, are you a ghost?"

"Um . . ." I'd just taken a big bite of a peach, and the juice dribbled down my chin.

"Ghosts don't eat peaches," Danny said.

"Really? The last time you were in heaven, Danny Berlov, what did they eat?"

"Ghosts eat . . ." Danny's eyes gleamed. "Worms!" We were ten years old, after all. "They get big plates of fat, juicy worms, and they eat 'em when they're still alive and wiggling."

"*You* eat worms!" Barbara cried, and took off toward the water, Danny sprinting after her.

I ran, too, laughing wildly as if I were the rowdiest, most fun-loving member of this happy trio. Instead of the outsider.

Why did I feel excluded, after having spent an hour with Danny by myself? Bantering was the special thing Danny did with my sister. They bickered over everything, from what they thought of their teachers to what candy bar was best, Hershey's (his choice) or Milky Way (hers), or their favorite movies—she liked Westerns, and he preferred gangster movies. Still, no matter how passionately Danny fought with Barbara, wasn't I the sister to whom he confided his tragic stories? And he never minded my being around when they argued; if anything, both of them liked having an audience. Whereas Danny told me about Gershon and Princess Verena only in private.

By that time, too, I had emerged from Barbara's shadow and claimed my own place in the world. If she was quick on her feet, able to fire off a retort to any insult, school had revealed me to have a quick mind. I was a child for whom the clumps of letters in our first-grade reader had leaped from the page and proclaimed themselves as *cat*, *father*, or *run*. Numbers, too, obligingly added, subtracted, multiplied, and divided themselves under my pencil. Even in Mr. Berlov's run-amok classes at the Folkschule, I learned enough Yiddish to understand when adults whispered in it, a skill I kept to myself.

Just as Barbara had her own set of friends, vivacious girls who took after-school dramatics classes, I gravitated to girls like Lucy Meringoff, with whom I competed amicably for the top grades in our class. Lucy and I knew every cranny of the Benjamin Franklin Library; the librarians greeted us by name whenever we mounted the white marble steps into the library for fresh armloads of books. Novels, poetry, history, biography—I loved them all for their enticing, sideways-printed spines, for the way they unfolded in my hands to reveal lives and events and language. I enjoyed the graceful type, even the whiff of mold on older volumes. As the principal had predicted on my first day of school, I had blossomed into myself—intellectually curious and praised not only for rote learning but for what my teachers called *comprehension*. No wonder Danny trusted me with his most tender secrets.

Oh, but Barbara was fun. No one else generated excitement the way she did, coming up with adventures and convincing everyone to go along. She started our neighborhood games and even got the adults to fall in with some of her plans. For instance, the year we were ten, she wanted to camp out on Colorado Boulevard in Pasadena on New Year's Eve so we'd have front-row seats for the Rose Parade on New Year's Day. She persuaded Papa, Aunt Pearl, and even Mr. Berlov to go. Mama, who stayed at home with Audrey, bundled us up in our warmest jackets and made us take every blanket from the house. For the first time, I stayed awake until midnight, drinking cocoa and telling ghost stories with Barbara and Danny, and the next day, the flower-covered floats in the Rose Parade were the most beautiful things I had ever seen.

Even when it was just Barbara and me, I never got bored. And I sometimes got in trouble, like when we took Mama's just-washed sheets from the line and built a fort in the yard. Once, though I protested all the way, I trotted after her to stand on the bank of the Los Angeles River when it surged with water during the rainy season. I couldn't stop thinking about Micky Altschul, the Boyle Heights legend who'd been swept away by the river in flood. Still, seeing the river in its glory as La Reina de la Puebla de Los Angeles was terrifying and thrilling. Barbara let out a yell of excitement, and I yelled, too, trying to outroar the river. It was worth the slaps we got when Mama somehow found out. On my own, I might have been a tediously good child, scolded only for spending too much time with my nose in books—and perhaps a tedious, line-toeing adult. Would I have become such a rabble-rouser if Barbara hadn't brought out the mischief in me?

But Barbara didn't just have a gift for mischief. My sister could be dangerous.

One afternoon in November 1932, not long after Roosevelt was elected president—we were eleven, and in the sixth grade—we went with Danny to Chafkin's grocery store. Barbara and I had a shopping list from Mama, and Mrs. Chafkin helped us find what we needed. After she figured out what everything cost, she took the strip of cardboard with our family's name on it from the collection of such strips hanging behind the counter and wrote down the amount to add to the total Mama and Papa would pay at the end of the month.

"There you go, girls." Mrs. Chafkin handed us the groceries and two pieces of bubble gum. She gave Danny a piece of gum, too, but ignored the items he'd placed on the counter—two cans of soup, a five-pound sack of potatoes, and a pint of milk.

"I want to get these," Danny said.

Mrs. Chafkin had seemed a little nervous when she was helping Barbara and me. Now discomfort streamed from her, though all she did was call out, "Eddie?"

Eddie was Mrs. Chafkin's energetic son, who had come into the business after graduating from high school a few years earlier. (Eddie Chafkin would eventually build a supermarket empire and become Los Angeles's leading promoter of Israel Bonds.) He hurried out from the back office.

"Danny Berlov," Mrs. Chafkin whispered, as if her voice had gotten trapped in her throat.

Eddie Chafkin glanced at the groceries on the counter. "Danny, have you got money to pay for these?"

None of us ever carried more than a nickel or two. "Put it on my father's tab," Danny said.

"Your father needs to come talk to us about his bill." Eddie took out the strip of cardboard with *Gershon Berlov* written on it and pointed to a black *X* next to the name.

"My father, he always forgets!" Danny laughed, but his cheeks flamed. "I'll tell him, and I'll just get this for tonight." He pushed one can of soup toward Eddie, who stood with his arms crossed. Everyone knew that, as well as being named for a dead ancestor whose Hebrew name was something like Efraim or Eliezer, Eddie Chafkin's parents had also named him for King Edward VII of England, and he always acted hoity-toity.

"That's not enough for dinner," Mrs. Chafkin said. "How about a few potatoes, too?" She took three potatoes from the sack Danny had placed on the counter and put them and the can of soup in a bag. Then she added the milk, too. "You'll need this for breakfast tomorrow morning."

"Ma!" I heard Eddie say as we went out the door.

Taut with shame, Danny mumbled that he had to get home. He hugged the small sack of groceries to his chest and ran.

"I hate Eddie Chafkin," Barbara muttered.

"Me too."

Of course, we understood what had just happened. Everyone was being hurt by the Depression, which had started with the stock market crash three years earlier and kept getting worse and worse. The Great Depression, as it was already being called, was a cataclysm in the larger world from which the adults were powerless to insulate us. All over Boyle Heights, people we knew—family friends, the fathers of classmates—had lost their jobs. Walking down the street, I'd seen neighbors with everything they owned—clothes, pots and pans, family pictures, whatever furniture they hadn't already pawned—put out on the curbside, the people hovering beside their possessions, some weeping, some holding their spines so straight they seemed about to crack. And it was never a surprise to walk into our kitchen and see a man with shabby clothes and downcast eyes eating the soup and bread Mama had given him when he knocked at the door and asked if she had anything to spare.

At least we had some soup to give them. Although Papa had had to take a salary cut, and lately Mama seemed tense all the time, some people still bought shoes, and Papa hadn't lost his job. But poor Mr. Berlov . . . who could afford the luxury of his Yiddish classes? He tried to come up with other ways to earn money, but he didn't have an enterprising personality, not like the Soy Bread Man, who walked downtown every morning and bought a dozen loaves of soy bread, then walked back to sell them in the neighborhood . . . and attracted everyone's attention because, when he came down the street selling the bread, he walked backward.

I knew there were relief agencies where Mr. Berlov could ask for help. Or he and Danny could eat at a soup kitchen. *A soup kitchen!* On trips downtown, I'd seen people lined up on the sidewalk for soup—often with their heads tucked into their collars, as if they were trying to hide their faces in case anyone they knew came by. I couldn't bear the idea of Danny—with the shame he'd always suffered, even before the Depression, on account of his father's poverty—having to stand in a soup line. I had to help him. But what could I possibly do?

That night I saw Papa sitting in his armchair after dinner, reading the *East Side Journal*, the local weekly newspaper. Papa especially enjoyed the letters people wrote to the editor of the paper; sometimes he'd read them out loud, and he'd comment to Barbara and me, "A letter to the editor, that's how an American speaks up!"

I took a pad of paper into the bedroom and started to write. *I saw a terrible thing today. A boy . . .* But I crossed that out, because I didn't want to point so obviously to Danny. *A person who lives in Boyle Heights tried to buy food for his family, but a grocer said his family couldn't get credit anymore.* As I would do one day in legal briefs, I laid the groundwork for my position by acknowledging the arguments that could be made against it: Grocers couldn't afford to just give things away. And there was help available for anyone who was in danger of starving. *But sometimes people need just a little help. What if the relief agency gave money to grocery stores? The grocers know which customers are having a hard time, and they could use the money to help them, without anyone having to ask.*

I carefully copied the letter with my fountain pen onto a sheet of good writing paper and signed it the way we did in school when we wrote letters to, say, thank a fireman or a nurse who came to speak to our class: *Elaine Greenstein, Mrs. Villier's sixth-grade class, Breed Street Elementary School.* I put it in an envelope and addressed it to the *East Side Journal*. When Mama wasn't looking, I took a stamp from the drawer in the kitchen where she kept them.

I mailed the letter the next morning. That was on Friday, and the newspaper didn't come out until the following Wednesday. In the meanwhile, Barbara came up with her own strategy to help Danny.

On Monday, she and I went to Chafkin's after school with Mama's grocery list. "You go get everything," she told me. While Mrs. Chafkin helped me collect the items for Mama, Barbara roamed in another part of the store, and she hung back as Mrs. Chafkin totaled up what I'd bought.

Excitement and secrecy and wildness zinged off of her, and the second we were out of sight of the store windows, I grabbed her arm.

"What is it?" I said.

"You'll see." She jerked away and kept walking, fast.

"What did you do?"

"You'll see," she repeated.

I'd thought we were going straight home, but instead she turned down Soto Street. To the rooming house where Danny lived.

I had barely seen him since the incident at Chafkin's the week before. That wasn't unusual—Danny had a gang of boys he hung out with, just as Barbara and I had our own girlfriends—but even when I'd waved to him on the playground, he'd pretended not to see me.

"What do you want?" he challenged when he answered Barbara's knock. He stood in the doorway, not asking us in.

"Is your father home?" Barbara whispered.

"No. Why?"

"Can we come in?"

He shrugged.

Barbara went over to the small wooden table that Danny and his father used for eating and as a writing desk. She folded back the flap of her school knapsack. "Look!" She took out several cans, a stick of butter, a bag of rice—about a dozen things in all—and placed them on the table.

"So?" Danny said.

"Barbara, where did you get that?" I said, thinking for a moment that she must have raided our own pantry before we'd left for school that day.

"Where do you think? Chafkin's," she answered. Then she said to Danny, "It's for you."

"We don't need you to buy us food."

"I didn't *buy* it."

Her words hung in the air.

"You stole it?" Danny and I spoke at the same time, with, I sensed, similar shock at this act, which every Boyle Heights kid understood on a small scale—swiping a piece of bubble gum—but which we had never encountered at this magnitude.

Then my disbelief turned into fear, and Danny's became anger.

"You stole this while we were in the store?" My knees wobbled with the inevitability that we'd be caught and held equally guilty.

"We don't need you to *steal* for us, either!" Danny snatched up the cans and shoved them back into her knapsack.

"Fine, take it back, then," Barbara challenged him.

"They'll think *I* stole it."

"Then you'll have to eat it, won't you?"

"I'll take it back," I threw out, but it was impossible. Either I'd be branded as the thief or I'd have to tell on Barbara.

"I don't care what you do with it." Barbara raked us both with a scornful glance and made her exit, slamming the door.

Danny surveyed the booty still on the table. Butter. Half a dozen eggs. Two cans of tuna fish, his favorite food.

"I'm sorry. I didn't know she was doing it," I said.

"You were right there, and you didn't have any idea?" But another quality entered his voice: admiration. For Barbara stealing! I thought of telling him about my letter then, but I didn't want to spoil the surprise.

"How was I supposed to know she was *stealing?*" I'd figured she was up to something, but my imagination for transgression was so limited, all I could think was that she was getting back at Eddie Chafkin by sticking chewed-up gum someplace or jumbling items on the shelves, putting a box of cereal with the canned peaches.

"Was Eddie around?"

"Just Mrs. Chafkin."

"Guess that'd be easier. Still." He rolled his eyes. "Your sister's nuts! Well, you take this."

"I can't. Mama . . ."

"I guess it's stupid for it to go to waste." He picked up the stolen items from the table and started putting them away.

In just two days, the *East Side Journal* would come out with my letter in it. Then Danny would really have something to admire.

On Wednesday I put on my nicest school outfit, a navy jumper and crisp white blouse. The *East Side Journal* got delivered (by Mr. Berlov; it was one of his ways to earn a little money) sometime during the morning, so it should be at our house when we came home for lunch.

Novice author that I was, it never crossed my mind that the newspaper might not publish my letter. But as a matter of fact, they did. I saw my letter in print when we returned to our classroom after the morning recess. Mrs. Villiers picked up a newspaper—the *East Side Journal!*—from her desk. Mrs. Villiers was one of my favorite teachers, a feathery woman of about forty who had been widowed in the Great War. She loved to quote famous sayings and always kept a pencil tucked into her blond chignon in case she was seized with the inspiration to write a poem.

"Look, children!" she said. "See how mighty the pen is!"

She had me come to the front of the room, and I saw that my letter occupied the place of honor at the top of all the letters to the editor, beneath a giant headline: "FDR, Listen! Boyle Heights Sixth-Grader Offers Relief Policy." Mrs. Villiers asked me to read my letter out loud. I had to push my glasses, new that fall, up my suddenly sweaty nose, and my legs got so tense from excitement I could barely feel them under me. Yet my voice rang out, thanks to Papa's elocution lessons and an unexpected stage presence, perhaps inherited from the *fusgeyers* on Mama's side. When I finished reading, Mrs. Villiers clapped, and everyone applauded with her. Then she cut out my letter and pinned it up on the wall. Mr. Roosevelt might invite me to Washington to give him advice when he took office as president, she said.

When school let out for lunch, I galloped out to the playground, certain that everyone knew about my fame—as if "Boyle Heights Sixth-Grader" were emblazoned on a banner that streamed out above my head. But my schoolmates hurried home the way they always did, the bold kids scuffling and shouting and the timid, gawky ones yearning toward a brief return to their real lives in which they were their mamas' treasures instead of the dull, easily bullied children they impersonated at school.

I told Barbara my news on our way home.

"You wrote a letter saying Chafkin's should give free food to . . . people we know?" She glanced at Audrey, whose six-year-old legs trotted to keep up with us.

"I didn't say any names. And it's not free food, it's money the government would give to the grocery stores, and then they . . ." My plan, so elegant in writing, sounded ridiculously complicated when I tried to explain it. "You'll see. Mama will have the paper at home."

"Did you print or do handwriting?" Audrey asked, focused on the mechanics she was just learning in first grade.

I groaned.

"Why didn't you write to the relief agency?" Barbara said. "Or the mayor?" She wasn't being obtuse to deflate me. The idea of writing to a newspaper was as foreign to her as stealing from Chafkin's—which I'd gotten her to promise never to do again—was to me.

Barbara may have failed to be impressed, but Papa appreciated the momentousness of this event. He'd gotten Mr. Fine to give him time off during the busy lunch hour, and he was waiting on the porch. As soon as I came into sight, he ran out and swept me into his arms. "Did you see the *East Side Journal*? And you didn't make one spelling error!" In the house, one *East Side Journal* lay open to my letter on the kitchen table, and another dozen copies sat pristine and untouched on the sideboard.

Mama, too, was all smiles and said she'd make anything I wanted for dinner that night.

"Meatballs!" I said.

Once Barbara saw my name printed in the newspaper, she joined in the fuss, showing the genuine pleasure in each other's triumphs that coexisted with our perpetual rivalry. On our way back to school after lunch, she carried an *East Side Journal* to show her class.

Everyone must have heard about my letter in their classes that afternoon, because I was the center of attention when school let out. The only person who acted oblivious to my exalted status was the one on whose behalf I'd attained it—Danny, who was waiting with Barbara in our usual spot at the edge of the playground. The one concession he made to my fame was to notice all the people looking my way.

"I have something to show you, but not with people staring at us," he said.

He had an air of suppressed excitement, and Barbara didn't balk at missing her after-school dramatics class. She and I went with Danny to the playground across the Red Car trolley tracks. He waited until we'd sat down on a bench, then made a show of reaching into his satchel. Was he going to pull out an *East Side Journal*?

"For you!" With a flourish, he handed Barbara two Milky Way bars. "And you." Another flourish, and he produced two Snickers for me. Last came a Hershey's bar for himself.

Candy bars, costing a nickel each, were rare treats during the Depression—far too great a luxury for a boy whose father couldn't afford a bag of potatoes. Barbara was always the one who challenged Danny, and I expected her to say something, but she had already peeled the wrapper from her Milky Way and was chewing her first bite.

"Danny, where did you get these?" I said.

"Chafkin's. Pollack's." The two local grocery stores.

"*How* did you get them?"

"Bought 'em. Snickers is still your favorite, isn't it? Did I get the wrong kind?"

"I love Snickers." I started to unwrap one. "It's just . . ." I had never before questioned Danny's versions of events. "No, you didn't."

"Didn't what?" he said through a mouthful of chocolate.

"You didn't *buy* five candy bars."

Danny hesitated and glanced at Barbara. She was taking tiny bites to savor her Milky Way.

"So?" he said.

"So, you could get caught!" The grocers kept the candy bars right at the counter, under their noses.

"Don't you want it?"

"Danny, since when is stealing the only way to get what you want? Didn't you see my letter in the newspaper?"

His face went cold. "The letter where you said my father can't pay his grocery bills?"

"I didn't say anything about your father."

"I can take care of myself. You want the Snickers or not?"

Barbara poked my arm. "Elaine, don't be such a stick."

"Of course I want it." I tore the wrapper off my Snickers and took a big bite.

"How'd you do it?" Barbara asked with the respect of one thief for another.

As Danny explained how he had pocketed the candy bars while the grocers helped him with small legitimate purchases, I devoured my Snickers.

The candy bar barely touched the ravenous emptiness gaping inside me. The sense of exclusion I had long felt around Barbara and Danny was no longer a mystery. Now I glimpsed the chasm that isolated me on one side while they stood, laughing, on the other. I played by the rules; I would eventually come to understand the rules inside and out, and fight to turn them to my—and my clients'—purposes. But believing in the value of rules was in my nature, just as Barbara and Danny were both natural outlaws.

That night at dinner, I stuffed myself with meatballs, as well as two pieces of the chocolate cake Mama had baked for the celebration.

BETWEEN ALL THE SUGAR and the excitement, the next day at school I felt sick. Mrs. Villiers put her cool hand on my forehead, then sent me home.

"Mama?" I called when I walked in the door.

She didn't answer. She must have been out. I was a little disappointed, but I had already been fussed over as much in the previous twenty-four hours as I usually was in months, and I was eleven, old enough to take an aspirin without any help and put myself to bed.

I pushed open the kitchen door to get a glass of water and saw . . . I didn't know what I was seeing. This was surely our kitchen: I recognized the green linoleum floor and primrose-flowered curtains, and the oak table standing in the middle of the room. A woman stood on the other side of the table; she had her back to me and didn't notice when I came in, but she was wearing Mama's blue housedress. And I recognized the black cast-iron soup pot and the smell of boiled onions. But . . .

Instead of being on the stove, the soup pot sat on a low stool.

The woman straddled the steaming pot, her legs wide and her knees slightly bent, as if she were going to sit on it.

And she was sobbing and talking out loud in Yiddish.

I stood frozen in the doorway. I hadn't thought I was very ill, but now I felt dizzy and my scalp exploded in sweat.

"Please, God, I can't do it this time," she said. "I know I don't talk to you as often as I should. Maybe you didn't hear I live in America now? Even here, a woman doesn't have much choice about getting married, all right. But you think I'm still in Tecuci, where the women have baby after baby—"

Tecuci was Mama's village in Romania. This woman talking to God *was* my mother.

"Mama?" I said.

She sprang up—and kicked the pot over. Steaming onions and water spilled onto the floor, onto her legs and bare feet.

"Ai!" Screaming, she ran toward the doorway. Toward me, shrieking, "What are you doing here?"

She shoved me aside, knocking my head into the swinging door. Once she'd escaped the kitchen and the scalding liquid, she staggered to a chair, moaning. "God in heaven, my feet!"

"Mama, should I call the doctor? Or Papa? Why don't I call Papa?"

"Elaine, no!"

"Please, can I do anything? I'll get you some Vaseline."

"Vaseline, yes. What did you mean, sneaking up on me like that?"

Weeping, I ran to the powder room. When I came back with the Vaseline, the rage had drained out of Mama. Her face was pale, and she whimpered when I applied the Vaseline to her feet and ankles and put gauze over it.

"Are you sure you don't want me to call the doctor?" I asked.

"I just need to sit here and rest a little."

"Is there anything else I can do?"

"I don't . . . Yes, could you clean up? In the kitchen?"

"Is it soup? Should I save what didn't spill?"

"Soup? You think like they say about old *bubbes*, I flavor my soup by pissing in it?" She started to laugh, but wildly. She must have seen she was scaring me, because she stopped and caressed my cheek. "Darling, it's not soup. Throw it out. And please?"

"What?"

"Don't tell anyone. This will be our secret, all right?"

I mopped the floor twice. Still, the house stank of onions for days. And Mama limped on her burned feet; she accounted for her injuries and the smell by saying she had knocked a pot off the stove.

Barbara had another explanation for the mystifying scene I'd witnessed. (Of course I told Barbara. I didn't breathe a word to anyone else, as I'd promised Mama. But sharing the story with my twin sister didn't count as *telling*; it was like trying to make sense in my own mind of what I'd seen.)

"You sit over a pot of boiled onions if you don't want to have a baby," Barbara said.

"What? That's stupid."

"That's what Sari Lubow's aunt said. Sari told me once she heard her mother and her aunt talking about it. Her aunt said it was old-country *meshugas*."

Barbara was my source of information about such things; she picked up every whisper about the facts of life the way I absorbed subjects in school.

A few weeks later, though, Papa announced that this year, instead of getting Hanukkah *gelt*, we were receiving a truly wonderful gift: a new baby was growing in Mama's tummy. So maybe Barbara had it backward and squatting over onions was what you did when you *wanted* a baby? Either way, I knew just enough about human reproduction to be certain Sari's aunt was right: the onions were *meshugas*.

And Mama didn't want another baby. "I can't do it this time," she had cried to God. Maybe I'd misunderstood her Yiddish? But despite, no, *because* of my confusion about the pot of onions, I felt certain of what I'd heard her say, the words burned into me by the very strangeness of that moment when I stood in the kitchen doorway and couldn't recognize my own mother. She had said, too, that women in America had little choice about getting married. Did that mean she didn't love Papa?

With all that on my mind, I was less upset than I might have been when Danny got caught shoplifting at Chafkin's, just before New Year's. Besides, even Eddie Chafkin felt sorry for the Berlovs, so the punishment Eddie devised was relatively mild: Danny just had to do ten hours of work at the store, sweeping and helping in the stockroom, to atone for his crime.

What did upset me was that Danny stopped telling me his stories. Maybe it was because of his embarrassment over my letter or because I, his unquestioning listener, had confronted him over the stolen candy bars. Maybe getting caught stealing was too great a collision with reality.

I suppose the stories would have stopped, anyway. We turned twelve that spring, too old for childhood fantasies.

When we went to the beach the next summer, rather than taking walks with me, Danny got obsessed with the muscle men. He spent every minute hanging out where they lifted weights and ran errands for them, and the men took him under their wing and got him started on bodybuilding.

I lost Princess Verena. And I gained a new sister, Harriet.

CHAPTER 7

ROAD TRIP.

I'M NOT GOING TO DRIVE ALL THE WAY TO COLORADO SPRINGS. OF course I'm not, I assure myself as I head east on the 10 freeway. That *would* be insane, especially for an octogenarian in pink Keds who has to stop every hour to pee and can't drive after dusk because her night vision is shot. I just couldn't stay in my house one more minute, couldn't bear the confinement of the walls. What does any true Californian do when she's jumping out of her skin? She gets in the car and hits the freeway!

I'm still jumping out of my skin, but at least I'm moving. I didn't own a car, didn't even drive, until I was twenty-six, when Paul's parents gave us a Plymouth as a wedding present. We drove the Plymouth on our honeymoon, four days at the Hotel del Coronado in San Diego, and when we weren't in bed or at the beach, Paul taught me how to drive on back roads lined with avocado groves. A born teacher, he was able to break down all of the actions an experienced driver does unconsciously. I learned well; I've always been a good driver. Sixty years of driving in L.A., and I've never had an accident.

But the one thing Paul never succeeded in getting across to me was having a lighter foot on the gas pedal. From the moment I learned to release the clutch without stalling, I loved speed! As I get beyond the perpetual Los Angeles traffic, I push the car—a silver Jaguar sedan, my gift to myself for my eightieth birthday—past seventy-five.

I'll drive as far as Victorville; it's just eighty or ninety miles from L.A. I'll treat myself to a date shake, the way Paul and I used to do when we drove to or from Las Vegas. Then I'll turn around.

But no matter how fast I go, I can't get away from what Josh told me earlier this afternoon.

"That card we found last week for the detective, Philip Marlowe," he said the minute he walked in, so excited that the words spilled out of him. "I did a little research. He was quite a character."

"He was rather well known back in the thirties and forties."

"*Rather* well known? I found newspaper articles about some big cases he helped solve. This one reporter wrote about him a lot. He made your friend Marlowe sound like a tough guy around thugs but a knight in shining armor if he was helping someone small and powerless." Josh shot me an oddly complicit look. "Turns out the reporter's papers are in a private collection of L.A. history from the 1940s. I'd heard about the collection, and I've been curious about it, so I went and took a look.

"And . . . voilà!" He reached into his banker's box and pulled out a nine-by-twelve envelope. "The reporter must have been friends with Marlowe, because he got all of his case files. I copied his file on your sister. At least I figured it was your sister—Barbara Greenstein, the one in the dance programs?"

"Yes, that's right," I said curtly. For Josh, following the card to Philip and then Barbara was nothing but a librarian's treasure hunt—a puzzle, a lark. But it was my life he was prying into, my hope that got kindled and, inevitably, dashed. Well, not this time. I already knew what was going to be in the file. I took the envelope and set it aside, then turned to the material I'd laid out on the table. "I promised you those letters to editors I wrote when I was a teenager."

But Josh was like a cat bringing in a dead bird and wanting to show off its kill. "Funny you didn't know Kay Devereaux was the name your sister used in Colorado Springs. When she worked at the hotel."

Obviously Josh had misread something. Still, I opened the envelope and pulled out the file, a thin sheaf of no more than half a dozen pages. My eyes raced over the top sheet, notes from talking to my family: Barbara's height, weight, date of birth, when and where we'd seen her last, the names of her friends, and so on. Continuing through the file, I could see how Philip followed those leads, though his actual notes were sketchy, a scatter of names or phrases he'd jotted for his own reference; I could piece them together because I'd already heard it all more than sixty years ago. Only one piece of information was new to me. Apparently it came from his interview with Alan Yardley: under Yardley's name, he'd written *Trocadero* and three women's names—women Barbara had worked with in the chorus?

"Fascinating, huh?" Josh said. "So can I ask you about Philip Marlowe sometime?"

I waved him off and dove into the rest of the file.

Performing in a nightclub is hardly the most stable profession, and it had clearly taken some digging to track down any of the showgirls; there was a page with multiple addresses and phone numbers under each woman's name, most of them crossed through, as well as the names of half a dozen nightclubs. Finally, he had found at least one of the women, though it wasn't clear which; he'd written "unhappy at home" and "heard Broadmoor Hotel, Colo. Springs, hiring." I figured that was what the woman had told him about Barbara. "Unhappy at home" gave me a twinge, but I could hardly argue that ours was a harmonious family from which no one would have wished to escape.

Then I came to the last item in the file: a letter, messily written in pencil and badly spelled but on a half sheet of good rag paper with the Broadmoor Hotel letterhead.

Marlowe—

    Theres a botle-blond, gos by Kay Devereaux, who might be your girl. Call if you want more infomation.

                               Carl Logan
                             House Detective

"Devereaux" was spelled out carefully, as if he'd copied it a letter at a time. My hand started shaking, and the words juddered in front of my eyes.

"Is this it?" I asked Josh, my voice tight and tinny in my ears. "Did you copy the whole file?"

"Everything except three or four copies of a photo, it looked like her high school graduation picture . . . Elaine, are you all right?"

"I can't meet with you this afternoon."

"Sure. Okay." He grabbed his banker's box. "Your sister came home, didn't she? After Philip Marlowe found her? You told me she got married and had kids."

"I'll see you next week, same time." I nearly pushed him out the door.

Then I went back to the file and read it again as I paced from room to room. It wasn't just that I felt too agitated to sit; with each change of location, each different set of furniture and fall of light, I hoped I'd be jogged toward some kind of clarity.

Carl Logan had it wrong, that was all. He hadn't been sure himself: *She might be your girl,* he'd written. And what was he going on, even to say that much? Philip might have mailed him Barbara's high school photo, we'd given him copies to show around, but she was eighteen in that photo! I have grandkids that age, and they all have the same shiny newness, their faces like just-minted pennies waiting for the stamp of experience. Logan could only have guessed he was seeing that high school girl in a bottle-blond chorine. And look at his letter, smudged and barely literate. Wasn't a hotel dick the sleaziest character in any detective movie? I'd bet Logan had insisted on being paid for his information, and he figured he'd get more money if he said what Philip wanted to hear.

Kay Devereaux wasn't my sister. It was the only thing that made sense!

Yet another explanation kept whispering in my mind, one that made me feel like I'd been punched in the gut. When I couldn't stand being in the house anymore, I got in the car and started driving.

AM I ALREADY AT Victorville? The diner where Paul and I liked to stop is still there, just off the highway. I use the ladies' room, get the date shake to go, and take a sip. Ah, the blend of dates, milk, and ice cream turns out to be one of the few revisited pleasures that's as good as I remember. I place the shake in the Jag's cupholder to enjoy as I drive home.

But instead of heading back to L.A., I obey Maxene, the name (after the middle Andrews sister) I've given the car's smooth-voiced navigator. Just for the heck of it, I'd programmed Maxene for Colorado Springs. Of course, I won't really drive that far. But Las Vegas—why not go there? Spend a day or two, see a show, play the slots? Is there anyone I need to call, anything to reschedule? I'm not meeting with Diane, the young attorney I mentor, until next week. And I taped my commentary for the legal affairs show on the public radio station yesterday.

Vegas, yes! I'll buy myself a toothbrush. And a swimsuit. One of the things I remember most fondly from trips we took to Las Vegas with the kids was swimming in those turquoise pools. Though I know that, unlike the date shake, which has held up to my memory of it, Las Vegas long ago stopped being the place I loved in the fifties and sixties, when you could still feel the desert grit beneath the glitz.

Vegas in those days was my cousin Ivan, a small-time operator who lived there and always treated us to a dinner at a steakhouse and introduced us to his latest lady friend. At least I reassured myself that he was small-time, involved in nothing worse than gambling scams. If he'd been doing anything really unsavory, wouldn't he have been able to afford something better than the series of modest apartments where he lived? And his ladies were invariably girl-next-door types from the Midwest.

Ivan was one reason we went to Vegas a couple of times a year. My parents had sponsored him to come from Romania in the late 1930s, and I felt responsible for him. And I like to play blackjack and the slots; gambling, after all, is something of a family pastime. Best of all, Las Vegas was a cheap, quick family getaway. I'm sure neither of my kids would set foot in Vegas these days—Carol's idea of a vacation involves backpacks and national parks, and Ronnie gravitates toward places where the entertainment features *museos* and string quartets, not feather boas—but we had some great times there.

Was I drawn to Las Vegas for another reason? I wonder now, sipping my date shake and pushing the car to eighty-five on the straight, flat interstate. Did I go because it seemed like a place where Barbara might have ended up? That's one of the futures I imagined for her, as a Las Vegas showgirl. Or she might have become a New York socialite or the wife of a fabulously wealthy oil sheik with homes in half the capitals of Europe—Barbara wouldn't have settled for anything small and ordinary. Not that I spent every minute thinking about her; I didn't have time. My missing sister was simply another instrument in my usual symphony of Paul and the kids and work and politics . . . an oboe, perhaps, sad and autumnal, that shaded every other tone.

No, I didn't *look* for her in Vegas, not like Mama peering into every store on her walks through Hollywood. Yet the one time I thought I spotted her, I took off like a runner exploding from the starting blocks, as if my muscles had been primed for just that moment. It was 1958, almost twenty years since she'd left. I was walking on the Strip with the kids. Carol was seven then and Ronnie four. Something about a woman walking half a block ahead of us, her back or her stride, riveted my attention, and I dropped my kids' hands and raced after her. "Barbara?"

She didn't react.

"Barbara!" I touched the woman's shoulder, and she turned. What was I thinking? This woman was barely twenty-five, whereas Barbara would have been nearly forty by then, the same as me. "Sorry," I stammered, and hurried back to my kids.

Ronnie was blubbering and Carol trying to be the reassuring big sister, although her eyes had gone wide in alarm. I hugged them, keeping my arms around them even when Carol squirmed and complained, "It's too hot, Mommy." I needed the comfort of my kids' sweaty bodies against the disappointment that the woman wasn't Barbara—and the jab of deeper hurt that shocked me in that moment with its force: while Barbara remained "missing" to us, she could have gotten in touch with our family anytime. But she didn't want to see us.

She didn't want to see me.

A PIT STOP AT a Denny's outside Barstow. I sit at the counter and order a slice of apple pie, not really wanting it but to "pay" for using the bathroom. The pie tastes great, though, and I take my time enjoying it.

I'm surprised, when I return to the car, to notice the first hint of dusk. It's not even five, but of course it's November. Well, I'm halfway to Vegas already; if I turn around now, I'll hit rush hour traffic in L.A. As long as I have to drive after dark, it's better with my lousy night vision to be on a straight-shot highway through the desert, I reason.

The austere landscape makes me think of the wild, beautiful desert photograph that Alan Yardley gave me, a black and white shot, all light and shadow. Yardley, when I went to ask him about Barbara, struck me as the gentlest man I'd ever met. I learned later, from Philip, that all the while Yardley was meeting my gaze with his sad, compassionate eyes, he was lying to me. I hung the photo in every office in which I worked—now it's above my desk at home—to remind me that trust must be earned, not blindly given.

Yet obviously I gave my trust too easily. As I race across the desert, the knowledge I've tried to push away all afternoon—the other explanation for Philip's card among my mother's papers and for the letter from Carl Logan in his file—worms into my mind: Barbara *was* living as Kay Devereaux in Colorado Springs. Philip found out, and he told Mama and Papa. And they all kept it from me!

"No!" I scream in the privacy of the car, the night, the desert.

It's no more than a second's inattention, but the Jag swerves, and I'm bumping over rough terrain, seeing nothing but shadows ahead of me. I pump the brakes. The car slows but continues to lurch forward. There's a scraping metallic shriek, and I sail over the edge of something.

I get walloped in the chest and rammed back against the seat. Then everything stops.

WHAT COMES NEXT IS a blur of pain and people in uniforms, first the Highway Patrol and paramedics, then white-coated doctors and nurses at the Barstow hospital.

I'm lucky, the emergency room doctor tells me; it looks like my worst injury is a cracked rib from the airbag slamming into me. Beyond that, "you're going to get some colorful bruises." They'll keep me overnight for observation, but I should be able to go home in the morning. He leaves, and a nurse who's been standing by says she'll take care of moving me into a hospital room.

Groggily, as I'm wheeled on a gurney, I wonder about the damage to my car. And hell, I'll have to call Ronnie to come here tomorrow and pick me up. But before I get out the words, the nurse says, "I hope you don't mind. Your cell phone rang while the doctor was treating you, and I answered. It was your grandson. He's on his way here. Hope that was okay," she says again.

"Fine," I mumble, my voice thick with whatever they gave me for pain. My grandson? But Ronnie's son, Brian, is in Argentina, working as a photojournalist. Then I remember that Dylan, Carol's son, moved to Los Angeles a few months ago; a former minor-league baseball player, he got a job coaching at Culver City High School.

It must be Dylan who called.

Still, the last thing the nurse says, as the drugs and shock drag me into sleep, mystifies me. "Your grandson must have ESP. He called because he was worried about you." ESP, indeed. What else would make Dylan worry about me?

HE'S THERE IN THE morning. The nurse who wakes me says, "Okay if your grandson comes in? He spent the night in the lounge."

"Sure." I'm touched—and so shaken up and vulnerable, in the wake of the accident, that tears spring to my eyes. I reach to brush them away, and flinch. Ow! I must have gotten a shiner.

A moment later, a young man—well, a blurry shape in the doorway, I don't know what they did with my glasses—enters the room and calls out loudly, "Grandma!"

But it's not my grandson. It's Josh. He hurries over to my bedside, whispers, "I had to say I was related, or they wouldn't have told me anything. And I didn't know how to reach anyone in your family." Once he's gotten that out, he takes a good look at me and adds, with real alarm, "Elaine, are you all right?"

"Better than I look. Really. Damn airbag." I try to laugh, but it hurts.

"Guess I oughta see the other guy, right?" he says.

"The Sierra Club will probably revoke my membership for what I did to the desert."

And my poor Jag! I ask Josh if he can find out what happened to it, if it was towed somewhere or is still sitting amid rocks and cacti. He rushes off, clearly grateful to have a task, and returns in fifteen minutes with the news that the car was taken to a Highway Patrol lot. I have no doubt the Jag is going to need extensive body work, but I'm hoping it suffered no serious internal damage. That turns out to be the case for me, I learn from the doctor, who comes by a few minutes later.

This morning's doctor, a soft-voiced blond woman, explains the difference between a broken rib and one that's merely cracked; I'm fortunate to have gotten the latter. She advises me not to stint on the Aleve because the biggest danger is that if it hurts too much to breathe and I avoid taking deep breaths, I can develop pneumonia.

The doctor is followed by a social worker who quizzes me about who'll take care of me when I go home. I placate her by saying I'll stay at my son's, though I have no intention of doing that; I can manage on my own. An aide helps me dress, and I'm good to go—more or, in this case, less. After the discomfort of getting out of bed and putting my arms into sleeves, I don't argue when the aide wants to transport me to Josh's car in a wheelchair, and I stifle a gasp when she and Josh help me get from the wheelchair to the passenger seat.

I'm reasonably comfortable once I'm settled in the car, a brown Subaru whose rear seat is jumbled with books, clothes, and fast-food wrappers (in striking contrast to the passenger seat, which he must have tidied up). Nevertheless, it's obvious that my plan of being on my own isn't going to work. As Josh drives—at a crawl, trying to avoid any bumps—toward the highway, I get on my phone and ask Ronnie if I can stay at his house for the next few days. That takes a while, as I have to assure him I'm not critically injured, explain why my archivist, of all people, picked me up at the hospital, and tell a half-truth about what I was doing in Barstow: "I got stir-crazy and felt like driving." Next I call my insurance company, report the accident, and arrange for them to tow the car to my dealer in L.A. And I leave a message for Harriet that I couldn't get to water aerobics this morning; we let each other know when we can't make it.

By the time I drop the phone into my purse, we've driven at least twenty miles, and I'm exhausted.

"Doing okay?" Josh says.

"Fine."

"Temperature okay? You want me to turn on the air-conditioning?"

"No, it's fine."

"How about some music? I've got Ella Fitzgerald, *The Great American Songbook*."

"I love Ella." Oh, I miss the abrasive Josh; his solicitude is driving me bonkers.

"I'm so sorry about—"

"I'm just going to close my eyes for a few minutes, okay?"

"Sure, of course. I'll shut up."

Ella starts crooning "Something's Gotta Give," and I must actually doze off, because the next time I look out the window, we're driving through the endless suburban sprawl between Riverside and Los Angeles.

"Almost home," I say.

"Can I ask you a question?" Josh says. "When you drove out here yesterday, you weren't by any chance going to Colorado Springs?"

"No. Las Vegas."

"*You* like Vegas?"

"Have you ever even been to Las Vegas?"

"Sure. But, you know, it's crass and shallow and phony. Well . . ." He shoots me a grin. "Guess Vegas has a lot going for it after all . . . Um, look, I really am sorry about yesterday. I took it for granted that after Philip Marlowe found your sister, she came home. Or at least she got in touch with you," he adds, clearly torn between his genuine concern for me and his rabid curiosity.

I have no doubt which is going to win. Maybe I'm just woozy with painkillers—or touched by his having driven all the way to Barstow and spending the night in the hospital lounge—but I don't mind trusting him with the real answer. "No, she didn't. I never knew what happened to her."

"You didn't know that he found her in Colorado Springs? Your parents didn't tell you about that letter from the hotel detective?"

"It must have turned out not to be my sister after all." Or maybe, I think, as Ella croons "Love for Sale," they found out something else, something Carl Logan confided when Philip called, that made them decide to cut her off—say, she wasn't just performing in the revue at the hotel but providing extra services for male hotel guests?

"Why did she leave?" Josh asks. "Did something happen?"

"No." What happened to push Barbara out the door is something I've revealed to only a handful of people—Aunt Pearl, Mama and Papa, Paul . . . and Philip.

"Enough about me," I say. "Tell me about your family."

"*My* family?"

I brought it up to change the subject, but it occurs to me that while Josh has talked about his doctoral studies, and I've heard all about meeting his Vietnamese girlfriend's family last month, I know very little about him. "You have parents, don't you?"

"My family, okay. Know the scene in *Annie Hall* where Woody Allen meets the Carol Kane character and sums her up? 'New York, Jewish, left-wing, father with the Ben Shahn drawings'?"

"And she zings him for reducing her to a cultural stereotype?" The scene had made an impression because Paul and I had three Shahn prints. "Is that you?"

"Jewish and left-wing, yeah. Different generation, so different cultural signifiers. Old roach clips in the junk drawer, every album by Bob Dylan, the Stones, and, in my mom's case, Joni Mitchell. And my dad's pictures were silk-screened posters for protest marches and rock concerts. They were made by the graphics collective he was in . . . until he went to work for an ad agency in Denver. That's one reason he and my mom split up—she thought he'd sold out."

"Do they still live in Denver?"

"My dad does, with his wife—she's a third-grade teacher. After they split up, when I was five, my mom moved to Leucadia, one of those beach towns north of San Diego. She does massage and holistic healing. Like I said, a cultural stereotype."

"Five, that's rough."

"Nah. My stepmom's great, and my dad is all left-brain practical, while my mom is right-brain visionary; I get to take what I like from each of them. And you ought to see me on an airplane. Nobody can get perks from the flight attendants like someone who's flown as an unaccompanied minor."

What did Harriet say? Each of us has a unique version of the history of our family. And I suppose everyone has reasons for coming up with—and believing—a particular story, like Josh's glib account of how painless his parents' divorce was for him. But I don't believe him. And I wonder which of my stories, my memories, would strike a listener as . . . well, not as fiction, since I happen to believe in objective reality. But what in the way I color my telling—my choice of words, whatever I emphasize or gloss over, tone of voice—might seem chosen to protect me or someone else from pain? Or blame?

It's relaxing to sit back, close my eyes, and listen. During the next fifteen minutes or so, I throw out a few questions and learn that Josh has two half sisters in Denver, and his mother has had a couple of serious relationships but mostly "she did the hippie single-mom thing" in a house that was tumbledown and drafty, but who cared, since it was two blocks from the beach.

He could be describing Carol, who named her son after Bob Dylan—the son with whom she got pregnant when she was a sophomore at Sonoma State. Paul and I pleaded with her to marry her boyfriend or (even better, since she was only nineteen) get an abortion, and no matter what, to stay in school. She did none of those things. Like Josh's mother, she bumped along, raising Dylan on her own, despite a number of relationships and making what I fear is a subsistence living working for the costume department at the Oregon Shakespeare Festival in Ashland. Aunt Pearl would be tickled; she taught Carol to sew. Carol is also a weaver and does her own original designs, intricately worked leaves and birds and flowers in subtle hues—not my taste, I like bold colors and abstracts, but they're works of art. If only she had a smidgen of Pearl's drive! She refuses to market her work. She's always disdained ambition . . . but of course, that's my perspective, the side I staked out in our fights when she brought home B-minuses, even C's from school. Playing out *my* cultural stereotype. Do any of us escape? Barbara, maybe she did.

We're coming into the city now, Boyle Heights is on our right, and Josh asks, "Do you want me to take you to your son's house?"

"Thanks, but I'd like to go home first and pack a few things." And, like any injured creature, I have an urge to return to my nest. "He can come and pick me up."

"Y'know," he says, "now that you've got the name Kay Devereaux, you could do some data searches. Legal records, things like that."

Of course, that's the way to proceed, rather than taking a cockamamie drive in the general direction of Colorado Springs. I could look for public records of marriages, divorces, real estate transactions, legal proceedings. Deaths. If she was ever charged with a crime or went to jail. *Is that why Mama and Papa kept this extraordinary secret? Because my sister, who had thought nothing of shoplifting as a child, was involved in something illegal?*

"I'm pretty good at that kind of thing," he adds. "Let me know if I can help."

"Thanks, I will." Though just thinking about having to fill Josh in, to give him an idea where to start looking, exhausts me. Have I ever had to tell anyone the whole story, starting at the beginning and trying to get across who Barbara was and how she left? Philip, I told him. But everyone close to me—my family, Paul, Boyle Heights pals, some of whom have remained my friends for life—they all knew what happened; they lived it, too. As for my kids, they picked up the story in bits and pieces, and gradually Paul and I filled in details and depth.

After all this time, is there really any hope of finding her? And do I want to? As Harriet said, finding her now could lead to any of a number of outcomes, not all of them happy. Despite being a Californian, I'm not someone who believes in omens, but look what happened when I simply drove in the direction of Colorado Springs. As if the universe were posting a giant "Keep Out!" sign.

At my house, Josh insists on walking me inside. I give him two twenties for gas. But buying him a tank of gas doesn't feel like enough thanks for what he's done.

"Wait!" I say.

I go into the den and survey the Ben Shahn prints, hanging in a cluster on one wall. I plan to give the subtle, almost Japanese-style "Blind Botanist" to Carol when I move and the Passover Haggadah illustration to Ronnie; my favorite, the surreal "Branches of Water and Desire," will come with me to the Ranch of No Tomorrow. But really, I'll have almost no wall space there. I reach for the print but feel a pang of resistance, almost a physical pain. I remember the day Paul and I bought that print and the spirited discussions we used to have about it, usually over drinks—was the giant bird perched on the roof of a house, or was the structure some kind of boat? What accounted for the bird's swagger, his wide-open, knowing eye? Well, I'm under no obligation to give Josh a Shahn. I can show my appreciation with a nice bottle of wine. Yet . . .

And then I realize what I want to give him. I go into my office and take down the desert photograph by Alan Yardley. It's part of the story of Barbara, a story to which Josh has added a fresh puzzle piece and, I think, acquired some small degree of ownership.

I dust the frame with a tissue, then bring the photo out to him. "I want you to have this."

"Elaine, I can't . . . Is this an Ansel Adams? All I did was give you a ride."

"It's an Alan Yardley."

"The man in Philip Marlowe's file?"

I nod, and he takes the photo from me.

"Wow. Thank you."

He asks if I want him to stay until my son arrives. I say no. I want a few minutes in my nest alone.

"Hey," he says on his way out the door. "I like road trips. Next time you feel like taking one, call me."

CHAPTER 8

UNCLE HARRY'S GHOST AND THE EARTHQUAKE

I FIRST NOTICED OUR FAMILY'S GHOST AT THE BEACH AT OCEAN PARK. It must have been the summer I was five, because I remember Audrey being there in a bassinet—and both Zayde and Pearl were present, so it was before Pearl got divorced.

On our weekend beach outings, the adults occasionally took a quick dip to cool off, and someone always accompanied Barbara and me, standing guard when we dug in the damp, ploppy sand at the shoreline, and clutching our hands in a death grip when we ventured into the sea. By far, though, the top adult pastime was lounging under umbrellas in canvas chairs. They ate, talked, read a little. They looked at the ocean—Mama sometimes stared at the water for hours—or lay back with their eyes closed, luxurious in their few hours of rest. The one exception to all of that indolence was Papa, who charged into the ocean and swam his mile.

Papa swam his mile whenever he got the day off and could come with us to Ocean Park, so I had heard variations of that phrase many times. "I'm going to swim my mile," he'd say, and stride briskly toward the water. Or someone would ask where Papa was, and another person would respond, "Swimming his mile." It was part of the casual flutter of language constantly swirling around me, one of many references to events in the adult world that I took for granted. On this day, however, *Papa swimming his mile* became a treasure chest of ideas so huge and thrilling and dangerous, I nearly burst trying to absorb them: *Swimming*, which involved lying on your stomach facedown in the ocean, but instead of choking and coughing the way I did when a wave splashed in my face, you moved through the water. A *mile*, the kind of distance you traveled by car or streetcar (on foot, you went for three or four or ten *blocks*), yet Papa was going that far in the ocean. *Swimming his mile* also meant Papa went into the ocean deeper than just up to his chest, which was the farthest I was ever allowed to go; even deeper than a step or two beyond where he could stand, as Pearl sometimes did, giggling and shrieking and then scrambling to regain her footing.

Papa went so far that, from the beach, I couldn't see him.

"What's gotten into you?" Mama asked when I clung to her. "Please, Elaine, it's too hot."

I didn't have the words to express the tumult of feelings my new awareness had stirred up—terror that Papa would never return, excitement that he was doing this thing that took strength and courage, and also the sense that I had shot to a more complex level of understanding everything, and I was on the edge of an exciting but challenging new network of meanings.

Mama put the back of her hand on my forehead. "Here, come into the shade. Drink something."

She poured me a cup of lemonade in which the ice had long ago melted. I sipped the tepid drink but could barely swallow. My gaze frantically swept past the dozens of bathers frolicking near the shore and fixed on the few bold specks beyond where the waves broke that were swimmers. Did Papa always come from the same direction after he swam his mile? Oh, why had I never paid attention?

At last I spotted him, his wavy black hair and mustache glistening with water, his wiry-strong legs jogging across the beach. I shot to him, and he gathered me up against his cool, dripping chest.

"What is it, Elaine?"

"Did you swim your mile?"

"I did." He laughed, for a moment as carefree as a boy. *How old was he then? Twenty-seven, twenty-eight?* "Do you want me to teach you to swim?"

"Yes!" I said, my faith in my athletic papa overcoming my timidity.

"Let me get something to drink first. Then I'll give you your first lesson."

Surprisingly playful, Papa trotted like a pony and carried me back to our cluster of umbrellas and chairs. There, my recent leap in awareness disappeared. The adults seemed to be talking in code, their conversation as foreign as when I heard the Yamotos down the street speaking Japanese.

"Forty-eight." Zayde shrugged and held up his arm to display his wristwatch.

"Actual swimming?" Papa said. "Or did you count getting into and out of the water?" His voice sounded light, like he was joking, but, held against his chest, I could feel how tense he'd become.

"Same way I counted forty-two," Zayde said.

"Pa." Aunt Pearl rolled her eyes. "Harry was just eighteen. And the water's rough today, isn't it, Bill? I heard them say there's a rip current."

"Harry" must be Uncle Harry, Papa's older brother, whom I'd never met because he died before I was born, fighting in the Great War. It was the one thing I understood. I tried to catch Barbara's eye, but she was playing with baby Audrey and ignoring the simmering tension among the adults, as I suppose I had done in the past.

"Pearl, forget it, will you?" Papa put me down without looking at me.

"Here, Bill." Mama's hand lingered on Papa's as she gave him a towel. "Do you want some lemonade?"

"Seventeen," Zayde said. "He was seventeen. It was 1914."

"Well, you see?" Pearl said.

"Is it too much to ask to have a towel that's not full of sand when I get back from my swim?" Papa shook the towel hard, without taking a few steps away, and the gritty sand blew on us.

His uncharacteristic anger made me think twice before approaching him. But I wanted to learn to swim!

"Papa?" I moved toward him as he dried himself with the towel. "Papa?"

Maybe he heard my voice tremble. Or he'd worn his anger out. "What is it, Elaine?" he said gently.

"You said you'd teach me to swim."

He hesitated a moment, and I braced myself for a no. But he smiled. "That's right, I did."

As a swimming instructor, Papa was more patient than when he drilled me in poetry or history. He made a game out of putting our faces in the water and blowing bubbles. That first day, I went from blowing bubbles with Papa holding me to not being held at all. Soon he taught me to do a dead man's float, and by the time I was six I could swim the crawl.

As I got a bit older, I sometimes swam out beyond the breakers with Papa. And as the tendrils of mature reasoning I'd first noticed that day at the beach grew, I realized that the key to the conversation that had baffled me was Uncle Harry's forty-two-minute mile, swum when he was seventeen—and that Harry's ghost stroked, always a little ahead, when Papa swam his mile.

A FRAMED PHOTOGRAPH OF Harry Greenstein, handsome as a movie actor in his army uniform, hung in our living room. He was also in another living room photo, a picture of Papa's whole family taken in 1911, the year after they moved from New York to the more healthful climate of Los Angeles. They made the move because our *bubbe* suffered from tuberculosis, but the change came too late for her. Seated beside Zayde at the center of the family grouping, Bubbe looked chalky and frail, and I knew she had died the next year. But the children! Impossible to believe that my pale, dull-eyed *bubbe* had ever produced these tanned visions of vitality!

Chubby and smiling, in dark dresses with white lace collars, nine-year-old Sonya and eight-year-old Pearl flanked the group. Bill—that was Papa—who was eleven, stood ramrod straight behind Bubbe; in his serious demeanor, I came to recognize myself.

Then there was Harry, dominating the photo with self-possessed grace. Although he was just fourteen, Harry displayed none of the gawkiness of adolescent boys, the resentful self-consciousness at being shoved inside bodies with which they're at war. If there had been a war within Harry, he had won. At five-six or five-seven, he hadn't yet reached his full height, but he'd clearly crossed the bridge from childhood to manhood. Standing behind Zayde's chair and between Papa and Sonya, he held himself straight like Papa, yet with just a hint of a slouch that telegraphed assurance, humor. Next to whippet-thin Papa, Harry was filled out, and not just because he was older; he had a naturally powerful body with broad swimmer's shoulders.

Harry swam his famous forty-two-minute mile in July 1914, which made it the centerpiece of an important summer, both for the Greenstein family and for the world. That June, Harry graduated from high school, and he and Zayde started the egg ranch. In August, Europe went to war.

Harry enlisted in the army a year later. The United States hadn't yet entered the war, but he knew it was coming. When it did, he was sent to the heart of the fighting and killed almost the moment he set foot in France.

"Did you fight in the Great War?" I asked Papa, about the time I became aware of Uncle Harry's ghost.

"I wanted to, but who would have helped Zayde with the egg ranch?"

A simple enough answer, but it concealed precarious fault lines that would deepen and slip and ultimately—at 5:54 p.m. on March 10, 1933—rupture.

FRIDAY, MARCH 10, didn't seem like a day that would change everything. On our kitchen calendar, the tenth was merely a blank square, a day whose primary significance was that it fell in the midst of three other dates circled in red: the previous Saturday, March 4, when President Roosevelt was inaugurated, and Barbara's and my twelfth birthdays, on March 28 and 29.

That Friday night, we would eat our first Shabbos dinner in an America led by FDR, an America that might emerge at last from the Depression.

Though the Depression shadowed everyone's life, it hadn't hit the Greensteins as hard as it hit so many others. Papa still had a job; Mr. Fine had had to lay two people off, but he had laid off single people, not a family man like Papa. And Papa had worked at Fine's for seventeen years! Mr. Fine often told him he was like family. We had to scrimp, of course, and Mama and Papa no longer talked about buying their own house someday, but we'd been able to install a telephone; and we always had plenty to eat and even new or expertly mended clothes, thanks to Aunt Pearl. Pearl was actually prospering in the hard times. She'd begun designing costumes for the movies, and movies were a comfort that all but the most desperate allowed themselves. For Uncle Leo, too, the Depression meant business for his bookstore on Hollywood Boulevard. People parted with rare books to get by, and Leo needed only a handful of still-wealthy collectors—or the newly wealthy, for whom there was nothing like a shelf of moldy classics to make them look cultured—to have a market. Zayde did all right, too, gambling being a comfort that even the desperate didn't give up.

We were the ones who felt sorry for *other* people. Papa gave money to charity, and Mama invited "less fortunate" families to Friday night dinners. Often that meant Danny and his father or—on that Friday—our next-door neighbors, the Anshels. Mr. Anshel, who worked as a printer, had gotten his salary cut in half, and with two small children to take care of, Mrs. Anshel couldn't go out to work. The whole Anshel family, including three-year-old David and the baby, Sharon, had thick, pasty skin. Mama said it was because they ate almost no meat but had to fill up on potatoes and beans.

To make sure the Anshels got meat that Friday—and to celebrate Roosevelt's inauguration—Mama was roasting two chickens, prepared by rubbing garlic, parsley, and oil under their skin and dusting them with paprika and her secret ingredient, a pinch of cinnamon. The fragrance filled the house as my sisters and I performed our Friday dinner chores. It was Barbara's and my job to transform the kitchen table. We moved the table into the living room, added two leaves, and spread out the good white cloth Mama and Papa had gotten for a wedding gift from Pearl. Then we set the table with the rose-patterned Rosenthal china, a gift shipped from the relatives in Chicago, and the crystal wine and water glasses, which

were also wedding gifts. It seemed as if every wedding gift Mama and Papa
had received was intended for Shabbos dinners, even though the only custom we followed was for Mama to light candles in the silver candlesticks
and mumble a prayer. The candlesticks were a gift from Papa's employer,
Julius Fine, and polishing them was Audrey's task.

Audrey had just placed the freshly polished candlesticks on the sideboard, Barbara and I were smoothing the tablecloth, and Zayde was relaxing in his armchair with a glass of whiskey when Papa came home. Was it
after six already? We'd better hurry. But I checked the clock, and it wasn't
even five-thirty. Mr. Fine had let Papa leave the store early.

"Papa! Papa!" Audrey danced from one foot to the other like a puppy
that couldn't contain its joy. Poor Audrey. The harder she tried, the
more Papa withdrew from her. She hadn't figured out that there were
times when none of us—not even me, his favorite because I did so well
in school—should approach Papa. When he got home from work, you
needed to wait until he'd put on his house slippers and had a few sips of
whiskey.

Predictably, Papa ignored us and walked into the kitchen. A minute
later, I heard Mama scream. Barbara, Audrey, Zayde, and I all ran toward
the kitchen and crowded through the swinging door.

Mama sprawled in a chair as if her six-months-pregnant belly were
a heavy beach ball that someone had flung at her and, catching it,
she'd fallen backward. Her eyes were open, but her face was as pale as the
Anshels'.

Papa stood over her, fanning her with a kitchen towel. "Water," he
said.

Barbara rushed to the sink and filled a glass.

"Should I call the doctor?" I said.

"No, it's all right." Papa took the glass from Barbara and raised it to
Mama's lips. "Mama just got a little too hot, with the oven going."

Mama sat up straight and glared at him. "Tell them."

Papa took a deep breath. He looked at the floor but spoke with his
elocution-champion enunciation. "I lost my job."

"Juli Fine cut your hours?" Zayde said, holding out against the full
disaster of what Papa had said.

Papa shook his head. "Mrs. Fine has a cousin who got laid off three months ago. He hasn't been able to find anything else."

"Why does that mean Papa lost his job?" Audrey whispered to me. I pinched her arm to shut her up.

"Charlotte, why don't you come sit in the living room and cool off?" Papa said.

"We'll finish fixing dinner," Barbara volunteered.

"How about I tell the Anshels someone's sick and we can't have company tonight?" Zayde offered.

"And let this chicken go to waste?" Mama said. "Barbara? Elaine? The chickens need another fifteen, twenty minutes. And can you boil green beans? I was going to fix them with bread crumbs, but . . ."

"I know how to do it," Barbara said.

Papa helped Mama to her feet, and they went with Zayde into the living room.

"What happened?" Audrey asked with tears in her eyes. Barbara and I explained. Then Audrey really cried. I grabbed her shoulders hard and said we had to act brave for Mama and Papa. Barbara had her sit down to snap the ends off the green beans, and I returned to the living room to finish setting the table.

Zayde had poured glasses of whiskey for Papa and Mama, who sat at opposite ends of the sofa.

"How about some music, Charlotte?" Zayde asked Mama.

"All right."

Every comment or gesture, however casual, felt stained by Papa's news. When Zayde turned on the radio to the classical station, I looked at the Zenith in its handsome cabinet and wondered how long we'd be able to keep it before we had to take it to the pawnshop.

As Papa, Mama, and Zayde sipped their whiskeys, they engaged in terse bursts of talk.

"What did this cousin get laid off from?" Mama said.

"Advertising."

"What does an advertising man know about selling shoes?"

"He's been out of work since December," Papa said. "He's got two kids and a mortgage."

"A mortgage! So he could afford to buy? Audrey, for crying out loud, put those candlesticks away."

Audrey, who'd crept across the room to put white candles in the candlesticks, jumped.

"I'm not going to pray over candlesticks we got from Juli Fine," Mama said. "I can't even bear to look at them! Put them away, Audrey. Now!" She took a gulp of whiskey, then said to Papa, "So, where is this house Mr. Advertising Man has got a mortgage on?"

"West side."

"Naturally. Did Fine at least give you severance pay?"

"Sixty dollars."

We paid twenty-two dollars and fifty cents a month just for rent.

"Mama?" Audrey whispered. She had returned the offending candlesticks to their place within the sideboard. Now she stood miserably, holding the candles. "What should I do with these?"

"Oy, how can I think about . . . I don't care, use other candlesticks."

Tears glistening in her eyes, Audrey looked around blindly. I realized she might not know there were candles in cheap brass candlesticks in the linen closet, in case the power failed. I was going to tell her, but then she ran into the kitchen.

"Seventeen years you worked for him," Mama said. "Long hours, overtime, any job that needed doing. You think Mr. Advertising Man with his mortgage on the west side is going to put in hours like that or get his hands dirty in the stockroom?"

"If it was your cousin and my business, wouldn't you—"

"Don't tell me you're going to defend him."

"Charlotte." Papa put up his hand: *enough.* He got up to refill his glass.

"Bill's right," Zayde said. "Of course Fine is going to help his cousin."

"His wife's cousin." Mama winced. "The radio. I don't want to hear it after all."

I leaped to turn it off.

How could they all be so silent? I was lifting each fork to put a folded napkin under it, oh so gently; still, the forks and napkins thundered onto the table.

"Where will you look?" Mama said after another minute.

"I'll start with the department stores downtown."

"To get another job selling shoes?" Zayde said.

Was it because Zayde was sitting under Uncle Harry's photograph? Somehow, his simple comment implied not just *Why would Papa want another job as a shoe salesman?* but *Why would anyone ever settle for such a job?*

"Maybe I should ask if they need someone to run the whole department store." Papa gave a sharp, dry laugh. "Or I'll just call the mayor and see if he wants me to help him run the city."

"All I'm saying, Billy," Zayde said, "is, this is an opportunity. You can make a fresh start."

"A fresh start, Pa. Why didn't I think of that?"

Mama should have touched his arm and said something; it was how she always defused fights between Papa and Zayde. But she just stared into her glass of whiskey. She almost never drank alcohol except for a Friday night glass of wine.

"There's always money to be made," Zayde said.

"A man who worked in advertising, a graduate of UCLA, is going to spend all day on his knees trying to force shoes that are too tight over Mrs. Scharf's bunions. What do you suggest for a man who doesn't have a high school diploma?"

"Feh, a piece of paper. You see how much good it did Fine's cousin."

Thank goodness, Mama finally opened her mouth. But all she said was, "His *wife's* cousin. That Trudie Fine, I bet she was at him night and day."

"You said it yourself," Zayde said. "If it was your business and a family member needed help, you'd help. Isn't that the idea, there's nothing like being in business for yourself so you can help family when you need to?"

"What kind of business am I supposed to go into with sixty dollars, in a depression?"

"Not just sixty dollars. I'm talking about a *family* business."

"Like the winery you wanted to get into, Pa. A winery, in the middle of Prohibition."

"Did Prohibition last? If we'd started then—"

"What did we know about making wine?"

"What did Julius Fine know about shoes when he got started?"

"Jesus Christ, Pa! Fine wasn't trying to make shoes, just to sell them."

"Bill, Bill," Mama murmured.

Zayde, to my amazement, grinned. "That's the spirit," he said. "That's the kind of fight it takes to get ahead. Bill, I say this because you're my son. You're as smart as the next fellow; in fact, you're smarter than most of 'em who make ten times what you ever made at Fine's and live in fancy houses on the west side. There's just one thing that holds you back."

He paused, and I thought of doing something to distract everyone's attention—dropping a plate? But I couldn't break a good plate. And I couldn't resist hearing what Zayde was going to say.

"Billy, you've always had a cautious nature. Nothing wrong with that, a little caution is good in business. But sometimes a man has got to take risks. To have a little—"

"Chutzpah," Papa said with a pinched smile. That's when I got scared.

Chutzpah, I had heard many times by then, was something Uncle Harry had possessed in abundance, and it was the quality Zayde prized above all others. "Harry could walk into any room in this city and have 'em eating out of his hand," Zayde often said. "Longshoremen or Torah scholars, didn't matter, he had the chutzpah to look 'em in the eye and tell 'em what he thought. Even the men who run Los Angeles." Or, more to the point, bankers who might have saved the egg ranch. Not that it would have needed saving. The ranch was Harry's idea, and he had had brilliant plans for everything, from getting the most output from the hens to advertising to transporting the eggs to stores. With Harry in charge, Green and Sons' Health-Wise Ranch would have been the biggest egg producer in the West, Zayde said. As I became aware of Zayde's tendency to embellish, I took that boast with a grain of salt. Still, how could you look at photos of Harry and *not* see a man who would have flung himself into the ocean of life . . . and swum faster and harder than everyone else?

I also knew, though this was never part of Zayde's stories, that Harry's enlisting in the army had forced Papa to drop out of high school at sixteen to take his place on the egg ranch. Though, of course, no one could take Harry's place.

And for all my uncle Harry's charm when he was alive, I'd come to dread the times when one of the adults—usually Zayde—brought him into a conversation. At the mention of Harry, Papa got tense and unhappy as he had that day at the beach, even if Zayde hadn't brought up Harry for the express purpose of comparing Papa to him; often, however, the comparison was at least implied, and it was a contest that Papa could never win. I felt bad on Papa's behalf. More than that, I sensed the story of Uncle Harry and Papa repeating between Barbara and me. I was studious, like Papa, and Barbara was a go-getter, a princess of chutzpah. There was a glow around her, as there had been around Uncle Harry.

And that afternoon, though no one had yet uttered Harry's name, I knew that his ghost had entered the room.

"That's it, chutzpah," Zayde said. "But you've got a point. Better to have a business we know something about. A betting shop, for instance."

"Pa." Papa stood up and took a few steps toward Zayde—casually, with his hands clasped in front of him, as if he were delivering a lesson in history or poetry.

"I've got ideas Melansky can't understand," Zayde said. "He doesn't know how to think big. But the two of us could—"

"Pa! Why do you think Harry enlisted in the army?"

Every nerve in my body crackled.

"Who said anything about Harry?" Zayde said.

"Why did Harry enlist?" Papa repeated.

"Why does anyone enlist? To serve his country." Zayde shrugged, but he stood, too, and his accent got stronger, a sign that Papa had upset him. I had an impulse to throw myself between them, but they seemed to be talking reasonably, and how dangerous could they be, two men in house slippers?

"Two years before we got into the war?" Papa said.

"He knew the war was coming."

"So he left a business he'd started just a year earlier. A business that was just getting on its feet."

"Look, I know it's hard to hear the truth about yourself. But don't—"

"The truth?" Papa said, his voice loud and rough. He took a step closer to Zayde. "The truth is, Harry enlisted to get away from your goddamn egg ranch."

"What are you talking about?" Zayde shouted. "The ranch was Harry's idea."

The yelling brought Barbara from the kitchen. We stood glued side to side as Mama, finally roused, cried, "Stop it! Both of you!"

"Harry hated the ranch," Papa said. "He hated chickens. He told me when he left for the army he never wanted to eat another egg."

"Your brother was a hero. Show some respect."

"Know what he hated most of all? He hated getting dragged into your crazy schemes. He was afraid he was going to be stuck doing that for the rest of his life."

"Crazy? Who doesn't eat eggs?"

"Please, Pa, he doesn't mean it," Mama said.

"Why do you think I had to go to work for Fine?" Papa said. "Because there was nothing left after that."

"Under this roof, I won't stay one more night," Zayde boomed.

"Harry couldn't wait to get away!"

"Not one night." Zayde skirted the table and pushed through the swinging door, toward his room.

"Bill, how could you?" Mama exclaimed.

Papa looked at his watch. "Girls, it's ten to six," he said firmly. "We have guests arriving soon. Is the food ready?"

"That's all right, I'll finish it," Mama said, but she didn't leave the room right away; she stood frozen, staring at Papa.

Barbara and I pretended to arrange things on the table; I was blinking my eyes, trying not to cry, and she squeezed my hand to calm me down.

Papa said to Mama, "How could I *say* it? Or how could I have *not* said it all these years?"

"You and your father—and poor Harry, dead all these years already—that's your business. But what are we going to do without your father's income? I'm going to go talk to him." Then Mama went into the kitchen.

Papa sank into the sofa. He looked dazed, the way he had one day when he'd swum his mile even though he was getting over the flu and he emerged from the ocean white-faced, his teeth chattering.

I looked at the elegantly set table and imagined the china and crystal stacked on the curb after we'd been evicted.

As if they had absorbed my fear, all of the beautiful things on the table trembled. But it wasn't just the table. The floor was lurching. Lights flickered. The whole house made terrible, deep grinding noises, overlaid by the shrill, ominous tinkling of crystal.

Barbara and I grabbed each other, screaming, "Earthquake!" Papa threw himself on top of us and pulled us to the shuddering floor as glass shattered around us.

Then it stopped.

For a few seconds, the stillness felt as strange as the shaking.

"Girls, are you all right?" Papa sat up and scanned our bodies for injuries.

We were whimpering like babies, but we hadn't been hurt. Not like Papa, who was bleeding from cuts on his head and arms! But he said he was all right. He told us to go outside—carefully, there was broken glass all over the floor—and wait in front of the house. Then he ran into the kitchen, yelling for Mama and Zayde.

Barbara and I tiptoed through the room, which had gone crazily askew. A table with knickknacks had toppled over, and all of the furniture, even the big, heavy sofa, had lurched into slightly different places. Outside, our wooden porch looked all right, but the three concrete steps were cracked, and a big chunk had broken off the middle step. Testing the ground each time I put a foot down, I picked my way over the broken steps and out to the sidewalk.

Neighbors were spilling outside, too, everyone dazed and eyeing their houses as if fearing what fresh revenge they might take for our living in them so heedlessly, with so little gratitude for their constant effort to squeeze joists and nails and boards together against the forces of chaos. Except for the porch steps and some broken windows, our house looked unharmed, but the porch roof had collapsed at the Lischers', three doors down. There was a horrid blaring sound—the horn of a car, one of several that sat askew in the middle of the street, with no drivers in sight.

"Is anyone hurt? Your mother, with the baby?" It was Mrs. Anshel.

What baby? I thought dully, wondering if she meant her baby, Sharon. But Sharon was right there in her arms. Then I understood she was talking about Mama's pregnancy.

"Papa's getting everyone else," I said.

"Tell him he needs to shut off the main gas line. . . . Barbara, Elaine, are you listening? Just come get me when your father comes out."

Mrs. Anshel turned out to be one of those people who get invigorated by a crisis. Wearing the navy and white dress and silver clip earrings she'd put on to come to dinner at our house, she bustled over to the Yamotos', two doors away. She told them about turning off the gas line—now I understood what she was talking about—and Mr. Yamoto went to take care of it. She mentioned the blaring car horn, and the two sons, Teddy and Woodrow, went and lifted the hood of the offending car.

Papa, Mama, and Zayde came around from the back of the house. Papa and Zayde supported Mama, who held a kitchen towel to her forehead.

"Mama!" we cried, running to her.

"I'm fine, girls. Something fell in the kitchen, that's all," she said, but she walked heavily and her eyes barely flicked over us.

But then, as if strength had flooded into her, she charged past us to the street. "Audrey? Where's Audrey?"

Barbara and I looked at each other, as if that would magically make Audrey appear. Together, we looked at the house. Audrey's face wasn't in any of the windows.

"Didn't she come out?" Papa asked me.

I shook my head.

"You said 'the girls' were out front. 'The girls,' you said!" Mama screamed at Papa.

He was already sprinting back into the house. Zayde was two steps behind him, and then Barbara and me, but, even holding her baby, Mrs. Anshel managed to plant herself ahead of both of us. "What are you girls thinking?" she said. "Take care of your mother."

Mama's face was ashen, except for the bloody gash on her head—no longer covered by the dish towel, which dangled in her hand. Mrs. Anshel led her to sit in one of the abandoned cars and told me to press the towel against the wound on Mama's head. I used it to dab at Mama's tears as well, while my own tears streamed and soaked the collar of my blouse.

The Yamoto boys had silenced the car horn, and we could hear Papa and Zayde calling for Audrey. No one answered.

"Barbara. Elaine." Mrs. Anshel made sure we were looking at her. "This is important. Was Audrey with you when the earthquake happened?"

"No," we said together.

"Where did you see her last?"

"Living room," I said. "But she was going into the kitchen." I glanced at Barbara.

"How was I supposed to notice?" she said. "I had to fix the dinner."

"Oh, was your mama not feeling well?"

"Yes," we answered quickly, both of us immediately understanding that we couldn't reveal what had really happened.

"Hmm." Mrs. Anshel clearly sensed there was more to the story. "Well, does Audrey have a hiding place? Someplace she'd go if she was upset?"

"I don't know," I said, as miserable as Audrey when Mama had snapped at her about the candlesticks.

Papa and Zayde returned, alone. Now Papa took over questioning Barbara and me, while Mrs. Anshel went to organize a search party. Were we absolutely certain we hadn't seen Audrey after the earthquake? Papa asked. What about before the earthquake? Did she go outside?

Yearning to help in some way, I mentioned the need to shut off the gas line. Papa asked Zayde to do it. Then he instructed Barbara and me to stay with Mama, and he joined the search.

Why wasn't Audrey in the house? Had she run outside in distress after I could have helped her but didn't? I asked myself miserably as, all up and down the street, people called her name. And then . . . had she been crushed under a falling building? Had someone taken advantage of the confusion of the earthquake and kidnapped her, like the Lindbergh baby last year? What could I promise God, if He brought her back safely? Of course I would never ever tease her again. But I needed to offer something bigger. What about helping my family, since Papa had lost his job? Some children, even as young as I was, had left school to go to work.

Then I heard a woman cry out, "Here she is! The little Greenstein girl!"

"Look, they found her!" someone else exclaimed.

I followed the pointing fingers and swiveling heads toward the end of

the block, and saw . . . it was Audrey! She rode on the shoulders of a handsome Mexican man. And wasn't that Auntie Pearl at their side?

Mama let out a cry and staggered toward them. Applauding and cheer-
ing, the crowd parted to let her through. The Mexican man gently lowered
Audrey from his shoulders, and Mama swooped to embrace her.

"I found her on the street outside my apartment," Pearl said. "I tried to
telephone you, but the line was down."

Now Mama was scolding Audrey but at the same time hugging her
and stroking her hair and weeping, while the rest of us surrounded them,
chattering and smiling, a happy family again.

"Bill? Charlotte?" Pearl said after the first few delirious minutes of relief that Audrey was safe. "Papa?" she added tremulously.

Pearl looked . . . not just pretty, but like women in the movies. Wearing
a clingy green sweater and high heels, and with red lipstick on her mouth,
my aunt was *sexy*. She placed her hand on the arm of the Mexican man
who had carried Audrey; and who hadn't, like the other helpful neighbors, drifted away. "I'd like you to meet Alberto Rivas," she said.

"Bert," the man said with a smile. "Pleased to meet you, Mr. Greenstein." He held out his hand to Zayde.

Zayde gave Pearl a long, cold look and walked away.

Papa, however, grasped Bert Rivas's outstretched hand. "Thank you
for bringing back our daughter." As if to emphasize how different he was
from Zayde, he added, "Please, stay and have dinner with us."

"Bill, you don't have to," Pearl said quickly.

"He brought Audrey back safe and sound. It's the least we can do."

Bert glanced at Pearl. She nodded, and he accepted Papa's invitation.
Even then, I kept telling myself he must be one of Pearl's neighbors; it was
a bit odd that he lived near Pearl instead of in the Mexican part of Boyle
Heights, but a certain amount of mixing went on, like the Yamotos living
on our block instead of in the Japanese area. And while the idea of Bert
being Pearl's neighbor was odd, it wasn't impossible, not like the other
idea that gradually forced its way into my mind: that Pearl had put on her
sexy sweater for Bert Rivas. That this Mexican man was my aunt Pearl's
boyfriend.

"I couldn't help it," I heard Pearl tell Papa as we picked our way over the broken porch steps. "The important thing was to get her home. What if there was another earthquake, or we had to get past buildings that were destroyed? It would have been crazy to bring her back by myself."

Back inside the house, we turned on the radio and heard that the earthquake had been centered in Long Beach, a terrible thing for the people there but a relief for us, since Long Beach was twenty miles away. Papa, with Bert's help, swept up the broken glass—almost all of the good crystal wineglasses, as well as several pieces of Rosenthal china. Barbara and I reset the table with everyday glasses, and the Anshels joined us for dinner, too, celebrating that all of us had come through the earthquake with little damage and that Audrey was safe.

Everyone was awkward at first around Bert, and no one breathed a word about Zayde having left for Sonya's. But by the time Papa opened a second—then a third!—bottle of wine, we were having the liveliest Shabbos in Greenstein family history. After dinner, the adults' cigarette smoke swirled deliciously. And Bert held Audrey on his lap and sang beautiful Mexican songs.

Papa sang along. I had no idea that he knew songs in Spanish. He dropped out during some of the verses but joined in enthusiastically whenever Bert got to a chorus:

Ay, ay, ay, ay,
Canto y no llores.
Porque cantando se alegran,
Cielito lindo, los corazones.

I'd learned that song, "Cielito Lindo," at school. "Canto y no llores" meant "sing and don't cry." I wondered if that was what Papa was doing, after losing his job and then having the terrible fight with Zayde. Did he wish he could take back what he'd said about Uncle Harry (whose photos hung askew; we had not begun restoring the house to its pre-earthquake order)? But I thought Papa looked defiant, even proud. As upsetting as the fight had been, he had finally stood up against . . . not even Zayde; what Papa had to fight was the ghost of Uncle Harry. And what an unfair fight,

Papa forever in the shadow of a golden boy killed on a French battlefield at twenty. Papa, whose imperfect adult life, with its inevitable disappointments and missed opportunities and sheer rotten luck, could never measure up to the youthful promise, the gleaming possibility, that was and always would be Harry.

CHAPTER 9

COUSIN MOLLIE
CHANGES
THE WORLD

THE 1933 LONG BEACH EARTHQUAKE KILLED 120 PEOPLE AND CAUSED
$50 million in damage. And the rifts that opened in my family that night
never closed.

Zayde had moved to Sonya's once before, after Barbara goaded him to
make the tin animals, but he'd returned just two weeks later, complaining
that Sonya chased after him with the Hoover anytime he walked on her
fancy carpet, and the only subject Leo ever talked about was his dyspepsia—
and no wonder, with Sonya's cooking. This time was different. Zayde didn't
come back. Not that he broke with Papa completely, the way he'd done
with Pearl. He still came over and ate dinner with us one or two nights a
week, and we saw him at family gatherings. But it wasn't the same as having Zayde living with us. I don't know if Harriet, born that June, ever
heard his stories.

And it's lucky I'd paid attention when Zayde took care of the fig tree in the yard. A few days after he left, I noticed the leaves beginning to wilt, and I hurried to water the tree, thinking at the time that I didn't want Zayde to come home to a dying tree. But as his absence dragged on, I became the tender of the fig tree.

Other things changed as well. Audrey had acted giddy and heroic on the night of the earthquake, laughing as she told everyone how, seconds after she turned down Aunt Pearl's street, all of the buildings shook, cars jumped crazily in the road, and she got thrown to the ground. "See!" She displayed her palms and knees, where Mama had washed the abraded skin and put on Mercurochrome and bandages. But for months afterward, Audrey had nightmares and wet her bed, as if she were a child of two and not seven. She was always sensitive, quick to tears, and now little things sent her into tantrums; she'd start with a sort of singing whine and build to a scream.

Papa spent a lot of time with her. He felt guilty for not having realized she was missing. And he was home a great deal; he couldn't find any work for two months after he got laid off from Fine's, and at first, when he did start to work again, it was only occasional jobs arranged through Pearl, purchasing shoes to go with costumes she designed for the movies. This would eventually grow into a moderately successful business that included, for big historical pictures, researching the shoes of earlier times and having a factory make dozens of pairs at a time.

Papa's success, however, still lay some years in the future. The summer after he lost his job, Barbara and I went to work. Barbara, who'd always had a knack for organizing our neighborhood gang of kids, started a summer playgroup for half a dozen children whose mothers worked or could afford a dollar fifty a week to get the kids out of their hair. My job was at Uncle Leo's bookstore on Hollywood Boulevard, which sounded perfect for a reader like me—except that, instead of reading any books, I was given tasks that Leo considered appropriate for a twelve-year-old poor relation, like dusting shelves and running to the drugstore for his bicarb. Danny was working, too, at Chafkin's grocery store. While doing his restitution for stealing, he'd impressed Eddie Chafkin by taking the job seriously; and once he paid off his debt, Eddie offered to hire him. Danny made fun of

Eddie's puffed-up manner and his constant schemes for squeezing a few more pennies out of the store. Yet he seemed to feel proud to be associated with his employer's energy and enterprise, qualities so lacking in his father.

Our jobs didn't end when we entered Hollenbeck Junior High School the next fall; we just switched to after-school and weekend hours. Overnight, it seemed, my childhood pals and I had become workers. *And isn't that the finest thing a person can be!* Cousin Mollie said.

Cousin Mollie Abrams came to stay with us in September when the union sent her to Los Angeles to organize the garment workers. She was the silver lining in the cloud of bad things that happened that year.

Even though Mollie was our cousin, the oldest daughter of Mama's brother Meyr, she was only five years younger than Mama, and the two of them had been like sisters when Mama lived with Meyr's family in Chicago.

"Mollie taught me English from her schoolbooks," Mama had told us many times.

"Mollie used to sneak her mother's cologne on hot days, and we'd rub each other's feet with it. We had the best-smelling feet in Chicago."

"Such beautiful English Mollie spoke. She was going to get a high school diploma and get a nice job, something in an office."

It didn't turn out that way. Meyr hurt his back and could no longer handle his job in the stockyards. Nothing else paid as well, and Mollie had to leave school at fifteen and work in a dress factory. Not that Mollie Abrams was the kind of girl who'd waste any time moaning that life had let her down! In the factory, her intelligence—along with a gift for rousing a crowd, no doubt inherited from Meyr with his *fusgeyer* theatricals—*did* help her get ahead. Before she was twenty, she became president of the union at her factory. Then she caught the eyes of the leaders of the International Ladies' Garment Workers' Union, and they asked her to help them . . . in Los Angeles. Cousin Mollie was coming to stay with us!

She was going to have the room off the kitchen that had been Zayde's—and either Barbara or I would share the room with her! But we had only a week's notice that she was coming. That gave me very little time to be excessively good and prove to Mama that I deserved the honor of rooming with our guest. Fortunately for me, the way Mama made her choice was neither rational nor fair.

It had to do with my being Audrey's chief tormentor, habitually mean to the sister immediately below me in the pecking order; Barbara, in contrast, treated Audrey like an innocuous pet, a canary or a gerbil on which she might lavish attention one day and then ignore for weeks. I was the one who pinched Audrey, made fun of her, and found her existence a frequent source of annoyance. True, I'd promised God that if He brought Audrey back safely after the earthquake, I'd never tease her again. But God never visited our secular household to hold me to my vow. And even though I felt sorry about the rough time Audrey was having, it was miserable for me, too, to wake up on a hot morning to the stink of her pee soaking the cot next to the bed Barbara and I shared. Worse, I would come home after being Uncle Leo's slave all day and riding back on the hot bus, and there was Papa on his knees like a horsey, with Audrey giggling on his back. I'd worked hard for my place as Papa's favorite through my diligence at his lessons and in school. For Audrey, he was willing to be a playmate.

All of that frustration went into the shove I gave Audrey when we were fixing Zayde's room for its new inhabitant.

The room off the kitchen had sat empty ever since Zayde left in March. At first we didn't touch the room because we expected Zayde to return. Once it became clear that his departure was permanent, Barbara and I begged to move there, but Mama and Papa were preoccupied with the new baby and with money worries; and the room needed a few repairs that no one ever got around to. The delay ultimately became part of the silver lining. Instead of the slapdash way we would have fixed up the room for Barbara and me, we were making it *beautiful* . . . for Cousin Mollie.

Papa, Barbara, and I painted the walls with fresh white paint. Mama made new curtains out of crisp fabric with a pattern of pink and blue flowers, and hemmed a square of the same fabric to drape over the orange crate that served as a bedside table. On Saturday night—just two days to Mollie!—Papa was hanging the pretty mirror edged with Mexican tile that Mama had insisted we buy, while Barbara oiled the wooden bed frame and dresser, and Audrey and I, on our knees, scrubbed every inch of the wooden floor. Mama, holding baby Harriet, stood in the doorway to supervise. That was a lot of people crowded into a small room, and Audrey kept getting in my way. Plus, she barely touched her brush to the floor, and I was desperate to do my job the best, so Mama would pick me to room with Mollie.

When Audrey bumped into me for the fifth time, I butted my hip into her.

"Ela-aine!" She crumpled to the floor, emitting the ominous whine that preceded her tantrums.

"Audrey, don't you dare," Mama said. Then she turned to me. I expected to be screamed at or slapped. Instead, Mama knocked me over with what she said. "That settles it. Elaine, you're moving in here with Mollie."

"What?" Barbara gasped. "How come *she* gets rewarded?"

"Not one more word. Barbara, you're able to get along with Audrey. Elaine can't. All I want is a little peace in this house."

"It's not fair!" Barbara wailed.

She was right. But my twinge of guilt was nothing compared to the delirious happiness that flooded through me. I went at the floor with vigor, as if energetic cleaning would speed the arrival of my cousin—who was so important that the union was sending her to Los Angeles on an airplane.

WE SOMETIMES MET PEOPLE at the railroad station, but I didn't know anyone who had traveled by airplane. Mollie's flight was scheduled to land at Glendale Airport on Monday evening, and we all went there to welcome her. Papa recruited Uncle Leo to drive his car, in which my family fit, but just barely, and we planned that most of us would ride back with Leo while Mama and Mollie would take a taxi.

Mollie's flight was supposed to arrive at seven-thirty. We got to the airport by seven and stationed ourselves along the chain-link fence that separated the waiting area from where the planes took off and landed. But seven-thirty came, with no plane from Chicago; then seven forty-five, eight o'clock, and, to Mama's growing consternation, eight-fifteen. "Chicago's always late," said a man whose nonchalant tone reminded me of movies where people dressed for dinner and sipped cocktails. The man had taken dozens of plane trips himself, he said. "Air currents over the Rockies, you can't predict."

Papa took advantage of the wait to give us a lesson on aviation. A plane could fly, he said, because the propeller—"See, the part that's spinning so fast?"—pulled it forward. If the pilot pointed the nose up, the propeller pulled up the plane. A man apologized for interrupting but informed us that what really made flight possible was the shape of the wings and something about a vacuum over them. None of us said much after that, except for Uncle Leo grumbling that he'd had to rush dinner and couldn't digest properly, and hadn't he told Papa that no one arrived at the airport as early as seven to meet a seven-thirty plane?

Mama kept staring at the sky, as if she could will Mollie's plane to appear. And it didn't matter if they announced that the next flight landing was from Denver or San Francisco—she hungrily scrutinized every woman who walked down the metal staircase. Only when the last person had left the plane did she pull back, an impression of chain links on her forehead.

For me, every minute at the airport was like breathing the freshest, sweetest air that had ever entered my lungs. Whenever a flight approached, I joined Mama against the fence, watching the airplane transform from high, distant pinpricks of light to a screaming, diving monster—my heart pounded in terror that it would smash into a million pieces. I sighed in relief when each plane touched down safely and juddered to a halt. At night, there were more flights landing than taking off, but it was even more astonishing to see a plane bump over the ground like an ungainly bus and suddenly rise into the air like a swan. *Vacuum,* I told myself; but how could a word I associated with Aunt Sonya's Hoover describe this miracle?

Just being at the airport was thrilling. Any other place I'd gone beyond Boyle Heights—the beach, downtown, Leo's bookstore in Hollywood—still felt like familiar territory. But not Glendale Airport, where everyone was dressed so nicely they might have been film actors costumed by Pearl, and the hum of talk was like listening to the radio, with no choppy accents or mangled grammar.

Papa gave nickels to Barbara and me and said we could go get Coca-Colas at the snack counter. Making the most of our freedom, we first visited the "ladies' lounge." I used the toilet, then went to the sink, but I froze when a Negro lady in a starched blue uniform came over and handed me the softest white towel I'd ever felt. "Here you are, miss," she said. I thanked her, but was that enough? Barbara, standing at the sink, had her own white towel; I tried to catch her eye, but she was absorbed in applying lipstick.

"Here. I'll meet you at the snack bar." She gave me the lipstick and breezed out.

As I stroked on the lipstick, the Negro lady picked up Barbara's discarded towel. "I'm done with mine, too," I said. "Thank you. Very much." I searched her face for a hint of what else might be expected of me. Then I saw a lady drop a coin into a dish on a table. I panicked for a moment. Should I use Papa's nickel? But I really wanted a Coca-Cola. I remembered I had some coins in my pocket, and I put the nickel in the dish.

At the gleaming snack counter, Barbara was talking to a blond boy who looked about our age. He was to her left, and she'd put her sweater on the stool to her right to save it for me, but when I got there, she didn't look at me.

I ordered my Coke and pretended to be fascinated by the menu.

"Oh, yes, we've flown four or five times," Barbara was saying, her voice bubbly and unfamiliar. "Mummy and Daddy say it's so much more convenient than the train."

"I'll say," the boy replied. "I can't wait until they have passenger flights to Europe. Ships are fun, but it takes such a long time, especially from Los Angeles."

What was a Monte Cristo sandwich?

"Wouldn't that be grand?" Barbara said. "Just like Lindy."

"You wouldn't be scared?"

"I'm never scared."

"How about you?" the boy asked. "Would you be scared? You," he emphasized, and I realized he meant me.

"I'd love to fly," I said.

He scanned my face. "Your sister?" he asked Barbara.

For a breath, I felt her hesitate. Then she said yes and introduced me—as Elaine Green—and without pausing for a breath, told me the boy's name, Gregory Hawkins.

"Yes, I can see the resemblance," Gregory Hawkins said. And then, "Well, nice to meet you. I didn't know it was so late. I have to go."

"Why did you do that?" Barbara said after he left.

"Do what?" I said. "Why did you tell him our last name was Green?"

She shrugged and slid off the stool. I followed her toward our family outpost at the fence.

She turned back suddenly, forcing me to stop short. "Don't you ever just want to pretend you're someone else?" she said fiercely.

And for a moment I glimpsed my family through the crowd as if I didn't know them. Mama was wearing the "smart suit" she'd had made for our first day of school, now seven years out of style and straining at the shoulders as she held Harriet. Papa and Uncle Leo were shorter and darker than most of the men in the airport, and although there were a few other young children present, only Audrey was squatting by the fence; somebody should make her stand up. And there was the sheer bulk of them—no one else was in groups of more than two or three—and the way they stayed in a clump by the fence instead of strolling around or going inside to have a drink.

Did I seem equally out of place? I wondered uneasily. And was it just that I was a poor girl among these well-off world travelers, or did I look glaringly, irrevocably Jewish? Was that what Barbara had accused me of "doing"? Was it the reason Gregory Hawkins had looked at me, seen the same largish nose and dark curly hair as Barbara had—but with my narrower face and glasses—and lost interest in flirting with us? I felt a wash of shame that stunned me. Where had the sense of "wrongness" come from? Yes, I had heard Mama's and Zayde's stories about how Jews were treated in their villages in eastern Europe, and I knew my life was nothing like the lives I saw in the movies. Still, growing up in Boyle Heights, I had never experienced scorn or hatred. Yet it was as if the humiliations and oppression Mama and Zayde had suffered had been lying in wait to ambush me. All it took was venturing beyond my narrow accustomed world, glimpsing myself as someone who belonged at the airport might see me.

My uneasiness lingered when I was back among my family. Harriet had pooped, but Mama hadn't brought a fresh diaper, never imagining we would have to wait so long. Harriet stank and fussed, and Mama made Barbara and me take turns holding her. I tried to get excited again about the airplanes taking off and landing, but I just wanted to be somewhere else. Or even, like Barbara, *someone* else? I glanced at Barbara, who, even though she had to hold Harriet, was standing a bit behind us, keeping her distance from the fence. The way she had chattered about "Mummy and Daddy" and lied about having flown . . . if I tried to do that, I would choke on the falseness. As always, I marveled at—and envied—my sister's audacity, her chutzpah. This time, though, something else stirred in me. True, I couldn't play a role like my chameleon sister. With every inch of my skin, every thought that crossed my mind, every word I spoke, I was Elaine Greenstein. And I was glad of it! I felt the integrity (even if I didn't have that word for it at the time) of being utterly myself, and it gave me an extraordinary sense of power; it was a way I would feel years later in courtrooms when I was at the top of my game. And Barbara—for a moment I saw past her facility at shapeshifting to her *need* for it . . . and I felt sad for her.

All of these thoughts fled, however, when a new set of lights appeared and someone shouted, "It's Chicago!"

"Mollie!" Mama called.

The plane landed, then jounced toward the fence and shuddered to a stop. Men in coveralls wheeled over the metal stairway, and from inside the plane a uniformed arm flung open the door.

The first passenger to emerge was a matronly lady in a lumpy brown suit and green hat. My eyes skimmed past her, but Mama screamed, "Mollie!" And the matron turned into a girl as she dashed down the stairs, yelling, "Charlotte!" and not caring that this wasn't the casual yet dignified way in which everyone else descended from planes. Mollie kissed Mama's fingers through the fence and hurried through the gate. Then she and Mama embraced, both of them laughing and weeping.

Finally Mama introduced each of us. "Elaine," Mollie said and gave me a kiss. "Your mama sent me the letter you wrote to the newspaper. I'm so proud that you're fighting for justice." She said a different special thing to

Papa, Barbara, Audrey, and even Leo, and she cuddled Harriet (and didn't wrinkle her nose at the smell) while we waited for her bags. Up close, Cousin Mollie looked a lot younger than when she'd first stepped from the airplane. She had springy dark hair like Mama's (and mine) that poked out untidily from her stylish green fez. And her brown eyes sparkled with energy.

When we got home Mama showed Mollie her room and said, "I hope you don't mind if Elaine sleeps on the cot."

"Mind?" Mollie clapped her hands. "It'll be like you and me, Char, when we were girls."

Oh, the wonderful talks we were going to have! The secrets I would share with the heroine of Mama's Chicago stories. But Mollie stayed up late that first night talking with Mama in the kitchen, and the next morning when I woke up, she had already left. That evening, Mama made a feast for Mollie's first dinner with us, and we waited an hour and a half before we finally gave up on her and ate. But she stayed out until long after I was asleep. When I awoke the following day, she was gone again.

It was like that all week. The same blazing energy that drew me to Mollie kept her working for the union from sunrise until midnight. In the morning, she left by six to talk to people on their way into the factories. Every evening, she attended a meeting or strolled around the Mexican center of Olvera Street—most of the dressmakers were Mexican—or visiting workers in their homes.

I tried going to bed early, hoping to wake up and talk with her when she got ready in the morning, but as the oldest of six children, Mollie had learned to be quiet. She slept with her alarm clock under her pillow and turned it off before the ring penetrated my sleep. She was extremely tidy as well. Other than her scents—a flowery toilet water and the nasty but tantalizingly adult smell of cigarettes—she left little sign that I even had a roommate. Alone at night for the first time in my life, I drew her brush through my hair and put a few drops of her toilet water on my wrists. I wished resentfully that I were a Mexican dressmaker. Then she'd be interested in me.

I wasn't the only one who felt slighted. Mama complained that Mollie might just as well have stayed in Chicago, for all the time she spent with us. "Your union is supposed to fight for better conditions for workers. Can't they give you one night off to see your family?" she said as Mollie prepared to head off to yet another meeting instead of having dinner with us.

Mollie embraced Mama. "Char, darling, with the union just getting off the ground here, we can't let up." She gave Mama a kiss, then left.

"Twenty-eight years old, and she's married to that union," Mama muttered.

On Friday night, Mollie called to say she couldn't have Shabbos dinner with us because she was being interviewed on a radio station. "What does she think this is, a hotel?" Mama said, and went to bed with a headache. Later, I awakened to voices from the kitchen. Mollie had finally come home, and Mama was weeping and talking to her in Yiddish.

Mollie took Mama out for lunch the next day, and on Sunday, though she spent the day visiting workers in their homes, she came back in the evening and joined us for a leisurely dinner. At first the dinner wasn't what I'd hoped for. All of us were greedy for our guest's attention, and the important things I wanted to tell her—that I was writing a report about Jane Addams, from Mollie's own city of Chicago, and that I'd been chosen to be an editor of the school newsletter—got drowned out by everyone else. Audrey recited a stupid poem. Zayde, who'd joined us that evening, boasted about the radical meetings he used to attend in his village. Barbara talked about her playgroup and answered Mollie's questions about the jobs held by the children's mothers and what kind of working conditions they had.

Then Papa cleared his throat loudly. "Mollie, may I ask you a few questions?" he said. "About your union organizing?"

"Absolutely," Mollie replied, at the same time that Mama said, "Bill," with a warning look. Papa had been grumbling that some of the garment factory owners were our neighbors, small businessmen who were having a rough time in the Depression just like everyone else.

"I voted for FDR," Papa said, "and I want you to understand, I'm all for unions at a big company like General Motors or in the coal mines. But why target the garment factories? You're talking about small businessmen, Jerry Bachman, for instance."

"You go to school with Greta Bachman, don't you, girls?" Mama said. "Mollie, would you care for a bit more kugel?"

"Thanks, Char. I've missed your kugel," Mollie said, but her focus stayed on Papa. "I met Jerry Bachman just the other day," she said.

"Sid Lewis is another one," Papa said. "He started out working in a factory in New York."

"Sid?" Zayde broke in. "A penny-pincher. Minute somebody becomes a boss, they forget where they came from," he said, smoothly sloughing off his admiration for anyone with the chutzpah to start a business.

Papa said, "You can't tell me Sid doesn't have sympathy for the people who work for him. He and Jerry, they'd pay their employees more if they could."

"Bill, I'm sorry to have to tell you," Mollie said, "but your friend Bachman is one of the worst offenders. He pays some women less than a dollar a week. Minimum wage for women in California is sixteen dollars, you know."

"Barbara, help me clear the table, and we'll bring out dessert," Mama said, again trying to defuse their disagreement.

But I didn't want them to stop. Unlike almost every other discussion I'd witnessed around our dinner table—about people we knew, alive or dead, or the minutiae of our days—Mollie and Papa were arguing about ideas! And Mollie was standing up for what she believed with no fear or apology. Not that Mama didn't hold her own in fights with Papa, but she fought only about household issues; only rarely and timidly did she venture an opinion about politics. Not Mollie. And she wasn't just throwing out inflammatory statements the way Zayde sometimes did, but calmly marshaling evidence, making her case. I felt as if our house—and beyond it, Boyle Heights, Los Angeles, and the world—had become more spacious, as if the next time I walked out the door, the streets would be wider and the figs on our tree fatter and sweeter.

Mollie paused for a second after Mama's interruption. Then, to my delight, she plunged back into the argument.

"Jerry Bachman is violating state law," she said. "They all are."

Papa bristled. "That is a very serious charge to make."

"The bosses!" Zayde said.

"Listen to all of you." Mama laughed uneasily. And then *she* got into the fray. "Who at this table has actually worked in a dress factory in Los Angeles? Why doesn't somebody ask me what I think?"

"You're right," Mollie said. "You're the authority, Charlotte. Did you feel you were paid fairly?"

"I . . . You know, an immigrant, you take any work you can get. You don't complain." Flustered, she glanced from Mollie to Papa. Her eyes settled on Papa. But she took Mollie's side! "And they know it. They know they can cheat you and get away with it. . . . Now, is anyone going to eat my poppy-seed cake?"

The discussion of Mollie's organizing continued, though Papa shifted to a less contentious tone. I dug into my cake with relish, thrilled by the power in Mollie that had sparked Mama to take a stand, that galvanized all of us and made us think about things beyond our narrow lives.

Mollie galvanized everyone she met. She began to appear in newspaper or radio reports as the forceful young woman shaking up the garment industry. And she did shake things up. Only a week after she'd arrived in Los Angeles, the cloakmakers walked off their jobs.

That was on Tuesday, September 25, 1933. The next morning, Mollie must have made some noise, or maybe it was the roar of her excitement that woke me.

"I'm sorry, dear," she said. "Go back to sleep."

"Are you going to the strike?"

"It's not a strike." She moved quickly and efficiently, buttoning a blue-and-white striped blouse.

"But the radio said . . ."

"Elaine, you know that what you hear on the radio depends on who owns the radio station? And that most of the radio station owners are friends with the men who own the garment factories?" she said as she fastened her hose and stepped into a brown skirt. *Never wear brown with blue,* I could hear Mama admonishing, even as I was transfixed by Mollie's words. "You know that, don't you?"

"Yes," I lied. I had learned that the government and the rich—though never FDR—made the rules to benefit themselves. But the radio! My family clustered around the radio as if we were hearing the word of God.

"So, what did the owners of the radio station say happened yesterday?" Mollie asked.

"That the workers left their jobs and went into the street, and they almost started a riot."

"Lying capitalist . . ." Mollie forced her brush through her unruly hair. "It was a peaceful march. We sang union songs. I'll bet the radio didn't say that. Or that so many people came to the theater where we held our meeting, they had to open another hall."

Inspiration seized me. "Can I go with you?"

"You have school, dear."

"Not until nine. I can catch a streetcar at eight-thirty." I jumped out of bed and grabbed for my clothes.

"There's nothing to come for. There's no strike."

"But didn't they leave their jobs? Isn't that going on strike?"

"I thought you were the shy one!" She laughed. "The way you won't let go of a point, you could be a lawyer."

That was how my future began. As Mollie explained the difference between a walkout and a full-blown strike, I savored the astonishing new self-image she'd offered me, the transformation from the first twelve years of my life as "the shy one" to a girl who was determined, *bold*, a girl who could be . . . well, I didn't know of any women who were lawyers. But the qualities she had attributed to me felt like qualities that described Mollie herself.

"Can't I help you?" I said when she finished, aware that bold Elaine wouldn't take no for answer.

She took my hands. "Tell you what. Would you like to come with me this weekend when I visit workers in their homes?"

"Oh, yes!"

That Sunday, I accompanied Mollie and a Mexican American union organizer, Patricia, to the barrio east of Boyle Heights to see dressmakers in their homes. The conversations took place in Spanish, which Mollie knew well enough not to need constant translations, so I didn't always follow. Still, it was impossible not to feel the women's excitement about the union, along with their terror that if they got involved, they might get fired or worse—some owners had threatened to deport them. And to see Mollie in action! She listened intently to the women, seeming to know just the right tone to take—sober or rousing or indignant—for each one. Sometimes she had to meet a suspicious husband before she could speak to his wife, and a few men refused to let her in; usually, though, Mollie won over the husband, who ended up laughing and joking with her or solemnly nodding and agreeing about *la justicia*.

It was impossible, too, not to see how badly the women needed help. I knew, of course, that Los Angeles had poor people, but the poorest home I'd ever been in was Danny's, and even though the two rooms where he and his father lived were shabby and cramped, at the very least the walls stood at right angles, and the building itself looked solid. In the barrio, I entered flimsy shacks that made me think of the house of sticks in "The Three Little Pigs." The houses were nicer inside, neatly kept and brightened up with pictures of nature scenes or movie stars cut from magazines, and many boasted a single luxury: a radio or a refrigerator. Still, the interiors were stifling on a warm early fall afternoon. And when I asked to use the toilet at one house, a blushing woman had her little boy lead me to an outhouse. Outhouses didn't sound so awful in Mama's stories of Romania, but she'd never mentioned the smell or the flies. I thought of trying to hold my pee, but Mollie planned to spend hours in the barrio. And I didn't want to disappoint her or insult the lady, whose son was waiting for me. Holding my nose, I lowered myself to an inch above the seat and peed as fast as I could.

The following week, I had no trouble hearing Mollie's alarm clock. I bolted awake every day at five-thirty when she did. Sitting in bed while she dressed, I heard about union members getting fired and the growing number of women joining the union in spite of firings and intimidation. And Mollie was starting to scout around for a building to be strike headquarters, if it came to that.

I wanted to visit the barrio with her again the next Sunday, but she gave Barbara a turn. I had talked excitedly about my experience all week, and Barbara had seemed eager to go, but she came home afterward complaining that she felt ill; she skipped dinner and went to bed with a hot water bottle on her stomach. Later that evening—when Mama and Papa were at a card party and Mollie at a meeting—she came into the kitchen wanting something to eat.

"How was it?" I asked, sitting at the kitchen table with her while she ate beef-barley soup and toast.

"I don't know. Okay." She stared into her soup, using her spoon to poke at a shiny blob of fat floating on the top.

"Isn't Mollie wonderful?"

"Isn't Mollie wonderful?" she mocked.

I fell silent, stunned by the venom in her voice. And because I always froze when someone confronted me. Especially Barbara.

She said crossly, "We talked to a girl named Teresa. She was only seventeen. She started crying, she was really scared, and Mollie held her. An hour later, I said something about Teresa, and Mollie didn't know who that was."

"Well, I guess . . ." I had noticed the kind of thing Barbara objected to, but I'd also seen that with all of the people Mollie spoke to in a day, she was absolutely present for each one; how could she do that if she was still thinking about the last woman she'd seen, or the dozen before that? Still, even if Barbara hadn't perceived what I had, it didn't explain her animus toward our extraordinary cousin. "Are you mad because I got to room with her?" I asked.

"Who says I'm mad?" She took a big, aggressive bite of toast.

"Why don't we trade next week? I'll move back in with Audrey."

"I don't want to trade."

"Come on. I'll promise Mama I'll be nice to Audrey."

"Elaine!" she yelled in my face. "Why would I want to room with Mollie? So I can stink of cigarettes like you do?"

"I don't—"

"Smell yourself. Your clothes, your hair. You reek just like she does!" Barbara grabbed at my hair, and I dodged away.

"What's wrong with you?" I protested. "You sound like you hate her."

"I just don't think Mollie Abrams is God."

"I don't, either."

"If she told you to jump off a cliff, you'd do it."

"That's stupid." I blinked back tears of frustration. Why, when Barbara argued with me, did words desert me? The same words that became my best friends when I sat quietly, pen in hand?

"She comes and treats our house like it's a hotel. She barely gives Mama the time of day. She's supposed to be a dressmaker, so how come her clothes don't fit? They don't even match!" It was the jumble of grievances we'd heard from the adults, delivered with Barbara's natural certainty. "And she never asks anyone about themselves. I bet she couldn't tell me one single thing about you."

"Yes, she could," I pushed myself to retort.

"Like what?"

"Like . . . I don't know . . ."

"See? Know what Greta Bachman's father calls his factory?"

"You don't even like Greta Bachman," I countered feebly, aware that this was a pointless diversion but lacking the skill to outmaneuver Barbara.

"Noni. He named it for his sister who died of influenza."

How could I argue against Mr. Bachman's poor dead sister? Then my eyes fell on the book I'd been reading. "She knows I'm reading *David Copperfield*! She said most novelists lie, but not Dickens. And she's got more important things to think about than her clothes. You went with her. You saw."

"You really liked it, didn't you? Going with her? Seeing those dirty, stupid Mexicans?"

"Dirty? Stupid? They're people! They're workers!"

"See, you sound just like her! You want to be like her, don't you?" She jumped up and ran from the room.

I sat trembling, shaken by the intensity of my own outburst and by having discovered Barbara's astonishing rancor toward Mollie. I even spat and said *kaynehora*, like Mama did, to ward off the evil eye on account of the awful things uttered so close to Mollie's bedroom door.

Another source of distress was the gap the fight exposed between Barbara and me. I understood, of course, that my twin sister and I had different personalities, and we had long ago established different interests and friends. Still, our lives were woven together so tightly, I would have sworn we held . . . not even the same beliefs; it was more intrinsic than that, like our speaking voices that no one could tell apart. But in the battle we had just had, along with the tussling and name-calling of our childhood fights, I'd felt stirrings of our adult selves declaring who each of us was at the core. And I was stunned to sense how profoundly unlike we were; I felt unmoored. My excitement about visiting the barrio with Mollie was visceral, like the immediate, unthinking pleasure of biting into a ripe plum. How could Barbara feel none of that? How could she loathe Mollie?

Something else had changed as well. I had stood up to Barbara. I'd found the words to make *her* run from an argument. The experience was exhilarating but unsettling. It was one thing to act bold around Mollie, who saw boldness in me, but to become that new Elaine all the time, even with Barbara! The change felt like the shifts and trembling that happened deep in the earth over centuries, shifts that had led to the Long Beach earthquake.

In the days to come, these nascent understandings merely whispered in the background, however. They—and everything else—got drowned out by the strike, which more and more each day appeared to be inevitable. Mollie sang union songs as she got dressed every morning, and she worried out loud about keeping any plans secret, so that neither the owners nor the rival Communist union could sabotage them.

I'd gotten used to Mollie's predawn alarm; still, I felt sleep-drugged on Thursday, when I opened my eyes and saw her dressing by candlelight.

"Wha . . . ?" I mumbled.

"Go back to sleep, dear. It's just four."

That woke me immediately. "Is this it? The strike?"

She took a deep breath. "Yes. The committee members are coming at five to get leaflets to hand out. They don't know it, but the leaflets will tell people to come to strike headquarters instead of going to work."

"Please, let me come."

"Absolutely not."

"I can help."

"Elaine." She switched on the light, then sat on my cot. "This can be dangerous." Leaning forward, she lifted her hair up from her forehead and exposed a dead-white scar an inch and a half long, just below her hairline.

"Oh, Mollie." I felt a shiver of nausea. "How . . . ?"

"Thugs in Chicago."

"Please, be careful," I said.

"I will, I promise," she said.

Then she went off to start the biggest labor action ever to hit the Los Angeles garment industry.

Once the dressmakers' strike started, Mollie spent nearly every waking hour at strike headquarters in the garment district. In our predawn conversations, though, she confirmed things I had read in the paper or heard on the radio: two thousand people were on strike, and it was clever Mollie who devised the "publicity stunt," as the newspaper called it, of having a dozen young, pretty strikers dress up in evening gowns and carry picket signs in front of a department store having a fashion show.

It was also true that there were disturbances on the picket lines, though Mollie said the owners' thugs were responsible, while the newspaper and radio blamed the picketers. So did the police, who arrested some of the women and put them in jail.

"That's terrible!" I said.

"No." Mollie grinned. "You refuse bail until the next day, and you stay up all night singing union songs. Drives the cops nuts."

She'd been arrested several times in Chicago and had no fear of jail. Nevertheless, she couldn't afford to get picked up here. Since she was a union leader, the authorities might twist the law and keep her in jail for days to try to cripple the strike.

I remembered that, but not until after I'd spoken to the man who asked about Mollie one morning, two weeks into the strike. I had left home early to work on the school newsletter. I was partway down the block when the man came up and tipped his hat at me.

"Morning, miss, sorry to bother you," he said. "I'm looking for Mollie. Am I too late?"

"She left already," I said. Any wariness I might have felt was dispelled by the fact that the man had an accent like Zayde's and a sharp, foxlike face, a hungry face, like many of the union men whose photographs I saw in the paper.

"Oy, I knew I shoulda got up earlier. I have some news I've got to get to her, about the union. You're her . . ."

"Cousin. Elaine."

"Pleased to meetcha, Elaine. Stu Malkin." He extended his hand for me to shake. "You don't happen to know where I could find her? I need to talk to her as soon as I can. Oy, I'm going to be in so much trouble."

"Strike headquarters," I said—and added, eager to be helpful, "Or else she goes around to the picket lines at the different factories."

Stu Malkin frowned and scratched his head. "That's what, fifty factories? A hundred? They're having a lot of trouble at Anjac, aren't they? Or Paramount? Or Kaybel?"

Mollie had mentioned the Paramount Dress Company. It was on the tip of my tongue, but then it hit me . . . if Stu Malkin were really with the union, shouldn't he have known there were eighty dress factories? And that Mollie always left before six?

I didn't answer him.

"Well, hey, thanks anyway, Elaine. You're a peach." He handed me a silver dollar. It was too much money, and then I knew: I had almost given Mollie away.

But what if I *did* give her away? Had I shown something on my face when Malkin, if that was really his name, said "Paramount"? He'd hurried over to a brown car and driven off quickly. Was he going to the Paramount Dress Company? Would he find Mollie there? And then what would he do to her? I had to warn her.

I kept walking normally until the minute his car turned the corner. Then I ran to the streetcar stop on Brooklyn Avenue.

Wild with fear, I caught the streetcar going downtown. Once my initial panic subsided, I realized I had no idea where to find Mollie. Instead of jumping on the streetcar like a silly goose, I should have run home and called strike headquarters; the phone number was on a card pinned up next to our telephone. Too late now, we had already crossed the gully that marked the Los Angeles River (dry this time of year).

Downtown, I transferred to the streetcar to the garment district. At Ninth Street, I spotted a picket line of about twenty women half a block away. I got off the streetcar and ran to them. No Mollie! But the minute I said her name, a brisk young woman came over and asked if she could help.

As I explained about needing to warn Mollie, I took in the women marching up and down on the sidewalk—and, standing between them and the grimy factory building, a line of half a dozen burly men.

The woman, who introduced herself as the strike captain, Norma, called over four picketers and sent each one to a different area of the garment district to look for Mollie. Then she turned to me.

"You're going to be late for school," she said.

"Can't I stay? Until I'm sure Mollie's all right?"

"I don't—"

"I'll march with you." I picked up a picket sign one of the messengers had left behind.

"Just like Mollie!" Smiling, Norma threw up her hands. "You decide you want something, and there's no way to stop you."

I basked in her words. I was like Mollie! Had Mollie brought out something brand-new in me? Or had she recognized an Elaine who'd been there all along? I proudly shouldered a picket sign and fell in line with the women, who greeted me warmly when they heard I was Mollie's cousin. And I became more aware of the men, who weren't just big but mean-looking.

The men noticed me, too.

"A little young, *chica*, aren't you?" one of them called out.

"Ignore them," Norma said firmly, and started up a union song. It was part of Mollie's morning repertory, and I joined in.

Fifteen minutes later, one of the messengers came back. Mollie was waiting for me, she said, and she led me to a car parked on a side street. The only person I saw in the car was the driver, a fox-faced man like Stu Malkin, but before I could panic, Mollie bobbed up from the backseat and waved.

She opened the rear door. "Get in. Quick . . . No, not on the seat."

I squeezed with her onto the floor in the rear of the car.

"Tell me exactly what happened," she said.

I explained.

"Okay, let's go," she said, and told the driver, Ed, to take her to an address in Hollywood.

Once we'd left the garment district, Mollie said we could move off the floor onto the seats. She and Ed speculated about whether Malkin was a policeman or a process server who wanted to hand Mollie an injunction; either way, whoever had sent him must be trying to keep Mollie from speaking at a big rally scheduled for that evening, so she needed to hide for the rest of the day.

She didn't act worried. In fact, she was jolly, as if this were a good joke. She said no cop or process server would find her where Ed was taking her. "And after that, young lady, he's going to drive you straight to school."

"Please, can't I stay with you?" I begged, though I knew what the answer would be.

But, to my amazement, Mollie laughed and said, "Well, why not? I guess you're getting an education today, aren't you?"

When we got into Hollywood, she surprised me even more.

"Have you ever had a manicure?" she said.

CHAPTER 10

MAMA AND THE
FUSGEYERS:
THE REAL STORY

OLLIE HAD FIGURED OUT A HIDING PLACE WHERE NO PO-
liceman would think to look for her: a posh Hollywood beauty salon. A
man in a uniform with gold braid said, "Good day, ladies," and held open
the door for us. Inside, a deep rose Persian rug led to a white reception desk
with carved designs decorated on the edges with gold paint.

"Hello, I'm Anne Simmons," Mollie said to the blond receptionist. I
stifled a gasp, realizing just in time that of course Mollie couldn't give her
real name if she was in hiding. Mollie said she was treating herself and her
cousin to a day of beauty treatments, and could she speak to the manager,
because we wanted "the works."

The receptionist relayed our message on a telephone, and the manager, Mrs. Barregas, bustled out to greet us. Everything about Mrs. Barregas was dramatic and artificial—jet-black hair piled high on her head,

bright red lips and fingernails, and the affected way she said, "Miss Simmons, enchanted." Mollie asked if there was a telephone she could use, and Mrs. Barregas ushered us to her tiny private office, decorated in unfussy black and white, at the back of the salon.

She closed the office door, then said in a perfectly normal voice, "Is there a problem? Laura, is she all right?"

Mollie assured her that Laura—Mrs. Barregas's cousin, who was a local union organizer—was fine, and Mrs. Barregas left us alone to use the telephone. I assumed Mollie wanted to check in with strike headquarters. I hadn't considered the obvious.

"Do *you* want to call your mother?" Mollie said. "Or should I?"

For the first time, in that day of hurrying to warn Mollie and huddling on the floor of the car to escape her pursuer, my legs turned to jelly. "You, please."

Mollie started by telling Mama that I was with her and I was safe, then that I had saved the day by coming to warn her. Mama got so loud then that I could hear her from the receiver at Mollie's ear. But no one was more persuasive than Mollie. In five minutes, she got Mama to agree to let me spend the day with her.

Mollie's charm wouldn't, I knew, spare me from punishment later on. But I didn't care. I was having an adventure with Mollie and even helping the union, albeit in a different way than I could have imagined. Trading my blouse for a pink-and-white striped cape, I entered a pink-wallpapered room for a "Hollywood facial," which involved reclining in a plush chair while expert fingers massaged creams into my face.

After Mollie and I both had facials, Mrs. Barregas showed us to a pink-upholstered settee in a spacious lounge to wait for our hair appointments—and, as Mollie remarked with a chuckle, to feel like ladies of leisure with no cares in the world beyond making ourselves gorgeous. Mrs. Barregas brought over two beautiful stemmed glasses. Mine held orange juice, while Mollie got a cocktail of orange juice and champagne.

Three other women occupied the lounge, one lying on a chaise with a mask over her eyes and the other two chatting and eating doughnuts. The doughnuts came from a doily-covered platter and were apparently provided for any of the customers.

"Good, there's one chocolate left!" Mollie reached for one with choco-late frosting, put it on a plate, and offered it to me.

"No, you have it," I said, and took a glazed buttermilk instead.

"Elaine." Mollie made sure I met her eyes. "Don't be afraid to ask for what you want. How about if we split the chocolate?" She broke the doughnut in half.

"I *like* the buttermilk," I protested.

"Really? Better than chocolate?"

Under her gaze, I admitted, "No, but I do like buttermilk."

"Fine. We'll split both of them." Mollie broke the second doughnut, then patted my hand. "You take everything so seriously, Elaine. Like your mama when she was your age. But your mama, poor thing, she had no choice. She got put to work cleaning our house the day she walked in the door. If she'd wanted the shame of being a maid, she used to say, she could have stayed home in . . . It was just an expression," she said, noticing my stunned face. "Some translation from Yiddish."

"I thought Mama loved living with your family," I said through a mouthful of chocolate doughnut. "She always says the day Uncle Meyr sent for her was the happiest day of her life."

Mollie looked confused, but just for a moment. Then she smiled brightly and said, "Yes, that's right. She and I, we had such good times. . . . How's the doughnut?"

"Delicious." I could tell she regretted having said anything about Mama and that she'd prefer I let the subject drop. But hadn't she just told me to ask for what I wanted? "Why did Mama say that, about being a maid?"

"You know." Mollie shrugged. "Everyone who came from Europe ex-pected life in America to be wonderful the second they stepped off the boat. They didn't expect to have to work in sweatshops. That's how the garment workers' unions got started, by immigrants who expected more."

It was hardly unusual for Mollie to bring up the union, but I sensed something evasive in her reply. During the next phase of the day of beauty, which was devoted to washing, cutting, and styling my hair, I thought about what she'd said . . . and became aware of gaps in what I'd heard from Mama about her life in Chicago, contradictions I hadn't noticed, I suppose, because when I first heard the story, I was barely older than a baby. Mama was just twelve when she'd come to Chicago—my age! So why hadn't she gone to school, instead of being put to work helping Aunt Ida? And all the time she was growing up in Romania, the one thing she'd dreamed of was to go to Uncle Meyr in Chicago. Why, when she finally got there, did she stay for only a few years? Why leave Meyr and move to California?

Mrs. Barregas appeared when the stylist finished giving me a marcel wave. "Look at you," she said. "A real young lady." She handed me my glasses. My hair was soft and wavy instead of bushy. But beneath my tamed curls, my mind roiled. Had everything I'd heard from Mama been a lie?

Mrs. Barregas escorted me back to the lounge, bustling now that it was midday. Half a dozen women talked, laughed, and ate; the doily-covered platter now held a stack of sandwiches. Mollie was already there, sporting her own marcelled hairdo and lunching on a sandwich and a cup of coffee. She had found a seat in the lounge's one quiet corner, where two chairs were partially secluded by a potted palm. I launched myself at her, but I had so many questions, I didn't know where to begin.

Fortunately, Mollie knew what was on my mind. After she'd admired my hair, she said, "What has your mama told you about how she came to America?"

"That Uncle Meyr came first? With the *fusgeyers*?" Surely Mama hadn't made up the *fusgeyers*! My heart sank at the thought of having to relinquish the most enchanting of my family's stories.

But thank goodness, Mollie said, "That's right."

"Then," I continued, "didn't Uncle Meyr help some of his brothers and sisters come over—first Uncle Nathan and Uncle Victor and Aunt Dora? And when Mama was twelve, he sent for her?"

Mollie took a sip of coffee from a cup as delicate as our Rosenthal china. "This is your mama's story to tell, so I don't really have the right to speak for her," she said. "On the other hand, she might be afraid of setting a bad example, or she might not want to say anything bad about my parents. Not everyone is willing to look at the truth squarely, like I do—and I think you feel that way, too."

She cast me an inquisitive glance, and I nodded so vigorously my marcelled hair shook.

"So this is just between you and me, all right?" she said.

"I promise." Secrets with Mollie, it's what I had dreamed of. Still, the prospect of hearing this secret—something Mama had deliberately hidden?—both excited me and stirred up a sense of dread.

"Your uncles and your aunt Dora were already grown up when they came to America, so they could look out for themselves," Mollie began. "But your mama—my father wanted to send for her, but my mother put her foot down. She said your mama was still a child, and we already had enough children in the house."

"He didn't send for her?" I said, absorbing the idea that the happiest day of Mama's life was something that never happened. But if that were true, and Meyr didn't send for Mama . . . "Then how did she get to America?"

"Ah." Mollie smiled. "She was very brave and very clever."

WHAT MOLLIE TOLD ME began much like the story I knew. Uncle Meyr had promised Mama he'd send for her when she was twelve. And not long after Mama's twelfth birthday, she heard that Avner Papo from her village was leaving with a band of *fusgeyers*, and she begged to go with him. There were two crucial differences, however. Meyr didn't send for her. Nor did Avner Papo agree to take her with him. So she went, anyway.

"By herself?" I breathed.

"Didn't I tell you your mama was clever and brave?"

Mollie must have adored her young aunt's story and asked for it often, because she remembered it in such detail, she might have been there herself.

At that time, it was a decade since the first hopeful *fusgeyers* like Meyr had set out for America. Hundreds of *fusgeyers* had passed through Mama's village since then, but they were no longer merry companies of youths embarking on an adventure. The later travelers were like this group, a bedraggled collection of some 150 men, women, and children. An initial contingent of young people entered the village singing, but the rest straggled; a family of eleven trudged in an hour after the first arrivals.

Mama observed the group's disorganization with delight. It would be easy to lose herself among them.

The night before Mama ran away with the *fusgeyers*, she was so excited she didn't sleep a wink. In the pitch-dark, not knowing if it was near daybreak or still the middle of the night, she slipped out of the bed she shared with two of her sisters, tiptoed into the kitchen and packed a bit of food— a half loaf of bread, some eggs, two jars of her mother's delicious plum preserves (but only one to eat on the journey; the other was a gift for Meyr). She had offered to take the *fusgeyers* some provisions, so neither the missing food nor her absence would raise an immediate alarm. Finally, there was the note she'd written, telling her parents she loved them and that she was going to Meyr. She slipped the note under the challah cover, which was used only on Shabbos; that was two days away, and she calculated she'd be far enough by then that no one would force her to come home.

As she crept out the door, the first light of dawn burned the sky. Every rooster for miles around started crowing. Had they ever made such a racket?

"She used to tell me," Mollie said, "she was sure the roosters were calling, 'Catch Zipporah! The little bird is getting away.'"

Pursued by the roosters' cries, Mama ran past the barn where the *fusgeyers* had slept and continued for two miles down the road they would take that morning. There she hid in a copse of trees, trembling with excitement and with the terror of getting caught.

Hadn't Avner Papo called her lucky, though? She'd never felt very lucky, but maybe God had saved all her good fortune and poured it into this one morning, because every instinct she had, every small choice she made, saved her from being discovered. I came to see my mother's luck that day as emblematic of her immigration to America. In the small details, she would succeed. It was the big things that would break her heart.

Soon the first *fusgeyers* came along, singing. She longed to join them. But these were the young people, their resilient bodies and spirits able to feel refreshed from eating a few crumbs of food and spending the night on a barn floor. Lively and sharp-eyed, the young people would notice in an instant if she appeared out of nowhere. She hugged herself to keep from running to them, and remained hidden.

A second group followed ten minutes later. Still she bided her time. She waited until she saw a clump of people of all ages, the adults looking exhausted already and the children fussing. No one even blinked when she slipped out of the woods and became one of them.

When everyone stopped at midday to eat something and rest a bit, Mama approached one of the girls among the young people and offered to share her food. "Plum preserves! Manna from heaven," the girl said. She and her friends ate quite a lot of the first jar of preserves, but the sacrifice was worth it, because they invited Mama to walk with them. And although these weren't theatrical *fusgeyers*, the young people planned to put on a play about a young girl who worked for a cruel factory boss, and who better than Mama, the youngest among them, to play the innocent girl? (I'd heard from Mama about her theatrical triumph, how she brought audiences to tears.) Striding down the road with the young people that first afternoon, Mama was bursting with happiness.

When the *fusgeyers* reached the town where they were going to spend the night, her joy changed to fear. A leader of the Jewish community gave a speech welcoming the travelers—and surely he was going to announce that a girl had gone missing from Tecuci and ask everyone to look for her. She hid, but she was afraid they would find her just by hearing her pounding heart. It was all right, though; no one said a word about her.

"Wait," I said. "Even if her parents didn't find her note, they must have suspected she'd gone with the *fusgeyers*."

"Of course they did. In fact, they sent a wire to Avner Papo, asking him to let them know if he found her, and would he look out for her? And when they heard she was there, they sent a little money, whatever they could spare."

"But she was only twelve!" My age. If I ran away . . . I could *hear* Mama's howl of anguish. And Papa would move heaven and earth until he found me. "Weren't they worried something bad would happen to her? Why didn't they try to make her come home?"

"Oy." Mollie sighed. "In Romania, children younger than twelve are still sent away from home to be apprentices and learn a trade. Right here in America, there are twelve-year-olds working in sweatshops. What did your mama's parents have to offer her if she stayed? And they must have seen that her mind was made up. If they forced her to come home this time, she was going to leave with the next *fusgeyers*, or the ones after that. Do you understand?"

"Yes," I said, though all at once I felt upset about everything. I ached for Mama, the ignored seventh child of nine, whose leaving caused barely a ripple in her family. I *didn't* understand—I refused to understand—Mollie's calm explanation for why Mama's parents let her go without a murmur. And to hear Mollie talk about her as if she were just another child in a sweatshop . . . in my mind, I heard Barbara railing against our cousin's coldness. Yet none of that changed my desire to be the Elaine that Mollie saw in me, a girl who didn't flinch from the truth.

This would hardly be my last experience of ambivalence, but it may have been the most wrenching. I had no conflicted feelings, though, about my hunger to hear the rest of the story.

I blinked back my tears and leaned forward. "Did Avner help her?"

"Ah." Mollie's eyes gleamed. "Avner fell in love with her."

"With Mama?"

"Why not with your mama? She wasn't a beauty, but she always had a way about her. . . . You haven't touched your lunch."

I hadn't noticed that a sandwich and a glass of milk had appeared on a settee next to me. I took a bite of the sandwich. Inside dainty triangles of white bread were slices of chicken, a delicacy that my family ate only on Friday nights. I kept on eating, though I barely tasted anything.

Avner found Mama and took her under his wing, Mollie continued, and they walked with the *fusgeyers* until they crossed the Austro-Hungarian border. From there, they took a train (the tickets provided by a Jewish agency) to the port of Rotterdam. The pennies Mama had saved were nowhere near enough money for the ship, but Avner was hardly going to abandon her. Crossing the Atlantic, she returned the favor. She turned out to have the stomach of a born sailor, whereas poor Avner broke out in a clammy sweat when they'd barely left port. Mama held a bowl for him when he vomited, coaxed him to eat bits of bread, and spooned soup into his mouth. After a week, he finally adjusted to the ship's motion, and she helped him up to the deck for a little fresh air.

At last the ship arrived in America. In the city where Avner's cousin lived, New York.

"Your brother is where?" Avner's cousin asked her, dismayed at having to squeeze not one but two greenhorns into his tenement apartment. "Chicago? How are you going to get there?"

"I'll walk!" Mama declared. She had crossed Romania on foot, hadn't she?

"New York to Chicago, she thinks she's gonna walk." The cousin guffawed, and his whole family acted like it was the funniest thing they'd ever heard.

"Your poor mama!" Mollie said. "She had no idea how big America was."

"What about Avner falling in love with her?"

"Ah, I'm getting there."

Once the cousin tired of bullying Mama, he sent a telegram to Meyr, asking him to wire her train fare. Two days later, Avner accompanied her to the train station and walked with her onto the platform to say goodbye.

Mama felt a lump in her throat, thinking of never again seeing Avner, who'd been kinder to her than anyone in her life. She told him she was going to miss him. He said he would miss her, too. Then, in a rush, he took her hand and said, "You're too young now, you're just a girl. But in three, four years, I could send for you." She had no idea what he was talking about. Until he said, "Or I could come there. Chicago. For you to marry me. To be my wife."

Heaven help her, she knew the look on her face was disgust. She loved Avner, but like a father; he was a grizzled old man! "I don't know. Maybe," she said, trying to smile. To take the hurt out of his eyes.

Looking back, she would see that moment at the train station in New York, when she had hurt Avner Papo, as the moment her luck ran out.

At some point Mollie and I shifted from the lounge to another area of the salon, where we had manicures and she told me what happened when Mama came to Chicago.

Meyr—though he had stopped being Meyr Avramescu and was now Mike Abrams—met Mama's train and brought her home to his wife, Ida. "About my mother," Mollie said. "Some people have hard times, and it makes them care about everyone who has hard times. But some people get so they just want to protect the little bit they have. I was there when your mama walked through our door for the first time; I was so excited to meet her. But my mother, before she even said hello, she said, 'You think in America, train tickets grow on trees?' "

Ida put Mama to work, helping cook and clean and look after her nieces and nephews (four of them when she arrived, and eventually Ida had two more); she had to pay back the train ticket and for the food she ate, the clothes she wore, and the little bit of heat in the apartment that warmed her body. School? There was no question of that. Even if Mike and Ida had been inclined to send her, twelve was too old to start school for someone who spoke no English.

"Didn't Uncle Meyr—Uncle Mike—stand up for her?" I asked.

Mollie sighed. "Sometimes, sure. But he was at work all day. And the stockyards, it's the kind of work that can kill a person's spirit." For the first time, it occurred to me that almost all of Mama's stories about Meyr took place in Tecuci. Her Chicago stories were about Mollie.

There was a thudding sameness to Mama's life in Chicago. At sixteen, she rebelled against four years of Ida's yoke and traded the drudgery of housework for the drudgery of working in a dress factory on Maxwell Street. She still had little talent for sewing, but her sister Dora was a supervisor and got her the job. Though she had to hand Ida her pay envelope, at least Ida no longer monitored her every breath. But Ida and Mike had new plans for her.

A friend of Mike's from work, Hy Slotkin, sometimes joined them for Shabbos dinner.

"Slotkin?" That name had fastened itself in my memory the day Mama locked Barbara in the closet.

There was nothing wrong with Hy Slotkin, Mama said, every time Mike or Ida said, "So, what's wrong with Hy Slotkin?"—which they did often, because Hy had asked for Mama's hand, and they wanted her to marry him. The truth was, Hy's laugh set her nerves on edge. "We called him 'Hyena,' " Mollie said. And Hy was ugly, with beefy arms and a permanent sort of grimace from closing his nostrils to the stockyard smell.

Mama was determined to escape. But she couldn't just take off the way she'd done at twelve; she no longer had that kind of daring. Then the Tarnows, from Mike and Ida's building, decided to move to Los Angeles for Mrs. Tarnow's rheumatism, and it was too much for a family with an ailing wife to pack up a household and get three small children across the country. They offered to pay Mama's train fare and let her stay with them, in exchange for her help with the move.

I already knew much of what happened next because it was the story of how Mama met Papa. Moving to Los Angeles at seventeen, she lived with the Tarnows in Boyle Heights and got a job in a dress factory. The Tarnows had promised Mike that they would treat her as if she were their own daughter. They kept their ears open and heard of a fine young man, son of a fellow who came from Mr. Tarnow's village in Ukraine—but American-born, with no accent! One thing led to another, and after a year, Papa dropped on his knee and asked Mama to marry him, an event that Mama, never much of a correspondent, reported in one of the rare letters she wrote to Mollie.

"But she didn't say yes right away," Mollie said.

"Did she have other . . . beaux?" I asked, getting used to the idea of Mama as a girl who'd "had a way about her." First Avner Papo, then Hy Slotkin; maybe men all over Los Angeles had bombarded her with flowers and poems.

"No. It's just, to be a wife and mother—it's a wonderful thing, but a girl needs to live a little first. She went on hikes in the mountains just north of Los Angeles. She went to the beach with friends. She tried out for a theater troupe."

"A theater troupe? Mama?"

"She wrote to me that some people in Boyle Heights were starting a Yiddish theater troupe. She'd been such a success with the *fusgeyers*, she decided to try out for their play. She and your papa—although they weren't married yet—had a big fight over it. He couldn't stand the idea of Yiddish theater in America. How could any intelligent person stomach a schmaltzy Yiddish drama when Americans spoke—"

"The tongue of Shakespeare." It was what Papa had said when he objected to my taking Yiddish classes from Mr. Berlov.

"Exactly." Mollie smiled. "She got so upset she told him she never wanted to see him again."

"No!" I burst out, stunned to imagine a situation that had brought me so close to not-being. And stunned to see my mother as a girl who had hungrily wanted things for herself and had so bravely, even ruthlessly, pursued them.

"She didn't mean it. Poor thing, the letter was covered with splotches from her tears. And in the next letter I got from her, a few months later, she said she and Bill had just gotten married."

"Did she try out for the play?" I asked.

"Funny, I guess she never said. But don't ask her. Like I said, this is between you and me. Okay?"

I nodded.

I spent the rest of the day hiding with Mollie at the beauty salon. In the early evening a union man came and drove her to her rally, then gave me a ride home.

OVER THE NEXT FEW weeks, my cousin Mollie made history. She gained recognition for the Los Angeles dressmakers' union and settled the strike. Then she was gone, sent by the union to the next city where working people needed her help.

The more I thought about what she'd told me, the surer I felt that Mama *had* tried out for the play, that she defied Papa just as she'd defied her parents by running away. And perhaps, if she'd still been the twelve-year-old who'd enchanted audiences in Romania—if she had retained any of the innocent hope that moved people to tears—she might have gotten a starring role and had a very different life. First the Yiddish theater, then the moving pictures that were beginning to be made in Los Angeles. But she hadn't been that hopeful girl anymore. And I understood why.

I thought I understood why Mama had changed so much . . . and why she would never whisper a word of how she had really come to America. I saw that what I had heard as an adventure tale, about her traveling with the *fusgeyers*, was in fact a love story. Mama's real theme was the great love of her life, between her and her adoring brother Meyr. How could she ever tell that story, if she had to admit that Meyr hadn't sent for her and that he'd let his wife work her like a domestic servant?

Beneath the anger that simmered perpetually in my mother, I saw the cruel disappointment. My heart broke for her. And at the same time, I wanted to repudiate her. I wanted never to be thwarted and chronically angry like she was.

I promised myself . . . it wasn't that I wanted to become exactly like Mollie. But I wanted to occupy Mollie's world, that spacious realm in which people didn't just worry about "me and mine" and who said what at the fish store today; instead, they passionately discussed ideas and fought for better lives for everyone. Decades later, I would encounter the Hebrew term *tikkun olam*, "repairing the world"—working for social justice, speaking out not only when your rights are stepped on but when anyone is denied justice. Mollie, whatever her flaws, had dedicated herself to the impossible, magnificent task of repairing the world, and she was leading the most meaningful life of anyone I had ever met. The kind of life I vowed to live.

CHAPTER 11

DANNY
THE SPY

A H, THANKSGIVING!

I wake up on Thanksgiving morning feeling . . . not terrific, that would be too much to ask for just two weeks after my car accident. But for the first time since the accident, I'd dare to call myself "energetic"—and looking forward to my favorite holiday.

I put on a sweat suit, pop *Tai Chi for Osteoporosis* into the DVD player in the den, and do my morning exercise. I'm still creaky and moving gingerly, but between my regular tai chi and water aerobics, I was in good shape for an eighty-five-year-old prior to the accident, and my doctor says I'm making "an A-plus recovery." I quoted the doctor to Ronnie and Harriet when I pushed to host Thanksgiving dinner here, as we'd planned. They didn't really try to talk me out of it. This will be our last Thanksgiving in the Santa Monica house, and they want it, too.

Thanksgiving is the one holiday that never held any traps for me. Not like Rosh HaShanah or Passover or Purim, which stirred up a maelstrom of feelings, my parents'—and later, Paul's and my—pleasure in the traditions and special foods coexisting with discomfort at old-country religiosity. And there was a sense of otherness about the Jewish holidays, of being separate from mainstream America, that brought up a complicated mix of pride and alienation. And fear: both Zayde and my mother had experienced pogroms in their shtetls, and when my kids were young in the 1950s, we were only a decade away from the Holocaust.

As for the holidays celebrated by mainstream America, Christmas especially became inescapable—and hugely tempting—when my generation settled outside Boyle Heights. Every December, most of the houses on our block in Santa Monica were festooned with twinkling lights, and the choir and orchestra at the kids' school gave a concert filled with glorious carols and Handel. One year, Paul and I gave in to the kids' pleading and got a tree—of course, emphasizing that our family didn't believe in Jesus, calling the tree a Hanukkah bush, and topping it with a silver Star of David. It was Papa, whom I'd seen as my assimilated parent, who refused to set foot in our house as long as the tree occupied the living room. (We moved it into the den.)

Thanksgiving, however, is celebrated by everyone fortunate enough to live in America. And we were happily, without a whiff of ambivalence, Americans.

Once I've done my tai chi, I prepare my contribution to our Thanksgiving feast, pumpkin pies. I'm nowhere near the cook Mama was, but pumpkin pie is easy as long as you use pre-made crust; it's hardly fair, but you get rave reviews for doing nothing but following the directions on a can of pumpkin and providing plenty of whipped cream.

The pies are baking and I'm eating cornflakes and reading the *Los Angeles Times* when Ronnie arrives. It's not even nine, but coming early to help was the condition he set, in our negotiation about having Thanksgiving here.

"Coffee!" He makes a beeline for the coffeepot, this six-footer who mysteriously emerged from Paul's and my compact family lines.

I may be the only one who calls him Ronnie, now that Paul's gone, but I still look at him—a gangly fifty-one-year-old whose fringe of hair, surrounding a bald spot, is more salt than pepper—and see the relentlessly logical boy who could outlast *me* in an argument. A born lawyer, as Cousin Mollie used to call me. Ronnie's mind works like mine, as if all the cogs and connections were built from the same materials and set of instructions. My easy child. (Carol won't be here. She's coming down from Oregon in two weeks to help me with the move.)

Over coffee, I ask him about his work. We're still talking, debating strategy for one of his cases, when Harriet comes over at ten. And then it's not too early, and there's plenty to do.

Ronnie gets the turkey, a twenty-five-pounder, into the oven, and then he, Harriet, and I figure out where to put extra tables and chairs. We're having a real gathering of the clan, twenty-two people, to bid farewell to the Santa Monica house, whose large dining room and yard made it the primary site for family events, even several weddings in the backyard. The yard is beautiful, still. I took out tension by gardening. Oh, I'm going to miss the garden, especially the fig tree, grown from a cutting I took from the tree behind our house in Boyle Heights.

By one, starting time for the touch football game at a nearby park, nearly everyone has arrived. Ronnie's wife, Melissa, insists on holding down the fort, staying in the house to baste the turkey and welcome any later arrivals, and I join the trek to the park two blocks away. Younger, fitter family members have brought lawn chairs and set them up for the spectators. I sit next to Harriet—and debate, as I have for the past two weeks, whether to tell her what I've found out about Barbara.

But what *have* I found out, really? Only that some hotel detective in Colorado Springs thought she might be a blonde named Kay Devereaux. I've done a bit of investigating since Josh dropped that bombshell, and I've discovered just one thing I'm sure of: the threatening reach of the Internet into every corner of our lives is overrated. For example, you can get online records of marriage licenses issued in Colorado Springs *if* the marriage occurred after 1981; otherwise, as I learned the old-fashioned way by making a phone call, you have to go to the county clerk's office and search microfilm—and there'd be acres of it, since I have no date for her marriage. Not to mention that I have no idea if she even stayed in Colorado Springs or got married there.

I've considered taking Josh up on his offer to help me search. Or hiring a detective, someone based in Colorado. But how far do I want to pursue this? Say I did find her, might I regret it? And the greater likelihood is that I'd invest time, money, and emotional energy, yet come up empty-handed. All over again. There's so little to go on—only her name and the fact that she worked at the Broadmoor Hotel in . . . I don't even know that, because Carl Logan didn't date his letter. But it must have been in the early 1940s, during the time—or not long afterward—that Philip was looking for her. And then . . . did Mama and Papa write her a letter? But why didn't Papa jump on the first train to Colorado Springs? And why didn't they tell me? Did they imagine they were protecting me? I had a right to know!

"Earth to Lainie," Harriet says.

"Yeah." I turn to my sister, who's wearing a Day-Glo lime green jacket and a Dodgers baseball cap.

"Are you doing okay with all of this? The move?"

"Yeah, I'm fine. I'm thankful. For all of this. For them." I nod my head toward our progeny scrapping and yelling over the football. "And for you. What about you, what are you thankful for?"

"The same. And I'm grateful that you only drove into a cactus when you . . . um, got it into your head to drive to Barstow." The look in Harriet's eye reminds me of Mama in those moments when I suspected she could see through me.

"Know what else I'm thankful for?" I say. "That we don't have to play football anymore."

"Nobody forced you to play."

"Ha! First I had to because all the Kennedy women played." Our Thanksgiving touch football tradition began in 1960, a few weeks after JFK was elected. Not that Paul and I were naive enough to mistake Kennedy for a real progressive, but who could resist the sense of hope, the youthful energy of those rollicking, tousle-haired Boston Irish Democrats? "Then it was because of the women's movement, having to set an example for our kids."

"You're feeling better, aren't you?"

"Much."

"Good. Look, there's something I've been thinking about since the day we went through those papers and books. But I didn't want to bring it up right after your accident . . ."

"What is it?"

"About Barbara."

"Barbara?" Did I say something out loud a moment ago? Or can my Wise Woman sister simply read my mind?

"You were asking, what if we could find her now. And I wondered, did you ever mourn for her?"

"Of course I did! The day she left, I cried my eyes out. At Pearl's." Even as I say it, though, I realize my mistake. It's true, I sobbed at Pearl's—the memory of my tears drenching the love seat is so strong, I can almost feel damp brocade under my cheek. But that happened the day before Barbara left. And my tears weren't for her.

"I mean grieving," Harriet says. "Acknowledging the loss. Saying goodbye."

"Like sitting shiva? I couldn't do that unless I knew she was dead." And I happen to know, because I've checked the Social Security Death Index, that there's no death record for a Kay Devereaux who'd be anywhere near the right age.

I have to tell Harriet! She has a right to know, too.

"Not sitting shiva," she says. "But what about creating some kind of ritual? We could do it together. Maybe on a trip to Rancho La Puerta this spring?"

"Definitely yes on the trip to Rancho La Puerta." We used to do an annual sister trip to the spa just south of the border, she, Audrey, and I, but we've gone less often since Audrey died (like Zayde and Papa, she had a stroke) six years ago.

"And think about doing a ritual?"

"Sure, I'll think about it."

I won't bring up what I've found now, during a holiday celebration. But sometime this weekend . . .

Still, it's one thing to have been told at the time, when there were decisions to make and things to do. All these years later, what do I achieve by sharing this news with Harriet except to torment her, too, with the suspicion that Mama and Papa lied about something that caused us such anguish? Our family tragedy, the loss that, she's right, we never mourned. Did we ever even call it a "loss," did we use that word? At first, when we found Barbara's note and couldn't locate her, she had simply "left." Over the following weeks and months, she'd "run away."

Her leaving wasn't like a death, unconditional. Clean. Marked by ceremonies brilliant in their power to tighten the screws on your anguish and push you into the physical release of weeping. *Now* you walk to the edge of the grave, jab a shovel into the damp, freshly dug earth, and drop the earth on the casket. *Now* you retreat from ordinary life for seven days, not going out and covering the mirrors. *Now*, when the seven days are over, the rabbi takes you on a walk around the block to symbolize your return to life.

Shiva or not, I've long been reconciled to Barbara being gone; I accepted it years ago. And yet, on this sunny Thanksgiving afternoon, as I wonder if I might have known where she was, might at least have known *that* she was, if it hadn't been kept from me . . . I feel the hole her disappearance left in my life as if the ground has ruptured and swallowed my children.

"Elaine?" Harriet says with alarm.

"What?" I say as my eyes race over the football players, atavistically seeking my own first: Ronnie, his daughter Zoe, Carol's son Dylan. Carol? In Oregon. And Brian in Argentina. They're all accounted for. Safe.

"Are you okay? You just moaned."

"That was a yawn."

Why put her through what I'm feeling now? As if I'd opened our family albums and every picture of Mama and Papa were corroded by acid?

FORTUNATELY, THE BLEAKNESS DOESN'T stay with me. At dinner, I revel in my raucous family, seated at three tables that spill from the dining room into the den. There's such a sad but sweet nostalgia when I catch, in the living, glimpses of the dead: Ronnie plunges a carving knife into the turkey with the same gleeful expression that used to come over Paul's face when he carved. I'm reminded of Papa's gravity in the serious eyes of

Harriet's youngest granddaughter. And all the tastes—Mama's sweet potatoes, now made by Harriet; Audrey's cranberry compote, the recipe
passed to one of her sons. It's as if I can look around the room, enjoy the
feast, and relive every Thanksgiving dinner that's taken place in this
house . . . and before that, our Thanksgivings in Boyle Heights. Harriet
and I are the only ones left from those days, the sole carriers of that
history.

But that's not entirely true, I realize. Danny was there, too; Mama always invited him and his father. It's the second time today I've thought
of Danny, and he stays in my mind as everyone pushes back from the
table with happy groans of satiation. I keep thinking about him during
a game of charades, and when we decide we finally have enough room
for dessert. My pies are a big hit, with reason; they're scrumptious. As I
said, you use pre-made crust and pile on the whipped cream, you can't go
wrong.

Then, three and four and five at a time, they say goodbye, and they're
gone, leaving my house cleaner than when they arrived. Danny, however,
lingers; multiple versions of Danny—the waif he was as a child, the muscular young man who built himself up lifting weights at Venice Beach, the
soft-eyed Danny I saw in private moments.

I check the international time zones. It's already eleven here, so it
shouldn't be too early to call him.

But I must have miscalculated. My call wakes him.

"Ken," he mumbles.

"Danny, oh, I'm sorry, I thought it was nine in the morning there." In
Israel, where he went to live after World War II—though it was Palestine
then. He put down his gun from fighting the Nazis and immediately picked
up another to fight for a Jewish state.

"I just sleep in some days. An old man's prerogative." His voice crisp,
he's gone from groggy to fully alert within seconds. The discipline of work
that he still, even in retirement, refers to vaguely as "imports and exports,"
I'm certain he was high up in the Israeli intelligence agency, the Mossad.

"Aviva lets you sleep in?" I say.

Danny's wife chose her name, which is Hebrew for "spring," when she
immigrated to Palestine after surviving a concentration camp. Danny

changed his name, too, from Berlov to Bar-Lev—"son of the heart." He and Aviva met when they were doing a sabotage mission against the British for the Haganah, the underground. Aviva is a formidable woman, a life force, whom I profoundly admire. She is also, not to mince words, intrusive, a person who, when you're enjoying your rye toast in the morning, will insist on slicing a cucumber and tomato for you, "an Israeli breakfast." And then stand over you until you eat it all. Aviva is one of the reasons that although Paul and I took half a dozen trips to Israel, we stayed with Danny and Aviva only once.

"Aviva . . ." He lets out a heavy sigh. "Is it that long since the last time we talked? Aviva has Alzheimer's."

"Oh, Danny, I'm sorry."

"Americans, always with the 'I'm sorry.' " Whatever hint of vulnerability crept in at the mention of Aviva's illness, it's gone now, replaced with combativeness—just like Danny as a kid, chin up against his father's poverty. Do we ever really change? "Could be worse. She's still at home. There's a nurse who comes, and our daughter, you remember, Shuli? She's just a few minutes away. Lainie, it's great to hear from you. How are you? Staying healthy, I hope?"

"I'm fine. I just had the whole family over for Thanksgiving."

"Thanksgiving, right. So what's new with you?"

"I'm moving. In two weeks."

"Mazel tov. You finally see there's no place but Israel for a Jew to live? There's an apartment by Shuli coming on the market. Owners are in a hurry to sell, they might offer some great incentives."

"Like armor plating for my car?"

"Like a sense of pride in being a Jew and realpolitik about the fact that the Arabs *do* want to push us into the sea, no matter what their prettied-up representatives say to get foolish American liberals to sympathize with them."

This is why Danny and I don't call each other often. He lives in a settlement on the West Bank, and you'd think, at our age, we'd be able to live with our political differences. For God's sake, I can do that with my grand-niece who became a Mormon and a Republican! With Danny, though, too many conversations over the years have deteriorated into my shouting about the destruction of Palestinian olive groves and his shouting about getting pushed into the sea; now it's as if just hearing each other's voices brings up all the old fights.

But that's not the discussion I want to have tonight.

"Danny," I say.

"What is it?" He's known me since we were five, and he picks up something in my voice. "Are you really all right?"

"Did you . . . Getting ready to move, I'm going through old papers. Old memories. Did you ever hear from Barbara?"

"Oy, that's ancient history. Why not let the past stay the past?"

"*Did* you?"

"Not a word."

"Did you try to find her?"

"I was already gone when she left." He joined the Canadian army in September 1939; he couldn't wait to get into the war.

"I meant later. You knew how to find people."

He chuckles but doesn't bother to deny that he was a spy.

"Not to get in touch with her," I say. "Just to know what happened, if she was all right."

"First of all, you're overestimating my capabilities. And I never had any doubt she was all right. All the stories I've heard from people who were forced to leave their homes and go to concentration camps, I wasn't going to waste my time worrying about . . . to be blunt, a vain, selfish girl who left of her own free will."

He's protesting a bit too much, but I have no idea if that means he actually did look for Barbara and won't admit it, or if it's because of what happened between him and me, wounds that penetrated deeply because we were so unguarded then, so young.

If we had slept together, just once, would it have eased the prickliness between us, the edgy subtext that turns stray remarks into jabs? (Is that the real reason for our intense political battles?) One time we came close. What a disaster. It happened on the first trip Paul and I took to Israel. We were staying with Danny and Aviva, who at that time lived in a spacious if decrepit old house in Jerusalem. One afternoon I stayed behind with a headache while Paul and Aviva went on an outing with the kids, theirs and ours. I was lying on the sofa in the living room, the coolest place in the house, when Danny came home from work. He massaged the base of my skull, a surefire headache cure, he said. Then . . . I mean no disrespect to Paul when I say that purely in terms of technique, no one could kiss like Danny. Kissing, shedding clothes, hungrily touching places our hands remembered, we made our way to the screened back porch (rejecting by tacit agreement the beds we shared with our spouses). It wasn't until we were lying together completely naked that I knew I couldn't go through with it. It wasn't that I was being noble or even that I feared getting caught. I saw it as a failure of imagination. Sleeping with Danny when I was married to Paul simply wasn't in me.

"I don't mean to sound harsh," he says. "But Barbara always had one foot out the door. Like your mother, I guess. Didn't she run away, too? With the, what were they called? The immigrants from Romania?"

"What do you mean, she ran away?" It must be just a figure of speech. There's no way Danny could actually know.

"What does anyone mean by 'ran away'? She snuck off in the middle of the night. Isn't that right?"

"Yes. But how did you find out?"

"I must have heard it from either you or Barbara."

But I didn't tell a soul, not until after Mama died. I'm certain of that, because sharing the story for the first time—with Audrey and Harriet— was a big deal. I saved it for one of our trips to the spa in Mexico and waited until we were on our second bottle of Cabernet to bring it up. And it stunned both of my younger sisters, albeit in idiosyncratic ways: Audrey got upset at having been excluded from yet another family secret, while Harriet expressed delight at having a new image of Mama as a sort of fugitive.

Barbara was the one person I was tempted to tell at the time. For the first few days after Mollie confided in me, I could barely keep from blurting out the story to her. But then time passed, and if I happened to think of the story, one of us was always on the way in or out, and it just didn't seem to be the right time. And why feel any urgency, when I saw Barbara every day?

Later I wondered whether it would have changed anything if I'd told

Barbara about Mama. Barbara must have thought she was making such a bold move, doing something that forever set her apart from our humdrum lives. Yet all the time, she was unwittingly (or so I thought) playing out our mother's drama of escape—unwittingly and far less spectacularly, compared to Mama setting out at twelve, on foot and penniless, for a country where she didn't speak a word of the language. Had Barbara only known, I wondered, would she have found some other way to distinguish herself?

But she did know.

"Is something wrong?" Danny says.

"No, not a thing . . . You remember Ronnie's daughter, Zoe? She just started graduate school in oceanography at UC San Diego."

As Danny and I brag about our grandkids, I chew on the new mystery he's given me. *How did Barbara find out about Mama running away? Who told her?* I suppose she might have heard the story from Mollie, as I did. Except Barbara wasn't at all close to Mollie. What about Papa or Pearl? I could see Pearl confiding in Barbara. On the other hand, Pearl tended to reveal truths to both of us; hard to imagine her telling Barbara and not saying a word to me. There's one more possibility—that Barbara's source was Mama herself. And as I absorb what Danny said, it's not a huge stretch to imagine Mama telling her favorite daughter that she'd run away, an act that had taken such courage. Surely, that was all she had confessed; Mama wouldn't have abandoned the face-saving fiction she'd created and revealed the heartbreaking truth—that the brother she worshipped hadn't sent for her. So why can't I shake the feeling that she was willing to be that transparent . . . to Barbara?

And now I'm no longer on the fence about looking for Barbara. I'm determined to find her, and not just to find out what happened to her. I want to know who she *was*, to understand the complicity between her and Mama, a complicity I always recognized but which went deeper than I had ever imagined.

It's midnight when I say goodbye to Danny, so rather than phoning Josh, I send him an email asking if he can do a data search for Kay Devereaux.

His reply arrives moments later. *Piece of cake.*

CHAPTER 12

LOVE AND DEATH

ONE OF DANNY'S JOBS AT CHAFKIN'S GROCERY WAS TO TAKE care of the signs around the entrance to the store and on the walls inside. He would tack up the latest advertising posters for Campbell's soup or Maxwell House coffee or Palmolive soap, and he kept an eye on the corkboard just inside the door, where people were allowed to post notices; the board in the 1930s was covered with offers of rooms to let and men willing to take any kind of work and "Rosenthal china, perfect condition: must sell." To keep the board tidy, Eddie Chafkin had a policy that no notice could stay up longer than two weeks, and Danny weeded out any whose time had expired.

There were also two prominent places, right next to the message board and directly behind the counter where people would look when the bill was being totaled, that Eddie dedicated to a rotating collection of posters. These advertisements (really, they were works of art) featured such images as smiling, sunburned youths carrying hoes, or luscious, crimson-fleshed watermelons—the handsome young pioneers and bounteous harvests of a life spent farming in the promised land of Palestine.

Eddie Chafkin was a Zionist, as everyone in Boyle Heights knew. And what a crackpot idea, most people agreed. *You want palm trees and nice watermelons, open your eyes—you're in Los Angeles.*

I doubt that it's even possible to look back at that time and *not* see it through the lens of the Holocaust. And in 1947, I wept when the United Nations voted to establish the State of Israel; everyone I knew was in tears. But in Boyle Heights in 1935, Zionists were seen as a fringe, even an anti-American organization.

As Aunt Sonya said, "Hershel Chafkin gets himself from Kiev to Los Angeles, breaks his back pushing a cart and selling vegetables door-to-door, and finally the man saves enough to start his own store so that when he drops dead of angina at forty-eight he can leave his beloved son a good business . . . and Eddie wants to go be a farmer in Palestine?"

I usually tuned out Sonya, who dripped scorn on virtually anyone of her acquaintance who wasn't within hearing. But Papa, who prided himself on his objectivity, also got heated on the subject of Eddie's Zionism. "The 'Promised Land,' that's the gift Eddie's father gave him by letting him be born in America," Papa said. "He should be grateful to be an American citizen. What if Franklin D. Roosevelt came to Boyle Heights and saw those posters? What would he think, that Jews aren't loyal Americans?" At least, Papa said, it was a relief that few people felt the way Eddie did; he'd heard that the Zionist Organization of America, to which Eddie belonged, had no more than fifty members in all of Los Angeles.

All of the adults had an opinion, and all of them were negative. Mollie—who wrote to me from the various cities where the union sent her—considered Zionism a reactionary movement because it made Jewish workers identify as Jews rather than uniting with workers of all faiths.

Zayde, too, despite occasional sentimental references to Eretz Yisrael, had no desire to actually go there.

So I was stunned, one day in April of 1935, when Danny was complaining as usual about working for Eddie, and I mentioned the ridiculous Zionist posters—and Danny jumped down my throat.

"What's so ridiculous about a Jewish homeland?" he shot at me.

"We have it a lot better here. In Palestine, it's all swamps with malaria," I said, parroting comments I'd heard for years.

"What if you were in Germany?"

"You think Eddie Chafkin's a fool. How come you sound just like him?" I said, automatically bristling against Danny's fourteen-year-old arrogance—and because I, at fourteen, bristled at everything. Either that, or I fought humiliating tears.

And I didn't know what to think about Germany. Adolf Hitler had become chancellor two years earlier, and he'd done crazy things, like firing Jewish government officials, boycotting Jewish businesses, even staging public burnings of books by Jewish authors. But that was just it: Hitler was crazy, and when the adults talked about him, the prevailing opinion was that the craziness would soon, like the bonfires of books, burn itself out.

"Shouldn't the German Jews be allowed to go to Palestine?" Danny said.

"If they want to, sure. But I bet they'd rather come to America."

"Wake up, Elaine! Haven't you seen For Rent signs in Los Angeles that say 'No Jews or Dogs Allowed'? You know how many hospitals here don't allow Jewish doctors to practice?"

"Do *you* want to go to Palestine?"

"I . . . yes."

I seized on his flicker of hesitation. "You want to be a farmer?"

"I want to live someplace where I don't have to apologize for being a Jew. Where a Jew can be free and safe and proud of who he is."

"That's America!"

America, not Palestine, was where our relatives from Romania wanted to come—and they wanted it desperately. The world might be keeping nervous eyes fixed on Germany, but things had gotten every bit as bad for Jews in Mama's native country, where two of her brothers and two sisters still lived, as did most of their children and a growing number of grandchildren. In letters that made Mama weep, they wrote about the harsh restrictions on Jewish employment and mentioned a popular political party that actually stated in its platform, "The sole possible solution to the kike problem is the elimination of the kikes." One of my uncles was kicked and punched in the street by uniformed thugs called the Iron Guards. A girl cousin escaped the Iron Guards by diving into a pile of trash, and she had to stay there for three hours until she felt it was finally safe to emerge from her hiding place. Mama and the Chicago relatives had agreed that each of them would file papers with the Hebrew Immigration Aid Society to sponsor one Romanian family member to come live with them—a young person, unmarried and healthy enough to take any kind of job. Mama and Papa had applied to sponsor the son of one of Mama's brothers, a boy named Ivan who was two years older than me.

"The point is," I told Danny, "they don't want to go to Palestine, they want to come to America!"

I made this point often, since Danny and I had the same argument again and again. And he always replied, "Jews from Romania, you think America's going to let them in? Jews need a place where, if they say they want to come, they're in."

Danny, I suppose, wouldn't let the subject drop because Zionism became a mission for him. He got involved in the Boyle Heights chapter of Habonim, a Zionist youth group, and he was constantly after me to join. And I railed against Danny's Zionism because I experienced it as a betrayal. I was the all-American girl that Papa had raised me to be, and I felt free and safe and proud living in the United States. How could Danny reject that? How could he feel more loyal to some abstract "Jewish people" than to America? I battled Danny over Zionism as if I were defending the law of gravity and the world would fly apart if I lost. And I battled well. Mollie had been the first to see the fighter in me, and she'd been right. I was actually developing a taste for combat, and Danny, persuasive and impassioned, made an ideal adversary.

There was another reason I persisted in these debates: to hang on to my friendship with Danny now that we'd entered the confusing terrain of adolescence. Instead of playing together in the park the way we'd done as kids, now he invited me to Habonim programs; I grumbled but went anyway, and we argued afterward. Just the two of us, since Barbara refused to have anything to do with Zionism. Which didn't seem to diminish her attractiveness to Danny. My sister and Danny found another way to preserve their childhood connection: they became sweethearts.

At first, when we got into our teens and there started to be dances and boy-girl parties, Danny asked both Barbara and me to dance, to the extent that he or any of the boys got on the dance floor at all. Then one night, the summer after we'd turned fourteen, everything changed. At a dance at one of the community centers, I was chatting with friends, and I saw Barbara come in from outside. Danny was right behind her. Both of them looked flushed, and they were holding hands. He put his arm around her, and they wove through the crowd to the refreshment table, never losing contact. As he filled two glasses of punch, she kept her hand on his arm.

I didn't know for sure what I'd observed, or maybe I just refused to accept it. But over the next few weeks, whenever a group of us went to the movies, Barbara and Danny sat next to each other; I'd glance from the screen and see that his arm had slipped around her shoulders. Then they had their first real "date," with Danny picking her up at the house. When she returned that night and came into the bedroom we shared (she'd joined me in the room off the kitchen after Mollie left), I feigned sleep.

Just as I'd loved Danny Berlov from the first time I met him, I had always noticed a special energy between him and my sister, a charge I would recognize when I saw the first Tracy-Hepburn movies in the 1940s. As a child, I had moments of hurt when I sensed that intimate friction between them. Those childhood pricks of distress were nothing, though, to the hideous toad that now squatted inside me, spewing out misery and envy, along with hatred toward myself, for not being the one Danny had chosen.

Barbara had movie dates with Danny, evening walks, times when they disappeared from a party for half an hour and came back smiling mysteriously. I maintained my closeness to him by having fights over Zionism.

It was after a Habonim lecture, one muggy night the following August, that Danny and I took our argument to the dark playground of our old elementary school. He had snuck a Schlitz beer and a handful of Chesterfields from Chafkin's. Sitting on the ground, my back against the school building, I smoked—which I enjoyed despite the harshness in my throat— and forced myself to sip the warm, nasty-tasting beer from the bottle that we passed back and forth.

"You don't like it, do you?" he said after he'd taken a swig and was about to hand the bottle to me.

"Yes, I do."

"Think I'll finish it myself." He raised the beer to his lips.

"No fair!"

I reached for the bottle. He grabbed my wrist, then pulled me closer and kissed me. It was a rough kiss—and awkward, my glasses jamming into his forehead, and beer splashing onto my hand.

I jerked back. "What was that for?"

"Guess I figured you should have your first kiss."

"That's generous of you. But I've been kissed, thank you."

"By Fred the dwarf?" he cracked. So he'd noticed one of the two times I'd gone off at a party with Fred Nieman, a brainy and witty boy who was cursed with being short and baby-faced. Not like Danny, who followed a regimen of push-ups and calisthenics he'd learned from the bodybuilders at the beach. Danny was no more than medium height, but he was muscular and tough, a boy the school bullies avoided.

"Fred's not a dwarf," I said. "And he kisses better than you do."

"Oh, yeah?"

"Yeah." I tossed my head.

Danny's kisses began softly, like Fred's. But they were also teasing, and he didn't just kiss my mouth; his lips touched my cheeks and eyelids and—who knew it could be such a thrilling place?—the hollow of my throat. With Fred, I had watched myself being kissed. Danny, I kissed back. He eased me from sitting against the building to half-lying on the ground, and something inside me melted. . . .

"No!" I tried to twist away, but he had me pinned. All that bodybuilding he'd done, he was strong. "Danny, no!"

He moved then, enough that I could turn to the side, but kept his arms around me. "Just a little more?"

"We can't do this." I pulled away. He didn't stop me.

"Right. Sorry, I shouldn't have. . . . You won't tell, will you?" he added as we stood and smoothed our clothes.

I knew whom he didn't want me to tell, and I briefly, intensely, hated him. "What kind of person do you think I am?"

"Smoke?" He held out a cigarette.

"No . . . Okay." Smoking offered a lull in which my hectic cheeks could stop burning, so I could face Barbara when I walked in the door.

As we smoked in silence, it occurred to me that I might be able to avoid seeing Barbara tonight. If I got home ahead of her I could use my standard ploy, pretending to be asleep, when she came in from spending the evening with the Diamonds, her club of eight girls who gathered at one another's homes, played big-band music on the radio, and danced. I joined them sometimes when they came to our house—Barbara had to include me— but I didn't fit in with the Diamonds, pretty, socially adept girls who acted in school plays, took "modern dance" classes, and were popular with boys.

I had my own club with Lucy Meringoff, Jane Klass, and Ann Charney. All four of us were great readers—hence our official name, the Brontë Sisters—and had been told ever since grade school that if we fulfilled our early academic promise, we might get college scholarships. Though we privately made fun of our reputations by calling ourselves the Plain Brains, our get-togethers were often study sessions—we thirsted for those scholarships—and we cultivated a smart, ironic detachment from the melodrama of high school romance.

Irony was an attitude I did my best to summon as I smoked after necking with Danny. It had a lot of competition. My body thrummed with sheer physical excitement, and my emotions ricocheted from guilt at betraying Barbara to rage and shame at the suspicion that Danny was using me. Maybe I was the one using him, my ironic self suggested, but without much success. (Irony would prove to be an ally throughout my life, but in those days I was an amateur at irony.) And on top of all that, I couldn't help it—I felt hope. Even the Plain Brains sometimes turned on the radio and swayed together with our eyes closed, imagining we were being whirled across a ballroom by Fred Astaire or Clark Gable. Or Danny Berlov.

"Walk you home?" Danny tossed the butt of his cigarette onto the playground, and the last shreds of tobacco glowed, then went dark.

"No, that's okay."

What if, I had dreamed, I were the sister Danny really loved? Barbara was lively and fun, and she was somehow born knowing how to flirt— a skill that, when I attempted it, made me feel like a giggling half-wit—and what boy wouldn't want to date a girl like that? But I had heard the Yiddish term *bashert*, the idea of two people destined for each other; when Danny was ready to get serious, I'd thought, would he choose Barbara, or would he pick his *bashert*, me? *Could he have kissed me like he just did if he didn't love me?* Coming home, I nearly danced down the street.

Audrey must have been watching for me, because when I was two houses away, she burst through the door and flung herself at me, sobbing. "Where were you? Where were you?"

"Habonim. What's wrong?"

"Zayde. They said you'd be home right away, and—"

I grabbed her shoulders. "What happened to Zayde?"

"He's in the hospital."

All I could get out of Audrey was that Uncle Leo had called and said Zayde was sick, and Mama and Papa had rushed to the hospital. They'd told Audrey to call Barbara at her friend's house and said I'd be home any minute—

"But you weren't!" Audrey cried. "And I tried and tried to call Barbara, but the line's busy."

Giving up on learning anything more from Audrey, I phoned Leo and Sonya's. My cousin Stan, now twelve and as sober as his father, reported that Zayde had been sitting listening to the radio, and suddenly he cried out and lost consciousness. Sonya and Leo couldn't revive him, and they'd called an ambulance. "The ambulance men think it's a stroke," Stan said.

I didn't need to ask which hospital Zayde had been taken to. *The* Boyle Heights hospital was the Seventh-day Adventist White Memorial, where my sisters and I had been born. It was close enough that I could walk there, but Audrey would have a fit if I left. Oh, no, poor Audrey! Having satisfied my urgent need to find out what had happened, I realized Audrey was ashen and trembling.

"I'm sorry, honey, it must have been scary for you." I opened my arms to her. As cross as I'd been, she still nestled into my embrace. I wasn't a *completely* terrible sister.

"Will Zayde be okay?" Audrey snuffled.

"He'll be fine." I rubbed Audrey's back and gave in to my own tears. When I was little, Zayde used to cuddle me in his lap and tickle me. He blew wet raspberries on my belly, and I shrieked in delight. Once I got too old to sit in his lap, we challenged each other to games of gin rummy and traded jokes we'd heard on the radio. Most of the adults in my life—Mama, Papa, my teachers, Uncle Leo at the bookstore—expected me to act responsible. But Zayde *played* with me.

Audrey and I were both crying when Barbara got home. What with having to deliver the upsetting news about Zayde, there was absolutely no danger that Barbara would take one look at me and *know* what I'd been up to with her boyfriend.

I never again felt so worried that my guilt would be written all over my face.

·Not that I intended to repeat my act of treachery! Especially not after Zayde died the next morning. It wasn't that I felt I'd *caused* Zayde's death by kissing my sister's boyfriend at the very time he fell ill; whenever that idea crept into my mind, I chided myself for being as superstitious as Mama. But I was no longer the kid who'd necked with Danny. Though only a few days had passed, I was no longer a child. In fact, Barbara and I were considered old enough to attend Zayde's funeral, which took place, following Jewish custom, the day after he died.

At the service, held in the Home of Peace cemetery just east of Boyle Heights, I held myself straight even though I felt dizzy from sadness and from having to wear my navy wool, my best dark skirt, under the August sun. Looking at Zayde's coffin (a fancy, expensive one; it was Pearl who insisted) and at the grave with freshly dug soil mounded beside it, I was grateful for Barbara, standing so close that we leaned together, gripping each other's hands. Because I'd studied Yiddish, which uses the Hebrew alphabet, I could sound out the words on a card given me by the rabbi, and for the first time I said kaddish, the mourner's prayer.

I balked, though, after the coffin was lowered and I saw what was happening. There'd been a shovel stuck in the damp earth, and people were walking up and placing a shovelful of earth right in the grave—Papa first, then Sonya, then Pearl, and everyone else was lining up to take a turn. I glanced at Barbara; she looked as stunned as I felt. "I'm not doing that," she whispered.

"Me neither," I said, and we hung back.

"Girls." I turned toward the gentle, Yiddish-thick voice—Mr. Berlov. "This is to help your *zayde*'s soul know it's time to return to God."

He soothed us forward. Through a blur of tears, I took the shovel, scooped up a clod of soil, and dropped it on the coffin. I handed the shovel to Barbara. She did the same and then ran crying—into Danny's embrace.

OVER THE NEXT SEVERAL months, Danny, as always, urged me to attend Habonim meetings, but he gave no sign that our kisses lingered in his imaginative life, the way they stubbornly did in mine. I said I was too busy to go to the meetings. It wasn't a lie. That fall we had entered Theodore Roosevelt High School, and I had a new set of teachers to impress, the crucial ones who would have the most say about whether I grasped the brass ring of a college scholarship.

Then in November, Habonim, along with several other youth groups, presented a talk I didn't want to miss, by a professor who had fled Nazi Germany and now taught at UCLA. Many people, not just members of the youth groups but adults, were going to the program being held in the meeting hall at the Yiddische Folkschule. Papa planned to go, and I thought Barbara might be interested, too.

I mentioned it while she and I were doing the dinner dishes that evening.

"Go sit in a boring lecture after I had to sit in school all day?" She plunged the soup kettle into the sink, splashing greasy dishwater. I jumped back—I'd already changed into a clean blouse for the talk.

"It's really important to Danny," I ventured.

I couldn't help being curious about whether Barbara and Danny fought over his love for Zionism and her disdain for it. Did she encourage his involvement in Habonim even though she had no interest, like asking a boy about his favorite sports team? Was the subject off-limits between them? Though I couldn't imagine Danny saying nothing about his passion in life. Ah, but maybe he and Barbara didn't waste time on conversation when they were together. Certainly that was Mama's fear; she hovered like a hawk whenever Danny came in with Barbara after a date, and she often issued the warning that pubescent girls seem to provoke in adults the world over: "Boys only want one thing." She also muttered darkly that women in our family were so fertile, barely a touch of a finger could cause a pregnancy. She had sat down with Barbara and me and, with unusually explicit language, made sure we understood exactly where babies came from and what we should never let any boy do to us.

As much as Danny might enjoy necking, however (and as skilled as he was at doing it, I thought with a shiver), he also loved to talk and argue, and he had always sparred with Barbara. When I was older, I would have said Danny used argument as a form of foreplay. So, did they argue about Zionism? I was hardly going to ask. I rarely talked about Danny with Barbara, or Barbara with him. Dangerous territory. As it proved this time.

"Is that why *you're* going? Because it's important to Danny?" She gave me a mocking smile, and I felt ripped open, my impossible love for Danny Berlov naked and pathetic like a newborn bird fallen from its nest. *Did she know?* Danny would never have told her; some other boy, a boy who was compulsively honest, might have felt a need to confess, but not Danny. Barbara must have just been referring to the torch I'd always carried for him; that was bad enough, a humiliation that made me squirm.

"Don't you care what's happening in Germany?" I lashed back. A crude defense, and she laughed.

"Oh, Elaine. You're going to spend two hours listening to a lecture, and you think you deserve a medal?"

"It's better than spending two hours giggling with your friends and trying out new hairstyles."

"What does it matter if I care? You're the serious one, the smart one." Her voice went raw, but for just an instant; then the mocking tone returned. "Say hi to Danny for me."

YOU'RE THE SERIOUS ONE, *the smart one.* Maybe it was just a dig, a reminder that *she* was the pretty, popular sister, the one Danny loved. Yet there'd been a crack in her voice, I was sure of it. As I sat in the packed hall, waiting for the talk to begin, I wondered if I'd received a glimpse of what Barbara suffered by being constantly compared to me. Though how

smart could I be, if in my resentment at being not-Barbara, I'd never imagined it might be hard for her to be not-Elaine?

It hit me that, of my two most important childhood companions, I had
made an effort not to drift apart from Danny. And I *knew* Danny: I understood what he cared about and could easily fall into a conversation with
him. When it came to Barbara, on the other hand, I guess I'd figured it was
enough to live under the same roof and share a room. But it was my sister
who'd become a mystery to me. We rarely talked about anything bigger
than "Did you see my hairbrush?" And the occasional times when our
conversation went beyond the mundane, how often did I belittle her—as,
I realized with dismay, I had done just an hour earlier? Barbara didn't get
the grades I did, but that hardly meant she was stupid. As the speaker
walked to the podium, I promised myself I was going to get closer to Barbara; I would make a real effort to find out what she thought about life and
the world, and I'd take her ideas seriously.

Then the talk began, and I was riveted. The professor, Dr. Blum, wasn't
the gaunt, hollow-eyed refugee I'd expected but a portly man with a rather
pedantic speaking style. His ordinariness made what he said more awful.
He spoke about losing his university post with no protest from Christian
colleagues he'd known for years, having his children barred from sports
facilities, and being stripped of citizenship and even forbidden to fly the
German flag by the Nuremburg Laws. And there was the constant fear of
physical violence, but how could you complain when the attackers wore
government uniforms?

The story had a familiar ugliness. Many people in Boyle Heights were
immigrants who had experienced similar injustices. But those things had
happened in eastern Europe and Russia, not in "civilized" Germany! And
there was a relentless pettiness to the Nazis' anti-Semitism. A relatively
minor law that chilled me was a ban on the use of Jewish names to spell
something to a telephone operator—you couldn't, for instance, say "*A* as
in Abraham"—a rule that burrowed so deeply into the minutiae of daily
life, it was as if the Nazis wanted the Jews, and I suppose all Germans, to be
aware of them from the moment they woke in the morning to when they
lost themselves in sleep at night.

Soon I was dabbing at tears; so were many people around me.

Following the speech, the first people who asked questions were leaders of the youth groups that had sponsored the talk; they were in seats of honor onstage. Mike Palikow, a senior who was the president of Habonim, asked Dr. Blum about pressuring the British to allow more Jews to enter Palestine.

"Is this a Zionist organization?" The professor looked startled.

"My group is," Mike said.

"Well," Dr. Blum said, "I hope all of you here will pressure *your* government to allow more people to enter America. I'm sure you're aware that the United States has a strict quota for immigrants from Germany, but did you know it is not even accepting half that number?"

Danny leaped to his feet in the front row and shouted, "How can you say that and then not support a Jewish state in Palestine?"

People shushed him, and Mike Palikow said, "Danny! We're not taking questions from the audience yet."

Dr. Blum smiled. "I'm sorry to disappoint you, young man. I don't happen to be a Zionist. Next question, please?"

Danny persisted, his voice hoarse with emotion, "You got into America because you had friends who guaranteed you a job. What about all the people who don't have important friends?"

Several people called out, "Show some respect!" and a burly boy—Dave Medved, a star of the high school football team—ran over and locked an arm around Danny's shoulders.

As he was muscled out of the hall, Danny kept yelling, "There's only one place where Jews can be safe—Palestine!"

On the stage, Mike Palikow began to apologize, but the professor said, "It's good to see a young man who stands up for what he believes. And good to be in a country where such a thing is permitted."

After a dozen more questions, posed with extreme politeness, the formal presentation ended, and there were refreshments. Dr. Blum particularly asked to talk to the ardent young Zionist, but apparently Danny hadn't lingered outside the hall. Someone even ran over to the Berlovs' rooming house but couldn't find him there, either.

I had a hunch where he might have gone. I went upstairs to his father's classroom in the Yiddische Folkschule. Gershon Berlov had set up a corner for Danny when he was little, with a few toys and a blanket where he could nap; he used to play there quietly while his father taught.

The room was dark except in *his* corner, where a cigarette glowed.

"Danny." I inched toward him, feeling my way past desks as my eyes adjusted to the darkness.

"Elaine?"

"Yeah. He wants to talk to you."

"That pompous *yekke*?"

"That's not fair." In our neighborhood of mainly eastern European immigrants, *yekke* was a slur, a term for German-born Jews who looked down their noses at us in both the Old World and the New. In Europe, the *yekkes* prided themselves on their urban, cultured ways, compared to Russian or Polish Jews who lived like peasants in *shtetls*. People who came to America from those *shtetls* at the turn of century discovered that *yekkes* had arrived decades earlier. They had established fine banks and department stores and carved out a place in America's gentile society—and they offered charity but cringed at being associated with their crude eastern "cousins."

"Cigarette?" he said.

"Thanks." I sat on the floor next to him and took the cigarette he offered. "Aren't you going to talk to him?"

"What, and apologize?"

"I don't think that's what he wants. He said he liked seeing a young person stand up for something."

"Did he? Well, I'm not going to go back there." Danny lit a fresh cigarette from the butt of his first. "What about everyone else? Are they all saying I'm a *putz*?"

"No one's even talking about you."

"Elaine Greenstein, if *you* lie to me, I won't believe anyone for the rest of my life."

"Some people thought you were rude."

"Dave Medved told me I was a *putz*."

"He did?"

"A little *putz*." He started laughing, a kid's release-of-tension giggle.

I laughed, too. And then I was crying, I didn't know why—the distressing things I'd heard in the talk, the still-fresh loss of Zayde, my being alone with Danny in the dark?

"Elaine, are you okay?"

"Fine." I shook with tears.

He wrapped his arms around me, in a way that started out as a comforting gesture between friends. Then the embrace became something else. I tried to shrug away, I swear I did. I pictured myself getting up and leaving. Virtuous, a good sister. I pictured the scene with that good Elaine as if it were a movie—detailed but two-dimensional, distant—while Danny kissed my teary cheeks and a shivering started inside me.

I tilted my face toward his, my mouth.

MY SEASON OF DUPLICITY began in earnest that night. For the first time I practiced the adult art of splitting myself into two Elaines, one who betrayed her sister and the other who—and this was the art—*genuinely* made nice with her. I had decided, on the night of the talk, to reach out to Barbara, to be not just a sister to her but a friend; and I did. We both did.

At first I tried to start the kind of probing conversations I got into with Danny or my friends in the Plain Brains. But Barbara didn't mull over ideas or devour books the way I did. Nor did it help that the one burning subject I could have discussed with her, Danny, lay like a stone on my tongue.

Perhaps because she noticed I was making an effort, however, she reciprocated. She invited me to her modern dance class. *Me*, dance? But she warmly urged me to give the class a try, and one Saturday afternoon I swallowed my self-consciousness and went with her to the community center, where Helen Tannenbaum taught the class.

Miss Helen, I learned, studied with Lester Horton. I had read about Lester Horton in the newspaper. He'd made a dance called "Dictatorship" about the evils of fascism, and another that celebrated the Mexican revolution. Miss Helen, too, combined dance and politics. After she led a series of warm-up exercises (which, despite my clumsiness, were fun), she told us to imagine we were garment workers, shackled to sewing machines but struggling to break free. I twisted and panted, so absorbed I didn't even notice Miss Helen watching me until she said, "Yes, you're a dancer!"— praise that made me giddy with pleasure.

"Why didn't you tell me you did antifascist dances?" I asked Barbara on our walk home.

"Antifascist?" She rolled her eyes. "You can go for the politics. I go to dance."

Dancing turned out to be reason enough, a balm for my inner voice that relentlessly analyzed, interpreted, and judged. Not that dancing was mindless. Watching Miss Helen demonstrate a movement and working to reproduce it in my body, I discovered a realm of physical intelligence; she called it "muscle memory." Yet dance was also intoxicating and primal, my bare feet on the wooden floor, the occasional exhilarating times when I didn't just do steps but inhabited a dance's essence—it was like the lines from Yeats I loved, "O body swayed to music, O brightening glance / How can we know the dancer from the dance?"

I experienced that blissful state in rare glimpses. Barbara, however, had a gift for immersing herself in an emotion or character. She could shed her identity like shrugging off a sweater and transform into someone or something else. Our class did a recital, and a woman ran up to her afterward and gushed that seeing her dance was like watching an angel. We giggled over that for weeks. Still, I thought the gushy woman had a point. Barbara was an artist.

Our shared love of dance—and my recognition that in the world of physical intelligence, Barbara was the smart one—helped us regain some of our childhood closeness; it even made us willing to be vulnerable with each other. She came to me for help with her schoolwork. I quizzed her for tips on attracting boys, which I applied with surprising success. Not that I ever became the bright, chatty girl she was, but I got in the habit of taking off my glasses around boys and casting glances at them; the boys didn't have to know that until they got close, I saw them as blurs. It didn't hurt, either, that I got breasts. In the fall they weren't much more than hopeful bumps, but by the time I turned sixteen in March I had a figure. Although there was no one special, I got asked out on dates.

Between my brighter social life and my renewed friendship with Barbara, it was inconceivable that I would go behind her back with Danny again.

Inconceivable but true. At first, like the time at the playground and after the speech, it happened only when circumstances threw us together. He came by one night in January to see Barbara, but she was at a friend's, I said; I was sitting outside on the porch, my retreat even on winter nights from the chaos in our cramped house. "I'll visit *you*, then," he said, and sat beside me, and . . .

The next time, a few weeks later, Mama had sent me to Chafkin's to pick up a few last-minute things for dinner. Danny was just getting off work. "I'll walk with you," he said. "Just come back for a minute while I sweep the storeroom." We ended up on a cushion of potato sacks. His tongue darted into my mouth. Danny had tried this in the past; so, by now, had a couple other boys. But this time, I didn't pull away; I French-kissed him back.

Soon we dropped all pretense and simply arranged to see each other. And even though I necked with boys I dated, Danny was always the first: my first French kiss, the first boy I didn't swat away when he put a hand on my breast through layers of sweater, blouse, and underclothes, and later the first to slide his hand under my clothes and actually touch my breasts. Our trysts took place every two or three weeks, often in Chafkin's storeroom—where else could we have privacy?

I didn't split completely in two. I felt guilty and insisted that we discuss how we were wronging Barbara. But he maintained that he didn't love Barbara any less because he cared for me, too.

"So you wouldn't mind telling her about us?" I said. "Or going to the movies with me sometime, instead of sneaking around?"

"If we were in Palestine, I would. The pioneers in Palestine are creating an entirely new society."

"But we're not in Palestine."

"What about your cousin Mollie?" he countered.

"What does Mollie have to do with—"

"Bet she believes in free love."

Mollie did believe in free love, and in one of the stories I told myself I was a forward-thinker, a revolutionary. Alternatively, I was an ironic intellectual who had no patience for the silly conventions of high school courtship, the dates and moony looks and fantasies of marriage. These were identities I struggled to claim on evenings when Barbara and Danny stole a few private moments on the living room sofa while I lay in bed with a book in front of my face, unable to take in a word. Or when I swam up from dizzy kisses into Chafkin's storeroom, into the shame of being kissed in secret amid the dark odors of root vegetables and slightly rotten greens.

CHAPTER 13

A FREE
WOMAN

For MONTHS AFTER WE MET AUNT PEARL'S BOYFRIEND, SWEET-VOICED Alberto Rivas, Barbara and I spun elaborate fantasies about their wedding. We imagined every detail of our roles—and our outfits—for the grand event, and we privately referred to Pearl's beau as Uncle Bert.

The first time I'd met Bert, I was shocked that Pearl was dating a Mexican. It was enough of a scandal when the son or daughter of one of our Jewish neighbors married a Christian; there were religious families that sat shiva as if the person had died.

But my initial shock soon switched to admiration for the modern American woman who was my aunt. Like the forthright movie heroines for whom she designed costumes, Pearl wasn't going to be bound by musty, undemocratic conventions. She would follow her heart. As for Uncle Bert, he was charming and funny and handsome, and I adored it when he sang.

Clearly, however, the other adults in my family weren't as open-minded as Pearl. Bert came to our house with her only a handful of times and never again with the giddy joy of that first night, when he'd borne Audrey safely home after the earthquake. Papa in particular, for all that he preached American acceptance for people of all races and backgrounds, always acted tense and cold when Bert was around.

Barbara and I had enough sense to keep our mouths shut. But one day when Pearl and Bert had joined us for a picnic, Audrey blurted out, "When are you getting married?"

"Audrey!" Mama gasped.

Bert winked at Audrey. "I'm waiting for you to grow up so I can marry you."

"Audrey, come with me," Papa said.

"But—"

"Now!" Papa grabbed her hand to lead her away for a private talk. And he glared at Bert with so much anger it shocked me.

At least Papa was willing to speak to Bert. Zayde had refused to shake his hand, even after he'd rescued Audrey. Barbara and I eventually concluded it was Zayde's opposition that kept Pearl from marrying Bert. It was one thing for her to defy Zayde by living on her own after her divorce, but she must have felt she couldn't get married again without his blessing. And as time passed with no hint of an engagement, we had let the subject drop.

But now, four years later, Zayde was gone, his absence a rip in my awareness that cruelly occurred again and again—when I caught an astringent, vinegary whiff from the pickle barrels at Canter's and had an impulse to buy a kosher dill and take it to Zayde at Melansky's. Or I heard a great joke on the radio and started repeating it to myself, and only then realized I had lost my audience. Sometimes, I was so certain I heard his voice in the next room I had to go look and prove to myself that he wasn't there.

The one consolation was that Pearl was at last free to marry Bert. Not that she had said anything about it. But wasn't she planning to buy her own house in Boyle Heights?

"A whole house, for one person!" I heard Mama say to Papa.

"She could afford a house in Hollywood or Westwood if she wanted to live there," Papa said.

In fact, Pearl was doing so well designing clothes for the movies that she no longer worked out of her apartment but rented an entire floor of a building in the garment district. She employed half a dozen people and had set aside a room for Papa's business of supplying shoes to go with her costumes. She had even bought a car and learned to drive! She needed the car, a Plymouth sedan, to carry samples and so forth. But those were all requirements for her business. Why would Pearl want to buy a house, except to live in it with Bert? Barbara and I concurred, and we happily resumed our fantasizing about Pearl's wedding.

"Will they make some kind of announcement?" Barbara said one evening when we were on our way to Pearl's apartment. This was just after we'd entered our junior year in high school, and we were going to Pearl's to choose fabric for new dresses; Pearl still did some sewing for the family at home, often using remnants from the outfits she made for movie stars. "Or will she just start wearing a ring and wave her hands until we notice?"

"Waving her hands won't get any special attention." I laughed. "She does that all the time."

"What if she stre-e-etches?" Mimicking our dance teacher, Miss Helen, at her most dramatic, Barbara thrust her arms above her head and skipped down the street. "Come on!" she called, and I danced beside her, my self-consciousness mixed with the thrill of acting like an uninhibited, madcap girl.

We tumbled into Pearl's apartment giggling and sweaty, and when she asked why we were in such good moods, it spilled out.

"We're planning your engagement," I said.

"Who am I supposed to be getting engaged to?" Her laughter had an edge, but I'd gone too far to stop.

"Bert, who else?"

"Darlings, I'm not going to marry Bert. Would you like Coca-Colas? I've got Coca-Colas for you. Unless you'd rather have tea, but you're probably too hot—"

"Coke, please," Barbara interrupted Pearl's choppy, strangely nervous chatter. And then added, "Why not?"

"You, too, Elaine, Coca-Cola?" Pearl said.

"Yes, please."

Pearl bustled into her small kitchen. We followed, hovering in the doorway. I felt a little the way I had dancing down the street, simultaneously wishing I hadn't started and wild to plunge ahead.

"It's not because he's Mexican, is it?" I said. "I think that's terrible, that anyone would object to—"

"Just let me get your drinks first, all right?" Pearl poured two bottles of Coke into glasses and handed them to us. Then she said, "Don't you think if Bert and I wanted to get married, we would have done that by now?"

"But you couldn't," Barbara said.

"Someone told you about that?"

"We figured it out," Barbara said.

"Well, then you know nothing's changed." She strode to the table, where she had stacked half a dozen bolts of fabric. "Careful with your drinks. Take a look at this beautiful challis. It's from the new Myrna Loy film." She started to unroll a bolt of sea-green fabric.

"But now that Zayde's gone . . . ," I said, my need to understand stronger than my fear of annoying Pearl.

"Zayde? What are you talking about?"

"You couldn't get married because of Zayde," I said. "Because Zayde didn't like Bert. But now you can."

"Oh." Pearl stopped unrolling the challis. "*That's* what you figured out?"

"Isn't it—" I started, but she held up one hand and stood still for a moment, her eyes closed. Pearl did that sometimes in the middle of a conversation if she needed to collect her thoughts.

Opening her eyes, Pearl said, "Your parents would kill me. But you're not children anymore. And better, I guess, that you hear this from me. All right, sit."

As always, when Pearl was about to enlighten us regarding the adult world, she sat on her love seat—which, thanks to her prosperity, she'd had recovered with rich rose brocade upholstery—and lit a cigarette. I sat next to her, and Barbara took the chair.

"You're right, I can't marry Bert, but it's not because of Zayde. Darlings . . ." Pearl glanced from one of us to the other, meeting our eyes. "Bert is married already. He has a wife in Mexico."

"Won't she give him a divorce?" Barbara adopted the cool, sophisticated tone of movies in which things like this took place, while my mind reeled. An avid reader and movie-goer, I knew such things happened. But they happened to Anna Karenina or Jean Harlow, not to my aunt Pearl.

"In Mexico, in his village, people don't get divorced," Pearl said. "And I wouldn't want him to divorce her."

"Do they have children? . . . I don't mind," Barbara said.

Ah, but didn't I know what it was like to be desperately in love with a man who belonged to someone else?

"Four children," Pearl said.

I let out a small sob.

"I'm sorry, darling." Pearl said. "You didn't know your auntie Pearl was such a terrible person."

Now I was crying too hard to speak. All the rationalizations I'd made about free love crumpled, and I saw the tawdriness of everything I'd been doing—betraying Barbara and, even worse, being so pathetically in love with Danny Berlov that I was willing to be his girl on the side. No stranger to self-criticism, I knew how it felt to be embarrassed or ashamed over something I'd done, but this was the first time I truly loathed myself.

Pearl hugged me and stroked my hair, at first apologizing—and, as I kept weeping, asking "Elaine, what is it? Is something else the matter?"

I found my voice then; I would have died before I let her suspect I had my own reason for tears. "It's just sad that you can't get married."

"Oh, no, it's not. Really," Pearl said. "I'm an idiot, I should have explained better. I don't *want* to marry Bert."

"But you love him," Barbara said.

"Love." Pearl sighed. "The two of you, sixteen years old, you should listen to all the love songs they play on the radio and think you're in heaven when a boy takes you in his arms on the dance floor. Just know that when you get older, it will be different. Bert is a very sweet man. But darlings, I don't want to be any man's wife."

"You married Uncle Gabe," Barbara said.

"And I found out that not every woman likes being married. To have a man telling you what to do, even what to *think*! Keeping you awake all night with his snoring. Sulking if you don't make your kugel with the exact number of raisins his mother put in hers."

Despite the cloud of misery that surrounded me, I was captivated by this revolutionary idea. I realized I had seen plenty of examples of unmarried women who, as far as I could tell, led fulfilling lives—Pearl, Mollie, many of my teachers. But no one had ever stated it outright: *not every woman likes being married.* And although Mollie always remained my model for activism, it was Pearl I would think of when the feminist movement came along.

My mind also buzzed with the reverberations of *snoring*, which forced me to consider what else went on when a man and woman shared a bed. Barbara and I had figured Pearl and Bert "did it," but it was different when I'd expected them to get married. Suddenly, things I had observed between Pearl and Bert—the clingy sweater she'd worn the night of the earthquake, the intimate looks he gave her as his baritone caressed the lyrics of a song—became a peek at the scary-thrilling mystery of grown-up sexual desire.

"What if a husband wouldn't *allow* me to work?" Pearl was saying. "Or he tried to take over my business and run it himself?"

"Bert wouldn't do that," Barbara said.

"Oh, *chiquitas*," Pearl said; it was what Bert called us sometimes. "You never really know a man until you let him put a ring on your finger. Then he thinks he owns you. I'm happy with my life the way it is. . . . But what's this nonsense your *meshuganah* aunt is filling your heads with?" She kissed Barbara's cheek, then mine. "So, do you want new dresses to wear to dances, so the boys will flock around you?"

Was Pearl only saying she didn't want to marry Bert so we wouldn't feel sorry for her? I wondered, as she unrolled challis and crêpe de chine. But Pearl did seem happy—invigorated by her thriving business, excited at the prospect of buying a house. Actually, sinful Aunt Pearl seemed like the happiest of all the adults I knew, a conundrum I chewed on for days.

IT'S TOO SIMPLE TO say that finding out about Pearl changed my life or Barbara's. It was more that the choices each of us made not long afterward reflected who we already were.

For me, hearing Pearl's revelation set off my first struggle with adult moral ambiguity. Carrying on an affair with a married man—that was the province of *bad* women, home-wreckers. (Now I understood Papa's and Zayde's coldness toward Bert.) Yet Pearl was one of the people I loved and admired most in the world. She was kind, principled, straightforward; although she didn't volunteer unpleasant truths, she leveled with Barbara and me whenever we asked. Look at the way she'd told us about Bert, making no excuses. And in her not wanting to marry, there was a freedom of thought that dazzled me.

Not that her choices lacked consequences. After that conversation, I felt a pang whenever I saw her cuddle my youngest sister, Harriet, and coo about her delicious baby smell.

"I'm not a baby!" Harriet protested. "I'm four!"

"Well, you still smell scrumptious!" Pearl burrowed her nose into Harriet's belly, making her gurgle with laughter. Even if Pearl had no desire to be a wife, I suspected she would have loved being a mother. But she seemed clear-eyed about what she'd given up and, as she had said, genuinely happy with her life as it was.

Yes, Pearl was dating a married man, but his wife was far away in Mexico. And she was seeing him openly, willing to face censure. Not like me—sneaking around, cheating on my own sister!

A few days later Danny whispered, after our history class, that he wanted to see me. And I said no.

He caught up with me after school. I was hurrying to catch the streetcar to get to my job at Leo's bookstore.

"What's wrong?" Danny said.

"I just don't want to. . . ."

"You mean this week?"

"I mean not ever. There's my streetcar."

"Elaine, wait. Can't we talk about this?"

The streetcar, one of the Yellow Cars of the Los Angeles Street Railway, pulled up. "I have to go."

To my amazement, Danny got on the car after me and dropped a precious nickel into the fare box.

"What are you doing?" I said. "Don't you have to work?"

"Eddie won't mind if I'm a little late."

The car was crowded, and we couldn't sit together at first. But at the next stop, my seatmate got off, and Danny slid in beside me.

"Did something happen?" he said.

"No."

"Is it something I did?" He looked at me as if I held his happiness in my hands. No one had ever looked at me that way, and to see that yearning in Danny's eyes! I felt a dizzying sense of power . . . and an urge to spare him any pain.

But I took a deep breath and said, "I just don't feel right."

"Can we still get together sometimes and talk? There's no one else I can talk to the way I can with you."

"We can talk."

He flashed me a rakish Errol Flynn smile. "If that's really all you want to do."

"We can *talk*," I said, weakening again at the intimacy, the smell of him, as he leaned close to me.

"Good, I'm really glad. Guess I'd better get to work . . . Uh, Barbara didn't say anything, did she?"

Of course, that was why Danny had jumped on the streetcar after me and why he'd looked heartsick—his fear of upsetting my sister!

"Do you and Barbara kiss?" I demanded.

"You're kidding, right?" he said softly, his eyes flicking toward the woman on the seat ahead of us.

"Do you kiss?" I whispered.

"What do you think?"

"French-kiss?"

"Elaine, are you nuts?"

The woman in front of us giggled. We were already downtown and almost to the car barn at Fifth and Olive, where I would transfer to the streetcar to Hollywood.

"Let's get off, okay?" I said.

"Fine!"

"You tell him, sister!" the woman called out as we left.

Somehow the constraint of being on the Yellow Car had made it easier to talk. On the street, I stared at Danny for a moment, then started walking fast.

"Do I let you do things she won't do?" I said. "Is that why you keep wanting to see me?"

"I thought you liked—"

"Maybe I should ask her."

"No!" He grabbed my hand. "If it matters so much, I do more with her. Elaine, please, look at me?"

I let him pull me out of the pedestrian traffic, under the awning of a music store.

"Danny, you have Barbara," I said. "What do you want with me?" I had wondered all along, but hadn't dared to ask.

He gave a bark of laughter—except it came out like a strangled sob. "*Have* Barbara? No one will ever have Barbara." Then he quickly made himself into Errol Flynn again. "You don't want to see me, suit yourself. It was just . . . it's not like you have anyone special, and you're a good kid. Guess I felt sorry for you."

"Felt sorry for me? I hate you!" I yelled as he sauntered away.

THE FIRE OF ANGER carried me, head high, through work that afternoon and school the next day. Too soon, however, my fury lost its all-consuming force, its ability to incinerate every other emotion. I crashed into misery. Around people, I managed to impersonate the Elaine Greenstein everyone knew, a girl who was smart and serious but no more or less happy than any other Boyle Heights sixteen-year-old. But, alone in my bedroom, I wept.

Again and again, I relived that moment just before Danny strode off.

Not when he said he was sorry for me, I knew he was lashing out then because he was hurt. But I kept remembering the uncertainty he'd revealed about Barbara. That, I understood wretchedly, was what Danny really wanted with me: it wasn't the thrill of having more than one girl nor his genuine attraction to me, though I suppose both those things were part of it. But more than anything else, Danny saw me as insurance, a rough replica of Barbara in his back pocket because he couldn't count on the real thing.

It was as if he had intuited something in Barbara that became more and more apparent during our junior year. That September she started attending the Lester Horton dance school in Hollywood; Miss Helen had recommended her for a scholarship. Taking the scholarship meant she'd had to stop running her children's playgroup, and at first Papa balked and said we couldn't afford to lose her income. Mama, however, went on a campaign to ensure that Barbara could go to the dance school. She discovered a dozen new places to pare household expenses. After years of insisting we didn't need charity, she applied for the free milk available for needy families. And she continually repeated the word *scholarship*—which Papa revered, even if the scholarship was to a dance school. For weeks that fall he started conversations with, "Did you know Barbara was awarded a scholarship?"

Barbara now went to the Horton studio most days after school and didn't come home until eight or nine. She spent every Saturday there, too, and often stayed in Hollywood and spent Saturday evenings with friends from her dance class. Her conversation bubbled with new names: Lester, of course, and Bella, the star dancer who taught some of her classes, and her fellow students. Most of all, she mentioned Oscar, who played piano to accompany the classes, although Oscar rarely played the keys, she said; instead, he plucked the strings inside the piano or drummed rhythms on its body. He offered singing lessons, too, and Barbara reported excitedly that he considered her "a natural talent."

The night of the dance studio's Christmas party, she didn't get in until after midnight. I woke up when she stumbled, trying to undress in the dark.

"Oops," she said with a giggle.

I switched on the light.

"Ow!" She shielded her eyes. "Could you just light a candle?"

I lit a candle and turned out the light. "Are you drunk?"

"Not really. Well, a little. Oscar made gin rickeys."

"Barbara, are you going out with Oscar?"

"It was just a party." With efficient, graceful motions, she shed her dress and dropped it on the floor.

"How old is he?"

"Want a ciggie?" She fished a pack of Chesterfields out of her dance bag. Even though I smoked on dates or at parties, I had never actually bought my own pack of cigarettes. Or smoked at home.

"In here?"

"Why not?" Still, she threw open the window.

We lit our cigarettes from the candle flame, and I emptied our tin of bobby pins to use as an ashtray. Barbara, clearly tipsy, lounged unself-consciously in her slip and said things she might otherwise have kept to herself.

"Oh, Elaine," she sighed. "He has the most exquisite hands. Musician's hands."

"Oscar?"

"Umm." She took a slow, luxurious inhale.

"Isn't he in his twenties?"

"God, it isn't like high school, where it's a huge deal for a sophomore to date a senior. We're artists working together."

"Does Danny know?"

"About Oscar's hands?" she teased.

"You know what I mean."

"Danny Berlov doesn't own me. No man is ever going to own me."

The words may have been borrowed from Pearl, but the sentiment, I came to understand, was pure Barbara. She continued to date Danny officially—the dates announced to Mama and Papa and Danny picking her up at the house—while she saw Oscar under the pretext of socializing with her dance-class friends. That lasted for a month or so. Then Oscar disappeared from her conversation, to be replaced by a dancer named Ted.

I had no idea if Danny was aware of the other boys—the men, really—in Barbara's life. Though I did my best to avoid him, there were times I couldn't help seeing him—for instance, if Mama invited him and his father to Shabbos dinner. I was at the table sometimes when Barbara gushed about her new friends, her classes, rehearsals for a student show. As for Danny . . . for all that he'd molded himself into a muscular, take-charge young Zionist, I kept seeing the barefoot kid I'd met when we were five, a boy who lied to cover up his shame over his absent mother and feckless father.

Love! In my mind, the word took on Pearl's weary tone. I loved—well, I used to love—Danny. Danny loved Barbara. And Barbara . . . Poor Danny, his real rival wasn't Oscar or Ted, it was something he could never compete with. Barbara loved freedom. Not that any of us—Danny or Barbara or me—could have articulated it at the time, but Danny felt it keenly. "No one will ever have Barbara," he'd half sobbed—and as the world of Hollywood and the dance studio became more and more her world, I saw that he was right.

Although part of me vengefully relished Danny's distress, I did feel sorry for him. And one Saturday in February 1938 I stopped hating him. Actually, my hatred had long since faded. My private tears had stopped a few weeks after our fight in September. And in November I'd gone to the homecoming dance with Fred Nieman, who'd grown enough during the previous year that he now looked like a short young man instead of a child; he even needed to shave. Fred didn't become my boyfriend, but he was a regular date. Eventually it was simply habit that made me go cold when Danny was around.

On the Saturday afternoon when I buried the hatchet, I got home after working at the bookstore and found Danny scrambling on his hands and knees on the living room floor; Harriet sat astride his back, kicking his sides and whooping, "Ride 'em, cowboy!" He often played with Harriet when he'd come by for Barbara, but had to wait because she was late getting home from the dance studio. I mumbled hello, planning to pass by and go to my room, but then Danny looked up with an expression so forlorn that instead I laughed and said, "Harriet, give the poor horsey a rest." I plucked her off his back and distracted her with some hard candies I had in my pocket. Danny asked me how things were going, and for the first time in months I did more than choke out a few polite words to him. By this time, I'd been promoted from just running errands at the bookstore to waiting on customers, and I told him about a bizarre woman who'd come in that day: she was six feet tall, wore a sort of magician's robe, and was looking for books about the worship of cats.

"You mean lions?" he said.

"No, house cats."

"A lion, I could understand."

"I want a kitty!" Harriet piped up.

"The ancient Egyptians worshipped them," I told Danny.

"No wonder their civilization died."

It was a silly, awkward conversation, but after that he and I were able to talk again. And we had very serious things to discuss.

HITLER'S FLURRY OF ANTI-JEWISH laws had appeared to culminate in the 1935 Nuremberg Laws, as if his madness really had burned itself out; or at least, as if ordinary, decent Germans had decided enough was enough. But in 1938, there was a fresh eruption of hatred.

The first signs of this new wave of insanity occurred at the end of 1937, not in Germany but in Romania, where the leader of the vicious anti-Semitic political party became prime minister. Within a few months, Romania shut down all Jewish-owned newspapers and fired every Jew who had a government position. Those two actions alone cost nine of our relatives their jobs. The terrible news led to the first long-distance telephone call Mama ever received, from Uncle Meyr in Chicago. Not one of their relatives had obtained permission to immigrate, and the Chicago relatives planned to hire lawyers, both in Chicago and in Romania; could Mama get a lawyer in Los Angeles? Desperate, Mama asked Aunt Pearl for help. Pearl had already guaranteed a job at her dress company for Ivan, the nephew whom Mama and Papa had applied to sponsor. Now Pearl gave Mama some of the money she'd put aside for a house. Mama never breathed a word about it to Papa; he would have been furious and ashamed that she'd begged his sister for funds he couldn't provide. I knew about it only because Mama asked me to go with her to speak to the Los Angeles lawyer and to draft several letters.

Events in Romania slipped beneath most people's notice. However, the whole world paid attention when Germany annexed Austria that March. Germany immediately imposed its anti-Semitic laws on the Austrian Jews. Then, as if having fresh victims had inspired them, the Nazis spat out new punishments for the crime of being born Jewish. In April, Jews had to register all property held inside the Reich—the word alone felt harsh and cruel in my throat. Then Jewish-owned businesses had to be identified, a task performed with gusto by jeering Hitler Youths who painted the word *Jude* along with rude pictures on shopwindows. At that point, President Roosevelt himself decided to admit more immigrants from Germany and Austria. Still, we kept hearing about Jews desperate to flee who had nowhere to go.

Danny devoured the news. He'd become president of Habonim, and he spoke wherever he could, at Habonim meetings and school and community forums, to alert people to the need for a refuge for European Jews. I didn't just attend the meetings but also wrote announcements to publicize them. And I helped Danny write articles for the Habonim newsletter and the school paper, even letters to the *Los Angeles Times* and other newspapers. The newspapers liked to air "the youth perspective," and several of our letters got published. Working together on a letter or an article, we hammered out the language in heated debates. I found his approach too inflammatory—"If you call people 'spineless,' they're not going to listen to anything else you have to say!"—and he said I was "just being a good little Jewish girl and not making waves."

I still disagreed with him about Zionism, but that became a quibble next to my urgency to *act* and the gift Danny revealed for moving people to action. A natural storyteller, he spoke about the big political events happening in Europe in terms of small, heartbreaking stories gleaned from people in Boyle Heights who had family members there. Just as he'd beguiled me with his tales when we were children, he could move his audiences to tears and persuade them to write letters to Congress or hand out leaflets on the street. I put my energy into Habonim because Danny made it the most dynamic youth group trying to do *something*, though it didn't matter to me if the refugees went to Palestine or America or Rhodesia or Cuba—any country that was willing to crack open its doors.

Danny was also an unwavering optimist. Whenever I got discouraged, he convinced me that if we kept raising our voices, someone had to listen. He turned out to be right. That June, America opened its doors to Ivan Avramescu, my cousin from Romania.

Or, as Barbara called him, the Rat.

CHAPTER 14

RANCH OF NO TOMORROW

GET OUT OF THE POOL AFTER WATER AEROBICS, SHOWER, AND DRESS. And then, for the first time, instead of going home, I drive to Rancho Mañana. I moved here yesterday. I check in at the reception desk—a requirement that makes me feel like I'm in kindergarten—and assure the too-solicitous young woman that of course I know how to get to my own apartment.

But for a moment, after I take the west elevator to the third floor, walk down the hallway to the right, and open the door, I think I must have gotten confused and entered someone else's unit, after all. The first thing I see, directly opposite the front door, is a depressing wall hanging, a blob of mustard and beige and brown. Strangely, however, right below the brown blob is a tomato-red and black love seat just like mine.

I hear Carol's voice. "Hey, Mom. . . . Do you like it?"

"Oh, it's beautiful. Gorgeous!" I sing out. Giving my inner art critic a swift kick, I go take a closer look at what's obviously Carol's handmade housewarming gift for me. "Ah, it's—what are these, moths?"

"Dragonflies. You don't like it, do you?"

"I do! I can't believe you gave each one of them so much detail. It's amazing. And the colors are so subtle." As I examine the hanging, I actually do appreciate it; with extraordinary precision, Carol has woven several dozen swarming dragonflies, some of them no bigger than a fingertip. And there's an extraordinary range of color—strands of gold, deep chocolate browns, delicate fawn beiges. So why, as genuine praise spills out of my mouth, does it sound less and less sincere?

Carol comes and stands beside me, twisting a fistful of her long hair, which is barely touched with gray; seen from the back, in her peasant blouse and jeans, my elfin daughter still looks sixteen. Between Carol and Ronnie, he got all of the genes for height. She's always been tiny, so small-boned we used to laugh and say she looked like she could blow away; a joke, but sometimes my heart caught in my throat, and I feared she really might take off like a seedpod on a gust of wind. We enrolled her in gymnastics when she was little, because she had a perfect gymnast's body and loved tumbling, but she turned out to have no taste for the drill or the competition.

"The colors are wrong. I knew it," she says. "Darn, I got some bright blue yarn and tried doing something contemporary for you, but . . ." She sighs. "The yarn just didn't speak to me."

"Carol." I give her a hug. "It's beautiful. Thank you." I wish I could convince her. I wish I could have adored the hanging the moment I saw it.

More than anything, I wish Carol and I weren't doomed to hurt and misunderstand each other. Still, neither of us has ever walked away. Even during the nightmare that was her adolescence, when my once-gentle girl embraced the 1960s trinity of sex, drugs, and rock 'n' roll, the one thing she didn't do, ever, was run away. There were nights when I was up at three in the morning, watching for her to come home, but she always did. As if she were honoring an unspoken pact, that vanishing like Barbara was one pain she wouldn't inflict on me. We have always stayed engaged, no matter how difficult it's been.

"I made a salad for lunch," she says. "Is that okay?"

"Perfect." I push aside papers on my former kitchen table, which has become my dining room table; like much of my furniture, the dining room table didn't fit here.

While we're eating, the phone rings. I start to let the machine pick up, but it's Josh, saying, "I've got something."

I snatch up the phone. "Hold on," I tell him, and retreat to the bedroom. "What is it?" I ask after I've closed the door.

"This thing just came in the mail. I can come by tonight and show you. I'm free by seven-thirty."

"Seven-thirty's fine." Carol should have left for the night by then. She's staying at her son's.

"Sure," Josh says. "How do I get to this place? Rancho something, isn't it?"

I give him directions, then return to the living/dining room and hang up the phone.

"What are you up to, Mom?" Carol says.

"Nothing."

"Come on. *I* used to be the one who took the phone into the other room."

"It was Josh. My archivist," I say.

"Oh, right."

"I need to meet with him tonight."

"We were going to see a movie!"

"Oh, I forgot. I'll call him back and reschedule."

But Josh turns out to be busy tomorrow. I could see him later this week, I suppose. *Impossible!* I can't wait for whatever he's found out about Barbara. I tell Carol we'll have to postpone and catch a flash of hurt in her eyes that has nothing to do with the movie. I consider letting her know what's going on, even inviting her to stay for the meeting with Josh tonight. Just thinking of it, my gut clenches. Barbara was *my* twin sister. This is my search. I don't want to have to listen to anyone else's opinion about how—or, worse, whether—to proceed. And right now, with the fresh wound of finding out my parents knew about her and said nothing, Barbara occupies a place in me that feels fragile and naked, astonishingly so. I'm not ready to let anyone enter that room. Josh, all right, he was involved from the beginning. And he's essentially a stranger, whom I've insisted on paying for his help. But no one else.

"Can we still have dinner?" Carol says. "The chicken teriyaki?"

She has decided that we, she and I together, will brave the Rancho Mañana dining room for the first time this evening; they're doing chicken teriyaki, apparently a favorite. I feel a bit as if Carol's walking me to my first day of school. And I *am* nervous about my first plunge into this tight little society of some 180 people, about half of whom I've crossed paths with at some time in my life

"Absolutely," I say. "I wouldn't enter the lions' den without you."

That afternoon, Carol focuses on the kitchen while I unpack my office. And I come across the folder of poems I'd planned to "lose." I suppose Carol might appreciate getting the poems; and sharing them with her is a vulnerability (unlike the search for Barbara) that I'm willing to risk. I flip open the folder, see a poem about night-blooming jasmine "perfuming Breed Street's dreams." On the other hand, maybe Carol would look at the poems and feel the way I did when I saw her wall hanging—touched, yes, but also awkward and torn.

THE CHICKEN TERIYAKI AT dinner lives up to its reputation. Not that this keeps one of my tablemates, a tiny woman whose face is dwarfed by eyeglasses with huge red frames, from complaining with every bite and regaling us with blow-by-blow details of the chicken dishes she used to make. I'm going to ask to be assigned to a different table. Yes, we're assigned, another kindergarten touch. What the hell, maybe I'll just sit wherever I want, start an insurrection.

After dinner, Carol takes off, and suddenly, as if someone stuck a pin in me and all the air whooshed out, I'm exhausted. I want to go home! On leaden legs, I trudge back to my apartment. Amid the chaos of moving boxes, I can't summon the energy to open a book or turn on the television but sit on the love seat under the mustard dragonflies.

The leaden feeling finally lifts when the receptionist calls and tells me Josh is here.

"Nice place," he says when he comes in. And heads straight for Carol's wall hanging. "Wow, what's this?"

"My daughter made it." My eyes are riveted on the envelope he's carrying—so small, just an ordinary business envelope.

"Dragonflies?" he asks.

"Yes."

"Wow. It's cool."

I'm ready to rip the envelope out of his hand. "What did you find out?"

He takes a piece of letter-size paper from the envelope, spends an eternity unfolding it, and finally hands it to me. It's a copy of a brief newspaper article with a group photograph of about a dozen young women and, standing behind them, several men. Someone has handwritten on the copy "March 9, 1942" and the headline reads: "Colorado Springs Entertainers Join USO Tour." The article says that fifteen local singers, dancers, and musicians had signed on for one of the first European tours being organized by the United Service Organizations, a group formed to provide entertainment and recreation for U.S. servicemen.

"I got in touch with a librarian at the Colorado Springs library and invoked the mutual help code that binds librarians all over the world," Josh says while I squint at the faces. "She tracked this down for me."

Bad enough that the photo, which looks printed from microfiche, is blurry, but the women had struck a chorus line pose, standing at an angle with one hip jutting and an arm extended in a flourish. Not one of them jumps out at me. I check the caption, match the name Kay Devereaux to a girl with platinum-blond hair and a close-lipped smile. She's one of the shorter girls; that would be right. But her face is turned sideways and it's partly obscured by her curtain of hair.

"It's her, isn't it?" he says.

"I'm not sure." I get up to grab the magnifying glass I keep near the telephone, then realize I no longer own the little stand that conveniently held the phone, directories, and various inordinately useful items; there was no room here. Shit!

Josh and I try blowing up the picture on my copier, experimenting with different settings. Kay's face dissolves into pixels.

"What about after this tour?" I ask. "Didn't the USO send her back to Colorado Springs?"

"The librarian checked the phone directories for the rest of the 1940s and didn't find any listing for her. And the Broadmoor Hotel has a historian—the librarian put me in touch with her. There's no record of Kay Devereaux working there again. The historian said some of these folks came back home after the one USO tour, but for a lot of them, Colorado Springs wasn't home, anyway. Or they liked the touring life, the excitement of being at the front and all that, and they signed on for additional tours. Does that sound like your sister?"

Did it sound like Barbara, to dye her hair the color of Jean Harlow's, leap into a dangerous situation, and run half a world away from Boyle Heights? I'm on pins and needles . . . even as I warn myself that this trail, if it is one, is more than half a century old.

"It's possible," I say.

"I'm thinking my next step is to check with the USO."

"Good idea. Oh," I add with a chill, "and check the military death records, too. If she got killed in a war zone, maybe they counted it as a combat death." I had never thought of her being in the war. All of the worrying I did about Paul and the other boys risking their lives, and I never suspected she might be there, too. In my stories about where she'd gone and what happened to her . . . always, somewhere, she was alive. And I still existed in her inner world, just as she did in mine. Imagining her lying all these decades among fallen soldiers—I picture a mist-shrouded graveyard in Normandy—it's as if part of *my* life were blotted out.

"Sure, I'll take a look," he says. "But didn't you already check the Social Security Death Index, and she wasn't there?"

"Right, of course," I say, relieved.

So there's a good chance Barbara is alive. Not Barbara but Kay, I caution myself. Still, I hear my own excitement in Josh's voice when he says, "What are you going to do when you find her?" This is another reason I don't want to tell my family: having them waiting on tenterhooks along with me would make the wait excruciating and the likely disappointment crushing. Josh, in contrast, just sees this search as an adventure. In fact, he shifts gears effortlessly from talking about Barbara to asking me to tell him about Philip Marlowe.

"Sure," I say. "But I don't have much to tell. Do you want a drink?" Thinking of Philip immediately brings up the association. "Scotch? Wine? Sprite?"

"Scotch is great. . . . Did you really work for him?" he says when I bring our drinks.

"Yes, but just a handful of research jobs over a few months. It was in trade for his looking for Barbara."

"What kind of research?"

"Nothing glamorous," I say in response to his avid expression. "It was mostly library research. The most exciting case I remember, I went to city hall and looked at plats, those maps that show who owns property. Then I looked up the owners whose names were listed. Turned out a lot of the property was registered in the names of dead people; someone was doing a swindle."

"Cool."

"But my job ended when I handed over my research notes. As I said, there's really very little to tell."

"How'd you give him your notes? Did you go to his office?"

"No, he took me out for steaks. Bloody ones." The memory makes me smile. "He always took me to this place in Hollywood. It looked like a dive, but they did the most amazing steaks. I think he worried that I didn't eat enough red meat."

"You *dated* him?"

"Good grief, no. I was just a kid."

"You were in college, right? You must have been twenty, twenty-one?"

"I was a Jewish girl from Boyle Heights."

"Was he anti-Semitic?"

"Philip? No more than most people in those days."

"Did he ever say anything?"

"What, like 'Hitler's got the right idea'? Of course not." How to explain to this twenty-first-century kid, with his Vietnamese American girlfriend, how insular America was when I was his age? "There was a jeweler—

Rosen's or maybe Rosenberg's—next to the steak place. One night, a man was standing in the doorway when we walked by, and Philip asked if I knew him. I said 'Who?' And he said, 'That Jew.' Was that anti-Semitic, referring to him as 'that Jew'? Assuming any two Jews living in Los Angeles knew each other? What he said was just the way people thought in those days. There was no malice in it."

"It didn't bother you?"

"If I'd gotten up in arms over every innocuous comment, I would have been at war with the world." Like Danny. "But who knows, maybe it did bother me, since I remember it after all these years."

I've surprised myself. I don't recall thinking any of that at the time. Or if I'd had a glimmer, I couldn't have articulated it then. Philip's remark might have stung for a second and then been forgotten as we entered the restaurant and were enveloped in the warmth and the enticing smells of meat and cigarettes.

But wasn't that the night when everything he said got under my skin? Wasn't that our last dinner, the night I made a fool of myself?

It occurs to me that there might have been another reason for the tension between us that night. What if he already knew, when he sat across from me at dinner, about Kay Devereaux in Colorado Springs—and he kept it from me? I hope not. I'd prefer to think well of him, to believe he didn't find out until later, when we no longer saw each other. Because after that night, he kept his distance. He didn't ask me to work for him again.

CAROL STAYS THROUGH THE end of the week, unpacking every box and helping me plant cuttings from the yard in the community garden. She even hangs every picture. "Otherwise, they'll still be in boxes six months from now. Believe me, I've done it," my vagabond daughter says. She moves her hanging to a bedroom wall. It looks better there—my bedspread, curtains, and chair are in various shades of blue with daffodil-yellow accents. But how I wish I could have had Josh's reaction the first time I saw it, that immediate visceral pleasure in response to something we instinctively perceive as beautiful.

At the last minute, when she's saying goodbye, I give her the folder of poems I wrote when I was a teenager.

"A few of them are love poems to my high school boyfriend," I warn her, already questioning the impulse that made me grab the poems and hand them to her.

But she says, "Thanks, Mom," and then she gives me an enormous, open smile, the smile that caught at my heart when she was a little girl: how could anyone be so open and survive? It catches at my heart now, and I'm glad about the poems.

Then she's gone, and I'm no longer "moving into Rancho Mañana." I'm living here. I have no regrets. Being at Rancho Mañana has given me an environment without stairs, nursing staff in case I need them, and a community of people I can see without having to drive for an hour. And several of them are people I genuinely like. I've gotten my table assignment switched so I'm sitting with Ann Charney Adelman, a friend since our Plain Brains club in high school. Ann has one of the most nimble minds of anyone I know, and although I'm only required to buy fifteen dinners a month, most nights I go to the dining room to enjoy her company. I keep running into cronies from countless political causes; now they commandeer the wheelchair van to go to rallies. There are "activities," too—bridge, mah-jongg, chair exercise, crafts, book groups, outings to theaters and the symphony, and Torah study. (Rancho Mañana is about 70 percent Jewish; I feel like I'm back in Boyle Heights. In fact, Ann isn't the only childhood classmate here.)

With the holidays have come nonstop parties. For New Year's Eve, last night, Rancho Mañana put on a soirée with a jazz trio hired for the occasion. Several musicians among my fellow residents, men who used to play professionally, sat in, and we had a rollicking time until nine, when we watched the ball drop at Times Square and welcomed the New Year on East Coast time with plastic flutes of passable champagne. That was followed by a party at Ann's; a dozen of us kept going until it was really midnight, then broke out more champagne (good stuff this time).

This morning I'm paying for every sip. But it was worth it. Everything, really, has been worth it. Except for God's latest, cruelest joke. To tantalize me with new "clues" about Barbara and then . . .

The USO's records were destroyed in a fire in 1979.

"You've got to be kidding," I said when Josh told me two weeks ago. "Burned records are a convenient complication in detective novels. Bad detective novels." I kept it light, but I felt flattened.

"No kidding. On to plan B. She was a professional entertainer, so she might have had a career after the war. I'm going to try the performers' unions and *Variety*, things like that."

But he tried all the entertainment industry sources, with no results. Neither of us has any idea what to do next.

Sitting in front of the television on New Year's Day, I nurse my hangover with black coffee and dry toast and watch the Rose Parade. Then the TV talks to me. Not "Hello, Elaine" or anything like that. But the navy band is marching across the screen playing "The Stars and Stripes Forever" and sparking all the ambivalence that the sight of marching servicemen stirs up in me—pride and patriotism from World War II, anger over the young people thrown into the Viet Nam and Iraq wars—and then, damned if I don't feel there's some kind of message for me.

I pick up the remote and silence the TV. I refuse to start receiving messages from home electronics. What's next, a communication from my toaster oven? Then it hits me: *Stars and Stripes*, the military newspaper that was a big deal during World War II.

I turn on the computer, see that the *Stars and Stripes* archives are online. And I find what I'm looking for. First there are a few articles that mention USO performances and a "chanteuse" named Kay Devereaux. Then comes this item from February 1946, datelined Berlin:

> We bid adieu to the divine Kay Devereaux, who just got hitched to Air Force Lieutenant Richard Cochran. Lovely Kay not only serenaded the troops throughout the war, she stayed on and bolstered the morale of the occupation forces. Alas, she's leaving us to return with her husband to his ranch in Cody, Wyoming.

In a fever, I look up Richard Cochran in Cody. Nothing. I can ask Josh to dig some more. But a ranch in Wyoming? Barbara thrived on nightlife and excitement. Yes, she loved Tom Mix movies, but that hardly meant she wanted to ride the range.

I get out the decades-old photo from the Colorado Springs newspaper and the magnifying glass (which I eventually located in a kitchen drawer). But the glass doesn't help; what I need is something that would let me pin back the platinum hair that half obscures Kay Devereaux's face.

Still, my own sister. Shouldn't I *know?*

CHAPTER 15

GOLDEN DOOR

"ELAINE! ELAINE, COME HERE!"

The urgency in Mama's voice sent me flying into the kitchen. She was gripping a piece of paper, her eyes wide and hands trembling.

"What is it, Mama? What's wrong?"

She handed me the paper. It was a telegram . . . oh my God, it was a telegram from the Hebrew Immigration Society. Ivan had been approved to immigrate! And we needed to wire his boat fare.

"Oh, Mama!"

Mama sang out words I had only heard from religious people: *"Baruch Ha-Shem!"* which I knew meant "Praise God." She caught my hand, and we whooped and danced, weeping with joy, until she sank into a chair, flushed and panting.

Still breathless, she said, "I'll call your father and tell him to go to the bank and arrange for the money." She'd been setting aside a little money every month in an Ivan fund.

"How soon is he coming?" I asked.

"Well." Mama chewed her lip, the way she did calculating sums in her head at the market. "He'll want to leave right away. But he'll have to get to a port first and then to New York, I suppose. Then take a train. Still, he might get here as soon as next month." Suddenly, her face clouded. "Oy! Where are we going to put him?"

I had to leave for work—school had let out a week earlier, and I was on my summer schedule at the bookstore. That evening, over a celebration dinner, I heard the plan Mama had come up with to accommodate Ivan.

"Barbara and Elaine," she said, "you'll move in with your sisters"—Barbara and I both let out yelps of indignation—"and Ivan will have your room."

"Four of us in one room?" I groaned. "That's impossible."

"Do you know how many of us slept in one *bed* when I was a girl?" Mama said.

"Can't he sleep on the sofa?" Barbara said.

"The sofa!" Mama slammed her hand on the table. "Do you have any idea what your cousin has been through? What is wrong with you girls, begrudging him a bed? And look at you, barely touching this pot roast. A person would think you weren't happy!" She took a bite of pot roast, her glare compelling me to do the same.

Papa stayed out of the discussion, but it turned out he wasn't deaf to our pleas. The next morning, he proposed another idea: Audrey would join Barbara and me in our bedroom off the kitchen, and Ivan could share a room with Harriet. She was just five, after all, barely more than a baby.

Ivan arrived three weeks later, on a Wednesday in mid-July. All of us went to the Santa Fe Station (magnificent Union Station wouldn't open until the next year) to meet his train. Harriet was so thrilled about her new roommate, she couldn't stop bouncing on the platform. I envied her unambiguous delight. My genuine gladness was nonetheless tinged by resentment over all the changes that had occurred a few days earlier: I'd had to jam my clothes into a single dresser drawer to make space for Audrey, and a looming bunk bed had displaced the sweet little cot (as I now saw it) in which I'd slept ever since I shared the room with Mollie. Priding myself on being grown-up, I uncomplainingly took the lower bunk when Audrey demanded the top, but then I had to switch with her four times because she kept changing her mind. And there was nonstop bickering as Audrey,

Barbara, and I blundered through the awkward choreography of making room for one another to dress, lay hands on our possessions . . . and *breathe*.

Still, I joined Harriet in jumping up and down when Ivan stepped off the train. *Yes, it's him!* He resembled the boy in the photo we'd been sent, and his head jerked up when Mama called his name. Mama ran toward him. I started to follow, but Barbara plucked at my sleeve.

"Look at those clothes! And he's dirty," she whispered.

"He's been traveling for days. Weeks," I said, touched by the small, frightened-looking boy enveloped in Mama's embrace. Ivan was supposed to be nineteen, but he was short and scrawny—and undeniably foreign with his too-big, formal suit and heavily brilliantined hair.

Mama pointed us out, and he smiled.

"Ugh, he's got pointy teeth," Barbara muttered. "He looks like a rat."

"Barbara, cut it out!" I said, and hurried to embrace our cousin.

If I had seen Ivan as boyish and frightened, however, I reconsidered when he met my eyes with a sharp gaze. And I knew enough Yiddish to understand him when we emerged from the train station and walked toward the Yellow Car stop, and he asked, "Where is your automobile?"

"Oh, we don't need an automobile," Mama said. "In Los Angeles, the streetcar and the bus go everywhere."

"All Americans have automobiles." His alert dark eyes shifted from side to side, as if he suspected us of hiding a Buick someplace.

He was clearly dismayed, too, by the smallness of our house and by having to share a bedroom with Harriet. Still, he smiled when Harriet chattered away at him; he had a sister just her age, he said in a mix of Yiddish and a little halting English. And no wonder he acted wary, after all he'd been through. At dinner, Mama loaded his plate with brisket, noodle kugel, and vegetables, and plied him with questions about the family. Ivan's father, a typesetter, had lost his job when the government closed down the Jewish-owned newspapers. The family moved to a smaller apartment, and his father eked out a living from jobs he got here and there, but the strain ruined his health; he suffered severe headaches, and on some days he couldn't get out of bed. Ivan, who'd been a promising student of mathematics, had had to leave school and help support the family. Even so, his parents had insisted he go to America when he had the opportunity.

It was too dangerous to stay in Romania, where Ivan had even been beaten by Iron Guard thugs.

"Those animals!" Mama cried. "Did they hurt you?"

"Just my wrist." He held up his left arm. His wrist was slightly crooked; it must have healed badly after being broken.

Tears came to my eyes, and Mama couldn't bear it—she ran from the table sobbing.

"I'm sorry to upset her," Ivan said. "For us . . . Such things happened to everyone, you know, many boys my age."

"Enough of the Old World," Papa said. "You're in America now. It's time to look ahead." He announced magnanimously that Ivan should take the rest of the week to settle in; he didn't have to start his job at Aunt Pearl's factory until the following Monday.

"I don't understand," Ivan said.

Papa repeated what he'd said, speaking slowly—assuming, I suppose, that Ivan hadn't followed his Yiddish with its Ukrainian and American inflections.

"But I don't really have to work there, do I?" Ivan said. "A *dress factory?*"

"My sister's factory," Papa said. "She was kind enough to—"

"I can't sew!"

"You said in your application—"

"One says whatever the authorities want to hear." Ivan's mouth twisted in a half laugh, humorless and world-weary. An expression that said he found us impossibly naive.

"Well," Papa said, "I'm sure my sister will find something for you to do. And you'll take night classes, learn English. No reason you can't look for another job then."

Later I translated the conversation for Barbara, who hadn't taken Mr. Berlov's Yiddish classes with me.

"He's a rat, you'll see," she said.

Barbara loathed Ivan's *heh-heh* laugh and darting eyes and the way Mama catered to him. And she chafed at Mama's and Papa's insistence that we take our cousin, who was glaringly foreign even in the American clothes Mama bought him, with us to social events.

"How can you be so mean?" I scolded her.

"Elaine, you don't like him, either. You just won't admit it."

I wish I could have said that Ivan was a gentle soul whom I defended naturally, out of true affection. Certainly there were times when my heart melted toward him, like the night Mama cooked a Jewish-Romanian stew, and at the first mouthful he sighed and looked as vulnerable as a child; or when he hoisted Harriet on his shoulders, as he must have done with his own baby sister. And maybe if I had grown up with a brother, I wouldn't have minded that he—and Mama—took it for granted that his new sisters would make his bed and clean up the mess he left in the bathroom after he shaved. But there *was* something sneaky about Ivan. Aunt Pearl, for instance, hadn't cared that he wasn't the skilled tailor she'd been promised; there was plenty of lifting, carrying, and cleaning he could help with. But she had to ask Papa to speak to him because if she didn't keep an eye on him, he handled dresses with filthy hands or crammed bolts of fabric onto shelves instead of folding them neatly. She'd caught him playing solitaire when he was supposed to be working and even smoking cigarettes he'd taken from her desk. And when I saw him displaying his crooked wrist to a girl at a party, I remembered a letter Mama had received five or six years earlier—hadn't Ivan broken his wrist playing soccer?

Even if he'd made up the story about being beaten by the Iron Guards, though, did that blot out the essential truth that he had suffered in Romania? And he had to be miserable now, a boy only two years older than I torn from his family, a top student forced to work at a menial job, someone who spoke three languages—Yiddish, Romanian, and French—constantly feeling stupid because he didn't know English. I tried to befriend him, but my Yiddish proved inadequate for anything beyond a stilted conversation. And it wasn't Ivan's fault, but his presence made our family dinners tense and constrained. Mama often spoke Yiddish to him privately, but Papa decreed that we use English at the table to augment the classes Ivan had started attending two nights a week. Our dinner conversations often sounded like classroom drills, and there were awkward patches when no one spoke, and I heard myself chewing every mouthful. Only Harriet, who seemed impervious to the rest of the family's moods, gaily prattled to Ivan, not caring if he understood her, and he regarded her with real warmth.

Other than Harriet, the one person with whom my cousin seemed at ease was Danny. Danny had been so eager to meet our real-life victim of European anti-Semitism that he came by the day after Ivan arrived, embracing him and greeting him with a flood of Yiddish (Danny's first language, which he and his father still spoke at home). Of course, he invited Ivan to speak at Habonim, with Danny translating. But he didn't just use Ivan to promote the cause. A real friendship developed between them. Speaking to Danny in Yiddish, Ivan actually laughed, not the tepid *heh-heh* that drove Barbara nuts but a big, relaxed laugh that made me wonder how he might act if he weren't burdened by being the recipient of our charity.

Years later, when I would see Ivan in Las Vegas, getting by, I assumed, on small-scale finagling, I'd think of the life he might have had. I'd wonder if he could have been a mathematician or a business whiz, if his life could ever have been as big as that laugh. And I would promise myself I'd go to see him more often. (He rarely came to visit us in L.A., he claimed he had too much business to attend to.) But I didn't. I knew that the qualities in Ivan that made Barbara's skin crawl—and which, I admit, I found distasteful—were survival skills that came from his being born in a rotten place at a horrific time. Still, by the time he was living with us, he seemed furtive and calculating as if by nature. When Barbara called him "the Rat," I felt, guiltily, that the name was apt.

"The Rat" was how Barbara continued to refer to Ivan, in spite—actually, because—of Danny's liking for him. She fumed that she couldn't go to a party anymore without Danny wanting to spend half the night yammering with her creepy cousin. And if she finally got Danny to dance with her, then Ivan mortified her by asking some girl to dance—if you could call his odd shamble *dancing*—and sometimes misinterpreting the girl's ordinary American friendliness and putting such a mash on her that she had to shove him away.

Danny pleaded Ivan's case. And he got furious one time when Barbara was supposed to bring Ivan with her to a movie but she came to the theater alone, saying that Ivan had stayed home with a headache; and then he found out she'd crept out the back door to avoid Ivan.

I got the feeling Barbara and Danny were arguing a lot. She came home early from several of their dates, tight-lipped and cross. And she spent even more time than before at the Hollywood dance studio.

Barbara did her best to keep her life at the dance studio separate from Boyle Heights. She never invited dance-school friends to our house, and when she went to their parties, she didn't ask Danny to come as her date. But her two worlds inevitably collided when she performed. That September, a few weeks after we entered our senior year of high school, she danced at the studio in a program of solos by advanced students. Our whole family went; Mama, Papa, Audrey, and Harriet piled into Pearl's Plymouth, while I went with Ivan and, of course, Danny by streetcar.

Barbara's dance was electrifying. To a soft tropical drumbeat (her one-time boyfriend Oscar played congas), she prowled the stage with a lazy, sensual stalk that nonetheless carried a sense of danger; she made me think of a panther leisurely closing in on its prey. The drumbeat built, and she pivoted sharply and sprang, arms and legs slashing—I could almost see claws. When she finished, I clapped so hard my hands stung.

Afterward, there was a reception with punch and cookies. Standing in a cluster of her dance friends, Barbara was flushed with the afterglow of performing. She shot a dazzling smile toward us—Danny, Ivan, and me—when we approached her. The smile must have given Ivan courage, because he went up and kissed her on the cheek.

"Beautiful! Beautiful!" he said in accented but clear English.

"Oh. Thanks," she murmured, then quickly turned away.

"Who's that, Babs?" one of her fellow students asked.

"Um, just . . . Aren't you just perishing of thirst? Let's get some punch."

"It's her cousin," Danny said loudly. "He's a Jewish refugee from Romania."

"Really?" The girl turned toward Ivan, clearly fascinated. "Would you like some punch?" she said, making a gesture of drinking.

"Sure. Okay."

She took Ivan's hand and led him toward the table. The other girls followed, vying for Ivan's attention.

That left Barbara and Danny—and me—in a tight little eddy in one corner of the room, the reception noisily swirling around us.

"Happy?" she said to Danny. Her low voice carried an aura of threat that made me think of her slinking across the stage, getting ready to pounce.

"*What* is your problem?" he said.

"Never do that to me again."

"Do what? Remind you that you're Jewish? Or expect you to act like a human being?"

I knew I should leave them alone, but I couldn't move.

"Don't you make yourself sick, being so self-righteous?" Barbara snapped.

"Don't *you* notice anything beyond your own selfish little world?"

"Selfish? Why, because the people I know care about art, instead of going on and on about how everyone hates the Jews? If the world stopped hating the Jews, would they have anything left to talk about?"

"*They?*" Danny echoed, staring at her with horror. "*They?* When are you going to get it through your vain head that it's not just your cousin Ivan that people hate? It's *you*."

"Ivan's repulsive. If the Jews in Europe are like him, no wonder people hate them."

Danny's hand flew up, and I was scared he was going to hit her. But he just gestured toward her chest. "What's in there? Do you even have a heart?"

Then he walked away.

"Well." Barbara glanced at me and gave a tight little laugh.

"Barbara, are you all right?"

"Dammit, would you stop looking at me like I just said 'Heil Hitler'?"

"I know you didn't mean it." Surely she had only wanted to hurt him. She couldn't have meant the hateful things she'd said.

She sighed. "You don't get it. I'm not good like you and Danny. Come on, let's get some punch."

"You're right, Danny is self-righteous," I said as I followed her to the refreshments table.

"Don't you see, the kind of girl Danny wants me to be, I'm never going to be like that. It would kill me." She gave me a smile I couldn't read. Mocking? Despairing? "You can have him," she said.

"I don't *want* him!" But I protested to the air. Barbara had plunged into the crowd around the punch bowl.

Didn't she know that I had long ago outgrown my childhood infatuation with Danny? I wished I could make her understand, but if I brought up the infatuation, I risked exposing too much.

And there was no chance to talk to her about anything. In the days after her fight with Danny, she made herself as inaccessible as Greta Garbo in *Grand Hotel*—"I want to be alone!" At home, she laughed too much, with brittle gaiety, and seemed to live on nothing but heavily sugared tea. "Dieting," she said when Mama noticed how little she was eating. And in our room at night, where we often whispered after Audrey had fallen asleep, she got into bed, turned to the wall, and closed her eyes while Audrey was still putting on her nightgown.

At school, she and Danny maintained an icy distance. If they happened to cross paths, their faces hardened, and they made a great show of turning away. And Danny extended his avoidance of Barbara to me. Anytime I approached him, he was rushing off on crucial Habonim business, self-important and swaggering—his grief and wounded pride so jagged, I was amazed people didn't scatter as he walked by, to avoid being raked.

Our classmates buzzed about the mysterious rupture between one of our golden couples. Apparently neither Barbara nor Danny confided in anyone, because even their close friends quizzed me about what had happened. I said nothing about the argument, and I agreed with everyone that the passion of their rift was so intense, it would surely lead to a passionate reconciliation. I didn't even tell the Plain Brains—with whom I could cast a bemused eye at the *Romeo and Juliet* playing out at Roosevelt High School—what I really felt.

Barbara and Danny were both deeply upset, I had no doubt of that. But I sensed that something irrevocable had changed between them. *Do you have a heart?*—Danny hadn't just asked, he had accused her. At first I wondered with horror if he could be right. And in that case, had Barbara ever loved him? Was my sister capable of loving anyone? Then one night about a week after their fight, Mama came into our room when we were getting ready for bed. In a whisper—Audrey was asleep in the top bunk—Mama asked Barbara if something had happened between her and Danny.

"We split up," Barbara said coolly.

"Oh, *mein kind*." Mama came close and put a hand on Barbara's cheek. "You and Danny, you've been sweet on each other since you were kids."

"Puppy love," Barbara said, but there was a catch in her voice.

"What happened?" Mama said in the caressing voice she used when we'd fallen and gotten hurt.

"Nothing."

Crooning, Mama reached out and stroked Barbara's hair. For a moment Barbara leaned toward her, as if she were going to melt into Mama's arms and dissolve in sobs. Then she shook off Mama's comforting hand.

"Nothing happened," she said harshly.

Rebuffed, Mama flipped from tenderness to suspicion. She reached toward Barbara's stomach. "You're not pregnant, are you?"

"Mama!" Barbara jumped away. "There's no way I could be pregnant."

"You and Danny, you never—"

"You don't believe me?" Barbara yanked up her slip and exposed her flat, dance-toned stomach.

"For shame!" Mama slapped Barbara's face so hard that she staggered. *"A shandeh un a charpeh,"* she muttered as she stormed out of our room. *A shame and a disgrace.*

Barbara let her slip fall and stood trembling. I put my arm around her.

"That was horrible of her," I said. "Are you all right?"

"I really got to her, didn't I?" She let out a snort of laughter—a jagged sound, painful to hear. "D'you want to smoke?"

I glanced toward Audrey, who was lying so still that I was sure she was feigning sleep. We threw on robes, went out to the back porch, and lit cigarettes.

"Are you really all right?" I said. "About Danny?"

She blew a smoke ring. "He and I should have broken up ages ago. I guess neither of us had the guts to be the first to say it. Now that it's happened, tell you the truth, I'm relieved."

I had just seen her trembling, though, a hurt child ready to weep in her mother's embrace. I think she *did* love Danny and was devastated at losing him. But what had she told me moments after their fight? That trying to be the girl Danny wanted would kill her. I'd heard her statement as hyperbole, a response to the drama of the moment. Now I began to feel she had hit on a profound truth. I had seen Barbara as the one in control, dangling Danny on a string all the while she didn't even fake an interest in Zionism and made no effort to include him in her life in Hollywood. Now it struck me that one reason Danny had persisted in dangling was that he simply refused to see her for who she was. To fulfill whatever fantasy he'd spun about her, she would have to extinguish something in herself. And along with her genuine misery, I sensed a visceral joy, the ecstasy of an animal tearing full tilt toward the woods after escaping a trap.

The next week, Barbara started eating again. And the dramatic cold shoulder she'd been giving Danny lost conviction and became a weary shrug. The steam went out of his response to her as well. Soon he started asking out some of the girls who'd always buzzed around him. And Barbara stopped splitting her social life between Boyle Heights and Hollywood and spent most Friday and Saturday evenings with her Hollywood friends.

The other person whose life changed in the wake of Barbara and Danny's breakup was Ivan. I don't know if he had any idea of his role as a subject of their argument, but he stayed out of Barbara's way afterward and pretty much avoided me, too. He even stopped seeing as much of Danny. Ivan was making his own friends, guys he'd met in his English class, he said. He went out with them several nights a week and always came in late—Pearl complained that he barely kept his eyes open at work. I got up to use the toilet one night at two in the morning and found him passed out on the sofa, stinking of booze and cigarettes. I prodded him awake, not wanting Mama or Papa to find him like that in the morning. The moment he was half conscious, his hand flew to his pocket, and bills spilled out, not just ones but some fives and tens.

"Ivan, what is that?" I said as he grabbed at the money and stuffed it back into his pocket.

"None of your business." That particular English phrase, he'd learned to speak with scarcely any accent.

"I'm not going to tell on you. It's just you might not know what's legal in America and what isn't. Where did you get that money?"

"Casino."

"Are *you* gambling?" How could he have turned his meager wages into so much money?

He shook his head. "I am good at mathematics. I help. You not tell?"

"I—"

He grabbed my hand and squeezed hard. "You don't tell."

"All right." As long as he was telling the truth about the casino—and somehow I believed him—then he wasn't engaged in some major criminal activity. And between Zayde's bookmaking and Mama's prowess at cards, gambling was practically a family business.

This happened in mid-October. A week later, Ivan quit working for Aunt Pearl and moved out of our house. He'd gotten a job on a gambling boat, one that was fitted up as a nightclub and anchored off Long Beach just past U.S. territorial waters, and a coworker offered him a room in an apartment in San Pedro. Mama fretted that she hadn't made her nephew feel at home, and what would her brothers and sisters say? On the other hand, wasn't the point of sponsoring Ivan that he should become able to make his own way, and who would have believed it would happen so quickly? That was America! Mama made him promise to come for every holiday, and he departed with kisses all around—even one from Barbara, who was thrilled to get rid of him and regain our two-sister bedroom, a sentiment I shared.

BY NOVEMBER, EVERYTHING HAD settled down, except that Danny still avoided me.

Herschel Grynszpan changed that.

Herschel Grynszpan was exactly my age, seventeen. If his parents had moved to Los Angeles when they left their native Poland, he might have gone to Roosevelt High with me. Instead, his family settled in Hanover, Germany, and when conditions there got bad, they sent him to live with relatives in Paris. In late October, the Germans expelled his family, along with seventeen thousand other Polish-born Jews. But the Poles refused to admit them, and they were stranded in a village on the border.

On November 7, 1938, Herschel bought a gun, went to the German embassy in Paris, and shot and wounded a Nazi official. Two days later, the official died. And the Germans took revenge. Unlike the scratchy, brutal word *Reich*, *Kristallnacht* sounded like something out of a fairy tale. *Kristallnacht* shimmered; it carried the hush of snow mounded on pine boughs that I'd seen in movies. *Kristallnacht* did shimmer, I suppose, the "night of broken glass" hurling glittering shards all over Germany and Austria as vandals attacked more than two hundred synagogues and thousands of Jewish shops.

In Boyle Heights, dozens of organizations joined forces and planned a rally to take place that Sunday. I heard that Danny was asked to speak at the rally as a representative of the youth groups, and two days later— I suppose after wrestling with the task on his own—he asked me to help write his speech. Of course I said yes; this was far more important than any petty hurt I felt because he'd barely spoken to me for weeks.

On Friday, we met after school in Eddie Chafkin's small office in the rear of the store; files for Eddie's and Danny's Zionist activities occupied a quarter of the pristinely organized shelves. Both of us were so upset about *Kristallnacht* that there was no constraint between us, no sign of the months-long break in our friendship. We quickly fell back into our usual wrangling over words and ideas. Danny, fists clenched as if he couldn't wait to pick up a gun himself, called Herschel Grynszpan a hero. I admired Herschel's bravery; still, he was an assassin. And since Danny would be speaking in a public forum, I wanted him to speak for the rule of law.

"What rule of law, when the laws are made by Nazis?" he demanded.

"Herschel took a life."

"What if he'd assassinated Hitler? Would you be against that?"

"Don't you think your speech should be about what the Germans did on *Kristallnacht*? And the need to help people emigrate?"

We fought for half an hour, forcing ourselves to a consensus only because Danny couldn't stay away from work any longer.

A week later, we returned to Eddie's office because Germany had retaliated further, banning all Jewish students from German schools, and we wanted to write a letter to the Los Angeles newspapers. But the urgency immediately following *Kristallnacht* had passed; this time it felt as if we were meeting for the first time since I'd witnessed his argument with

Barbara, and we were ill at ease. We drafted the letter with little of our usual bickering. In fifteen minutes, Danny stood up to return to work.

"Thanks, Elaine," he said.

"Sure." I turned to Eddie's typewriter and rolled in a sheet of Habonim letterhead.

Danny cleared his throat. "Really, thank you. I don't always say . . . that is, I hope you know how much I appreciate . . ."

This was a Danny I hadn't seen before, bashful and tongue-tied.

"I'm happy to do it. Not *happy*, that's not the right word," I said, afflicted with my own self-consciousness. "But this is important."

"See, that's what I mean. You're a . . . a good person." He started out the door, but turned back.

"What?"

"Well, I guess . . ." His eyes flicking away from mine, he blurted out, "I wanted to say, I realized that for me to really care about a girl, she has to be a person I respect."

He dashed out of the room.

If Danny was trying to say he cared about *me*, he was too late, I thought as I attacked the typewriter keys. He'd had his chance, and he'd put me through the humiliation of being his girl on the side. But what did it matter what Danny wanted? Even if I'd once been in love with him, I'd been a kid then. To echo Barbara, it was nothing but puppy love.

Damn! I'd shifted my left hand one key over and mistyped an entire line. I ripped out the paper and started fresh. When I finished the letters—to the *Los Angeles Times*, the *Herald*, and the *Herald-Express*, as well as the Boyle Heights newspaper—I left them on the desk and hurried through the store, hoping Danny would be busy with a customer and I could just wave goodbye.

But he was stocking shelves, and he called out, "Wait!"

"I've got to get home," I said.

"Have you seen *The Lady Vanishes*?"

"The Hitchcock movie?"

"Want to go on Friday?"

"I . . ." I went mute, aware of Eddie Chafkin, who wasn't even pretending not to eavesdrop.

"Friday, then? Good."

What an idiot I was! I'd seen *The Lady Vanishes* two weeks ago when it first came out—I could have just said that. But the Berlovs didn't have a phone, so I couldn't call Danny that night and set things straight. I'd tell him the next day at school.

In bed that night, I kept going hot and then cold, pushing off my blankets and a minute later piling them back on. *For me to really care about a girl, she has to be a person I respect.* Wasn't it what I used to dream, that Danny needed to get Barbara out of his system, but his truest connection was with me? *And look where that dream got me!* I thought, throwing off the covers. *Sneaking around in Chafkin's storeroom.* This wasn't sneaking, though. He'd asked me on a real date. Shivering, I grabbed for the blankets again.

In the morning, I ached all over and lurched to the breakfast table. I must have looked awful, because even Harriet asked if I was sick. Mama placed her blissfully cool hands on my face and ordered me back to bed. She even called the doctor.

I'd caught an influenza that was going around, the doctor said when he came by that afternoon. This flu wasn't severe, he assured Mama. Still, just the word *influenza*, to someone who'd lived through the 1918 epidemic, struck terror. Mama muttered *kaynehora* against the evil eye that had spotted a foolish girl who called too much attention to herself by getting so many A's in school, and she prayed that the forces of darkness wouldn't notice her other daughters. She moved Barbara out of our room onto the sofa and banished everyone, even Papa, from visiting me.

Only Mama entered my sickroom—Mama at her most tender, bearing chicken broth and hot milk with honey; propping me up, her arm around my shoulders, and coaxing me to sip. She gave me sponge baths and Bayer aspirin for my fever and held me, crooning in Yiddish, when I shook with chills. Sick as I was, I basked in Mama's coddling and in the feverish lassitude that made me feel like a small animal, all my awareness telescoped into my body with no room to think about anything else.

I slept for most of two days. Then, around the time my fever broke, Audrey, Harriet, and Papa all got sick, and Mama had to take care of them.

Still weak but no longer consumed by illness, I longed for distraction. I was thrilled when Barbara snuck into the room.

"Look what I found." She held out a book.

It was a book of poetry by Muriel Rukeyser, a pristine brand-new copy like the ones I got to handle at Uncle Leo's bookstore but couldn't afford for myself.

"Barbara, thank you!"

"Oh, it's not from me. I found it by the front door." She smiled. "Guess he was afraid of running into me."

There was a note stuck between the pages. *Dear Elaine, When I said* The Lady Vanishes, *I didn't mean you! Get well soon. Lucy said you'd like this book. Sincerely, Danny.*

"Danny never gave *me* any books." Barbara's tone was teasing, but I searched her eyes for signs of hurt.

"Do you mind?"

"When do you ever see me sit still long enough to read anything?" She picked up a brush and coaxed it through my fever-matted hair. "Yecch, bet you can't wait to have a shampoo."

"That's not what I mean."

"Darling, I don't mind at all."

Her nonchalance might have concealed deep pain. Nevertheless, I heard condescension, the noblesse oblige of the naturally attractive toward those of us who have to work to be loved. *Just like Danny!* I thought, regarding his gift with loathing and for a full day refusing to touch it.

But my boredom became unbearable, and a new book was too tempting to resist. And reading poems about a West Virginia mining disaster, even if Danny had given them to me, didn't weaken my determination to resist *him.*

When I returned to school after two weeks of convalescence, he asked me to the big New Year's Eve party, a youth dance at the Workmen's Circle hall. I should have made it clear then that I didn't want to date him, but I was still shaky from being sick; that was the excuse I gave myself. Instead, I hedged and said I didn't know if I'd be feeling well enough by New Year's Eve to go out. I hoped another boy would invite me to the party—you didn't have to have a date to attend, but who wanted to walk into a New Year's Eve dance with her girlfriends? No one else asked me, though, and I decided to stay home.

Ah, but then New Year's Eve arrived, and everyone was going out. Barbara had a party in Hollywood, although she told Mama and Papa she was going to the Workmen's Circle dance. The rest of the family was spending the evening at Sonya and Leo's. I'd die before I tagged along to the family party, the gawky daughter who at seventeen didn't have big plans of her own. But why did I have to spend New Year's Eve by myself just to avoid Danny?

And how could I pass up the chance to wear my first evening gown, a Hanukkah gift from Pearl made out of coppery brown silk? The gown had a bias-cut bodice, a nipped-in waist, and a skirt that draped snugly over my hips. When Pearl was fitting the dress, I worried that it was too sophisticated for me. She said a girl who was almost eighteen deserved a grownup dress and that the color would pick up the gold flecks in my hazel eyes. And it did!

I went to meet Lucy and Jane at Jane's house. Our fourth Plain Brain, Ann, had a boyfriend—Bill Adelman, the class math whiz—and she was going to the party with him. We fussed with one another's hair and makeup, spritzed on Jane's mother's Chanel No. 5, and passed around a bottle of Scotch that Lucy had gotten from her older brother. It was cheap Scotch, raw in my throat, but the buzz—and the swish of my copper silk dress against my thighs—made me feel daring and adult as we walked to the dance.

In the cloakroom, Lucy and I took off our glasses and slipped them into our bags; Jane promised to watch out in case either of us started to stumble into a punch bowl.

I walked into the hall, dazzled for a moment by the noise of the band and the hubbub of people, all of them fuzzy to my nearsighted eyes. Instantly, as if he had been watching for me, Danny was at my side.

"You made it! You look . . ." He took a step back and really looked at me. "Wow! You look beautiful."

He held out his hand and led me onto the dance floor.

I had danced with Danny before, at parties where everyone partnered everyone else. But this time, on the final night of 1938 . . . it wasn't just that he held me closer. Dancing together that evening felt more intimate than our long-ago necking sessions, as if some psychic distance had melted between us. When a song ended, he kept his arms around me and whispered things into my hair. "Elaine, you're so beautiful. . . . What a fool I've been." He ran his hand down my back, the glide of silk and the warmth of his palm becoming a single delicious sensation, as if he were caressing my bare skin.

I didn't let him take possession of me for the evening. Not at first. I'd have a dance or two with Danny, then return to a cluster of girls, making ourselves available to the stag line. But as he kept asking me to dance, as we talked between dances with our faces nearly touching—and at midnight, when he gave me a long kiss in front of everyone—I didn't feel like second best. I felt like the one he had always been waiting for.

CHAPTER 16

BASHERT

"NOT DANNY BERLOV AGAIN!" MAMA MOANED WHEN DANNY RESUMED coming by the house, this time for me.

"What's the matter with Danny?" I said.

"With a father who never has two dimes to rub together, and the son's a *meshuganah* dreamer who wants to go farm in Palestine—what's he going to make of himself?"

"You never said that when Barbara was going with him."

"I never worried that Barbara was going to marry him. But you . . . you'd go to the ends of the earth for that boy."

"Well, I'm not going to go farm in Palestine!" I retorted, annoyed by her pitying look—and because she understood Barbara so well, but she was so wrong about me. How could she look at me and still see the timid little girl who used to follow her sister's lead? Had she really not noticed what a determined young woman I'd become?

I felt a similar frustration when I was "talked to" by Aunt Pearl, who warned me about the pain I might be inflicting on Barbara and the danger that Danny was dating me because I was Barbara's sister. Didn't she see that Danny had chosen me for myself? Didn't anyone see *me?*

Actually, one person in my family acted delighted for me—Barbara. I had screwed up my courage on New Year's Day and told her that Danny and I had spent much of the previous night's dance together; I wanted her to hear it from me rather than through the school gossip mill. "Lainie, I always knew," she said, and gave me a hug. My nerve went only so far. I didn't ask *what* she'd always known; I didn't want to find out if she was aware of our clandestine meetings . . . which would remain in my mind as the lousiest thing I ever did. In the 1970s, I occasionally found myself at a party where someone would insist on playing a pop psychology game. One question was invariably "What is your deepest secret?" Those trysts with my sister's boyfriend always leaped to mind, and I never mentioned them.

But whatever she knew or didn't, Barbara quickly adjusted to the new state of affairs. And so did Danny. One evening in February, she happened to be at home when he came to pick me up for a movie. The two of them chatted casually, with no hint of still-wounded feelings between them.

As for the rest of our world, once people got over the surprise that Danny was dating "the other Greenstein twin," everyone agreed there was a rightness to Danny and me, as if we'd been destined for each other—*bashert.* The intellectual intensity that already existed between us, our passionate engagement with ideas, ignited now that we were going together. Collaborating on articles and letters to newspapers, we debated more heatedly than ever. And with our high school graduation coming up in June, we had fervent arguments about what we planned to do with our lives. Danny and I had radically different ideas about our futures because we had radically different visions of the world and our place in it.

For me, college was the pot of gold at the end of the rainbow, the prize that had dangled in front of me for years. At last I was actually filling out applications to UCLA and USC . . . and even beginning to look beyond college and consider what I wanted to do with a college degree. Mollie had said I could be a lawyer, and in her letters, she kept telling me that I was "born with a legal mind." Well, why not? I dreamed of going to law school and fighting for working people in the courts. I broached the idea to Papa, but he frowned and said it was one thing for a family to invest in a son entering a profession like medicine or the law, but teaching was a fine, respectable job for an educated young woman. The ideas Mollie put in my head! Even my favorite teacher, Miss Linscott, said, "For a Boyle Heights girl to go into teaching, that's something to be very proud of."

Danny, however, was all for my becoming a lawyer—and, in a larger sense, doing something that mattered. His quarrel with my ambitions, like mine with his, came back to our debates about Zionism. All of my visions of the future took place in America: I couldn't imagine being a lawyer anywhere else, couldn't imagine living anywhere else. Danny burned to go to Palestine and fight for a Jewish state; he simply burned to fight, so much so that he saw no point in making any plans for a life in Los Angeles.

"Don't you want to take Eddie up on his offer?" I asked him. Eddie Chafkin had proposed that if Danny studied business at Los Angeles City College, Eddie would arrange his work hours to accommodate the class schedule; on top of that, he'd give Danny management responsibilities and raise his salary. "He'll *pay* you to go to school."

"So I can be a shopkeeper?" Danny paced in front of the bench where I sat in Hollenbeck Park. His need for action was visceral, like the need with which his hands pushed under my clothes when we were alone.

"So you can learn how to run a business. Don't you think Palestine needs people who know how to run things? At least fill out the application for City College."

"What's the point? There's going to be a war."

"You sound like you *want* a war."

"I want someone to stand up to Hitler."

"But you heard what he said—*Vernichtung*." The hideous word meant "extermination." Hitler had announced in January that if war broke out, *Vernichtung* would be the fate of all the Jews in Europe.

"Don't you think he's going to do that anyway?"

Of course I didn't think that. What sane mind, in 1939, could have *imagined* the machine-like design and screaming evil of the Nazis' *Vernichtung*?

"Wise up, Elaine," Danny said. "The rest of the world doesn't give a rat's ass what Hitler does to the Jews. How much more of Europe do you think they'll let him take?"

This was in March, and Germany had just occupied the whole of Czechoslovakia, expanding beyond the Sudetenland region that France and England had signed away the previous fall.

As the spring progressed and our class moved closer to graduation, growing talk of war magnified the restlessness everyone felt as we perched on the edge of our lives beyond high school. Good news, such as college acceptances—including mine to USC, with a full scholarship—or someone landing a job, provoked a frantic gaiety. Especially when it involved the boys' future plans.

At our graduation in June, I looked at my male classmates in their caps and gowns and couldn't help picturing them, even the smallest and gentlest boys, wearing uniforms and carrying guns.

But not yet. First we all had to go to work.

For me, work simply meant more of what I'd done since I was twelve: helping at Uncle Leo's bookstore. I still had to unpack and shelve books and run to the drugstore for Leo's bromo, as I'd done from the beginning. I was no longer the only schlepper, however; Leo had given his son, Stan, who was now fifteen, a part-time summer job so he could learn the business "from the ground up." And over the years Leo had come to trust me to wait on customers, search for rare books, and place orders. I had a pleasant voice—the "radio voice" for which both Barbara and I were praised—and I handled routine telephone contacts. The one difference, now that I had a high school diploma, was that Leo gave me a ten-cents-an-hour raise.

Graduation led to big changes, however, in Danny's and Barbara's lives.

A week after we graduated, Danny quit working at Chafkin's. He'd found a job that paid much better and fed, at least a little, his hunger to fight Hitler, at a factory in Long Beach that built ships for the United States Navy—ships on which he hoped to fight as soon as America got into the war. It was the kind of place that didn't hire a lot of Jews, but the job required lifting and carrying, and Danny said the boss was a good guy who didn't care what kind of name Berlov was; he just looked at Danny's strong shoulders and back and hired him. Not everyone at the shipyard was so tolerant. Once a week, it seemed, Danny got into a fight with a coworker over some anti-Semitic remark. The first time I saw his face after a fight, I kissed every bruise. But I came to suspect that he looked for fights—broadcasting that he was Jewish, taking offense at the needling we'd all learned to ignore, and then hanging around after work where he'd be sure to run into the offender.

"You want me to be a good little Jewish boy?" he said when I questioned him.

"A lot of these people aren't evil, they're just ignorant. They'll get used to seeing you every day, and if you joke with them sometimes—"

"Elaine, you work in a goddamn bookstore. You have no idea."

He was right that I didn't understand the rough male world of a shipyard. On the other hand, I had worked in Hollywood since I was twelve, and this was his first job outside Boyle Heights. But nothing I said changed the swagger that had come into his step, the sense that Danny was already at war.

Barbara, too, found work that paid well, though we were forbidden to tell anyone about it. Through a friend from her dance school, she landed a job singing and dancing in the chorus at the Trocadero on Sunset Strip. An elegant, classy club, it boasted a movie-star clientele, she emphasized when she broke the news to Mama and Papa.

"No, it's not respectable," Papa said.

"Papa, it's like in the pictures, Ginger Rogers." Barbara had brought him his evening whiskey and told Mama to relax on the sofa and let her finish cooking dinner. She had asked me to be there for moral support.

"Any girl can show her legs in a nightclub," Papa said. "A girl lucky enough to graduate from high school . . . You get an office job."

"There aren't any office jobs. Look!" She held out the page of last Sunday's *Los Angeles Times* with the "Help Wanted—Female" ads, a paltry two columns of listings. I had suggested she use the ads to bolster her argument, though I had my own misgivings about the Trocadero job. For one thing, she was underage, something Papa clearly didn't realize. She must have gotten a fake ID.

"What about this?" he said. " 'Receptionists, operators. Positions open now.' "

"It says they want people with experience."

"Here, this is made for you. 'Women who can talk clearly, desiring to become radio announcers.' "

"Papa, it's a school. They just want you to pay them to train you, but then where are the jobs? . . . At the Trocadero, they're very careful about the girls in the chorus. There's even a chaperone to make sure no one bothers us."

Papa shook his head. "A nightclub, it's not a place for a decent girl to work. Why don't you talk to your aunt Pearl? She might need someone to answer the phone. Or—"

"Is Aunt Pearl going to provide employment for every person in this family?"

Barbara had gone too far. Papa's face flushed and his jaw set.

"No daughter who lives under my roof is dancing at a nightclub," he said.

"Fine!" Barbara shot back.

I held my breath. Was she threatening to move out? If it wasn't respectable to dance at a nightclub, living on her own would be a scandal.

"You said there's a chaperone?" Mama broke in.

We all stared at her. She repeated her question.

"Yes, to make sure no one bothers us," Barbara said. "And they send you home in a taxi."

"They pay the fare?" Mama asked. "They don't take it out of your wages?"

Barbara nodded.

"Then here are the rules. You come straight home after work—Elaine, I expect you to tell me if she doesn't. You don't date any man you meet at this nightclub. You *never* take a drink there. Do you understand?"

"Yes!"

Papa cleared his throat. "Charlotte, what do you plan to tell people when they ask what our daughter is doing?"

Barbara had anticipated that question. "What if you say I'm a receptionist at a hospital and I have to work the evening shift?"

"I was on the stage once, you know. With the *fusgeyers* in Romania." Mama looked wistful. And I thought of the part of the story she hadn't told, the secret I'd heard from Mollie: that Mama had tried out for a Yiddish theater troupe in Los Angeles.

If Mama saw her own unfulfilled dreams in the nightclub job, that didn't mean she cut Barbara any slack. The first week Barbara worked at the Trocadero, Mama or Papa waited up for her every night, to make sure she came straight home and to see the taxi themselves. I knew the nightclub wasn't paying for the taxi. But Barbara told me the job paid so well that she could afford it.

Even after Mama and Papa relaxed their vigilance, she didn't push her luck. She returned home from the Trocadero as promptly and soberly as if she really did work at a hospital—well, as far as I knew, since I developed the ability to go on sleeping when she tiptoed into our room in the wee hours. As the summer went on, she and I almost never saw each other awake. When I quietly dressed in the morning, she sprawled unconscious in a tumble of sweat, stale cigarettes, and Shalimar cologne. I didn't smell alcohol, though. She may have had a drink or two, but there was nothing that hinted at wild parties after hours.

Our paths might have crossed between the time my job ended (when I had a day shift) and hers began, but she went out hours before she had to report at the club. She was taking dance or singing classes, she said, or making the rounds of film studios. She showed me the photos she'd had taken, glossy head shots, to leave at the studios. There were two different photos. In one, she projected a youthful wholesomeness "for ingenue roles." The other was a glamour shot with a teasing half smile that reminded me of Paulette Goddard. "Weren't those expensive?" I asked. She replied that a friend—whose name, Alan Yardley, was printed with an ornate stamp on the back of the photographs—had done them for almost nothing, as a favor. Certainly that wasn't impossible. Nor did it mean anything that she'd never before mentioned Alan Yardley; had I heard her talk about anyone she'd met at the Trocadero? Maybe it was only that we'd gone so abruptly from living in tandem for eighteen years to barely seeing each other that made me uneasy, that made me sense she had a secret life.

Not that I devoted much thought to Barbara. I was immersed in *my* life, scared and excited about entering USC in September, avidly following the news from Europe . . . and intoxicated by love. The thrill was sexual, of course. Things I had once said no to—when I was just fifteen, and when I was Danny's second choice—I craved now. His hands and lips on my breasts. His fingers slipping beneath the edge of my panties and inside me, the first time a man ever touched me there. And my hand in his trousers, until he groaned and twisted away. Touching and kissing were as far as we went. He carried a rubber in his wallet—all the boys did—and he sometimes asked wouldn't I, please? But he didn't pressure me. For one thing, we were in constant danger of being caught, whether we were outdoors in a park or on the sofa in my house with my parents sleeping across the hall. And for all our ardor, neither of us lost sight of what we wanted to do with our lives. If I got pregnant, it would ruin everything—for both of us, since Danny would do the right thing and marry me. Of course, we wanted to get married someday—we didn't discuss it, but it was understood—but first I had to go to college, and Danny had to make his way in the world. (Another thing we didn't discuss: I hoped that by the time we were ready for marriage, he'd have come to his senses and decided to live in America, not Palestine.)

The most exciting time, we didn't touch at all. We were in the living room late one night in July, necking on the sofa, and Danny sat back and said, "Let me look at you."

"All right," I said, lying in my disarray of opened blouse and unhooked brassiere. I wasn't wearing a slip; it was too hot.

"No, let me *see* you." Gently, he edged my blouse toward my shoulder.

I sat up. Moved to the end of the sofa. Took off my blouse but not my bra. Danny had seen my breasts, of course, pushing aside my clothes as we clung together, but this was different. My shoulders hunched forward protectively.

"Please?" he said.

I slipped off my bra. Glad that, a few feet away from him, I was too nearsighted to see his face clearly.

This was all he'd asked for, I knew. But a strange boldness seized me, and I walked into a pool of moonlight coming through the window. I stepped out of my skirt. My panties. I stood before Danny naked.

Neither of us spoke for a minute. Then he said, "Elaine Greenstein, I will always love you."

"Danny Berlov, I will always love you," I responded.

I returned to the sofa and put my skirt and blouse back on, though I didn't bother with underwear. But I reached for my glasses. "Your turn," I said.

"What?"

"I want to look at you."

"Your parents."

"You weren't worried about them when you asked me. Scared?" I dared him. Though I held my breath for a moment, alert for any stirring from my sleeping family.

He walked into the patch of light and shed his clothes. I had stroked him to climax, but always with my hand in his trousers, and I stared first, greedily, at the mystery of his penis—which dangled limply, because he was nervous. What excited me most, I discovered, was what I already knew, the body so familiar to me from beach outings that I could have sketched it from memory: the torso and limbs sculpted by weight lifting and toughened by his job. The firm jaw and spill of black hair over one eye.

Naked in the moonlight, Danny was so beautiful that tears filled my eyes.

I waited until he scrambled back into his clothes, then went over and kissed him lightly. He pressed against me, but I said no. The moment was so perfect, I wanted to preserve it forever.

I am my beloved's, and my beloved is mine, I read in "Song of Songs," one of the poems I devoured. And I wrote poems; sitting under the fig tree in the yard or riding the streetcar to and from work, the words spilled out of me. *I* was poetry, able to be myself, nothing hidden, and be loved. I even sang when no one was around, "Bei Mir Bist du Schön" and "Over the Rainbow" (*The Wizard of Oz* had just come out).

Had anyone ever been as shiny and full of promise as I was in the summer of 1939? Things I had yearned for all my life were no longer vague dreams but what I woke to every morning. I was going to college. The boy I had loved from the moment I saw him loved me. I was so dazzled by my own happiness that any concerns I had about Barbara were mere flickers next to the delirious glow that enveloped me.

Then one night in August, something made me jerk awake. It was the sound of Barbara weeping. She lay on her stomach, her face mashed into the pillow, but she was crying too hard to muffle the sound.

"Barbara, what is it?" Sitting beside her, I rubbed her back through the scratchy sequins of her costume. She wasn't supposed to wear the costumes home. "Did something happen at work?"

She said something, but her words were lost in choking sobs.

"Do you want some water?"

She nodded.

I ran into the kitchen and filled a glass, and she sat up and gulped it like a thirsty child. Then she leaped to her feet. "Get me out of this thing! Now!" She turned, and I unzipped her costume, essentially a tight se-quined bathing suit. She shed it as if she were fighting to brush cobwebs from her skin, then grabbed her nightgown and slipped it on.

"Cigarette?" I said.

She grimaced. "I breathe so much cigarette and cigar smoke every night, I have smoke in my lungs instead of oxygen. Glamour job, huh?"

"Is that what's wrong? The job?"

"Uh . . . yeah, the job. Sore feet, sore back, and every night I've gotta fight off these pigs who . . ." Her cool cynicism crumbled. "Pigs who . . ."

"Barbara, what is it?" I put my arm around her. "Did someone hurt you?"

"Oh." She buried her face in my shoulder and sobbed.

"Did someone hurt you?" I said again, when her tears had quieted.

"You can't tell anyone."

"I won't."

"Promise! Not Mama or Papa. And not Danny."

"I promise."

She took a deep breath. "Guy sends me a note at the club—he's a pro-ducer, and I should come see him in his office at Warner Brothers. I'm a big girl, I know—if he wants to kiss me, cop a little feel, I don't care as long as he puts me in a picture. . . . I'm shocking you, aren't I?"

"No." *Yes.*

"He . . . he . . . Shit, I'm so stupid! I'm so . . ." Under my arm, I felt her shudder. "I knew just to tease him, okay, not to let him lay a finger on me unless he promised me a part. But he did promise. He showed me a contract with my name on it! He signed it, and he had me come to his side of the desk to sign my name. And then he unzipped his pants. He made me . . . he . . . in my mouth . . ." Then she shrugged away from me, and her voice went hard. "Big deal, you do that with Danny, right? An old man's smelly pecker, you just need a bottle of Listerine after. But he said he was going to contact me about a film, and he didn't. Then I found out he's not a producer at Warner Brothers, he's some kind of accountant there. Stupid, stupid! Tonight, I saw him at the club. I asked to talk to him, and he said we could talk in his car. Asshole was just trying to get another blow job. I almost said yes, so I could bite off his little hairy prick!

"Well?" she said after a moment. "Aren't you going to say anything?"

"Ah . . ." I wouldn't have been surprised if no sound came out of my mouth, if I were in the limbo of a dream. It wasn't just that I was appalled by the nasty thing the man had done to her. I was appalled by her! She had walked into his office expecting something like this; she'd gone along with it. If the man had turned out to be a real producer, would she have felt it was all worth it?

"Elaine! Here." She lit a cigarette in her mouth and passed it to me. "Shit, I should never have told you."

I stared at the girl next to me and couldn't believe she'd grown up with me in the house on Breed Street. Someone had replaced my sister with a streetwise chippie.

But she wasn't streetwise. For all her veneer of toughness, Barbara was only eighteen. I found my voice.

"He's a monster."

She rolled her eyes. "He's a man."

"Can you do anything?"

"Like what? Call the guy's wife and tell him what a jerk she's married to? She probably already knows. Or maybe I should complain to Jack Warner?" She shook her head. "Look, I don't know why I got so upset. I bet every girl I work with could tell the same story."

"What if you get a different job?"

"Doing what?"

"What about dancing in Mr. Horton's company?"

"Some people in this family need to make a real living. It's okay. I just needed a shoulder to cry on. Thanks . . . Hey, I'm beat. I have to get some sleep."

"Barbara, are you sure you're all right?"

"Nothing hurt but my pride." She turned away from me, burrowed under the covers.

She was sleeping when I left the next morning. I waited up for her when she got home from work that night, but she didn't want to talk. I suspected she regretted having revealed so much, and I didn't push. But I worried about her after that. I feared that her tendency to leap without looking might get her into a worse situation than what happened with the phony producer, something dangerous.

On top of my concern for her, one more thing lingered from our conversation. I kept hearing her say, *Big deal, you do that with Danny*. But Danny and I had never done *that*. Had he done it with Barbara? I fantasized about trying. When we necked and I was holding his penis, I could slide down his body and put my mouth where my hand had been. But I didn't have the nerve. And he didn't ask.

Then something else screamed into my awareness. War.

On August 23, the Soviet Union signed a nonaggression pact with Germany. That night after dinner, Danny and I sat at Canter's with several friends: my pal Ann and her boyfriend, Bill; Burt Weber, who was one of Danny's cronies from Habonim; and a recent addition to our group, Paul Resnick.

Paul had graduated from Roosevelt High two years ahead of us and joined the Abraham Lincoln Brigade, the leftist Americans who had fought with the Republicans in Spain. He'd come home in April, after the Republicans were defeated, and he was about to enter USC like me. Paul made no secret of his membership in the Communist Party nor of his disdain for Zionism, and he and Danny, both natural scrappers, argued over their competing ideals with the gusto of men on a football field. The two of them gravitated toward each other, and now whenever Danny and I got together with friends, the group usually included Paul—wiry, sandy-haired, his ironic smile a reminder that he, alone among us, had broken free of the cocoon of Boyle Heights and *lived*. He had fired a gun at other men, and their bullets and grenades had whizzed past him. He had guzzled *vino* from the bottle and sung partisan songs; he sang some for us, in a surprisingly sweet baritone. There were women, too. He only alluded to them when I was present, but clearly Paul had crossed the chasm that the rest of us trembled on the brink of. He'd had sex.

I jumped into Paul and Danny's debates, though I lacked their true-believer faith—I didn't think any *ism* could save the world. But I enjoyed the sparring. And I was determined to hold my own around Paul, because he rattled me. I couldn't stand the way Danny and the other boys became wide-eyed kids whenever Paul told war stories. To be fair, Paul didn't paint a glorified picture of his life as a soldier; still, all the boys listened as if they were sitting in the National Theater watching a war movie, and they couldn't wait to experience the thrill of battle themselves.

What disturbed me even more about Paul was the shiver in the way he looked at me. And the shiver I felt in return. Even when I was dating other boys, no one but Danny could just meet my eyes and spark that kind of sexual awareness, as if his gaze were a caress. Paul became the second man to evoke that response. Perhaps because of his greater sexual experience, I think he knew he had the power to unsettle me, which made me determined not to show it. It felt like a contest: he'd win if I wavered, but if I gave no sign of the fluttering he provoked in me, then it was my victory. In retrospect, my sense of being in a constant state of subtle combat with Paul made me fling myself into spats with him—as I did on the night of the nonaggression pact.

Danny lit into Paul first. "What do you think of your comrade Joe Stalin now?"

"I think Stalin understands how devastating war can be. He knows it's not some kids' game." Paul's challenging gaze lingered on me, and I felt embarrassed that I'd ordered a Coke; he was drinking black coffee.

Refusing to let him intimidate me, I glared back. "What about the Communists' high ideals? Aren't you dedicated to fighting Fascism? There's no worse Fascist than Hitler."

"No, there's not. But why should the Soviet people go fight Hitler when the capitalist countries are sitting on their fat rumps?"

"What if France and England declare war?" Burt said.

"France and England sat back and said, 'Take Austria. Take Czechoslovakia.' They said to Franco, 'Take Spain.' "

"But what if they do?" Burt said.

"Then I'm on the next ship to England to join up," Danny said. "Anyone with me?"

Danny had said it before—all of the boys talked about fighting for England or France, whichever country had the guts to say no to Hitler first—but in that moment it became real. There was going to be a war, and Danny was going to fight in it. I grasped my Coke glass, clung to the slippery cold of the condensation on the side.

"I'll go!" Burt said.

"I will, too," Bill chimed in, but Ann turned to him sternly.

"You're going to do the world a lot more good as a physicist than as a soldier," she said. Bill had a scholarship to Princeton. (Yes, he ended up working at Los Alamos.)

A moment of fidgety silence followed.

"What about you, Paul?" I said. "You got Danny and Burt to decide to join the British army. Are you going to go with them?"

"I'll join up when the U.S. gets into it."

"So when Danny and Burt are fighting Hitler," I said witheringly, "I guess you'll be going to football games at USC."

"Elaine!" Danny said, and everyone looked at me open-mouthed. "Paul just spent two years fighting. And no one is forcing me to do anything. I decided this on my own."

Within a few weeks, Danny got his wish. He was going off to war.

On September 1, Germany invaded Poland. France and Britain declared war two days later, and Danny started trying to raise the money to get to England. Then on September 10, Canada got into the fray, and all he needed to do was travel up the coast to the nearest Canadian city, Vancouver. That was a Sunday. The next morning, Danny quit his job and bought a train ticket. Burt did, too. They were leaving on Wednesday at 7:45 a.m.

I longed to spend every remaining minute with Danny, but I had just started at USC, and even students from wealthy families—much less a scholarship girl from Boyle Heights—didn't dare cut classes the first week of freshman year. And when I did have a chance to see him, the flurry of leave-takings meant we were always in a crowd of people. Even on his last night . . . I planned to stay up all night with him and see him off at Union Station the next morning, but our entire group of friends would be present; the all-night farewell party was taking place at Burt's home.

When I got off the streetcar from USC that Tuesday afternoon, I didn't go home. Instead I walked to the rooming house where he and his father lived—the territory Mama had declared off-limits because it was too easy for us to be alone. Finding Danny alone that afternoon was what I hoped for . . . and feared. I had made a decision: I wanted to make love with him before he left.

Clammy with nerves, I entered the rooming house and climbed the stairs to the second floor. Approaching Danny's door, I heard him laugh— not the hearty laugh he'd have in a group of friends but a low, intimate chuckle I associated with our times alone. Another voice laughed with him. A girl?

I knocked. The laughter abruptly stopped.

"Danny?" I called. "Danny, it's me."

"Elaine! Just a sec."

There were scrambling sounds. And a giggle. Definitely a girl.

I tried the door. It was unlocked.

Danny, his face flushed and hair damp with sweat, was fumbling with the zipper of his pants. Behind him, equally sweaty and tucking in her partly buttoned blouse, stood Barbara.

Their mouths were moving. But I couldn't hear anything except the roaring in my own head. Danny started toward me. I ran.

"Elaine, wait!" he called.

I don't know if he came after me. I kept going, the streets of Boyle Heights a blur of speed and heat and tears. I had no idea where I was running until I got there—Aunt Pearl's, the small, neat two-bedroom house she'd bought that spring in an older neighborhood a few blocks from Danny's.

Once I was at Pearl's, I hesitated, catching my breath by the azalea bushes on either side of the steps. Could I bear to tell anyone what had happened? Did I *know* what had happened?

"Elaine." Pearl was standing in the doorway. "What is it?"

I stood speechless, my stomach churning.

She hurried down the steps to me. "Darling, you must be so upset about Danny leaving."

The heady fragrance of the flowers made me think of standing in Danny's doorway, smelling scents I hadn't consciously identified but now gave names to. *Shalimar. Sex.*

I threw up on the azaleas.

CHAPTER 17

SWEETHEART
OF THE
RODEO

S HE WAS THE SWEETHEART OF THE RODEO, A BELOVED SONGBIRD and voice on the public address system for the Buffalo Bill Cody Stampede, an extravaganza that ran July 1 to 4 every year, and for the smaller, summerlong Cody Nite Rodeo. At any rate, that's what happened to Kay Devereaux Cochran—who later became Kay Applegate, then Kay Farris, and finally Kay Thorne—according to articles from the Cody, Wyoming, *Enterprise* that Josh has given me. The stories date from 1946—an announcement that Richard Cochran had brought his bride, described as "a USO star," back to Cody—to 1999, when she was one of the "legends" featured in an issue of the paper dedicated to the Stampede's eightieth anniversary.

That's not all Josh has brought me. There's also a glossy brochure for the OKay Ranch Adventure—Kay's dude ranch.

"It was a regular ranch when she moved there with Cochran," Josh explains while I search for my sister in photographs of a blond woman perpetually sporting fringed cowgirl garb. She's generously built, voluptuous in the early shots and hefty over the years, but her teasing Mona Lisa smile suggests she has no doubt of her appeal to men. Four husbands— I guess she had proof of that.

"Five years later, they turned it into a dude ranch, the KayRich," he says. "Must have been her idea, because she kept the ranch after they split up."

"But it's called the OKay now?"

"She changed the name after the movie came out in the late fifties. *Gunfight at the O.K. Corral?* Great marketing decision."

Here she is, in the ranch brochure, though the word *brochure* doesn't do justice to a catalogue offering everything from river rafting to cattle drives to courses with naturalists to spa services; anyway, she's perched astride a monstrous horse with the ease of someone born with a saddle attached to her butt. The ranch is run these days by her son, George Applegate Jr. Also photographed on horseback, he's a bit paunchy but powerful, with a craggy Robert Mitchum face set off by thick silver hair. George junior looks like every dude's fantasy—and like no one in my family.

As for Kay, even the earliest of these photos was taken nearly ten years after Barbara left, and the images are blotchy, probably copied from microfiche. The clearest photos—and the only ones in color—are from the rodeo anniversary spread and the ranch brochure, and in those Kay is in her late seventies or eighties. Her hair determinedly blond and her face a good-humored truce between plumpness and the leathery skin of years spent outdoors, she resembles . . . not Mama or me as we aged, or my other sisters. She looks more like the good ol' gal who was governor of Texas.

I pick up the magnifying glass.

"It's got to be her!" Josh sounds like a kid insisting there's a Santa Claus.

I respond cautiously, "She's the right height." In group shots, everyone else towers over Kay. I wish I could make out her eye color. Or find one photo where, instead of her perpetual Mona Lisa smile, she's got her mouth open, and I could look for a gap between her front teeth, a trait Papa bequeathed to all four of us.

"The right height and the right age," he urges. "And her voice sounds like yours."

"Her voice? Is there something online?" In spite of my determination to examine the facts calmly, I feel a surge of excitement.

"Well, actually . . . ," he says, uncharacteristically tentative, "I talked to her. On the phone."

"You called her? What the hell were you thinking?" What was *I* thinking, trusting a twenty-four-year-old kid with something this delicate?

"I only called because—"

"Did you think this was some kind of game?"

"Of course not." He reddens as if I'd slapped him. Good! "Elaine, just listen, please. I called because of the librarian. None of the newspaper archives are online, so I had to call and request everything. The librarian got suspicious about some guy from L.A. asking for everything they had on 'Miz Kay.' So I came up with a cover story. I said I was researching a documentary about women who were in the USO in World War II. And then I started thinking, seems like Cody's so small, what if she says something to Miz Kay? I figured it'd be less suspicious if I called her myself."

"What did you say?" All the weeks of carefully following every step of Kay Devereaux's trail . . . how much damage has he done?

"That I'm just doing preliminary research, but was she available if I wanted to come out there and film an interview? Really, that's all." He risks a smile. "And don't you need to know if she's at her ranch or spending the winter in Florida? Aren't you going to contact her?"

"I . . ." All of the times I've rehearsed in my mind what I'd say if I could talk to Barbara again—but it was the way I might fantasize a chat with Eleanor Roosevelt or Cleopatra. And I imagined talking to *Barbara* as she existed in my memory . . . not to the formidable reality of Kay Devereaux Cochran Applegate Farris Thorne.

If Kay Devereaux Applegate Farris Thorne *is* Barbara. I need to really examine the material Josh brought me, weigh the evidence. *Is her voice really like mine? Or is that just what Josh wanted to hear?*

After he leaves, I go one by one through the newspaper articles; in neat chronological order, they let me follow Kay's rise as a rodeo entertainer. But much more than that, they offer a window into her life. Every landmark is there—marriages, divorces, births. She has three children: a daughter, Dana Cochran, born in 1949, and two sons, Timothy Cochran, born in 1952, and George Applegate Jr., born in 1957.

And Kay didn't just get into the paper because of the rodeo; quite a few articles concern her business dealings. Along with running a successful dude ranch, she opened the area's first multiplex cinema in the mid-1980s—a controversial move, since it raised fears that the multiplex would threaten a beloved 1930s movie palace. But Kay cherished the grand old theater as much as anyone, she told a reporter; in fact, she had loved going to the movies in such theaters when she was growing up. Where was that? the reporter asked. "All over," she said evasively (to my mind). "My folks moved a lot."

And maybe it was to make up for her evasiveness—she was, after all, trying to smooth ruffled feathers in the town—but then she opened up and said, "We used to call the movie theater the Polly Seed Opera House, because people brought sunflower seeds for snacks. By the end of the movie, you'd have hulls all over the floor."

I read it again. And a third time. Boyle Heights can't be the only place where people munched on sunflower seeds at the movies, I warn myself. Still, the Polly Seed Opera House! I dive into the rest of the articles, no longer reading carefully; now I'm skimming for clues. I come across obituaries for three of her four husbands, including the latest, Thorne; so she's alone now, like I am. I see nothing else that shouts "Barbara" to me. But I'm too excited to concentrate; my eyes are jumping over the pages. I'll give the articles a close read later. Right now my apartment feels far too small to contain me. I grab my jacket, purse. Hesitate for a breath, remembering what happened the last time I took out my agitation by driving. But nothing else will satisfy the urge to be in motion.

There's just one thing I have to do first. I call my sister—Harriet—and invite her over for dinner tonight. This news belongs to her, too.

Then I jump in the Jag. I don't care where I go; I just need to drive.

HARRIET COMES BY AT seven-thirty, after seeing her last therapy client of the day.

"Yum, shrimp pad thai," she says, lifting the lid off one of the contain-ers of the takeout I picked up.

"And the other one's chicken curry. Cabernet okay?" Better to let her settle in a bit before I break the news. And I wouldn't mind having a glass of wine first. Okay, a second glass. I started on the cab before Harriet ar-rived, as I read the rest of the articles—and careened between gratitude that Barbara has had a good life and bitterness that if she was doing so well, then there's no excuse for her not getting in touch with us.

"Cab's perfect." Harriet spoons generous portions of rice, shrimp, and chicken onto her plate and sighs with contentment at her first bite.

Harriet might be described in English by the soulless, clinical term *overweight*, but really she's *zaftig*, the Yiddish far truer to my youngest sis-ter's sexy plumpness and appetite for experience. A *zaftig* gal chomps off as big a bite of life as she can get her jaws around and chews with gusto. I've been thinking of Harriet, but I realize I could be describing Kay; she cer-tainly looks like a woman who wouldn't pass up a succulent prime rib or a slice of chocolate cake.

I, on the other hand, am one of those boring women who count calo-ries. Except for the negligible calories in wine. When I refill my glass a third time, Harriet gives me a sharp look.

"You said we had to talk," she says. "What's up?"

She's as impatient with beating around the bush as I am. But I've had the chance to absorb all this in bits and pieces over two months, and I try to ease in.

"Remember those boxes of papers I came across, from Mama's apart-ment? Well, I found this in one of them." I take Philip's card from the top of the documents I've stacked on the chair next to me.

She stares at the card for a moment. "Philip Marlowe . . . would he have come to the house to see Mama when I was six or seven? A big man—muscular big, not fat?"

"That sounds like him."

"And he was a detective!" Harriet spears a shrimp. "Funny the ideas kids get. I remember thinking he was some kind of doctor. Mama shooed me out of the house so she could talk to him in private. A detective! Was Mama in some kind of trouble? And who was Kay Devereaux?"

I had hoped that seeing the card would prepare her a little. But she was so young, and clearly she was told nothing about what Philip was doing for our family.

"Harriet." My tone makes her put down her fork and meet my eyes. "What if Kay Devereaux was Barbara?"

"Our sister Barbara?" she says dubiously.

I nod.

"Lainie, it's just a card."

"It's only the first thing I found."

I launch into the story, showing her the "evidence" in the order in which I found it: Philip's case file, the photo of Colorado Springs entertainers who joined the USO, articles about Kay Devereaux's marriage in Berlin and her life in Wyoming. Harriet skims the various documents and throws out an occasional request for clarification, but she doesn't react, not even to the reference to the Polly Seed Opera House. It's as if her mind were a quiet pool receiving everything I say with barely a ripple. Her calm is a bit unnerving. On the other hand, I recognize what Harriet is doing: she's falling back on her professional identity, in which she feels confident and in control. She's hearing me out as if I were a patient in therapy . . . just as I'm presenting my case the way I would in court.

She continues acting the therapist after I finish, her gaze compassionate and her voice soothing. "I know how much you've wanted to find her. Seeing that card and then the detective's file, you must have felt it had to mean something."

"I did find her." I start to spread the newspaper clippings over the table, amid our plates and takeout cartons.

"Wait a second!" She holds up her hand. "You don't have to convince me that you tracked down this woman Kay from Colorado Springs. But if she'd turned out to be Barbara, Mama and Papa would have told us."

"That's what I thought at first, too. But the Polly Seed Opera House?"

"Back in the twenties and thirties, that was probably a nickname for movie theaters all over the country. Come on. Do you really see Barbara ending up on a ranch in the middle of nowhere?"

"Look what she made of her life! She figured out a way, living in the back of beyond, to be a star!" I argue, even as doubt trickles into me. The comment about the Polly Seed Opera House is the only "proof" I've found. The remainder of the articles yielded no other ahas.

"Lainie." She takes my hands. "I can only imagine what it must mean to you to think you've found her—your twin sister."

"You sound like you *don't* want to find her!" I throw out, bristling at the possibility that I'm being blinded by my desire . . . not just to find Barbara but to claim for her the successful, colorful narrative in the articles about Kay. The woman posed on the back of a powerful horse like she owns the world, that's who I want Barbara to be.

Harriet reaches for the nearly empty bottle of Cabernet. "Share the rest?"

"It's all yours."

She pours the wine, takes a sip. "Most of *my* memories of Barbara are about her leaving and the impact it had on everyone else. Before that . . . Every so often, this glamorous older girl who smelled fantastic—I remember this wonderful perfume—"

"Shalimar."

"Every so often she noticed me, and this cloud of Shalimar swooped down and kissed me or sang me a song. But she wasn't around a lot. Wasn't she always going to Hollywood for something?"

"Dance classes. The Horton School. She had a scholarship. Harriet, you have to remember that!" I say when she looks vague. It's not just that Barbara's scholarship and her success at the dance school were family triumphs. But the eagerness with which she ran to Hollywood, her hunger for a life outside Boyle Heights, were iconic parts of our family story—the kind of events you look back on when you're trying to understand what happened later.

"That's my point," Harriet says. "I had nothing like your connection with her. I told you when you brought this up earlier, I was ambivalent about the idea of finding her. And I was only thinking then about how fraught it would be to try to contact her. But this! If finding her means I have to accept that this detective tracked her down and told Mama and Papa, and they never told us . . . Jesus!" She gets up and paces, as if she'd like to walk away from all of this. "You're asking me to trade the old, dull pain of being abandoned by a sister I barely knew for the pain of feeling so betrayed by Mama and Papa I want to go to the cemetery and scream at their graves. I hate it that after all these years, Barbara could poison my memory of them. Now, *that* sounds like the Barbara I remember, poisoning everything."

Her rage, I feel it, too. Yet in spite of it, every time I look at the photos of Kay in her Western regalia and think *Barbara*, my heart lifts.

"So you do think it could be her?" I venture.

Harriet's gaze goes inward, a look so like Pearl's fierce concentration that for a moment it's my aunt in the room with me.

"You have some pictures of Barbara, don't you?" she says. "Say, from when you were in high school?"

My photo albums are actually organized; Carol put them in order when she helped me unpack last month. I find the right album, while Harriet brings a bright standing lamp over next to the table. She gets out her reading glasses—I give her the magnifying glass, too—and she starts to look back and forth between photos of Barbara and shots of Kay Devereaux. Forcing myself to give her some space, I go into the kitchen and make a pot of decaf. And I bought one of those giant brownies they sell these days; I cut it into four normal-sized pieces and put them on a plate. Then, having run out of distractions, I hover—I can't help myself—as Harriet scrutinizes photos under the magnifying glass.

Looking over her shoulder, I see Kay in her thirties, forties, fifties, and beyond, and I remind myself that these same photos didn't convince me this afternoon. But now it's not just that I glimpse Barbara in the curve of Kay's cheeks or the assertiveness of her stance; rather, it's the kind of primal recognition that happens on parents' day at summer camp, when you scan the crowd of kids and zoom in on *your* son, *your* daughter. What if I had kept my discovery of Kay to myself? I wonder. Might it have been enough simply to *believe* I knew who and where Barbara was, a last filament of connection far too delicate to expose to a cooler mind like Harriet's?

My God, was *that* why Mama and Papa said nothing? Because they couldn't be sure, and they needed for Barbara to be Kay Devereaux, alive and well in Colorado Springs? And wouldn't I at twenty have taken apart every "proof" Philip gave them, more intent on truth than on comfort?

Harriet spends nearly an hour examining photos, one hand holding the magnifying glass and the other tensely twisting her hair; she doesn't even touch the brownies. Then at last she takes off her reading glasses, rubs her eyes.

"They say that twins have trouble forming attachments as adults," she says. "It's especially true of identical twins, but it can apply to fraternal twins, too. They're always looking for the kind of closeness they had with the twin."

"Are you saying . . . what, that I have a neurotic need to find her? That I haven't been able get close to people because of her?"

"I wasn't talking about you. Look at *her*. Four husbands."

"Then you do think this is Barbara?"

"Yes. Maybe. No. All of the above." She runs her hands through her tangled hair. Then she gives me a therapist look. "What happens when we call and Cowgirl Kay says, 'Barbara who?' "

"She might not say that," I reply, though again I think of the daunting reality of Kay Devereaux Cochran Applegate Farris Thorne.

"Oh, Elaine."

"So do you think we *shouldn't* contact her?"

"I just think we need to anticipate how she's going to respond—and how we'll feel. And I'd like to consider the option that you've achieved one of the best possible outcomes by solving the family mystery, and maybe we *should* leave it at that. But let's not make any decisions now. How about if we both sleep on this and talk tomorrow, all right?"

"All right."

"No decisions right away. Promise me."

"Um," I say noncommittally.

We embrace. I give her half the brownie to take home.

"Promise," she says again as she leaves. As if she can see the idea that's entered my mind.

It's a crazy idea. She's right about sleeping on all of this. But after she leaves, I'm too keyed up to go to bed. I turn on the television.

There's a TV show on that I actually like, but after ten minutes, I realize I'm not following it. I take out a deck of cards; solitaire is a surefire way to distract myself.

I can't do it. Really.

Still, I abandon the solitaire game and turn on the computer and swear out loud because it takes so long to boot up. I feel . . . impatient. Annoyed. *Alive.* As I print out flight schedules, I dance around the room, a fierce old woman's dance.

Harriet with her "Barbara who?" got me thinking. There is no satisfactory way to contact Barbara, for the first time in more than half a century, over the phone. I have to be there, to see her face the moment I say, "It's me. Elaine."

Cody has an airport. From there, I'll need to get to the OKay Ranch, which, according to the brochure, is thirty-seven miles out of town, twelve of them on a "scenic highway"—in the Rocky Mountains. In the middle of winter. It would be smart to wait until spring. That would give me time to plan my approach carefully, and I wouldn't have to drive on mountain roads in January.

But what did Josh say after he drove me back from Barstow? *Call me the next time you feel like taking a road trip.*

CHAPTER 18

GONE

PEARL PUT HER ARM AROUND ME WHILE I RETCHED OVER HER FLOWERS. Then she led me inside to the familiar site of our serious conversations, the love seat, which sat against a cream stucco wall in her Spanish-style home.

"I'll be right back," she said, hurrying into the kitchen. She returned a moment later with a glass of water, as well as a damp towel that she mopped over my face and arms.

And I sobbed out my story.

"He never stopped loving her, did he?" I wept.

"Shh, Elaine. Shh."

"You knew! You warned me he might just be going with me because I was her sister."

"But I was wrong. Anybody who's seen you and Danny together wouldn't doubt that he loves you. Danny and Barbara, I don't know. There's just something between them."

"Sex?"

"Oy. Any eighteen-year-old boy, it's sex. Elaine." She searched my eyes. "You and Danny, have you . . ."

"I wanted to! Today. That's why I . . ." *And Barbara got there first.*

Oh! I felt like I'd been punched in the stomach. I'd been focusing my hurt and anger on Danny. Now the sense of betrayal shifted to Barbara, and I was shattered. As if, compacted into that irredeemable moment when I opened Danny's door and saw her, was the pain of her having been his first love; and so much deeper than that, it was the rivalry I'd felt all of my life as I competed with Barbara for Mama's love . . . and again and again, Mama chose her. I let out a wail.

"Elaine! Elaine!" Pearl cried, but I raged around the room sobbing, pushing away her efforts to calm me. Why had I run away like a child? I wanted to be back at Danny's, to pound my sister until my fists were bloody. At least Danny had a reason for betraying me: he had never gotten over her. But Barbara? I pictured her standing behind him, disheveled and flushed—*triumphant?* Was she deliberately trying to destroy me?

"Elaine!" Pearl grabbed my arm and thrust a glass of amber liquid at me. "Drink this."

I took a gulp. Whiskey, nasty-tasting. I downed the whole shot and found my voice. "How *could* she? Does she hate me?"

"Darling, I don't know why she . . . Here, sit." She wrapped her arms around me. "I wish there was something I could say that would make this not hurt so much."

Pearl held me as the afternoon softened into dusk. Between my spasms of tears, there were also quiet times when I simply floated, exhausted and empty.

During one of those calms, the phone rang. Pearl had ignored several calls earlier, but this time she asked if I'd be all right and went into the kitchen to get the phone.

"Your mother," she said when she came back a few minutes later. "I said you were going to have dinner with me. All right? I was just going to make a salad and boil some potatoes."

"Fine," I said, though I couldn't imagine forcing anything down my throat.

"She asked about the party tonight. I said you were upset about Danny leaving, and you didn't think you were going to go."

Oh, no, the party. But maybe the excuse Pearl had given Mama would work for my friends, too. Certainly Danny wouldn't breathe a word of the real reason I was missing.

"Tonight do you want to stay here?" Pearl asked.

The question thrust me into the future, the eternity in which I had to sleep barely three feet from Barbara. Just thinking of it made my skin crawl.

"Aunt Pearl, please," I begged, "can I move in with you?" She hesitated, and I pressed on. "I'll tell them I need more quiet so I can study."

Pearl sighed. "You and your sister are going to have to talk."

"Please? I'll pay you for room and board."

"Lainie, I don't know. . . . I'm going to go make dinner now, okay?"

She returned to the kitchen. And I huddled on the sofa, a girl whose problems a few hours earlier had been limited to the challenges of being a freshman at USC and Danny's departure for war.

Unless I'd been living in a fool's paradise. With a floaty clarity (I'd drunk the whiskey on an empty stomach), I considered the possibility that this wasn't the first time Barbara had been at Danny's. Hadn't I wondered what she was up to, leaving the house every afternoon long before she had to be at work? Maybe her secret was that she was seeing Danny on the sly . . . the way I used to see him when he was *her* boyfriend, I thought, the guilt from that time flooding me. If Barbara had walked in on us in Chafkin's storeroom, how would she have felt?

"It's not the same!" I protested out loud. If God was trying to give me a taste of my own medicine, God had it wrong. Not that my behavior hadn't been contemptible, but we'd been kids then. Now we were on the brink of our adult lives.

But they couldn't have been seeing each other behind my back. Even if I believed Barbara was capable of something so lousy, Danny never would have hurt me like that. *Would he?* In the venomous whisper of doubt I heard the rationalizations he used to give for sneaking around with me, and I wondered if I had utterly misjudged his character, if instead of complicated, forgivable reasons for his behavior, he was simply a manipulator who liked playing one of us against the other. I would come to see Danny as a man who enjoyed subterfuge for its own sake. I don't think he had become that man yet; it wouldn't happen until the war. But that afternoon I glimpsed it, and it chilled me—or so I imagined when I looked back and dissected my failed first love. But that cool, rational exercise wouldn't happen until years later.

That day at Pearl's, I was like a wounded animal, burrowing into her love seat . . . and freezing into stillness when I heard someone walking up the porch steps. A voice called through the screen door, "Mrs. Davidoff?"

Danny.

"Mrs. Davidoff?" he called. "I'm looking for Elaine."

It was dusk, the room in shadow. Hoping he couldn't see me, I held my breath.

But Pearl came in from the kitchen. "Danny, wait just a minute," she called.

I jumped up. Whispered, "No."

Pearl put her hands on my shoulders. "I'll send him away if you want me to. But you're not going to have another chance. If you don't see him and he goes and gets killed in the war, will you be able to forgive yourself?"

"I'd like to kill him myself! Now."

"I know. And he deserves it."

But Pearl was right. Everything that Danny had been to me, I couldn't refuse to see him the night before he left for the war. "Let him in," I said.

"Light?" She nodded toward the lamp.

"No!"

Pearl told Danny I was here and held open the door for him.

"I'm sorry," he mumbled to Pearl.

Then he was inside. My *bashert*. He stood tentatively, facing me . . . in a way that reminded me of the glorious night when he'd stood naked before me. A roaring filled my head, and my legs dissolved. I sat down, willing myself not to faint.

"Danny, you take care of yourself, all right?" Pearl said. Her back was to me, so I couldn't see the look she gave him, but he seemed to shrink several inches.

"Yes, ma'am."

Then Pearl left the room. Left me alone with him.

He took a few steps toward me and fell to his knees. "Elaine, I'm sorry. I'm so, so—" He choked on a sob. I had never seen Danny cry, not even as a child. For an instant, my eyes welled up. That made me even more furious at him.

I slapped his face so hard my hand stung. "How could you?"

"I'm sorry. I'm sorry." He took the slap, just kneeling there and weeping.

"How could you? With her?" I slapped him again, feeling a savage joy at hurting him.

"Elaine, please!" He grabbed my hands.

"Let go of me!"

"Please, I'm leaving tomorrow. Can't we talk?"

"Let me go!"

He released me but scrambled to his feet, out of range of my slaps.

"Did you *fuck* her?" I spat out. I had never spoken that word before. Saying it made me feel grown-up and mean.

He wiped his eyes on his sleeve. "No. I didn't . . . make love with her. Elaine, I love *you*."

"Have you been seeing her?"

"What do you mean?"

"Have you been seeing her in secret?" I studied his face, alert for any subtle shift in expression that would tell me I'd hit a nerve. But he looked stunned, and I believed him when he said no. Yet that didn't dampen my rage.

"Please, the whole thing was crazy. It's like I'm in some kind of fever, getting ready to leave. She came by to wish me luck, and she gave me a kiss goodbye, that was all, but then . . . you know."

"Then *what?*"

"I feel terrible that I hurt—"

"Did she give you a blow job?" *You do that with Danny, right?* she'd said to me.

"Elaine, won't you let me apologize?" Now *he* sounded angry. Had he thought shedding a few tears would fix everything? Did he think I was so hopelessly in love with him?

"Did she?" I said. "Don't lie to me!"

"Okay, yes. But it was only—I'm being completely honest with you, okay?—it was because she used to, back when we were going together."

"How come you never asked me to?" I demanded.

"To give me a . . . You've got to be kidding! I have too much respect for you. I didn't ask *her* the first time, she just did it. . . . Look, I don't blame you if you hate me right now. I deserve it. But I'm leaving tomorrow. Won't you wish me luck?"

I hope you get killed! But just thinking that made me feel sick.

"Good luck," I said.

"I love you."

He paused, and I formed the response in my mind: *I love you, too.* I had felt that way until only hours ago. I had loved Danny with no reservations, nothing held back. As deeply as he'd hurt me, still in the balance between love and loathing, there were years of love. And this might be the last time I would ever see him, the last time I could tell him. Part of me ached to say those words. And part of me felt like saying them would twist a knife in my gut. I had clamped down on my tears, but now I wept.

"Elaine." To my horror, he dropped to one knee in front of me. "It's a terrible time to do this, but I was planning to, tonight. And I'm not going to have another chance."

"Danny, don't," I murmured, though I felt mesmerized as he took something out of his pocket and held it on the palm of his hand. A small box.

"Elaine, will you marry me?" He flipped the box open, and in the dark room I saw the shape of a ring.

"No!" If he was only proposing because of what he'd done, as a sort of grandstand apology—if he thought that would make me forgive him and fall into his arms—it was demeaning. And if he were telling the truth and he'd actually planned this, then how could he have betrayed me with Barbara?

"It's my mother's ring. I told you, I was planning to ask you. Tonight."

"Danny, go!"

"Tell me you'll think about it, at least?"

"Go!" I pushed him.

After he left, I sobbed in Pearl's arms. And begged her again to let me move in with her. Just as Barbara had led sexually when she and Danny were going together, I suspected she was the one who had turned this afternoon's goodbye kiss into something else. That hardly excused Danny, but my sister? I couldn't bear spending one more night breathing the same air she breathed.

Barbara must have felt the same. The next day she was gone.

I DIDN'T KNOW ANYTHING was wrong until I got home from USC the next afternoon. I was planning to eat dinner at home and then return to Pearl's; she'd agreed to let me stay at least one more night.

I steeled myself as I turned onto our block, about to face Mama for the first time since my life had disintegrated—and anticipating an argument over my staying at Pearl's. It was a fight for which I had no strength. After a wretched, sleepless night, I had forced myself through the day at school, fumbling if a professor asked me a question and fleeing to bathroom stalls for bouts of tears. The last thing I wanted on top of that was Mama grilling me about why my own home wasn't good enough for me. But if I didn't get it over with now, she'd storm over to Pearl's.

"She's here! She's here!" called Harriet when I came up the porch steps.

Mama pounced on me before I'd taken three steps inside the door. She brandished a sheet from a notepad with a few lines written in black ink. "What do you know about this?"

"About what?" My frayed nerves crackled as I took in my whole family—everyone but Barbara—gathered in the living room. Mama, Audrey, and Harriet were all on their feet, Audrey with tears trickling down her face. Only Papa, sitting in his chair, looked calm, but he, too, stared at me expectantly.

"Charlotte, let her put her books down!" Papa said. Glaring at Mama, he continued, "Elaine, it's a letter from your foolish sister, who should *never* have been allowed to work in a nightclub."

"What nightclub?" Audrey whispered.

As I set my books on the end table, Mama explained that she'd peeked in on Barbara at noon, because Barbara always came into the kitchen for coffee by then. But the room was empty. "And I found this on her pillow!" She thrust the note at me.

Dear Mama and Papa,

>*Don't worry about me. I'm fine. I just need to make my own life. I love you.*

>>*Barbara*

"Why would she do this to me?" Mama moaned. "If you knew the chill that went through me when I found that letter! I know I'll never see her again."

"You'll see her this very evening," Papa replied. "We'll go to that night-club and talk some sense into her."

"Is there a man?" Mama shot at me.

Besides mine? "I'm sure she's just moving in with a friend." And I was. I felt no concern, not a flicker of twin-to-twin intuition that anything was wrong beyond my selfish sister pulling this melodramatic stunt and throwing the entire household into turmoil.

"Elaine," Papa said, "do you know if there's anything wrong? Some problem your sister is having that we should know about before we see her tonight?"

"She probably just wants to live on her own."

"Live on her own?" Mama pinned me with one of those looks that made me feel transparent. "What happened between you and your sister?"

"Barbara and I hardly even see each other awake anymore."

"On the same night, she leaves and you skip Danny's going-away party and stay at your aunt Pearl's," Mama persisted.

"I was upset about Danny leaving. I needed to be someplace quiet."

"You're upset that he's leaving, so you decide not to see him?"

"Charlotte," Papa intervened. "Let's have some dinner. Then you and I will go to this nightclub and talk a little sense into our daughter."

"As if I could eat," Mama said, still scrutinizing me.

She and I threw together some eggs and fried potatoes for a meal at which Papa tried to pretend everything was normal, asking my sisters and me about school. Harriet went along with the fantasy; enjoying more attention than she usually got at the dinner table, she chattered about which of her classmates she liked best, who already knew how to read a little, who had a dog, and couldn't we get a dog?

After dinner, Mama put on her best dress, a hunter-green silk with a draped bustline, one of Pearl's creations, and she and Papa called a taxi, a luxury, to take them to the Trocadero.

I settled my sisters in front of the radio for *Amos 'n' Andy*, then phoned Pearl to say I didn't need her offer of a bed tonight because Barbara was staying with a friend. "No, nothing's wrong," I said. *At least, nothing that wasn't already destroyed by my hateful sister.* I hoped Mama and Papa didn't succeed in making her come home. Even better than moving in with Pearl would be to have the cozy room off the kitchen all to myself.

WHEN MAMA AND PAPA returned, a little after ten, Papa had his arm around Mama, and she staggered as he guided her to a chair.

"Elaine, make your mother some tea," he said.

"What happened? What did she say?"

Papa sighed. "Your sister wasn't there. She quit her job last night. I'm sure she's fine, but no one could tell us where she is. . . . You! Back to bed," he ordered Audrey, who was crouching on the stairs.

"I'll make the tea." I hurried toward the kitchen, dying to have a few minutes to think.

"Forget the damn tea!" Mama had shaken off her stupor. Her voice was like a blow. "Elaine, come here and look at me."

I did.

"What went on between you and Barbara yesterday?"

I'd thought I couldn't hate Barbara any more than I already did. But she had left me to bare my humiliation to Mama and Papa while she was hiding out at a friend's, having a good time . . . wasn't she? *Though why did she quit her job?* I thought with my first stir of alarm. If she planned to live on her own, she needed the job more than ever.

"Elaine!" Mama said.

"I . . ." But there was no point in fudging; Mama had guessed it already. "I went over to Danny's, and she was with him."

"Doing what?"

"Necking."

"Necking, that's all?"

"How am I supposed to know?"

"Elaine!" Papa said firmly. "Did you and Barbara have a fight?"

"No, I just left."

"And went straight to your aunt Pearl," Mama sniffed. "Not to your own mother."

"I just . . ."

To my relief, Papa stayed focused on the problem at hand. "Think, Elaine," he said, "Where would she have gone? Who are her closest friends?"

I started with Barbara's friends from the Diamonds. "Susie Graf. Alice Wexler—"

"Listen to the two of you!" Mama rolled her eyes. "Don't you realize that now we know exactly where Barbara is?"

I stared at her. "Where?"

"Well," Mama said, "I guess a person doesn't have to have a college scholarship to be smart."

"Charlotte!"

"Where else would she be," Mama announced, "but on the train to Canada? With that good-for-nothing Danny Berlov."

"No," I said. "Danny wouldn't have. . . ."

"Why not?" Mama pounced on my hesitation.

I had thought I had no secrets left, that no corner of my life remained private, but I couldn't bear to expose the fact that Danny had proposed to me. "He's enlisting in the army, it's not like she can be with him," I said. "He won't even be staying in Canada. Maybe he'll have a month of training, but then they'll send him to England."

"*You* would think of all that," Mama said, "but would your sister? Would Danny Berlov?"

"Charlotte, that makes no sense," Papa said in his let's-be-reasonable voice. "Elaine's right. Danny will be going into the Canadian army. And how could Barbara afford a train ticket to Canada? Or a place to stay after she gets there?"

Mama insisted, though, and Papa agreed to go to Western Union tomorrow and send a telegram to Barbara at the Vancouver train station.

"Don't send it to Vancouver," I broke in, despite my reluctance to say anything that would support Mama's fantasy about Barbara being on the train. "The train doesn't get there for another day and a half. Send it to the station in . . ." I'd gone over the timetable with Danny, a lifetime ago. Sacramento? No, the train had already left Sacramento. "Portland, that's the next city where the train stops for an hour, and there'd be time to deliver a telegram."

"Write to Danny Berlov, too," Mama said. "Say we hold him responsible for our daughter's safety . . . or for marrying her. What if that no-goodnik got her pregnant? And then he runs off to war and gets killed, and there she'll be, alone with a baby, in Canada."

She couldn't be pregnant! They hadn't gone that far, Danny had sworn to me.

While Papa gave in to Mama's whim, he also asked me to make a list of Barbara's friends for us to call and ask if she was staying with them.

"What if I go tomorrow and talk to some of them?" I suggested.

"Don't you dare," Mama said. "Start asking where she is, and you'll get everyone in Boyle Heights gossiping that the Greensteins' wild daughter has run off."

"Elaine," Papa said, "*you* go to the university and keep up with your classes. And I don't see any point in contacting anyone right away. Let's wait another day, and I'm sure she'll come home on her own."

"She's on that train, you'll see," Mama declared. Then she came over and stroked my arm. "Oy, Elaine."

"What?" I said, more wary of her sympathy than of her third degree. I could defend myself against Mama's probing. But if she switched to her rare comforting mode, I feared I'd melt into an inconsolable three-year-old.

All she said, though, was, "Don't waste any tears on Danny Berlov. You're well rid of him."

THAT NIGHT I MADE the list Papa had asked for, starting with the girls in the Diamonds—though if Barbara really meant to hide, she would never go to anyone in Boyle Heights. I had met a number of her dance school friends, too, or heard her talk about them, and I added the names I could remember.

I also considered the Trocadero. They had let Mama go into the dressing room this evening and talk to the chorus girls, and they'd all claimed to know nothing about where Barbara might be. I wished I knew if she had a special friend there, a girl who might reveal something one-on-one—and to Barbara's sister, a girl her own age—that she wouldn't have told Mama. But Barbara and I had had so little contact all summer, I had no idea who her friends were.

Even as I prepared to look for Barbara in Los Angeles, though, I couldn't help finding a crazy logic in Mama's theory. Not that I thought she'd left *with* Danny, that the two of them had planned it—it was one thing for him to succumb to the temptation of the moment, but not even the Danny I currently reviled would run away with my sister scant hours after asking me to marry him. But Barbara must have panicked after I walked in on them, afraid of my anger and even more terrified I was going to tell Mama and Papa and she'd catch hell the minute she walked in the door. Desperate to get away, what if the first thing that popped into her mind was the one train she knew left the next morning? It was a rash act—an infuriating one—and just the kind of thing I could see my sister doing.

When I went to bed that night, I discovered that in addition to the note she'd left for Mama and Papa, there was a second note under my pillow.

Lainie, I'm sorry. I love you.

I had an urge to rip the note into shreds in rage. Instead something made me slip it into the treasure box I'd gotten from Aunt Pearl as a child. Did I have some premonition that the note would be the last thing I heard from Barbara? What I remember feeling toward her was still-fresh anger and rage, along with a hint of worry—but no more than a hint. I was able to sleep that night. And the next day at school, I found I could focus on my studies. I even held my own with my economics professor, who quizzed us with the bloodlust of a tiger tearing apart prey. Not even my anguish over Danny dimmed the glow I felt after I answered a tough question and the professor nodded as if he were making a mental note of me; it was the kind of recognition I experienced at the start of every school year, the moment when a new teacher identified Elaine Greenstein as one of the smart students—only this time it was happening not in the Boyle Heights public schools but at the University of Southern California.

Nevertheless, Barbara's absence afflicted me with a need to do *something*. After my last class, I called home to see if there'd been any word from her. Not a thing, Audrey reported. So I went to Barbara's dance school in Hollywood. I found four of her friends there. I told them she'd gone to stay with a friend but forgot to leave us the name, and did they know who it was? They said no but gave me the names and telephone numbers of a few other people to try.

I planned to make the calls as soon as I got home, but Mama wouldn't hear of it. I'd blabbed about Barbara too much already, she fumed.

"Mama, none of those girls lives anywhere near Boyle Heights!"

"How do you know they don't have relatives here?"

"We aren't living in Jane Austen's time. It's not going to ruin our whole family if people know—"

"There's no reason to go stir up trouble," Mama grumbled. "We know where she is—on that train."

The train was due to reach Portland at seven-forty, and that evening after dinner, Mama's anticipation became so palpable that just sitting in the same room with her, I wanted to jump out of my skin. I retreated to my bedroom and opened *Beowulf*, which I had to read in Old English as well as in translation. But though I forced myself to stare at the book, all I could see was the train speeding closer and closer to Portland. At seven-thirty I gave up on studying and joined the rest of the family in the kitchen. They were gathered around the table, within grabbing distance of the wall-mounted telephone. Papa was playing a game of fish with Audrey and Harriet, and Mama was aimlessly straightening things in the cupboards.

At seven-forty we started stealing glances at the phone and the clock, and by eight we simply sat and stared at them. When the phone finally rang, at eight-fifteen, Papa lunged for it. "Barbara!" Mama exclaimed, hovering at his elbow. We all hovered, listening to his end of the conversation.

"Sol, how are you?" Papa said.

It was an ordinary call, and I started back toward the table. Then I heard Papa say, "Burt called you long-distance from the train station in Portland? That's good."

"Sol Weber," Mama mouthed. Burt Weber's father.

"She's not missing, of course not," I heard Papa say. "Just thoughtless. She went to spend a few nights with a friend and didn't tell us who. . . . Just this crazy idea my wife had." He frowned at Mama. "But of course, she's at a friend's. . . . No, we don't need any help. Thank you for letting us know."

Papa hung up and then told us what he'd heard from Burt Weber. Papa's telegram, delivered when the train arrived in Portland, had made Danny so frantic that instead of just sending a telegram in reply, he had insisted that Burt call home (Danny's father still had no phone of his own) and make it clear that Barbara wasn't with Danny. And in case anything had given us the idea she might be on the train, Burt assured his father that he and Danny regularly stretched their legs during the long trip by walking up and down the entire length of the train, and they would both swear Barbara wasn't there.

"Sol Weber!" Mama groaned. "He's got a bigger mouth than the worst yenta. What did you say in that telegram to make Burt Weber get so upset?"

"Who was so sure she was on that train?" Papa snapped in retort.

"Papa?" Audrey said, her voice tight with anxiety. We had seen Mama and Papa argue, but not like this. Usually Mama nagged and Papa got coldly disapproving; he rarely raised his voice.

"What is it, Audrey?" Papa tried to smile at her.

"If Barbara's not on the train, is that bad?"

"No, in fact, it's very good news. It means that your foolish sister is here in Los Angeles, after all."

"When is Barbara coming home?"

"Soon. Look what time it is. You and Harriet should be in bed."

"What if we write to Mr. Keen?" Audrey persisted. She was referring to *Mr. Keen, Tracer of Lost Persons*, a show on the radio.

"Go to bed!" Mama said. "Now!"

Audrey's eyes brimmed. Poor kid, she was nervous by nature, and with all our attention glued to Barbara, no one had attempted to ease the impact of the family crisis on her.

"Hey," I said to her. "How about if you get ready for bed, and I'll read to you from *Nancy Drew?*" I put my arm around her, took Harriet's hand, and led them to their room.

Harriet was too young to fully understand what was happening, and she was too naturally cheerful to be distressed by family storms. (At least, that's what I assumed at the time, observing my ever-smiling youngest sister.) Audrey, however, was visibly frantic. I did my best to respond patiently to the questions she flung at me: What kind of job did Barbara have, and why had it been a secret? Why had Mama and Papa thought Barbara had left with Danny? Wasn't Danny my boyfriend? I was able to answer those questions, albeit in edited form. But what could I say when she asked, "Is Barbara all right? Why doesn't she call? Did something bad happen to her?" How could I soothe her anxiety when my own was churning?

I hadn't really believed Barbara was on the train, but Mama's speculation had given me a narrative to set against her absence, a story in which she combed her hair, drank coffee, and sat safely watching through the window as California passed by and then Oregon. She must be hiding out with a friend in L.A.—that had always been the most likely explanation—and it made me want to shake her until her teeth rattled. But she'd been gone for two days now, without a word, and I was no longer just irritated, I was scared.

The news from Burt had affected Mama and Papa the same way. When I returned to the kitchen, Mama was no longer trying to keep Barbara's absence a secret; instead, she was going down the list I'd made of Barbara's friends and calling them. Between calls, she moaned that this was God's judgment for the heartache she'd inflicted on *her* parents. Then she took a deep breath and called the next number on the list. And Papa . . . I'd never seen him so unnerved. Pacing and chain-smoking, my usually de-

liberative father careened between railing against his thoughtless daughter and worrying that she was in real peril. One minute he said we
shouldn't put ourselves through the aggravation of searching for her,
since she was certain to waltz in tomorrow, blasé about the havoc she'd
stirred up. In the next breath he wanted to call the police. "But why would
the police get involved?" he said. "She's eighteen, and she left a note, and
look at where she worked . . . But that's the point. A girl with a job like
that, how is she going to have the good judgment to stay out of trouble?
Elaine, what do you think?" He turned to me with imploring eyes. I started
to stammer out a response, but he'd shifted back to cursing Barbara's self-
ishness.

Since he was already on his feet pacing, Papa bolted into the living
room when we heard someone at the front door. I was a few steps behind,
and Mama quickly finished her latest phone call and followed, calling out,
"Barbara!"

But it was Pearl, her face scrubbed of makeup and her hair in pin curls,
as if she'd been getting ready for bed and rushed over. "I tried to phone,
but your line was busy," she said. "I got a call from Ruth Eder. What's this
about Barbara going to Vancouver with Danny?"

"Let's sit." Papa switched on a lamp and sat down heavily, as if he had
just that moment turned old.

He got out Barbara's note, which he'd been carrying neatly folded in
his wallet, and told Pearl what had happened over the past two days. "Why
didn't you tell me?" Pearl exclaimed at one point, but she clearly wasn't
going to waste time being miffed.

When Papa had finished, she sat silently for a moment, her eyes closed
in thought. Then she asked, "Does she have much money?"

Mama shook her head. "She gives most of her pay to me. Why?"

"I wondered if she could afford to get a hotel room for a night or
two. Or even leave town. There are plenty of places to go, not just Vancouver. . . ."

Suddenly my map of where Barbara might be swelled from Los Angeles to the entire world, a universe in which she was lost forever. I choked
back a sob.

But Mama was saying, "She has a little spending money, that's all."

"Well, she's going to need any money she's got," Pearl said. "Why don't we leave a message for her at her bank?"

"What bank?" Mama said. "Since when does she have a bank?"

"She asked me about opening a savings account—it must have been last winter. I told her I use Union Bank downtown, and I think she was going to go there."

"You didn't think you should tell us about this?" Mama said, ruffled as always that one of us had confided in Pearl. And her nerves were frayed; she'd just called eight or nine of Barbara's friends, fighting to keep the panic out of her voice as one girl after another told her they had no idea where Barbara was.

"Charlotte, I assumed you knew," Pearl said. "But I didn't see it as something I needed to warn you about. I thought it was a fine idea, very responsible, for her to get a bank account."

Mama bristled. "Isn't that up to her parents to decide?"

"This note," Papa broke in. "You'll ask them to give it to her?"

"I'll take it there first thing tomorrow and talk to my banker. He can alert the tellers and ask them to give it to her when she comes in."

All of us went back into the kitchen so Papa could sit at the table to write. Mama resumed making phone calls, although it was ten-thirty by now. She woke several people up and had to endure their irritation, and she was no longer keeping the panic out of her voice.

Papa started several letters but kept crumpling them up. "I blame myself," he sighed to Pearl. "I never should have let her take that job."

"Oh, Billy," Pearl said, patting Papa's hand. "If it wasn't the job, it would've been something else. Nobody could have stopped Barbara from spreading her wings."

"Spreading her wings?" Mama, who was between phone calls, turned and glared at Pearl. "Is that the kind of advice you give *my* daughters, Pearl? To spread their wings?"

"Of course not. Not like that."

"I'm sorry you don't have children of your own, but if my daughters need advice, you send them to me."

"Please," Papa said. "The last thing we need is to argue."

"Don't tell me you're going to take her side," Mama said.

Pearl stood. "Bill, if you want to write that note and get it to me first thing in the morning, I'll take it to the bank," she said, and stalked out.

"Aunt Pearl!" I hurried after her onto the porch.

"Elaine, if you have something on your mind, talk to your mother," Pearl said loudly. Then she put her arms around me. "How are you doing? How's school?" she whispered.

"All right."

"Keeping up in your classes?"

"Yes."

"Don't you dare let your sister take that away from you."

I DON'T KNOW WHAT Papa said in his note, but he went out early the next morning with Pearl to take it to the bank. Mama planned to continue calling the families of Barbara's friends. I offered to help, but if there was one thing on which Mama, Papa, and Pearl agreed, it was that nothing should disrupt my education.

I had to force myself out the door to leave for school, pulling away from my family's trouble as if it were a magnet sucking at me. Once I broke free, however, USC was a refuge. Everyone in Boyle Heights knew me as my parents' daughter, one of "the Greenstein girls." At USC I was simply another freshman. I didn't come trailing my entire family.

Was that how Barbara felt when she went to Hollywood?

I wasn't completely anonymous, of course. I ran into Paul on the quad. He had heard about Barbara and asked if there was anything he could do to help.

"No, thanks," I said, on guard for some knowing look or comment, since Paul, like all of Boyle Heights, must have heard that we'd suspected Barbara had run off with Danny—and how could Paul Resnick resist the chance to throw me off-balance? But in his warm voice and eyes, I sensed only concern.

"I'm serious. Call me if I can help," he said.

My Friday classes ended at noon. On my way home from the streetcar stop, three people asked me if there was any word about Barbara; and when I opened the front door, I heard, "The college girl, here she is!"

It was Aunt Sonya, planted on the sofa with her mending basket—though there was no sign of actual mending going on.

"I came over the minute I got the kids off to school this morning," Sonya told me. "Anything I can do. Though why your parents let her work in a place like that! Well, I guess they paid even better than anyone realized."

"What do you mean?" I hated to let Sonya bait me, but she clearly knew something.

"Your father went to the bank this morning, and guess what? Your sister had a savings account there, but not anymore. First thing Wednesday morning, she went in and withdrew every penny. One hundred and thirty dollars! Can you imagine?"

No, I couldn't imagine. Barbara kept only two or three dollars from each of her paychecks, and she spent it on clothes and cosmetics and car fare. "How could she have so much money?"

"Not from anything respectable," Sonya said darkly.

"You don't know that," Mama said, coming in from the kitchen. She was wearing her nicest housedress and a slash of lipstick, as if refusing to show any weakness in front of Sonya.

"Charlotte, face facts," Sonya said. "Has my brother ever managed to earn a hundred and thirty dollars in an entire month?"

"Where *is* Papa?" I broke in.

"The nightclub," Mama said. "He made an appointment to see the manager. Pearl took the afternoon off and drove him. He wants to find out what was going on there."

"As if a man who runs a nightclub would admit anything!" Sonya sniffed. "And they're gone two hours already. Didn't I try to tell them, you don't just walk in on a man like that and accuse him of—"

"Well, Sonya!" Mama forced a smile onto her face. "It was very nice of you to come over, but I don't want to keep you from cooking your Shabbos dinner."

"That's all right. My girl is taking care of everything." Sonya employed a Mexican American girl to help with the housework. "That much money, there has to be a man. What is it with the women in this family? Hasn't anyone heard of saving yourself until you're married?"

"Sonya!"

"Pearl with that *schvartze*," Sonya continued. "And now Barbara—"

"Sonya, shut the hell up!"

Both Sonya and I turned toward Mama in shock. I couldn't count how many times I had heard her say, *If we didn't need Elaine's job at Leo's bookstore, what I wouldn't say to that woman.* Now she had said it.

"If I'm not welcome here . . ." Sonya made a show of stuffing the shirt she hadn't touched back into her mending basket.

"If you'll excuse me, I need to start cooking dinner," Mama said. "Elaine, don't you have schoolwork?"

Gratefully I followed Mama through the swinging door into the kitchen. I offered to help her with dinner, but she told me to go study.

In my room, I contemplated my sister's wealth—and her seeming willingness to use sex as currency. She'd gone to see the "producer" expecting something like what happened; what upset her was being cheated out of her part of the deal. Still, what would she have had to do for $130? It was a fortune.

PAPA AND PEARL DIDN'T return until late in the day. By that time, Audrey and Harriet had come home from school; Mama had sent them to the Anshels' next door. She hadn't, however, succeeded in dislodging Sonya from the sofa. So the three of us—Mama, Sonya, and I—heard what had happened that afternoon. The nightclub manager had been quite willing to see them, Papa said; he even commiserated with them in Yiddish. And he showed them an account book with everything he had paid Barbara; it wasn't a penny more than she'd turned in to Mama, plus the little bit she kept for herself. There was nothing that came close to explaining the money in her bank account.

"But he told us that some of the girls make extra money by modeling," Papa said.

"Modeling?" Mama said. "In department stores?"

"For photographers." Papa stared at his hands. "You know, pinup pictures. Pretty girls in bathing suits."

"*Gevult,*" Sonya said. "There's a man who has a bookstore a few blocks from Leo—Mr. Geiger, you must know him, Elaine. He has photographs of girls in a back room."

"Barbara would never do that!" I said.

Not that I had seen any of the "specialty" items Arthur Gwynn Geiger was rumored to sell from his back room. (In the front of his shop, it was said, the same handsome volumes never moved from the shelves.) But Geiger occasionally came into Leo's store—all of the Hollywood Boulevard book dealers knew one another—and I'd rarely felt such a visceral dislike for anyone as I did for the pudgy, affected, fortyish Geiger. His left eye was glass, his gaze cold and fishy, and he insisted on looking me in the eyes, bullying me to look back or else feel I was being rude. The idea of Barbara having any connection to Geiger made me cringe.

"Of course she wouldn't," Pearl said, and glared at Sonya. (With Sonya present, Mama and Pearl had buried the hatchet from the night before and were a united front.) "All he said was that *some* girls modeled!"

"That much money, whatever she was selling, it wasn't apples on the street corner," Sonya said.

"As a matter of fact," Papa said, "he gave us the names of three photographers." He held up a sheet of cream-colored notepaper imprinted with the Trocadero letterhead, which bore some writing in an expansive hand. "We went to see them—that's why we were gone for so long. But none of them knew Barbara."

"Oh . . ." I caught my breath.

Fortunately, Sonya spoke at the same time—"As if they'd admit anything to *you*!"—and my reaction went unnoticed.

While they discussed what to do next, I debated whether to mention that I'd recognized the name of one of the photographers: Alan Yardley. He was the friend who'd done Barbara's glossies for "almost nothing." Did she pay for the glossies by modeling? And maybe she had done additional modeling for the money? The fact that Yardley denied knowing her suggested something unsavory had gone on. Certainly I wasn't going to bring it up in front of Sonya. But why even tell Mama and Papa, when it would only upset them? The important thing now wasn't how she'd come by her $130. What mattered was that she *had* money; she wasn't on her own and penniless.

I said nothing.

The next morning, Saturday, Pearl came by in her car for Papa, and they set out for the train and bus stations. If Barbara had cleaned out her bank account, then she might have left Los Angeles, and they planned to show her graduation picture to the ticket agents and ask if anyone remembered selling her a ticket, and to where.

I went to my job at the bookstore. On my lunch break, I took a walk and found myself drawn toward Geiger's shop. I wondered if he sold photographs that were taken by Alan Yardley. I walked through the door. Geiger wasn't there, but a hard-looking woman in a tight dress strode toward me as if to prevent me from going any further. "Sorry, wrong address," I said, and left.

If I could just see for myself if there were any pictures of her, I'd have a better idea what to do. But my brief foray into Geiger's shop had made me realize there was no way *I* could ask to see his special stock. Paul, on the other hand . . . A college fellow could walk into Geiger's and be welcomed, and Paul, worldly from having fought in Spain, could pull it off. He had invited me to call him, and he'd seemed sincere. But did I want to ask for Paul Resnick's help? It would mean confiding in him that my sister might have posed for pinup shots. And what if he did find pictures of her at Geiger's? Could I trust him?

To my surprise, the answer that came to me was yes. I phoned Paul at his father's scrap metal business. He came by the bookstore an hour later, and I explained what I had in mind.

His visit to Geiger's took twenty minutes. When he came back, he handed me a flat parcel, the dimensions of a four-by-six-inch photograph, wrapped in brown paper and tied with string.

"You were right," he said.

"Thank you." I was grateful not only for his help but for his lack of childish embarrassment. And although I felt wild to rush someplace private and rip the parcel open, I didn't want Paul to leave right away. I found his presence steadying. "You asked if he had any photos by Alan Yardley?"

"That Geiger's a piece of slime, isn't he? When I asked about Yardley, he said, 'Obviously you're a connoisseur.' He said he'd just gotten the latest shots of her yesterday. I wondered if they were taken after she left home."

"The latest?" I glanced at the parcel, clutched in my clammy hand.

"I got four different ones, I got the feeling they were from different modeling sessions."

"How will I know which is the latest?"

He shook his head. "You'll know. . . . Elaine, I hope this doesn't sound like empty comfort, but I've seen a lot worse."

"Thanks. And thanks again for your help."

"Please, if there's anything else, promise you'll call?"

After he left, I went into the bathroom and edged the string off the parcel. Paul had said he'd seen a lot worse, and I naively expected saucy shots in lingerie, even some nudity. She *was* wearing lingerie in one photo—a transparent peignoir that left nothing to the imagination as she faced the camera with a teasing smile. That was the tame one. In two others, she was completely naked, striking provocative poses, her face pouty and her back arched to push out her breasts.

And Paul was right: there was no doubt which was the last shot. She sat on a bench, leaning back slightly. One leg was raised so that her foot was on the bench and slightly to the side. You could see everything. Her eyes looked empty, and she hadn't pretended to smile. She knew no one was going to care about her face.

These weren't pinup shots. They were smut.

I reeled with revulsion. And rage. I wanted to run to Geiger's store and smash the windows, take a baseball bat to Geiger's smug face, burn every filthy picture. Next I'd destroy Alan Yardley's camera. And then I'd go after my rotten sister! In the first three pictures, she was flirting with the camera. Did she see "modeling" as a lark? She had to know her photos would be pawed, drooled on, and worse. Didn't she care? Did she *enjoy* the idea?

I heard Leo clearing his throat outside the bathroom door. I'd been in there for ten minutes. I flushed the toilet and ran the water in the sink hard. My hands felt filthy. I scrubbed them under hot water, then washed them again after I'd remade the parcel of photographs and shoved it into my purse.

I tried to get back to work, but I felt genuinely ill: queasy, wobbly. I told Leo I wasn't well and left early. I couldn't stop seeing that last photo in my mind. However Barbara had felt doing the other poses, sitting with her legs open was no lark. And despite her pretense of sophistication, she was only eighteen. Look how she'd fallen for the line the "producer" fed her. What kinds of people was she around now, and what lines were they giving her? Should I push Papa to go to the police? At least he needed to talk to Alan Yardley again. If, as Paul surmised, the last photograph was taken after Barbara had left, maybe Yardley knew where she was.

But to make any of that happen, I'd have to tell Papa about the photographs. And it wouldn't be enough to tell. He would insist on seeing them. Still, if Barbara was associating with men like Yardley and Geiger, did I have the right to keep her secrets? *I* was only eighteen. This was too big for me.

I would tell no one but Papa, I decided. I just had to talk to him away from everyone else. That turned out to be easy. I walked into the house expecting the anxious hubbub that had greeted me every day since Barbara's departure. But Papa was alone in the living room, sitting in his armchair reading a book. Mama was in bed with a headache, he said, and Pearl had taken Audrey and Harriet to a movie.

Papa told me about the latest phase of the search. He and Pearl had gone to the train and bus stations, even the steamship lines, but they found no one who remembered selling a ticket to Barbara. Ticket agents worked different shifts, of course, and they planned to go back during the week and try again.

"How are *you* doing?" He regarded me with surprising tenderness, and I fought tears.

"All right," I said.

"Your first week of college, and we haven't even talked about it. Tell me about your classes and professors."

As I answered Papa's questions about USC, my fingers kept wandering to the dirty photographs of Barbara in my handbag.

But I couldn't let Papa see her like that. I decided to burn the photographs. Barbara would come home; at least she'd get in touch with us when it suited her. I would just have to wait until she felt ready.

I couldn't do that, either.

CHAPTER 19

AN INTELLIGENT JEWESS

ALAN YARDLEY'S PHOTOGRAPHY STUDIO WAS ON A SIDE STREET off of Hollywood Boulevard. I went there after my classes on Monday. I was nervous, expecting the sliminess of Geiger's shop. But instead, the tiny lobby, where a pleasant middle-aged Japanese American woman announced me over an intercom, looked like an art gallery; the pristine white walls held just half a dozen cleanly spaced photographs, harshly beautiful desert scenes.

Yardley himself surprised me by being . . . the word that comes to mind is *courtly*. I'd figured he would keep me waiting, and I was prepared to stay there for hours, but he immediately opened the door to the studio and invited me in. And there was such gentleness to Alan Yardley. He was in his fifties, I guessed, and he was slender and quite tall, over six feet, although he walked with a stoop, as if to keep people from being intimidated. And even though I jumped in the second I walked into his studio and accused him of lying to Papa, his gaze remained kind and a little sad.

"You do know her! I have some of the pictures you took of her!" I said.

"The pictures?" he said softly.

"From Arthur Geiger's store."

"Ah." He regarded me with his sorrowful eyes. "I'm sorry, but I didn't see any point in mentioning the pictures to your father. I thought it would only upset him. Does he know?"

I shook my head.

"So you thought that, too. You didn't want to hurt him."

Ridiculously, I started to cry.

"Oh, dear," he said. "Let me see if the tea is ready. I asked Harumi to fix some. Please do sit down."

He went out to the lobby, giving me a few minutes alone. I got control of myself, then looked around.

An open area at the far end of the room was where Yardley staged photographs. The space currently held a stool draped in gray velvety fabric, and a rice paper screen provided a soft background. Two cameras mounted on tripods and several lights on poles faced the "stage." Just behind the cameras, in the center of the studio, were a low table and two wooden chairs. On one side of the room, he kept various props: stools, chairs, platforms, drapes, and so on. The opposite side was a working area with a light table and more photographic equipment. And on the wall above the light table hung more of the austere desert photographs I'd seen in the lobby.

Yet despite the accumulation of objects, the studio was surprisingly peaceful. Even as I anticipated a further confrontation with Yardley, something about the desert photographs made me feel calm.

Yardley came back in carrying a tray with a white ceramic teapot, two handleless white cups, and a plate of almond cookies.

"Joshua Tree National Monument," he said, following my glance toward the desert scenes. "Have you ever been there?"

"No."

"The most beautiful place on earth. Sit, please," he said as he placed the tray on the low table.

"All right."

He poured the tea, a transparent golden liquid, nothing like the inky brew we drank at home.

"Sugar?"

"Yes, thank you."

"It's Japanese green tea. I wouldn't recommend milk, but if you'd like some . . ." There was a small pitcher.

"It's fine," I said impatiently. As gracious as he seemed, I reminded myself that this was the man who had talked Barbara into exposing her vulva for his camera. "Mr. Yardley—"

"Alan."

"When did you take the most recent picture?"

"The most recent . . . ?"

"Where she's on *that* bench." I had spotted it among his props. "With her legs open."

He sighed. "You saw that one? Hmm, I suppose a few weeks ago."

"Arthur Geiger said he just got that one in his shop last weekend."

Despite my combative tone, he responded evenly, "That sounds right. It takes a few weeks for me to develop the film, make the prints, and then get them to my customers. Please, why don't you tell me what you want, and maybe I can help."

"Did you take that picture last week, after she left home? Did you see her?"

"Oh, and you think I might have some idea where she is! I'm so sorry, no. This must all be a terrible shock for you. I knew Barbara wanted to live on her own, but I was surprised she left so abruptly—"

"How *well* did you know her?" What else had he talked her into?

"No, it's nothing like that. I don't get involved with the girls who model for me. Even if I were inclined to, and I'm not, Harumi would never allow it. My wife." He nodded toward the lobby. "But the girls and I always drink tea and chat a bit first. And they usually talk about why they're modeling, what they want to do with the money."

"How much money is it?" I said, thinking of Barbara's savings account.

"About thirty dollars a session. More if a girl gets a following."

"Or if she opens her legs?"

"Ah, well. It's a sordid little business, I won't insult your intelligence by pretending otherwise. But I do treat the girls with respect. And men being the way they are, there happens to be an excellent market for this sort of thing. Spending a few hours posing lets the girls pay for singing or acting lessons. Or for college. And it lets me afford to do what *I* love." He gestured toward the desert photos.

Yardley was just a smoother creep than Geiger, I cautioned myself. Still, it was easy to imagine Barbara feeling comfortable with him, confiding in him. His kindness felt genuine and not simply a facade to deflect me. But was he nonetheless *trying* to deflect me with his refined manners and delicate tea and breathtaking photographs? Was he hiding something about Barbara? And was there any way I could pierce the facade and get him to tell me?

"Mr. Yardley, if you could see how this is upsetting my mother, my whole family . . . ," I said. "If there's any small thing you remember from talking with her . . ."

"I wish there was."

"You said she wanted to live on her own. Did she give you any idea where she might go?"

"I suppose I thought she wanted to get an apartment with one or two girlfriends."

"Anyone in particular? Did she mention any names?"

"Let me . . . No, I don't recall any names."

Everything he said was plausible: that he'd taken the last photo weeks ago, that Barbara had spoken only vaguely of her plans. But I kept feeling I was being outmaneuvered by a master. Yardley knew exactly how far I was able to go. At five-three and 120 pounds, I was hardly going to rough him up like a tough guy in the movies and force him to talk. Nor was I going to come back with Papa, because then I'd have to show Papa the photos. The police? But would they get involved? And if they did, would an investigation just drag Barbara and the rest of us through the mud?

"Did she ever talk about leaving Los Angeles?" I tried.

"Not that I remember."

To have come this far, to have found out he'd taken dirty pictures of Barbara and confronted him, and to leave with nothing!

"Alan!" I slammed my teacup onto the table, was gratified by the knock of porcelain against wood. "You saw her last week, I know it! Where is she?"

Even during my outburst, his face remained quiet. (Years later, when my kids' generation gravitated to yoga and Zen Buddhism, I'd wonder if he had studied some Eastern discipline.) But for the first time that afternoon, he spoke vehemently. "I swear to you, I don't know where she is. If it's any comfort, Barbara struck me as a girl who will always land on her feet. I wish I could help you. But I'll make a promise, Elaine. Unless she's left Los Angeles, I'm sure I'll hear from her when she wants to model again. I'll do everything I can to convince her to contact you."

"And you'll take more pictures of her?" I shot back.

He shrugged. "That's her decision."

Suddenly—I don't know where it came from—I became a dragon. "Alan, my sister is eighteen. She's underage. You're not going to take more pictures of her. And the ones you've already taken, stop selling them."

Or else? I could hear him think it. But he said, "All right."

"The negatives, too?"

"The negatives, too. Would you like another cup of tea while I get them for you?" he said mildly, as if we'd simply been sitting, politely chatting, all along.

"No, thank you."

He started going through file drawers. And I finally began to grasp how thoroughly Barbara had disappeared. In less than a day, she had quit her job, emptied her bank account—an account she must have built up over weeks or months by modeling—and then vanished. I had figured she'd taken off in an impulsive panic. But an impulsive act leaves loose ends, and if Barbara had left even one loose end, we hadn't found it. Instead, it was as if she'd calculated in advance how to cover every track. My catching her with Danny had pushed her to leave when she did, but had she planned her escape all along?

Yardley handed me an envelope bulging with photos and negatives. "I can see why she was so proud of you," he said. "You just started at USC, didn't you?"

"That's right."

"And you're going to be a lawyer?"

"She told you all that?" I said, surprised to think that, as Barbara had sipped fragrant tea and talked to this gentle man who invited confidences, some of the confidences were about me.

"As I said, she was proud of you. And envious."

"Of me?"

"You have such important things ahead of you. College, a career. I'm afraid your sister had found out her glamorous job meant having to slap away men's hands and soak the bunions on her feet. And she was floundering, as lots of young people do. But having met you, I'd venture to say you know who you are and where you belong in the world."

"That's not true!" I protested, not only because I didn't feel that way at all but to deny his attempt to define me.

"Yes, well, who am I to say?" He gave me a rueful smile. "I'm just a pornographer who likes to pretend he's some kind of artist."

PAUL HELPED ME BURN the negatives one night later that week at his father's scrap metal lot. But nothing else ended so cleanly.

Papa went back to talk to ticket agents a few more times over the following weeks. And he, Mama, and Pearl, in various combinations, made the rounds of nightclubs; even $130 runs out eventually, and Barbara might have gotten another chorus line job. They started with the posh places, visiting all of them within the first two weeks. But gradually the clubs got seedier and the outings more sporadic. Papa went to the police, too, but, as he had feared, they weren't going to mount a search for an eighteen-year-old girl who had worked in a nightclub and left home of her own free will.

How many ways can you look for someone who's determined not to be found? And why keep looking for a girl who had plenty of money, wherever she'd gotten it, and was too heartless even to send a postcard and let her mother know she was still alive? But anytime one of us—Mama, Papa,

Pearl, or I—ventured the opinion that we had exhausted the search and it was time to give up, someone suggested a new avenue to try. Papa spoke to the only private detective we knew of, Ned Shulman, who had an office on Soto, but he was offended by Shulman's insinuating questions and what he had the gall to charge. Better to spend our money—well, Uncle Leo's and Aunt Pearl's money—on ads in the personal columns in Los Angeles and other cities in California, and on the reward offered for information.

We ran the ads for six months, and Papa checked out any responses that seemed promising; the responses trickled in for another year. Several times the police called, and Papa went to the morgue and viewed the body of an unidentified dead girl, a task from which he returned white-faced but forcing a smile, to let us know immediately that the girl wasn't Barbara.

But time passed. People we ran into in Boyle Heights eventually stopped asking if we'd had any word. We went on. Well, all of us except Mama did.

The rest of us were fortunate to have lives outside the house, but Mama . . . at least she didn't spend all day in her nightgown weeping, like a neighbor who'd had to go to a sanitarium. Mama got dressed in the morning. With help from Audrey, especially, she cooked and kept the house reasonably clean. (No wonder Audrey was the one who inherited Mama's culinary skill.) She took part in conversations. Yet she stumbled through these things as if none of them—none of us—were real to her. One afternoon I was riding the streetcar to Leo's bookstore, and I glimpsed her walking down Hollywood Boulevard, peering into shops and restaurants. Something told me not to approach her. But I mentioned it to Audrey later and found out that once or twice a week, Mama left home in the morning and didn't come back for hours.

I still awoke every morning in the bed that had been Barbara's (we had put away the cot) to the fresh awareness of my dual losses, Barbara and Danny. An ache. A moment, depending on my mood that morning, of sadness or worry or anger. But then I went out the door, took the streetcar to USC, and got immersed . . . not just in my classes but in a lively social world, a group that congregated at "our" table in the student union for passionate political discussions and got together on weekends to continue our debates, drink cheap wine, dance, and flirt. It was a society in which, to my pleased amazement, I felt deeply at home.

You know where you belong in the world, Alan Yardley had said. I hadn't believed him then; how could I, in just my second week at USC, when everywhere I looked, I saw smartly dressed blond girls and beefy, football-playing boys, people who talked about fraternities and sororities and the cars their parents had bought them? It was alien territory in which I'd figured on being a perpetual outsider. But as the overwhelming newness subsided, I discovered quite a few of my classmates who took their studies as seriously as I did and cared what was happening in the world. It wasn't just the bookish kids with Jewish surnames and glasses, either. A girl in my English class with a sweep of blond hair à la Veronica Lake urged me to come to a forum on the class struggle, and she became a friend.

And toward the end of my second month at USC, Hank Graham asked me out. Hank was the quarterback of the junior varsity football team and also the star of our economics class. He grasped concepts with astonishing quickness; a self-described conservative, he even had the confidence to challenge our New Dealer professor. Sometimes, on the way out of class, he argued with me—not in a bullying way but out of his engagement with ideas. When he invited me to a movie, at first I figured he was joking. He meant it, though. Not that he ever took me to one of his fraternity dances or a party with his friends. He was the first boy I'd gone out with who owned a car, and whether a date started at the movies or a concert (Hank introduced me to chamber music, which became a lifelong love), we ended up parking someplace like Mulholland Drive. He was a gentleman, cajoling but never forcing. At some point, though, I realized he saw me as a sexual adventure, a girl with the fabled licentiousness of the "exotic Jewess." The idea amused me: Elaine Greenstein, someone's sexual adventure? And to be fair, the adventure took place on both sides. Hank was the first boy I'd dated since Danny, and I took a fierce pleasure in necking with someone, anyone else; all the better that it was a boy I didn't love. More than that: as if Barbara had carried the wildness for both of us, in her absence I discovered my own wild streak. Wherever she'd gone, was she now drawn to libraries? Did she pick up books and adore their smell?

Still, it disturbed me to be the Jewess whom Hank hid from his friends.

At least, that was what I told myself when I started turning down Hank's invitations. (I said I was busy, and he didn't seem to mind.) But I think something much larger had shifted. I no longer felt a compulsion to get back at Danny.

At first, after that day when I'd caught him with Barbara, my anger and hurt burned as hot as my love. He sent me letters, pleas for forgiveness, daily that first month or so. Just seeing a letter from him made me want to scream. I refused to open the letters and told Mama to throw them away; and then sometimes, weeping and cursing, I'd fish one out of the garbage and read it in spite of myself. Then his unit left for England, and the letters dwindled to two or three a week. And though he still said in every letter how much he loved me and how sorry he was for hurting me, he also told me about being in England and about army life. I knew what was in those letters because I started to read them, even if I still didn't write back. The moment when I'd opened the door to his room and seen him with Barbara hadn't stopped haunting me; for years, one thing or another—seeing Mr. Berlov on the street, smelling Shalimar perfume, even hearing a low, intimate laugh—would thrust that memory into my consciousness, and I'd feel as if I'd been sick. But something had changed. I'd stopped thinking about any kind of future with Danny; I was able to read his letters with the part of me that saw him as one of my oldest friends and hoped for his safe return from the war.

Later I'd ask myself how, after loving Danny from childhood, I could so quickly let him go. *Did* I glimpse something in him that day that forever changed who he was for me? On the other hand, maybe everything would have been different if only he hadn't been leaving the next day—if there'd been time for my rage to soften and for him to approach me in small steps, for us to do a subtle dance of apology and blame and eventual reconciliation.

And maybe none of that mattered. Over the years, I would see generations of high school romances in all their drama—and their evanescence. And I wondered if Danny and I had been outgrowing each other already, as we moved from high school into the world; and if that was why, the next spring, I was ready to fall in love with Paul.

Paul had been part of my life all along. We had two classes together, history and English, and we gravitated to the same group of campus left-wingers. I was grateful for the help he had given me after Barbara left—and for his discretion. Word got around Boyle Heights about her dancing at the Trocadero, but I never caught wind of any rumor about the girlie pictures. Seeing Paul around campus or at a party, I occasionally caught a hint of the shivery, caressing look he used to give me, but he no longer tried to unsettle me. I supposed he felt sorry for me, or embarrassed, since he'd seen the photos.

Then, one afternoon in May, we got on the same streetcar from campus at the end of the day and sat next to each other. And when we got off in Boyle Heights, he asked if I wanted to take a walk.

"I've got at least two hours of reading to do," I said.

"It's spring," he said. "Smell." We were standing beside a night-blooming jasmine, just unfurling its petals in the late afternoon and emitting an indolent perfume.

On the streetcar, we had discussed what the entire country was obsessing about: the war. The week before, Germany had launched simultaneous blitzkrieg invasions into Holland, Belgium, Luxembourg, and France. Holland and Luxembourg had already surrendered. Now France and Belgium were fighting for their lives—with help from the British Expeditionary Force, which included Danny and Burt's unit from Canada.

On our walk, though, the war didn't exist. *It's spring,* Paul had said, and it was as if by announcing it, he made spring the central fact of the universe, more real than anything else. It was one of those perfect late afternoons in May, the sun pleasantly warm yet soft, a sun that kissed everything—the streets, buildings, Paul, and me—with golden light. Flowers bloomed riotously, the jasmine and also California poppies in orange, yellow, and crimson. Walking to Hollenbeck Park, I noticed my legs gliding in my hip joints with an animal joy I hadn't experienced since I used to dance.

There was another kind of awareness, too, a return of the current I had once felt between us. But it was no longer a flicker, a *could-this-be-sexual* frisson. As if the current had gained force from months of lying dormant (months, Paul told me later, when he had held back, giving me time to get over Danny), it permeated that afternoon. It was present in the glances

Paul and I gave each other, in the brilliant poppies, in the softness of the grass on my bare feet when I took my shoes off in the park. And the heady jasmine—whenever I remembered our first kiss, that afternoon in the park, the memory was drenched with the fragrance of jasmine.

I didn't love Paul with the sweet abandon of my love for Danny. Thank God. A college woman now, I cringed to think of the girlish sweetness and naivete I had only recently escaped. That summer of 1940, Paul became the first and only man with whom I would ever make love. Still, I reserved parts of me he couldn't enter, keeping him from getting too close through ironic remarks. He fought back avidly. How we thrived on our battles! Going with Paul—and, later, being married to him—had the kind of charge I used to envy between Danny and Barbara.

I wrote to Danny to tell him I was going with Paul; I felt I owed him that. He didn't respond, but I didn't know if that was because of my news or because he'd started a dangerous new job. I had heard through the Boyle Heights grapevine that following the evacuation from Dunkirk at the end of May, Danny, whose first languages were Polish and Yiddish, had volunteered to go behind enemy lines as a spy.

On September 12, 1940, exactly one year after the last time I'd seen Barbara, I was on edge all day. All of us were, privately, unable to bear mentioning it. Surely, wherever she'd gone and whatever filled her day, she was thinking of us. And her persistence in *our* thoughts, in our yearning, was so intense, I felt as if we could will her into physical presence, at the very least that we could summon her voice on the phone. Magical thinking. Of course, there was nothing. Then the day ended, and it was September 13, then September 14, and so on and on.

LIFE STUBBORNLY CONTINUED.

I completed my sophomore year at USC, making the dean's list as I had the year before. Paul and I broke up after one of our spats exploded, and for those moments I loathed him—and loathed knowing I'd given him power to hurt me. But the fight also made me realize how much Paul meant to me. And by the time we got back together a week later, with fevered makeup sex, I couldn't remember the specifics of the fight. (During our marriage, we used to joke that neither of us ever thought of divorce, but we often contemplated murder.)

The war spread. Germany attacked Yugoslavia, Greece, and even the Soviet Union, to the anguish of our leftist group. There was constant debate about whether the United States should get into the fight, and more Boyle Heights boys went to enlist in the Canadian army, two of them immediately after the terrible news that Burt Weber had been killed fighting in North Africa.

In my house, there were just five places at the dinner table; no one made a mistake and set six anymore. I knew from Audrey that Mama still went out a couple of days a week, and I assumed she was going to Hollywood, but she no longer acted as if she were sleepwalking; she seemed herself again.

I hated anniversaries, those false markers on the calendar that raised a flutter of anticipation I couldn't suppress. The following March 28 was Barbara's twentieth birthday, March 29 mine. I stayed out late both of those nights, refusing to wait at home for a letter or call that wasn't going to come. And both nights I got drunk, which in my case didn't involve dancing on tables; when I drank, I really did get "tight"—wound up, archly funny, and, according to Paul, sexy in a sort of dangerous way, as if I might have a switchblade concealed in my bra. When the next September 12 came along—two years— I did the same.

It was 1941. I was an adult, a junior at USC, and no longer a virgin. A boy I knew had died in battle. If there were times when I ached to share a story with Barbara or hear her laugh—if, alone in *our* bedroom, I opened the lid of my treasure box and held her note, or found a scarf she'd left behind and pressed it to my nose to catch a whiff of her—the next morning I was brisk and cool again: Katharine Hepburn in *The Philadelphia Story*, Rosalind Russell in *His Girl Friday*, Bette Davis in anything.

I felt as if I were in a movie, delivering lines that surprised me with their sophisticated bite, the first time I spoke to Philip Marlowe. I guess he brought that out in me.

It happened that October at Leo's bookstore. I was working alone that afternoon. An ominous sky and thunder growling in the foothills had discouraged paying customers, leaving just a handful of regulars, people who would read entire books as they stood in the aisle—and whom I trusted not to steal anything. It was enough to glance at them occasionally from the office, where I was studying for a pre-law class.

I looked up, alerted by the bell over the door, when Philip came in. I kept looking because he didn't belong. Not because he was handsome in the rough-hewn style of movie thugs; we got customers who looked like that. But those men entered the store like every other book lover—even as their feet carried them forward, their eyes kept darting toward the shelves on either side, and after a few steps, they paused, enticed by a title or the look of a binding. This man headed straight toward me, and though he was polite as he elbowed his way down the narrow aisle, I sensed a contained violence in him that put me on alert and intrigued me.

He opened his wallet and flashed a star at me. Apart from chatting with the beat cops who stopped by the store, my only experiences with the police had involved helping Mollie hide from them and having them call Papa to look at girls in the morgue. I said nothing, collecting my thoughts. And I took off my glasses, distancing myself; though a moment later I realized it was the gesture I'd adopted as a teenager around boys. Well, the cop *was* good-looking; more than that, his eyes hinted at intelligence and humor.

He asked if I'd do him a favor.

"What kind of favor?" Whoever this cop was chasing, I figured I might be on their side.

But he wanted to know about Arthur Gwynn Geiger. And he asked as if he wanted something bad to happen to Geiger, which made me inclined to help him in any way I could. I hated Geiger for ruining Barbara, even though blaming him wasn't rational. He had only sold the photos; I should have turned my wrath toward Alan Yardley for taking and peddling them, or the capitalist system for turning girls into commodities, or why not Barbara herself for being such a little fool? But no matter; it was Geiger who repelled me.

Still, I didn't know what the cop wanted with Geiger. And was this man really a cop? Anyone could make up a badge with a star, and something about the man felt slightly off. Stalling as I debated whether to trust him, I parried his questions. And flirted a little. He parried back. I had never met a cop with such an agile mind. I'd been right about the intelligence in his eyes.

He asked for an 1860 edition of *Ben-Hur* with a specific erratum. I looked it up and saw that Ben-Hur hadn't been published until 1880.

"There isn't one," I said.

"Right. The girl in Geiger's store didn't know that."

"That doesn't surprise me." I had seen the girl who worked for Geiger, a slithery sexpot; I questioned whether she even knew how to read.

Then the man told me he was a private detective, and the things that had seemed wrong about him fell into place. I gave him my impression of Geiger, not saying a word about Barbara, of course. And not mentioning Geiger's business in smut—clearly he already knew about that.

Two days later, every bookseller on the boulevard buzzed with the news that Geiger had been shot. Murdered.

The next week, the detective returned to Leo's bookstore. He introduced himself this time—Philip Marlowe—and asked if he could buy me dinner when I got off work.

"Did you shoot Arthur Geiger?" I asked. I would have cheered to hear about Geiger's public disgrace or financial ruin. I wouldn't have minded in the least if he'd been beaten to a bloody pulp. But murder . . .

"Didn't you see the newspapers?" he said. "He was killed by a business associate. A falling-out among thieves."

"Do you believe everything you read in the papers?"

He laughed. It was a good laugh, with nothing mean in it. When he finished laughing, he regarded me seriously. "I didn't kill Geiger. But I killed another man. I was protecting someone. Maybe you wouldn't see it that way, though, and you might not want to have dinner with me."

I considered it. Not just his having killed someone but the dangerous, tantalizing spark I felt with him.

"On the other hand," he drawled, "you might want to tell me what *your* beef was with Geiger, and if it's settled now."

How had he guessed I had my own reasons for hating Geiger? "Is this just an invitation for hamburgers?" I said. "Or will you buy me a steak?"

Dinner turned out to be steak, although it bore no resemblance to anything I knew as "steak"—the cheap cuts that Mama cooked on rare occasions and parceled out among us. At the dimly lit Hollywood dive to which Philip took me, the waiter placed a slab of porterhouse in front of me. It was the most mouthwatering meat I had ever tasted.

I hadn't planned to say anything about Barbara. But I'd had a glass of Scotch, and the place was smoky and intimate, and Philip listened with such deep attention, his surprisingly gentle eyes offering understanding but not, thank God, pity. I ended up telling him everything over dinner that night, about the dirty photographs and Arthur Geiger and Yardley, whom I suspected of having lied to me, but how could I have forced him to talk? I even shared the awful moment in which I found Barbara with Danny. I'm sure that getting people to open up was one of Marlowe's professional skills, but what really made me trust him was that he reminded me of Paul. He had the same essential . . . *Goodness* is an old-fashioned word, and it seems an odd choice for a man who'd just told me he had killed someone. But in Philip, as in Paul, I saw a good man—fair, generous, compassionate, a man of principle who would choose his battles wisely but, once he decided to fight, wouldn't back down.

After I told him about Barbara, he made a proposal. He'd do a bit of sleuthing and see if he could find out anything about her. In exchange, would I help him with occasional library research, things like that?

I didn't say yes right away. I'd gotten my hopes up too many times already, only to have them crushed. And after two years there seemed even less chance of success. But I decided it was wrong not to tell Mama and Papa about his offer. They insisted on meeting him. Mama, especially, adored him. In my mother's living room, the muscular detective came across like a big, gentle dog, albeit one who was extremely well-spoken. He listened with respectful kindness when she talked about leaving her village as a girl and never seeing her parents again, and he asked for a second piece of her apple cake. And so our agreement began.

He called a few days later with my first "assignment"—going to the library and perusing the newspaper society pages for the past six months, looking for connections between a society matron and a handsome young man who I figured was a con artist. It was a tedious task that cured any illusions I might have about detective work being exciting. He had me give him the results over dinner, his treat at the dive with the fantastic steaks.

He had news for me, too. He had gone to Alan Yardley's studio in Holly-wood but discovered Yardley had closed his business nearly two years ago; he'd moved to Twentynine Palms, near Joshua Tree National Monument, according to the dentist who had an office next door.

"He wanted to be an *artist*," Philip sneered. "You must have scared him. Sounds like he ran a few months later . . . What's the matter?"

"I'm thinking what an idiot I was. I *liked* Alan Yardley."

"Why?"

"I suppose because he was good at feeding me a line, and I was naive enough to believe him."

To my surprise, Philip said, "You're smarter than that. Tell me what you liked about him." He listened intently when I explained about Yardley's gentleness and said that his quietly beautiful photographs made me feel as if the earth possessed a deep, inherent order that would outlast all of the chaos that humans unleashed upon it.

He wouldn't be able to follow up right away, Philip said, but he sometimes got jobs that took him out Yardley's way, and he'd drop in on the photographer then.

A few weeks later, I got another assignment and another dinner, though no new information. Philip had a job coming up, however, that would take him to Palm Springs, and he should be able to make a side trip to Twentynine Palms to talk to Yardley.

That dinner took place during the first week in December.

On that Sunday, December 7, 1941, the Japanese bombed Pearl Harbor. All of Los Angeles, all of the country, went into turmoil. On Monday the United States declared war on Japan; declarations of war against Germany and Italy followed three days later. Many of the boys I knew enlisted immediately; there were long lines outside every recruiting center.

Paul resisted the rush to war. Like a number of my male classmates, he planned to wait until the end of the semester, which was just six weeks away; there'd still be plenty of war left to fight, he said. I understood that after fighting in Spain, Paul had no boyish illusions of glory, and he hardly needed to prove his courage; that was one of the things I loved about him, that he was an adult, a man. And the thought of him going to war and risking his life filled me with anguish. Yet I had caught war fever, too; how could I not? Every time another Boyle Heights boy enlisted or a former classmate strode across campus in his uniform, I felt a thrill of pride. I was filled with urgency to act now, not to schedule the war after exams. I never said any of this to Paul, because I understood that he was acting rationally while the rest of us danced to a primal drumbeat, but his coolheadedness enraged me. I was furious at myself, too: how dared I judge him when no one expected *me* to put on a uniform and be willing to die?

Constantly on edge, I woke up every morning tense and snarly after disturbing dreams, and I threw inflammatory adjectives into papers I wrote. At least when school was in session, I could sit in my private funk in classes. Over Christmas break, I worked full-time at the bookstore, and I had to act pleasant all day.

With so much craziness going on, it wasn't until a few days after Christmas that I saw Philip again. We got off on the wrong foot from the start. He was carrying a large, flat parcel wrapped in white paper under his arm—had he gotten me a Christmas gift? I didn't have anything for him, but was I supposed to? It was one of those awkward moments when I felt as clueless about American culture as a greenhorn just off the boat. Then he made it worse. We were walking from his car to the steak place, and he said, "Do you know him?"

"Who?"

"That Jew." He nodded toward Rosen's Jewelers, where an olive-skinned man with wavy hair about the color of mine lounged in the doorway. Wearing no coat despite the chilly evening, the man looked as if he worked in the store and had stepped out to take a break. Perhaps he was Rosen himself.

"No," I said. "Of course not."

It was nothing, a stray comment from a man who'd asked me about Boyle Heights as if it were on another planet. But I suppose it made me even testier than I was already, quicker to take offense.

In the restaurant, after we got our drinks, he said, "You'd make a good cop."

"Is that a compliment?" I shot back.

"Take it easy, sugar."

"Well, you don't have the highest opinion of cops."

"A *good* cop, was what I said. Would you like to hear why? Or would you prefer to take that steak knife and stick it through me?"

"Sorry. It's . . . everything." I took a sip of my drink and stopped glaring at him.

"Phew! I can see why Alan Yardley repented of his evil ways and went off to have visions in the desert."

I had no idea what his cryptic comment meant, but the important news was that he knew something about Yardley. "Did you see him?"

"Yup. You were on the money about him. He's okay."

"What did he say about Barbara?"

"As you suspected, she went to Yardley after you caught her with the boyfriend. Seems she felt safe with him. Good instincts, like you. They did, as he so delicately put it, another modeling session; she wanted the money. Then he and his wife put her up that night at their house. Maybe I'm getting all schoolgirlish and gullible, but I think he was on the level, no hanky-panky."

I nodded. "I've met his wife."

"Next day, he drove her to her bank downtown and then to the train station in Riverside."

"Why all the way out there?" Riverside was a good fifty miles from Los Angeles. If she was going to get on a train anyway, why not catch it in the city?

"Apparently she was worried that your family might show her picture around the train stations. She didn't want anyone coming after her."

Even though I'd accepted by now that Barbara had been planning her escape, it stunned me to understand how thoroughly she'd anticipated our moves and preemptively foiled them. Had she been that desperate to get away?

"Eat your steak," Philip said. "It's good for you."

I'd barely noticed that a steaming T-bone had been placed in front of me. I dutifully ate a couple of bites.

"I suppose Yardley lied about helping her leave because he'd promised her?" I said.

He nodded. "Can't say I hold his former profession in high regard, but I'd say he was a man of his word."

"Then why did he tell you now?"

"Funny thing," he said with a wolfish grin. "I'm told I'm the kind of fellow people can't stop themselves from confiding in. And by this time, who at the Riverside train station is going to remember her?"

"Did your persuasive powers extend to getting him to divulge where she went?"

"He said he didn't know."

"Didn't know or wouldn't say?"

He chuckled. "I should have brought you with me. You got him to quit taking dirty pictures and dedicate his life to art. Maybe you could have—"

"*What* are you talking about?"

"It was that visit from you that made him decide to get out of the smut business." He raised an amused eyebrow, and my volatile, touchy mood returned.

"Are you making fun of me?"

"I wouldn't do that. According to Yardley, meeting you changed his life. Taking a hard look at what he did through your eyes. In fact, he asked me to give you this. To thank you."

He handed me the parcel he'd brought into the restaurant. I unwrapped it. It was one of Yardley's desert photographs: sand, scrub, and sky exquisitely etched in black and white.

"Does he think that makes what he did all right? I don't want it," I said, even as I imagined how beautiful the photograph would be on my wall, and something in me felt glad that Yardley was living in the desert he loved. But I was wretched that night, on the verge of either tears or rage, and I chose rage.

"Well, it doesn't really go with my décor," Philip said. "Keep it, anyway. It might be worth something one day. So Yardley's story was, your sister told him she was going to stick a pin in a train schedule and decide that way."

"How could he let her do that? She was only eighteen."

"He figured she had enough money—and enough moxie—to take care of herself."

"If we got the schedule of trains that left Riverside that afternoon—"

"Elaine." He regarded me with what looked infuriatingly like pity. I wanted to slap him. "You figured it out for yourself. She'd been planning her getaway for a long time. She did work that she may have found de-meaning so she could save up the money to leave. She went to the trouble of catching a train in another city so she couldn't be followed. Sweetheart, look, for some people, it's not enough to leave the family nest. Some people—for reasons they probably can't explain themselves—feel like they're running for their lives."

"People in my family *did* run for their lives!" I said. "My grandfather was being chased by men who wanted to kill him. My mother, if she hadn't gotten out of Romania . . . do you know what's happening there now?"

"I think I have some general idea."

"No, you don't! You have *no* idea."

Later, I understood that I reacted so strongly because what he'd just said and the new evidence he'd brought me suggested something I refused to *think*: that Barbara had eagerly, happily, severed everything that con-nected her to us. To me. It made me feel blotted out of existence. Not just who I was now, but the dual identity I'd had from the moment of my birth seventeen minutes after hers: Barbara-and-Elaine, "we."

"Where are you going to look next?" I asked, my eyes daring him to suggest giving up the search.

"I think I'll go get chummy with a few chorus girls. Chorus girls seem to appreciate my charm." He gave me such a woeful grin, I had to laugh.

I had another drink, and we settled into the flirting and bantering of our previous dinners.

The flirting didn't mean anything. Philip inhabited a different Los An-geles than I did, a city where people carried guns and had their first drink of the day before lunch, a place where the most ordinary conversations crackled with sexual innuendo. He flirted with me as instinctively, as insig-nificantly, as he breathed. I knew that.

But I was in a reckless mood. The war, the tension I'd been feeling with Paul, and now having to imagine Barbara running for her life—running from me. When Philip was driving me home after dinner, I pressed close to him and kissed him.

"Well," he said. He turned onto a side street and pulled the car over to a curb.

He kissed me back. For a moment. Then he gently pushed me away.

"Can we go to your apartment?" I said. Despite the cocktails I'd had, I wasn't drunk. I wanted to live in his Los Angeles, if only for that evening.

"Oh, sweetheart," he said. "You're not that kind of girl. You'd hate yourself in the morning."

"I wouldn't!"

"Then *I'd* hate myself in the morning."

"Liar," I teased. My fingers darted to his crotch, confirmed that he was hard.

He grabbed my wrist so tightly I yelped. "Cut it out. Go sit over there." He directed me to the edge of the seat, next to the window.

In silence, he drove me home.

Philip was right. I wasn't that kind of girl. I felt guilty for even thinking of cheating on Paul. And I dreaded seeing the detective the next time. Should I pretend nothing had happened? Apologize for acting like an idiot and blame it on too many drinks? I decided to take my cue from him; he had surely weathered awkward situations like this one. But weeks passed, and I didn't hear from him. Finally, in late January, I called and reached him at his office. In a terse, uncomfortable conversation—had he been embarrassed, too?—he said he'd struck out with the chorus girls, and I could consider our trade completed.

I said goodbye to Barbara then. What else could I do? I was saying so many goodbyes in 1942. Paul enlisted in the army. All of the boys were going to war.

CHAPTER 20

BLACK ICE

AN IMMENSITY OF SNOW COVERS THE PLAINS STRETCHING TO THE horizon on either side of the highway. The road itself looks clear, but the woman who rented us the Explorer at the Cody airport warned us about black ice.

"Highway surface'll look fine, but there's a coat of transparent ice on it," she said. "Gotta keep testing your traction."

The warning came too late. I'm out of control already: I've been lurching and careening as I booked flights and hotel rooms for Josh and me, aired out my wool coat, bought snow boots, and duplicated family photographs to bring. It's all happened in just the past week since Josh brought me the information about Kay Thorne. I told myself I had to act quickly to get this trip in during Josh's winter break . . . as if I were somehow orchestrating this headlong rush. In truth, it's like falling down a flight of stairs.

I did that once; it must have been thirty years ago. One minute I was starting down the stairs from the bedroom, carrying a stack of files and thinking about the case I was working on; the next I was hurtling at a remarkable velocity yet with enough time to marvel at how fast a

130-pound woman could travel—and at my utter inability, despite kicking out at the railings, to stop. When I landed finally at the foot of the staircase, I lay still for a minute, amid a flurry of escaped papers, and scanned my body for anything that hurt so much I shouldn't try to get up on my own. I was lucky. I suffered nothing worse than two broken toes. Later I could summon a distinct picture of taking the first steps onto the stairs, and I vividly, with a sort of detached curiosity, remembered the fall itself. What I couldn't retrieve was the instant when my feet went out from under me.

Was it when I discovered the Kay Devereaux card?

Was it when Barbara left?

Or did the spill of events that brought me here begin long before, at some moment in our childhood when our eyes locked in perfect understanding, or we were laughing, and our two laughs, identical in pitch and rhythm, blended into a single voice?

Harriet, the one person in my family to whom I told the truth about this trip, tried to persuade me to let the news about Kay Thorne settle before I did anything; she offered to come with me if I still wanted to go this spring. But she didn't insist that she needed to be there. And even if I were capable of waiting, when I imagined Harriet and me arriving at the OKay Ranch and approaching my twin sister for the first time in more than sixty-five years, I understood that this is something I need to do alone.

That is, with no one except my sidekick from the beginning of this quest, Josh—who's driving the Explorer down the main street of Cody.

"This is it, right?" he says. "The Buffalo Bill Village?"

I look up and see the sign for the hotel I booked (which despite the picturesque name, is a Holiday Inn). Flying here took all day, half the time in the air and half waiting between flights in the Denver airport, so we're staying in the hotel tonight and driving to Barbara's ranch in the morning.

Josh unloads our gear, not just suitcases but a huge black case holding a professional video camera—unnecessary, and it was murder to get through security in Los Angeles. But he's so delighted with his cover story, that he's filming a documentary on World War II USO entertainers, he almost believes it himself. His enthusiasm has its value. He got on the phone to Kay Thorne right after I called him, and she eagerly agreed to be interviewed; she even invited him to stay at the ranch. I'm grateful he wasn't so caught up in his fiction that he accepted.

Actually, Josh has turned out to be a good companion on this journey. He threw out a few questions in the Los Angeles airport this morning—how was I feeling about seeing my sister again and what did I plan to say to her?—but when I changed the subject, he took the hint and didn't ask again.

I spend half an hour settling into my room, then meet Josh for dinner at the hotel restaurant. He relieves me of the effort of talking by nattering about the bars in town he's scoped out to hit that night. After dinner, I go to my room and watch television for a while.

At eleven I take an Ambien, turn out the light. And remain stubbornly awake.

The lighted display on the clock says 11:42 the first time I peek.

Then 12:26.

And 2:10.

The room is stifling. I've already shut off the heat vents. In Los Angeles, I never turn on the heat at night; on cold nights, a warm quilt is enough. I get up and open a window to a blast of frigid air. I can see the dark outline of the mountains to the west. Where *she* is.

In that visible distance, is she asleep, or does she, too, remain awake? Fighting insomnia? Maybe she's a night owl and stays up watching old movies on cable. Having a geography for her at last, a place on the map, makes her more real; she's in color instead of black and white. Did she ever cast her mind to Los Angeles and imagine me? Or did I always occupy a far smaller place in her life than she did in mine? Perhaps no place at all? I'm about to learn the answer to that.

I don't want to know.

I don't want to risk finding out I mean nothing to her. *Elaine? Sure, I remember. How ya doin'?* Better if she's furious at me for showing up, if she chases me off her ranch with a shotgun. Hate or fear, at least I matter.

What do you hope to get out of this? Harriet asked me. A reasonable question, and reason is my touchstone; I'm an attorney not only by training but in my deepest nature. And the answer? I want to glimpse the real woman behind the oh-so-public Kay of all the newspaper articles and the glossy dude ranch publicity, I told Harriet. I want to see for myself if she's all right. To follow our family mystery all the way to its conclusion. To attempt some kind of reconciliation, even *healing* (though that's Harriet's word, not mine).

All of the answers I gave Harriet make sense. I could argue each one and convince a jury. Reason, however, has nothing to do with the force that sank its teeth into me, picked me up, and dropped me here—in Wyoming at three in the morning, fishtailing over a sweep of black ice.

Finally I fall into a sleep in which I clench my teeth so tightly that when I wake up at quarter to eight, I feel like I've taken a punch to the jaw.

"You okay?" Josh says when I meet him for breakfast.

"I will be after two cups of coffee." I say; I hope. "How about you?"

He groans. "Country music, it always makes you feel like you've gotta have one more beer because of the girl who dumped you and you were so miserable you went and totaled a car, and the next day you lost your job . . . But hey, there's nothing like a few beers to get people talking about one of their local legends."

"Kay?"

"*Miz* Kay. First thing everyone said is that she's an amazing business-woman, one of the people who invented the modern version of the dude ranch. After some more beer, the story got really interesting. She's got a reputation for being a ballbuster."

"They used that word?" It's what the right-wing pundit called *me*—"brainy ballbuster," the slam I found so amusing that I cut out the column and had it framed. Does Barbara know *she's* seen that way? How does she feel about it? I can ask her! My nerves zing with anticipation.

" 'Ballbuster,' 'tough as nails,' and I recall something about 'chewing up her husbands and spitting 'em out.' Not that people saw that as a bad thing. They all respect Miz Kay. Except her own kids. She gets along fine with the son who runs the ranch—George junior, from her second husband. He and his wife live out there with her. But the son and daughter from her first marriage, that's another story. The son fought in Vietnam and came home with a drug problem. He moved away years ago; story is he finally got himself clean, but he calls a couple times a year and asks for money."

"How would anyone know that?"

"Good point. Could be that's just what fits the legend. Anyway, people *say* she and her daughter, Dana, fought like cats and dogs when Dana was growing up. Dana got married and moved to Seattle years ago. But she had to move back to the ranch last year with her youngest kid. Messy divorce."

So Barbara was a less than perfect mother. Like me. Like every woman.

The morning is clear and chilly. According to the display on the Explorer's dash, it's twenty-six degrees when we leave the hotel shortly after nine. As we head west, the temperature drops. We're steadily climbing, even though the mountains are peaks in the distance, while we're traversing a rolling prairie, a sprawling-to-forever space in which the meager signs of human industry—occasional fences, huddles of cattle—dwindle to specks against the snow.

And maybe this is all I need—to inhabit, briefly, this landscape she chose as her own, under a sky so vast that high, thin cirrus are mere thoughts of clouds. Maybe having come this far is enough.

Well, I'm no longer a child, quivering at the top of the slide. If I tell Josh to turn around now, no one will jeer at me for chickening out. I just wish I didn't feel so much like that child, my spine turned to liquid, my hands and feet like remote outposts I don't trust to obey my commands.

"Is this it?" Josh says as we approach an exit from the interstate onto a county road.

I check my written directions—unnecessarily, because I have them memorized. "Yes."

Now we're *in* the mountains. Josh has to slow to thirty miles an hour, sometimes twenty, to negotiate the curving two-lane road. And I settle into the limbo of being in transit, in which we will drive on this road forever; in which I haven't backed down yet never actually have to confront her. I am content.

Too soon, though, I see a carved wood sign that bears the ranch emblem, a stylized outline of a horse, and announces that the turn for the

OKay Ranch is a hundred yards ahead. The emblem is a bit crudely drawn, as if by a child, but the childlike quality is its charm; it sparks an instant sense of recognition. It makes me think of Saturday afternoon cowboy movies, and I'll bet it has the same effect on potential customers planning their dude ranch vacation.

"Looks like we've hit the north forty," Josh says.

A well-plowed entry road leads to an arched wooden gate with "OKay Ranch" and the distinctive horse emblem carved into the arch. Rustic but high-tech, the gate smoothly swings open after Josh announces himself over an intercom, and then closes behind us. The road makes a slight bend, and guests must get a thrill at their first view of the lodge, a graceful building made of whole logs and perched against the mountains.

"No wonder she's a successful dude rancher," Josh says, echoing my thought. My sister knows how to put on a show.

We come into the parking lot, large enough to hold perhaps fifty cars, though it's empty today. The lodge is closed for the winter, and we're supposed to continue to the family home a quarter mile on.

"Give me a minute," I say as Josh consults our directions to figure out which of several side roads we need to take. I hate it that I feel so fuzzy. The rotten night. The altitude. My terror.

But I don't have a minute. Zooming toward us, a snowmobile skims over the packed snow beside one of the side roads. It's sixteen degrees outside, but the snowmobiler didn't bother to wear a hat. Her blond curls fly, and I wonder if the granddaughter was dispatched to meet us.

She speeds into the parking lot and pulls up beside the driver's side of the car. And I see that the face above the electric blue parka is as old as mine.

"Josh! Welcome," she booms. Even with a touch of Western drawl, it's *my* voice coming from her mouth.

Josh jumps out and goes to greet her, and she pumps his hand. Glancing past him at me, she does a double take, then shrugs. "Follow me to the house," she says.

A tight U-turn, and she takes off in a spray of snow, a vigorous woman at home in this wild terrain. Zesty. Free. My sister.

It's nothing like any of the lives I imagined for her. Yet as she tears ahead of us, I see the Barbara who shoplifted groceries for Danny, the girl who yelled for joy on the bank of the river after a heavy rain. The girl who could leave us forever and not look back? But that Barbara I've never understood; that's the sister I want to shake until she gives me an answer. Ah, now I feel ready, my back straightening and senses on alert; it's the rush I experienced when I entered a courtroom.

"You okay?" Josh says.

"Fine."

The side road leads to a house that looks big enough to hold a family of ten. What must be an original log ranch house sits at the middle of the structure, surrounded by log and limestone additions. It has none of the architectural majesty of the lodge; this is a place where people live. She pulls into a big garage—it holds two trucks, a van, and three SUVs—and parks in a line of about a dozen snowmobiles.

Josh stops just outside the garage. And I get out of the car. Walk toward her.

Getting up from the snowmobile isn't easy for her. She has to perform a series of negotiations to extricate herself from the low seat; then she braces herself on the snowmobile and accepts Josh's arm to come to standing. She must be in pain, but there's no sign of it when she turns and gives me her close-lipped smile.

"I didn't know Josh was bringing anyone." She extends her hand. "I'm Kay Thorne."

I hear Harriet warning me that I'm chasing an illusion. Then Kay Thorne smiles, revealing the gap between her two front teeth. I take a deep breath.

"Barbara," I say. "It's me. Elaine."

I have imagined this moment so many times. I've seen her recoil. Or look perplexed and pretend not to know me. Or weep with joy.

For a heartbeat, she is so still, she might have stopped breathing. Then she breaks into a belly laugh.

"Holy crap!" She looks me up and down. "Holy, holy crap! Lainie, you're an old lady."

"Seventeen minutes younger than you!" I pull her into a hug, and she hugs me back. My God, she still wears Shalimar! I can feel her body shaking. Or is the shaking mine?

I take half a step back but keep my hands on her shoulders.

She brushes my face. "Don't cry. It'll freeze." She glances at Josh. "He's not filming any USO documentary, is he?"

"No."

"Hell of a bullshitter. It's not nice to trick old ladies," she teases him. Still a flirt. "Especially old ladies who are crack shots."

"Sorry, ma'am." He grins back.

"Your grandson?" she asks me. "He's got Danny's eyes."

"A friend. Barbara, I didn't marry Danny."

"You're kidding. Well, Jesus, Elaine, are you okay? You didn't come here in the dead of winter because you're dying of cancer or anything like that?"

"I'm fine. I came now because I had no idea where you were until a week ago." But I bite back the sharpness that entered my voice. I don't want to get angry, not when this is going so well. "How about you? Are you all right?"

"Can't complain. Well, I *can* complain, and I do. But nothing's seriously wrong."

"Hey!" Josh breaks in. "Mind if a California boy goes inside out of the cold?"

The minute he says it, it hits me that my wool coat, fine for winter visits to my daughter in Oregon, feels no more protective than a paper hospital gown. I turn toward the house.

Barbara doesn't move. Maybe she can't?

"Do you need help?" I ask.

"Elaine!" She fixes me with my own Acid Regard. "Wait. My family's here. You're not going to tell them, are you?"

"For crying out loud. Barbara, I didn't come here to expose you."

"Kay. My name is Kay."

"Fine!" What does it matter if she calls herself the Queen of Sheba? No one else has ever been able to jerk me around so completely or twist me into a tighter knot of helpless rage. Forget her voice and the gap between her teeth; now I know beyond the shadow of a doubt that this is my sister. "Are you going to at least let me use your bathroom? My bladder is screaming."

"Who do I tell them you are?"

"How about," Josh breaks in, "she's an old friend of yours from the USO? And I'm using her as an advisor?"

"I don't suppose you brought a camera?" she asks him. "They're expecting me to be a movie star."

"In the car. I'll get it."

I go to the car with him and get my bag of family photos, and we catch up with her as she hobbles toward the house. "Arthritis has got to be God's revenge against dancers," she says.

I refuse to feel sorry for her. Still, I offer my arm, and she takes it as we go to a side door. I follow her up four steps that have solid metal bars installed on either side.

Then my sister opens the door to her home.

We enter a mudroom. Two dogs launch themselves at us, a flurry of barks and eager tongues. I laugh and let them slobber on my hands.

"You have dogs?" she says, surprised.

"I used to. Spaniels. The last one died three years ago." I'm unbuttoning my coat as fast as I can—I wasn't kidding about my bladder—but my fingers are numb and the mudroom tight. Besides the three of us and the dogs, the walls bulge with parkas and fleece jackets hanging on hooks, and there are enough boots scattered on the floor to stock Fine & Son Fine Footwear.

I struggle out of the coat at last. "Bathroom?"

"Dana!" she calls. "This is my friend Elaine, from the USO. Show her where the bathroom is."

"Sure," says a fiftysomething woman who's been hovering just beyond the mudroom. Dana, the daughter. Despite my skepticism about the local rumor mill, Dana does look like a woman who's dragged herself home after a messy divorce. Her skin is pasty, and her streaked hair shows an inch of gray roots.

"Are you in the movie, too?" she asks as she leads me down a short corridor; but she says it like she doesn't particularly care.

"Yes."

"That's great," she mumbles.

Dana waits for me, then leads me into a beamed living room and introduces me to George and his wife, Lynn. Kay—no, *Barbara*! I'll call her what she wants, but I'm not going to censor the way I think about her—is nowhere in sight.

"She went to change clothes for the film," Josh says, sensing my anxiety. "She'll be back in a minute."

"That's what you think!" George has the tooth gap, and so does Dana; it must be one of those traits that bully any competing genes into submission. "You never tried to get my mom away from a mirror."

Along with his Robert Mitchum handsomeness, George has an easy, at-home-in-his-own-skin assurance that might even be able to persuade *me* to get on a horse. He ushers me to a somewhat threadbare but comfortable chair next to a hearth that, hallelujah, appears to hold an entire blazing tree. And it hits me where I've seen that visceral self-confidence before—in photos of Uncle Harry.

Lynn, who manages to be both down-home and chic with cropped white-blond hair and turquoise stud earrings, matches her husband's cowboy charm with a good innkeeper's gift for chitchat. She throws Josh some questions about his film and me about my USO tours; I'm lucky that years in courtrooms taught me to think on my feet.

Lynn's filling the time while we wait for Barbara. As ten minutes pass and then fifteen, even George fidgets. They've probably got work they need to get back to. Surely I'm the only one who's worried that Barbara will grab some diamonds from a safe, jump onto her snowmobile, and never be seen again.

"Let me go finish making the cinnamon buns," Lynn says. "And how about some cocoa? Or would you prefer coffee? Tea?"

"Don't pass up Lynn's cocoa," George says. "She's the reason people say the OKay has the best grub of any dude ranch in the country."

"Cocoa sounds great," I say.

"How about you?" she asks Josh, and he nods.

"I'll take some, too, with real whipped cream on it, not that healthy crap," Barbara says. She's back, standing just inside the doorway. She's changed into a black suede skirt and a fringed black vest over a red turtle-neck, along with black cowboy boots. Like Barbara Stanwyck in *The Big Valley*, and not just because of the outfit; it's the way everyone deferentially turns toward her.

"As if I'd dare try to keep you from clogging your arteries," Lynn says fondly. "I'll have Jen bring it in here when it's ready."

"Not here!" Barbara says so vehemently that her family looks at her in alarm. She tosses her head, announces, "We'll be in my office."

"Mom, don't you think . . . ," Dana begins, then pauses. "We got the living room all ready for you to film here. The light, you know? And your office must be freezing."

Poor Dana, having to come back home to her ranch-matriarch mother and the Western power couple of George and Lynn. I wish I could be for her what Aunt Pearl was for me. I settle for shooting her a smile.

"Josh can stay here and set up," Barbara says. "Elaine and I have some private catching up to do."

I force myself to stand up; I'm loath to leave the fire. But Barbara and I *do* need to talk behind closed doors.

Using an ornate cane, dark wood with silver filigree, she leads me to a newer wing of the house. We enter a spacious room with a desk at one end and three chairs grouped around a low table at the other. There's a big picture window with a view of the mountains. It's gorgeous. And so cold that frost coats the inside of the window. When I sit down, I let out a gasp; the chair seat is a block of ice.

But she's adjusting a thermostat on a photograph-covered wall, saying, "It'll warm up fast." Then she pulls up a chair next to me and leans close, searching my face. "It's really you. I missed you. . . . No, I mean it. Tell me about yourself. Did you graduate college?"

"Didn't you ever look me up on the Internet or at the library? Weren't you a little bit curious?"

"I tried. But computers are a complete mystery to me. And I tried 'Elaine Greenstein' and 'Elaine Berlov.' What *is* your name?"

"Resnick. I married Paul Resnick. Remember him?" I say. She looks blank as I continue, "He was a couple of years ahead of us at Roosevelt, and he fought in the Spanish Civil War."

"So, did you graduate?"

"Yes, from college and law school."

"You *did* go to law school! And did you become Eleanor Roosevelt?"

"I defended some people against Joe McCarthy in the fifties. Later I did civil rights and antiwar cases. And women's issues . . . I got a reputation as a ballbuster."

"No shit." She chuckles. "I've heard that's how a few people see me. But you really did all that?" She beams at me. "Lainie, you were always so brave."

"Me? *You* were the brave one. The way you threw yourself into things."

"I was just wild. And stupid . . . I don't suppose you have any cigarettes?"

"I gave up smoking in 1964, after the surgeon general's report. And again in 1967. And for good in 1971. When Aunt Pearl got diagnosed with lung cancer."

"Oh." A shadow crosses her face. Then she says, breezy again, "God, I adored Pearl. Did she ever marry the Mexican boyfriend? Or anyone?"

"No. But she and Bert lived together after she moved out of Boyle Heights and got a house in Los Feliz. And he took care of her at the end. He was wonderful."

"That Pearl! I wasn't as good at staying away from the altar. . . . I guess you already know that, don't you?" she says tartly. "You could probably tell me things I don't even know about myself."

We fall into the awkward silence of people who have too little to say to each other. Or too much.

"This is a beautiful place," I say.

"We like it. . . . God, it's been so long. So . . . Danny, did he get killed in the war?"

"No. After the war, he moved to Israel—it was still Palestine then. He became some kind of high-up in the Mossad, Israeli intelligence. Not that he'll ever admit it."

"He's still alive, then? You stay in touch?"

"We talk every few years. We argue about politics."

"Is that why you didn't marry him? Because you didn't want to live in Israel?"

"I didn't marry Danny because I grew up. And I fell in love with Paul! It had nothing to do with . . . anything else." Ridiculous to get prickly more than half a century since I last faced her in Danny's doorway, the air thick with sex and betrayal. I grab the bag next to me, change the subject. "I brought photographs."

"Oh, I'd love to see them."

I've brought several dozen pictures, snapshots from vacations and family gatherings as well as posed group photos at weddings, graduations, bar mitzvahs. Going through them gives us a way to fill in the stutters in our conversation. I tell her she can keep any of the photos she likes, and she says no thanks. Still, she looks avidly at the pictures of people she knew as we aged. And I fill her in on our lives—and deaths.

As she looks at the photos I brought, I scan the ones on her walls. Most of them are of people wearing Western clothes and straddling horses or standing next to them. But some pictures don't have humans in them at all. Her *family*. Not us but horses! Suddenly I'm seething.

Her eyes are on a shot from my wedding when she says, "Water under the bridge and all that, but I'm sorry about what happened . . . that day with Danny."

"Water under the bridge," I echo, but then I explode. "Who gives a damn what you did with Danny? But how about your disappearing without a word? How about letting Mama and Papa die not knowing where you were, that you were alive!"

"Would you have left me alone? Look at you—you have the nerve to do a background search on me, and a week after you find out where I am, here you are!"

"Did you think they were going to jump on a plane to Cody, Wyoming? Mama and Papa, in the 1950s? Or that hordes of embarrassing Jewish relatives would book vacations at your dude ranch? Is that what you were so afraid of, that people would find out you're Jewish?"

"I'm *not* Jewish!"

It's so preposterous, I stare, openmouthed, as she jabs her cane into the floor and pushes herself to standing. "Elaine, you don't get it. You think I'm living some kind of lie as Kay Thorne. But Barbara Greenstein was the lie. Trying to be *her* made me feel like I was suffocating."

Some people don't just leave the family nest; they feel like they're running for their lives. I jumped down Philip's throat when he said that, and I jump down Barbara's now, standing and shouting in her face, "That's the best you can do, to explain why you broke Mama's heart?"

"Is that why you came all the way here, to tell me no explanation is good enough? Big surprise, Elaine. I was never good enough for you."

"That's not—"

"Shh!" She cocks her head toward the door.

"Gram?" a girl's voice calls from the hall.

In the panicked glance that jumps between us, we could be eight years old, with Mama about to walk in on something we want to hide.

"Gram, are you okay? I've got the cocoa."

"Fine!" Barbara bellows. "Just hang on a sec, Jen, okay?" She sits back down, painfully—I can almost hear the joints gnashing in her hips and knees—and shoves the photos we've spread over the table into a pile before she calls, "C'mon in."

"Cocoa train," says the young woman, wheeling in a restaurant cart. A girl who has Dana's rangy build, along with my family's delicate features and dark curly hair, caught in a ponytail. I look for the tooth gap, but she gives only a slight, closed smile.

"My granddaughter, Jen," Barbara says. "And this is Elaine. A friend from the USO."

"Right, the technical advisor," Jen says. In her watchfulness, I see myself.

Jen transfers items from the cart to the table. There are two big cups of cocoa topped with whipped cream, a plate with half a dozen pastries, and individual plates, cutlery, and gingham napkins.

"Be sure to try one of the cinnamon rolls," Jen advises me. "Aunt Lynn won third place in the Pillsbury Bake-off with them—as we have to tell the guests six thousand times every summer. They really are fantastic, though. . . . Gram, I brought you a treat," she adds in a half whisper. From a pocket of her bulky sweater, she pulls out a flask and tips a generous amount of something into Barbara's cocoa.

"That's my girl," Barbara says.

It occurs to me that this may not be my sister's first drink of the morning. Was that the reason for her family's unease when we waited for her earlier? Well, so what if she drinks a bit? Here she is, living in her own home in a mountain paradise, eating her fond daughter-in-law's cinnamon rolls. And I've got the Ranch of No Tomorrow's teriyaki chicken.

The bite of envy is visceral. And familiar and comforting. Like smelling my mother's kitchen again or hearing Papa declaim poetry.

"Scotch?" Jen asks me.

"Please." So Scotch is Barbara's drink, as well as mine.

When Jen leans toward me to doctor my cocoa, something gleams between the edges of her thick cardigan. Oh, can it be . . .

"Can I see that? Your necklace?"

Jen pulls out what she's wearing on a cord around her neck. "I begged to have this for years, and Gram finally gave it to me when I graduated high school."

I barely hear her. I'm staring at the crudely fashioned tin horse. The model for the ranch's emblem. The horse Zayde made.

CHAPTER 21

TIN HORSE

"Can I?" I reach for the horse. My hand is shaking, and tears well in my eyes.

Jen looks confused, but she takes off the necklace and hands it to me.

Barbara jumps in. "It reminds Elaine of when we were in the USO together. The horse was my good-luck charm. . . . Brings it all back, doesn't it, Elaine?"

I'm weeping as I clutch the horse, feeling the surprisingly smooth edges—did Zayde make it that way, or did Barbara hold it so often she wore it smooth? She took the horse when she left. She *treasured* it.

I feel her hand on my knee. She's pulled her chair around so she's facing me. "Have some cocoa. Drink." Gently she takes the tin horse from my fingers and holds out the cup.

The cocoa is delicious, as promised—and well laced: I can taste the Scotch behind the chocolate. I glance around for Jen, but she must have slipped out of the room.

"How could you let us go?" I implore, finally giving voice to the question I have asked her in my imagination so many times. "How could you bear to live the rest of your life apart from us?"

She takes a swig of cocoa, then says, "I don't think I can make you understand. *I* don't understand why I do most things; I just do them. I'm sorry I hurt you. Really. And I did miss you. Sometimes in Europe during the war, I felt so lonely, and I'd get out an aerogram and write 'Dear Elaine' or 'Dear Mama.' But I never finished any of those letters—and don't ask me why, I can't tell you. I'm not like you. I don't take things apart. I just put one foot in front of the other. One day at a time."

One more cliché, and I'll throw my cocoa in her face. Could she really have cut us off with so little thought or regret? I understand that she isn't reflective by nature; she operated on instinct. But she wasn't just instinctual, she was secretive; I remember how opaque she became once she started leading a separate life in Hollywood. And now she's had a lifetime of keeping secrets—she's a pro. Still, I'm determined to get behind the barricade of platitudes.

"In Europe, when you didn't finish those aerograms, you were just in your twenties," I say. "But what about later? Why didn't you let us know when you got married?"

She reaches for a cinnamon roll. "If we don't do justice to these, I'll never be able to explain it to Lynn. I'll have to feed them to the dogs."

"Fine." I pick up a pastry and bring it to my mouth.

"Good, yes?"

The prizewinning pastry dances in my mouth, warm yeasty dough and sugar and cinnamon. But I persist. "When you had your first child, didn't you want Mama to know she had a grandchild?"

"Bet you were one hell of a lawyer," she grumbles. "What is it they say these days? 'It's complicated'? I met Rich, my first husband, when I was in Berlin, and I told him the same thing I was telling everyone—that my folks were dead, and I didn't have any other family. By the time it got serious, I knew him well enough to know that if he found out I'd lied to him, he'd never let me forget it." She gives a tight smile. "Richard Cochran turned out to be one mean, jealous bastard. Handsome, though."

"But you divorced him. What about after that?"

She heaves a dramatic sigh. "Look, by the time I threw Rich out, everyone knew me as a girl who had no family. Even my own kids! And why would I want to tell anyone . . . That's just it. What would I have told them—who I *really* was? It's like I said, Barbara was the lie; trying to be her was killing me."

"Would you have told Rich if your last name were Jones instead of Greenstein?"

"It was sixty years ago. And *my* last name was Devereaux."

"You don't just stop being Jewish, like canceling a magazine subscription."

"Would that satisfy you, Lainie? Would you feel like you got what you came here for if I said the reason I didn't contact you was that I didn't want anyone to know I was Jewish?"

Would it? In that story, this wild place under its endless sky becomes a bunker in which my gutsy sister hid from a world that scared her. Hid from herself. And me? She said it: *I* was the brave one.

"Not," she says, "that I think anyone in their right mind would be Jewish if they had a choice about it. I was in Berlin for a year after the war. Everywhere, you'd see the DPs, the people who'd been in concentration camps." She shudders. "But it wasn't that. It was the family, Boyle Heights, that claustrophobic little world. Lainie, it was different for you. People always expected you to go to college and make something of yourself. Know what I heard from everyone—Mama, Papa, my teachers, even Pearl? That the best I could hope for was to marry a good provider. Look at this!" She gestures toward the window and the ranch beyond. "I haven't done too badly. If I'd stayed in Boyle Heights, sure, I might have married some doctor and had a life of PTA and charity lunches and a house in the Valley . . . and I would have gone out of my mind."

A song from a musical tinkles in my mind: *You gotta have a dream, if you don't have a dream, how you gonna make a dream come true?* Did she have to get out in order to imagine herself? The thought brings a glimmer of understanding. But only a glimmer. I recognize that there are terrible impulses, even the will to murder, lurking in the crevices of my own psyche. But what she did . . . I remember Danny pointing at her chest and crying, "What's in there? Do you have a heart?"

"You felt trapped, and you had to get away, all right," I say. "But didn't you have a shred of compassion for us? At the very least, you could have written and let us know you'd landed on your feet, that you hadn't gotten murdered in some alley . . ."

"What are you talking about?" she says, indignant. "You knew that."

"No, I didn't."

"Elaine, come on! A couple of years after I left—it was the spring after Pearl Harbor—somehow you found out my name and where I worked in Colorado Springs. . . . Why are you shaking your head? Mama wrote to me there."

As on the day I found Barbara's dance programs, I feel as if I were standing beside the Los Angeles River in the rain, but this time the flash flood roars from the mountains and smashes into me. Mama and Papa *did* know, and they kept it from me. This is what I've suspected for some time; it shouldn't come as a huge shock. But hearing her confirm it . . . It reminds me of when Paul died. No matter that I'd heard the terminal diagnosis months earlier and watched him gradually slip away, or that the home hospice staff had walked me through what was going to happen. Still, the actual moment when I heard his death rattle and then the agonized breathing stopped, I refused to accept it. I kept talking to him, touching his cheek, *willing* him to flutter his eyelids. What Barbara's telling me can't be true.

"Elaine, what's wrong?" Barbara says.

"They never told me."

"What, about Mama writing to me?" Her voice goes thin.

"About anything! About your new name or that they'd found out where you were."

"But you're here," Barbara insists. "How else could you track me down?"

As I'm telling her about finding Philip's card, her face crumples. "Excuse me," she says, and does her best to hustle out of the room; but her arthritic limbs slow her down, and as she goes through the door, I hear a sob.

I get up, too, and pace, looking out the window at her glorious view and trying again to comprehend my parents' silence, sifting the information I've just heard into the speculations that have obsessed me for the past two months.

So it was true, as I'd thought, that Mama wrote a letter to the woman Philip had found. And then? No matter what explanation I come up with—that she and Papa couldn't be sure the woman was Barbara, or Barbara wrote a reply so hateful that Mama couldn't even bear to keep the letter—nothing makes me understand how they could deny us the comfort of thinking they'd found her. What did Harriet say when I told her? That she felt so betrayed she wanted to go to the cemetery and scream at Mama's and Papa's graves. That's how I feel now.

Fifteen minutes have passed, and I'm about to find my way back to the living room, when Barbara returns. She looks like she's put on fresh mascara, but her eyes are red and puffy, and she says ruefully, "Aren't we a couple of sob sisters?" Then she takes a deep breath. "You really didn't know. Mama didn't tell you."

"No."

"Jesus. Mama said, but I never believed she meant it. After I got her letter, I kept thinking Papa was going to show up on the next train. And you, Elaine—I was sure I'd get a letter from you. Unless you hated me so much you never wanted to see me again. You had plenty of reason to feel that way."

"Are you saying you wanted to hear from me?"

"Oh, I don't know, I . . ." She picks at the crumbs of cinnamon roll on her plate. "Mama reamed me, and I figured it was nothing compared to what I'd get from you."

"Would you have written back?"

She thinks about it, then says, "I'd like to tell you yes, but how can I put myself in the state of mind I was in back then? Getting Mama's letter threw me for such a loop, and everything was crazy then—the war, and I'd signed up for the USO. What I remember, the one thing I can swear is true, is that after I heard from her, every day I looked for a letter from you. I'd go to the office in the hotel where they sorted the mail. . . ." Her eyes go distant, as if she's seeing it. "I never, ever believed Mama would keep her promise. Elaine, I am so sorry."

I struggle to take it in, hugging myself . . . as if I could contain the tumult inside me. All of the years when I feared I had meant nothing to her, that she had coldly blotted me out as if I'd never existed. . . . After nearly a lifetime, that story about Barbara—and the hurt and anger I felt because of it—became one of my deepest truths. To imagine her as a twenty-one-year-old kid waiting for my letter and fearing the same thing about me. . . .

I take her hands. "I'm sorry, too. Over the years, I did look for you. I hired detectives." Then something she said tweaks my awareness. "What . . . promise?"

"Mama said—this was in her letter—that she was the only one who knew about me, and she promised not to tell anyone else."

"It's not true!" It can't be. Thinking that Mama and Papa had decided not to tell us was already devastating. But for Mama alone to offer concealment to Barbara like a gift . . .

"Lainie." She holds my gaze. "Like I said, I couldn't believe it, either."

"She said that? She actually said 'I promise'?"

"Well. First she reamed me for being a horrible daughter, and she loaded on the guilt—saying not a day went by when she didn't weep over leaving her family, and the one thing she wanted most in the world was to see her mother's face one more time."

That sounds like Mama. Whatever else she'd said, Barbara must have twisted it.

"But after all that," Barbara continues, "she said if it was what I wanted, she promised—she used that word—to let me live my own life."

I have a flash—so vivid that it brings back the feel of Mama's sweaty hand clutching mine—of our first day of school, the vertiginous moment when I grasped that Barbara and I would be in different classrooms. My disorientation wasn't just because I had to change my mental image of school and create a new one in which my twin and I were separated for the first time in our lives. Radiating out from that image were the streets around the school, then all of Boyle Heights, and from there Los Angeles, America, and the world. My entire internal landscape fractured, and I had to reconstruct it, though it was never again so reliable and whole. And *that* world had been only five years in the making.

"Why would she promise that?" I say.

"Your guess is as good as mine."

But it's not. There was always an uncanny connection between Mama and Barbara, as if they heard the same restless music in their heads. "What's *your* guess?"

She throws up her hands, a gesture that, even crabbed by arthritis, is so deeply familiar that the woman sitting before me could be Mama or Pearl or Harriet—or me. If she had stayed, our common vocabulary of gestures, the visceral traces of our entwined history, would have emerged every time we saw each other, and they might have faded into a background hum. Now each one brings a trumpet fanfare of recognition.

"When you got the letter, you must have had some idea," I say.

"I guess . . . I thought about what happened to her before she married Papa. You know, when she got kicked out of the place where she was living and felt like she'd run out of places to go. I guess I thought maybe she understood how trapped I'd felt."

"I *don't* know. What do you mean, she got kicked out?" Mama had told Barbara about running away from her family in Romania. What else did she confess?

"You never heard this?"

I shake my head.

"I guess Mama only told me because she could see I was headed for trouble—this was when I was sixteen or seventeen—and she was trying to get me to shape up."

The story Barbara tells begins like the one I know. Mama moved to Los Angeles with a family from Chicago, the . . . we grope a bit but come up with the Tarnows. She lived with them in Boyle Heights and got a job at a dress factory. The Tarnows knew Zayde because they had come from the same village in Ukraine; they arranged for Mama to meet Papa, which led to her taking his English class, and that led to Papa proposing.

After that, however, Barbara enters new territory. And I revisit another sensation I remember—the breathless excitement of hearing a secret from my sister. Excitement and apprehension, because uncovering the secret could be like peeling a bandage from a wound.

"It's not that Mama didn't care for Papa. She did," Barbara says. "But it was the way everything happened, meeting him because the Tarnows knew Zayde, and when Papa proposed, they knew all about it because he'd asked Mr. Tarnow's permission, and they kept pressuring her to say yes. She used to go to the beach and just stare at the ocean. Remember, she did that when we were kids? Anyway, she sat there and thought—how did she put it?—that she'd crossed Europe and then the Atlantic Ocean and then the entire United States. And after all that, she was being pushed into an arranged marriage just like in her village. The only difference was that now she had no place left to go. And then . . ."

"What?" I say in response to her pregnant pause.

"She met a man."

"Mama?" Though as I say it, I remember Mollie telling me, *Your mama always had a way about her.* "What man?"

"The director of a Yiddish theater company. She auditioned for a play they were doing, and she got a small part."

That part of the story Mollie hadn't told me; I wonder if she'd known.

"I don't know if she and this guy slept together," Barbara says. "She was vague about the details. But I guess she was staying out till all hours and having a few drinks. So the Tarnows threw her out. Literally, they put all her things in a sack and put it on the street. She went to the jerk of a director, but he washed his hands of any responsibility for her. In a way, she was relieved—she wasn't in love with him, he was just a smooth talker. At least, that's what she said. But she had no place to go. The first night, she slept on the street."

"She told you this?" As the story begins to settle in, I can see my passionate, capricious, maddening mother tumbling into a romantic involvement, even a full-blown affair. What I can't imagine is that she'd tell a soul. Yet she did. She was willing to reveal even that humiliation . . . to the daughter of her heart. The scald of hurt I feel—ridiculous after all these years—mortifies me, and I try to quell it. But the hurt, the sense of exclusion, has a life of its own, as if it's racing along some of my earliest, most deeply grooved neural pathways.

"Only because I was so wild," Barbara says, as if she senses how I feel—old pathways for her, too. "Most of what she talked about was the trashy way I was behaving and how a girl who lost her reputation could never get it back. And how I had to stop expecting my life to be like the movies and grow up. She told me about her mistakes in the hope of scaring me shitless, so I'd start acting like a respectable girl. It's just that the part of the story I paid attention to was the juicy stuff about her and this man. Naturally." She shakes her head, gives a small laugh. "It's so strange to talk about this after all these years. And with you."

"What happened—after she slept on the street?"

"She stayed the next few nights with a friend, but the friend didn't really have room. Then Mr. Tarnow came and had a talk with her. He told her if she said yes to Papa, they'd let her move back in until she got married. And then . . ." But she hesitates.

"What?"

"Phew! It's crazy, but I got this chill, like Mama's looking over my shoulder, knowing I'm about to spill her worst secret. As if it matters anymore. That night she went to the beach. She decided there was one place left that was even farther than California—she could walk into the ocean and drown."

Ocean Park at night is so clear in my memory I can smell the salt-tangy air as Barbara says, "She walked in with her clothes on until the water was almost to her neck. But then she got terrified of dying, and she had to struggle to get back to shore."

For a moment I'm there, feeling the water rising to my thighs and waist and chest, feeling the sodden pull of my clothes as I fight the suck of the waves. Poor Mama. I had thought, after the talk I'd had with Mollie, that I understood my mother's thwarted dreams. But I had only glimpsed her desperation, and I ached for her.

And poor Papa!

"Did Papa know?" Did the awful knowledge that Mama had nearly drowned herself rather than marry him account for the perpetual strain between my parents, his sternness and her simmering anger?

"She said he didn't."

"But she told you," I marvel again.

"She was really worried about me. With reason." She chuckles. And then gasps. "Holy crap! Holy, holy crap."

"What?"

"I just now realized I did take what she said to heart. I just got a different moral from the story than she had in mind. She was trying to tell me not to be such a dreamer and to settle for what I could get. What I heard was that I should never run out of places to go. And always, always have money of my own. Damned if I didn't live my whole life by what she told me. . . . Those pictures you brought. Can I see them again? I'd like to have one of Mama."

She chooses a shot of Mama and me, taken at Ronnie's wedding. "Thanks, Mama. For everything," she says, not hiding her tears. Then she swipes a hand over her eyes and announces, "Well, I guess we've got a movie to make."

She starts to haul herself to her feet, not bothering to hide the effort. I go over to help her, and she lets me. Then we're standing face-to-face. She caresses my cheek. And we embrace.

My arms around Barbara, I realize that what she yelled at me earlier is true: no explanation she can give is good enough. So she believed, at twenty-one, that I loathed her. But the lifetime of silence afterward—nothing can make that all right.

Yet . . . It's not that I forgive her. But forgiveness feels irrelevant. What matters is hearing her voice, holding her, looking out the window at the view she sees every day. It's the physical reality, flesh and blood and bone, of this person with whom I spent the first nine months of my existence, the two of us pressed together in the chrysalis of Mama's womb more closely, for longer, than we would ever touch anyone else.

What matters is my grandniece wearing Zayde's tin horse over her heart.

"I love you," I murmur.

"Me too. Lainie, thank you for coming. It means a lot to me."

As we leave her office, I say, "Harriet and I are going to a spa in Mexico this spring. Want to come with us?"

"Do they put you on a diet of watercress?"

"Food's fantastic. And we bring our own booze."

She shrugs. But doesn't say no.

DURING THE COUPLE OF hours we were talking, Josh filmed outdoor footage of the lodge and the mountains; Jen showed him where to get the best shots. And she helped him experiment with locations for the interview, sitting in various spots in the living room while he checked the light.

"I'm your body double, Gram," she quips.

Barbara forces a smile, and I can see that she's exhausted. I realize that I am too. I'm awash in fatigue.

"Show time," she says. And goes ahead with the "interview" like the trouper she is, faking it for the audience of Jen, who hovers, and anyone who might peek in.

Josh asks her to sit at one end of the sofa and does a little preliminary shooting—fiddling with sound levels, he says, and letting her get comfortable in front of the camera. Not that the Sweetheart of the Rodeo suffers from stage fright. When he starts filming, she launches into her USO stories as smoothly as if she's rehearsed them. In fact, all her stories have the polish of tales repeated dozens of times, delivered with professional timing.

I want to pay attention, to get a window into at least a few of the missing years in my sister's life. But I'll be able to watch the video Josh is making, I can share it with Harriet when I get home.

Sitting next to the fire, physically and emotionally wrung out, my mind drifts to the story I've just heard and to the person I *can't* forgive—Mama.

Never run out of places to go. That was the unintended moral that Barbara took from Mama's cautionary tale. But *was* it unintended, accidental? Or did Barbara hear exactly what Mama meant to tell her? Did Mama deliberately—though no doubt unconsciously—project her own yearning for escape onto Barbara and give her the strength to leave? And not just the strength but the resolve, as if she virtually pushed Barbara out the door?

Every person grows up in a different family, Harriet said. And I get it that my sisters and I each experienced a different version of Charlotte Avramescu Greenstein. Nevertheless, a Mama who refused to tell us Barbara was safe, a woman who chose Barbara's—and, even more than that, her own—fantasy of freedom over relieving our anguish, is someone I don't even recognize. That woman is a monster, condemning her other daughters to suffer and letting Papa keep going to the morgue to look at dead girls!

Condemning Barbara, too? I *would* have written to her. In fact, *I* might have taken the next train to Colorado Springs. And then? I can't imagine her coming home with me—I understand how stifled she felt—a lifetime of estrangement, is that what she would have chosen?

The rage . . . it's as if embers have leaped out of the fireplace and set me alight. My body is smoldering, my brittle hair a torch.

"Elaine?" Josh's voice pierces my concentration. For a moment I wonder if I've actually burst into flame. But he's just telling me they've finished filming. Apparently Barbara has called a halt to the interview.

"Gram, no way!" Jen is protesting. "You know, they have to film for hours to get five minutes they can use."

"That's plenty, isn't it, Josh?" Barbara says.

"Your grandma's a natural," Josh tells Jen. "It'll be fine. I'll let you all know if the funding comes through for me to finish it."

"Lynn's got lunch for us," Jen says. "I'll go tell her we're ready."

"We just filled up on cinnamon rolls," Barbara says. She's drained and anxious to get rid of us. I'm every bit as anxious to go, to be alone with this fury. I'm afraid that if I try to speak, venom will shoot out of my mouth.

"It's beef barley soup," Jen says.

"They've got to get going if they want to get back to Cody before dark."

But Jen is a girl who sticks to her guns. "They'll have time. And I promised Josh a snowmobile ride."

"Couldn't you have done that earlier?" Barbara snaps.

"We could have if we'd known you two were going to be talking for hours!" Jen turns away for a minute, helping Josh pack his gear. Then, with a coaxing voice that takes me back seventy-five years, she says, "Come with us, Gram?"

Barbara rolls her eyes. "Elaine, do you mind hanging out for half an hour? You can have some soup."

"I . . ." I look outside. The pale northern sunlight glitters on the snow. "I want to go snowmobiling, too."

"Have you ever driven a snowmobile?"

"Sure," I lie.

Jen finds me snow gear that more or less fits. I suit up like a chartreuse Michelin Man to match Barbara's electric blue and listen impatiently to Jen's lesson on how to start, accelerate (by pressing a lever), stop, and turn.

Finally we're moving. Slowly at first, making our way through trees, but then we hit an open field. "Take it easy," Jen cautions, but Barbara shouts, "Yahoo!" and presses the accelerator. So do I, yelling at the top of my lungs.

Icy air smacks my face. Deeper than anger, I feel the sting of an ancient wound—my earliest, infant awareness of the intense bond between my mother and my sister, the magic circle from which I was excluded. That was the real twinship in our family, Mama's and Barbara's twin souls. And me standing at that bright window, gazing at my mercurial, sparkling mother and sister, longing to be let in.

Tears half blind my eyes. Still, I squeeze the accelerator, relishing the speed, the risk. I hear yells, and suddenly a stand of trees rises ahead of me. I'm shooting straight at them.

For one more split second, I hurtle toward the trees. Then a small jerk on the handlebars and I'm back in the open, slowing down and waving in response to the panicky shouts behind me. Is this how Mama felt when she walked out of the ocean in her sodden clothes? Shaken and exhilarated? And suddenly clear?

Jen races up to me on her snowmobile. "Are you all right?" She looks terrified.

"I'm fine. Sorry I gave you a scare."

She rolls her eyes. "You've never driven one of these before, have you?"

"No, but I drive on the Los Angeles freeways. I figured, how hard could it be?"

"You and my grandmother! The two of you must have raised hell back in the day. Do you want to go back to the house? I'll go with you."

"Are you kidding? Now that I've finally figured out the controls? I'm fine. Really," I say. And I am.

Snowcapped peaks rise ahead of me, Barbara's mountain paradise. But what I'm seeing is the landscape of *my* life, the breathtaking vista in the photographs I brought with me—pictures of Mama and Papa holding my kids on their laps, lounging in my yard on a sunny afternoon, sipping drinks out of coconuts on a family vacation to Hawaii. Papa looks as if he finds this last activity undignified but nonetheless delightful. And the smile he's giving Mama . . . Did she keep Barbara's secret even from him, or did she tell him? How can I know what went on in their private moments, what their story was, when I was so mistaken about my own?

My envy of Barbara's bond with Mama took root when I was so young, it became part of my Elaine-ness. The pain of being left out was so intrinsic and unconscious I didn't go back and revise the story, didn't notice that I long ago stopped standing in the dark, my nose pressed to the window; I am inside, at the hearth. Barbara, it's true, had an extraordinary connection to Mama, a moth-to-a-flame closeness, intense and ephemeral . . . and perilous. And I have had the life in those photographs, the bumpiness and mess and ordinary daily happiness of all those years with Mama, Papa, Audrey, Harriet, Pearl, Sonya.

In my favorite photo, taken by Ronnie when he got his first camera, Mama is just sitting, holding a cup of coffee, at my kitchen table. She was in her sixties then, her hair completely gray but her cheeks still softly rounded and her skin smooth, the blessing of being plump. It's a candid shot; no one had moved a plate of toast crumbs from the table or straightened the day's *Los Angeles Times*. Mama's eyes are wide as if she's been startled, but I can tell she's exaggerating her surprise for Ronnie's benefit, because she's smiling at him with such love. Such astonishing love.

"Hey, slowpokes!" Barbara has circled back to us. "Come on, Elaine, want to race?"

We take off.

The dogs scamper behind us, barking their joy. Dogs are allowed at Rancho Mañana. I ought to get one.

I let out a whoop. She whoops back, the two of us tearing through the snapping cold. Flying, Barbara and me.

ACKNOWLEDGMENTS

F OR HELPING ME ENTER THE WORLD OF JEWISH BOYLE HEIGHTS IN
the 1920s and '30s, I owe particular gratitude to author-historian Harriet
Rochlin, who grew up in Boyle Heights—and who not only provided thor-
ough, thoughtful responses to my questions but invited me to look through
her personal archives. Thanks also to Elizabeth Fine Ginsburg, who told
me about going from Boyle Heights to study dance at the Lester Horton
studio; and to the Jewish Historical Society of Southern California, where
I spent hours exploring a treasure box of Boyle Heights oral histories. For
information about train schedules—and for saving me from putting Elaine
on the wrong streetcar—I'm grateful for the patient assistance of James
Helt, librarian at the Erwin Welsch Memorial Research Library at the San
Diego Model Railroad Museum.

The insights and encouragement of writer friends started with Abigail
Padgett and Sara Lewis, who pushed me to write this story that kept
knocking at my door. For deep, truly constructive feedback, kisses to the
Flaming Tulips—Abigail Padgett, Anne Marie Welsh, Carolyn Marsden,
Lillian Faderman, Oliva Espin, Robin Cruise, and Sheryl Tempchin—and
to Ann Elwood and Mary Lou Locke. Another important reader was the
person who made me fall in love with books: my mom, Harriet Steinberg.

It's a rare joy for an author to find an insightful reader who engages deeply with her work. When I approached the publishing world, I had the great fortune of finding a dream team of such readers. My agent, Susan Golomb, was my first brilliant editor and has been my champion throughout the journey to publication. Elaine became as real and important to Kendra Harpster, my editor at Random House, as she was to me. More than that, Kendra expanded my vision of what the book could be; she saw what wasn't yet on the page but was in Elaine's heart and in her world. And Susan Kamil at Random House had an astonishing ability to zero in on big-picture issues. Thanks also to Eliza Rothstein at the Susan Golomb Literary Agency and Kaela Myers at Random House.

My husband, Jack Cassidy, lived the book with me from the beginning—touring Boyle Heights with me, listening as I talked through problems, celebrating every triumph, and keeping my spirits up the rest of the time. My gratitude to him is beyond measure.

ABOUT THE AUTHOR

JANICE STEINBERG is an award-winning arts journalist who has published more than four hundred articles in *The San Diego Union-Tribune, Dance Magazine, Los Angeles Times,* and elsewhere. She is also the author of five mystery novels, including the Shamus Award–nominated *Death in a City of Mystics.* She has taught fiction writing at the University of California, San Diego, and dance criticism at San Diego State University. A native of Wisconsin, she received a B.A. and M.A. from the University of California, Irvine. She holds a blue belt in the Nia dance-fitness practice and teaches weekly classes. She lives in San Diego with her husband.